SPIRIT

The Cartographer Book 3

AC COBBLE

Cobble Publishing LLC

KEEP IN TOUCH AND EXTRA CONTENT

THANKS FOR CHECKING out the book! You can find larger versions of the maps and series artwork at accobble.com. You can connect with me on Facebook. I put the best stuff on Patreon. If you want exclusive updates, early access, and a chance to help steer future projects, that is the place to be.

If you'd like a free prequel novella in exchange for signing up to my newsletter, you can do that on accobble.com. One e-mail a month, never spam, unsubscribe at any time.

Happy reading!
AC

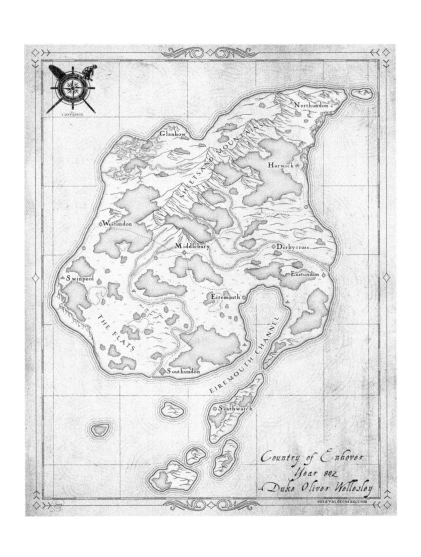

Northundon

Glanhow

SHEETSAND MOUNTAIN

Harwick

Westundon

Middlebury Derbycross

Swinpool Eastundon

Eiremouth

THE FLATS

EIREMOUTH CHANNEL

Southundon

Southwatch

Country of Enhover
Year 992
Duke Oliver Wellesley

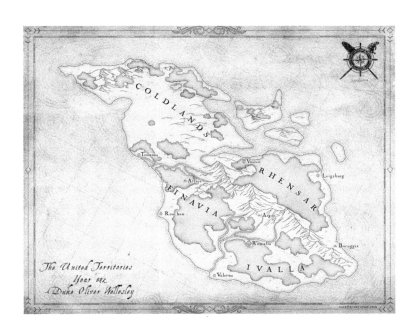

The United Territories
Year 882
Duke Oliver Wellesley

The Known World
Year 992
Duke Oliver Wollesley

THE SPECTATOR I

"MARQUESS BARTHOLOMEW SURREY, M'LADY," announced her maid.

Lannia Wellesley looked up at the woman. "Who?"

"The Marquess of Southwatch, m'lady."

"What does he want?"

"To offer his condolences, m'lady," answered the servant. The woman twitched uncomfortably, hands nervously fluttering to adjust her livery.

Lannia pursed her lips. Condolences. That was all she'd heard for two straight days. A seemingly endless procession of dour, grim-faced men had knocked on her door, offering somber assurances that everything would be all right, that they felt truly sorry for her loss, that they were there for her.

Some of them meant it.

With her father dead and his estate passing entirely into her uncertain hands, she was one of the wealthiest women in Enhover. In the world, she supposed. She was still young and beautiful, with a reputation for enjoying herself. There were few eligible bachelors in Enhover who wouldn't crawl on hands and knees to woo her.

Had they come with a bottle of sparkling Finavian wine and

promises to sweep her away to sunnier, more cheerful climes, had they begged to help her forget it all, then she might have been tempted. Instead, they asked about the funeral arrangements or how it was coming along with the dispensation of her father's assets and responsibilities. They asked whether the king had come to offer his regards or whom they should contact about business inquiries with her father's estate.

The king had come by, he and his sons, John and Oliver. Like the others, they'd clutched their hands in front of their waists and mumbled worthless platitudes. Oliver, who had been there when her father had fallen on the hunt, hadn't been able to hold her gaze. He'd barely looked at her as he'd stood trembling in front of her. A brave man, she knew, but he'd been humbled by delivering the awful news to his close cousin. And they had been close once, partners in an endless succession of childhood naughtiness, but when he'd come to see her, he had been just as gloomy a presence as the rest of them.

Duchesses Matilda, Duke John's wife, had been the warmest, but for years now, she'd been busy raising her growing brood of children. She and Lannia had never been friends.

"What shall I tell the marquess, m'lady?" asked her maid.

"Let him in," replied Lannia, steeling herself for another painful appointment.

She felt her eyes well with tears, more at the thought of how many more such meetings she'd need to take rather than sadness at the loss of her father. She made no effort to wipe away the tears. It was expected of someone in her state to show emotion, and Lannia had spent her entire life doing as expected.

She would miss her father. He'd been a kind man, thoughtful of his only daughter's needs, even if he'd never understood them. That had been their relationship, cheerful and warm, but always they were strangers.

A man cleared his throat, jarring her out of her reverie, and she looked up to see Marquess Bartholomew Surrey standing in the doorway of her sitting room.

"Apologies, m'lord," she murmured. "It has been a terrible day, and I'm afraid I don't quite know what to do with myself. I appreciate your concern, and your condolences are welcome."

"I haven't offered them yet," remarked the man.

Tall, thin, black hair swept away from his narrow face, he had the look of a sharp-tongued tailor rather than a peer. His clothes, several months out of fashion, were the only thing that spoiled the image.

She offered him a wan smile. "I thought you had. I've taken appointments from so many men these last two days... Can I offer you something to drink? Tea?"

The man's lips curled up at the corners and he shook his head. "You need offer me nothing, m'lady. May I pour you a glass of wine?"

"Wine?" she replied. "It's a bit—"

"A bit early, yes, unless one is dealing with a terrible loss," he interjected. "In such circumstances, I've found a small drink is the best way to soothe one's nerves."

Without further comment, he strode to the side of her sitting room and selected a green glass bottle off of a mirrored cart. He poured two glasses to the brim.

He offered her one and sipped the other himself. "A bit sweet to my palette."

"In a lady's sitting room, one should expect to find sweet-tasting wines," she retorted, pausing to gulp her wine in unlady-like fashion. She watched him sit across from her, and remarked dryly, "Please, sit and join me."

"The famous Wellesley wit," said Marquess Surrey. He crossed his legs and cradled his wine in his lap. "Known for your wit almost as well as your beauty and your penchant for sharing it. But I imagine with your father gone, it will be your inherited wealth your callers are interested in. Funny, isn't it? As if William would have found other causes to contribute to had he lived longer. His wealth was always destined for your hands. Why should his passing make any difference to a suitor?"

Lannia frowned at the man.

"I've not come to court you, Lannia," he admitted, "though you are worthy of such attention."

"I do not believe I know you well, m'lord," stated Lannia, staring at the man in consternation. "Not nearly so well that you may feel free to speak bluntly to me."

"You are right. We do not know each other well," agreed the man. "In fact, I believe we've only met two or three times, and then only briefly. It's so hard to find time for real conversation in the midst of a party. But while I do not know you well, and I daresay you do not know me at all, I knew your father."

Lannia blinked at the man and sipped her wine.

"I respected William greatly," continued Bartholomew, slowly turning his wine glass but not drinking from it. "Not because of his role as prime minster and not because of his qualities as a father."

"Why, then?" she asked, unsure if the man was intriguing or annoying. She was on the verge of demanding he stand and leave, and then telling her uncle, the king, about how rude the marquess had been, but it was that thought that stopped her. The man must know she could complain to her family and have him ostracized, yet he had said what he had said.

"Do you know what your father did in his free time?" asked the marquess.

"I didn't know that he had any," she retorted.

The man smirked. "Fair enough. William was a busy man, but not all of it was in service of the Crown. Not in the way he spoke about publicly, at least."

"What are you saying?" asked Lannia.

"Would you like to know how your father died?" inquired Bartholomew.

She gaped at him, unsure how to respond.

The man waited patiently, politely.

"I know how he died," she whispered. "A hunting accident. He fell."

"Is that so?" drawled the marquess. "Common was it, that your father would go hunting in the environs near here? Didn't you say he rarely had free time?"

"My cousin saw the accident," responded Lannia.

"Perhaps he did," acknowledged Marquess Surrey. "Oliver, right, the Duke of Northundon? Is he also an avid hunter?"

"Stop toying with me and say what you came to say," demanded Lannia.

"That's a girl," replied Bartholomew. "Wit and steel. You are a true Wellesley, and a true Wellesley does not stop until they have answers."

"Answers? I don't even have questions," said Lannia. "Do you think it wise to accuse my family of lying?"

"No, it is probably not," agreed the marquess. "You and I have a common interest, though. We can help each other."

"What interest is that?"

"We both want to know what happened to your father," explained Bartholomew. "I am so interested, in fact, that I'd like to ask him, and I need your help to do it."

THREE GIANT BRAZIERS WERE SET AROUND THE CIRCULAR, STONE room, each one roaring with two-yard high flames. It lit the space with a bright orange glow. Brighter than she preferred for these circumstances, but at least the light of the fires gave her some warmth, some sense of safety.

In front of her was the black, silk-clad back of Marquess Bartholomew Surrey. The peer, impolite and direct, but sincere, had finally convinced her over the course of too many glasses of sweet Finavian wine to agree to his bold scheme.

During the preparations for the ritual, she had sobered, but she was still curious. The attire, the symbolism, and the explanation of the rite all felt familiar yet strange. She'd performed similar activities in service to the Feet of Seheht. She had risen in that society from acolyte to priestess. She'd witnessed the workings of the upper echelon and participated in rituals that were secret even from other priestesses of her rank. She'd flung herself whole-heartedly into mastering the arcane practices and knowledge, but at no time had she thought it was real. At no time had she expected their midnight frolics to actually accomplish anything.

Her involvement was the result of abject boredom and a jaded disregard for the usual entertainments of the incredibly wealthy. By her twentieth winter, she'd reveled and rebelled, and grown tired of it. She had been raised in a palace with everything provided for her but nothing for her to do. At her fingertips, she'd had access to any entertainment the city had to offer. She'd been courted, wooed, and fawned over by most of the eligible men in the nation of Enhover, and no small number of ineligible ones. There'd been nothing out of reach for her, nothing her father or uncle could not provide. Nothing for her ever to work for, to be proud of. Nothing except the forbidden teachings of the Feet of Seheht and half-a-dozen other societies that she'd breezed through. Knowing the society's activities were banned by the Church, frowned upon by her father and uncle, had excited the young baroness.

She'd known it was theatre, though. She'd always known it was theatre.

Marquess Bartholomew Surrey, on the other hand, seemed entirely earnest in his plan to contact the spirit of her father. The man spoke with such certainty, such intense need, that'd she'd begun to believe him.

The marquess turned, his bright eyes burning like cold counters to the open flames in the room. Those eyes were the only part of him visible beneath his jet-black robes and mask.

Behind her, six similarly attired priests spread out around the circle of the stone room, taking places in between the flames of the braziers. They moved silently, and so far, only the marquess had spoken. She had no idea who the other participants were.

"Before we begin," intoned the marquess, assuming a practiced baritone that was as common in practitioners of secret ceremonies as it was on the stage, "I want to ensure you understand what we will do tonight, what you are agreeing to."

"You will not tell me it is too late to change my mind?" she asked, glancing back behind her to the unlit hallway they'd walked through on the way to the chamber. In the tunnel, she'd heard the heavy steel gate slam shut. She'd heard the clank of a lock as one of the society members had sealed them within the chamber. It had sent a trill of fear and excitement down her spine, knowing they'd trapped her inside.

"Would you prefer there be no choice?" asked Bartholomew.

The marquess moved to the altar in the center of the room. It was a rectangular table, waist-high to the men and draped in black silk that was stitched with silver thread depicting the symbol of Seshim. A spirit she was only passingly familiar with, but she knew the spirit was allied with Seheht. Two legs of the dark trinity, she'd been told long ago.

"If you'd rather," continued the marquess. He pulled up a corner of the silk sheet. Beneath it, she saw an iron manacle dangling from a stout length of chain.

She studied the restraint then looked to Bartholomew. "That is not necessary."

He shrugged. "Some prefer it that way. If you are ready, then disrobe."

Trying to hide her shaking, Lannia unclasped the black silk she was clothed in and let it fall to the floor. She felt the warmth from the fires on her bare skin, and following Marquess Surrey's direction, she climbed onto the altar, his hand on her back, helping her up. She lay down, her bare skin sliding across the smooth silk, the flickering fires caressing her with their warmth.

Bartholomew took a place beside the altar at her head, and the other six robed and masked figures stepped forward and surrounded her.

The seven men let out a low, sonorous hum. Motionless, they

continued the sound. So far below the streets of Southundon, the crackling of the fire and the steady buzz of the men's humming were only noises in the stone chamber. The echoes rolled back and forth, bouncing off the walls as the men continued their wordless chant.

She felt her body begin to respond to the warmth of the fire, to the seven men looking down at her nakedness, to the hums from their throats that seemed to course through her, washing over her body in waves. Her heart beat faster, her breath came in expectant bursts, and she shifted, parting her legs slightly.

The men around her stayed motionless, humming.

Bartholomew moved, and she followed him with her eyes as he collected a silver thurible. Swinging the censer from three thin chains, he waved it in a circle, and fragrant clouds of incense trailed after it, drifting down over her face and her shoulders.

She breathed deeply, inhaling the scent and feeling its comfort.

Bartholomew began to pace around the backs of the other participants, swinging the thurible, his low-voiced chant overlaying their humming. He spoke words she could not understand in a muddled drone that never seemed to break.

She did not know the meaning of his intonation, but she began to move on the altar, her excitement rising, looking into the eyes of the men surrounding her, feeling the hums from their throats penetrating her. The smoke from the incense covered the altar and began to fill the room, undulating tendrils moving along with the rise and the fall of Bartholomew's low, strange incantation.

There was something in the incense, something other than herbs burned for their scent, something that was intoxicating her, but she did not care. The thrill of the ritual, the fear that it would not work, and the panic that it would work, all raced through her. She wondered about tomorrow, when they emerged into the bright light of morning, what she would feel, what she would think, but she forced the thought away. There was no tomorrow, no tonight even. There was only now.

Bartholomew continued his slow rotation around the room,

spreading the smoke from the thurible and filling the stone chamber with echoes of his chanting. It was familiar and strange, like she'd heard it long before, but she did not know when.

Beside her, the two men closest to her head shifted. One produced a long strip of black silk. The other placed soft hands below her head, lifting it slightly, letting the first man wrap the silk around her, blindfolding her.

Her sight gone, she dove into her other senses, smelling the fragrant smoke, listening to the deep hums and chanting. She felt warmth from the palm of the man's hand against her cheek. She twisted her head so that the first man could tie the blindfold behind her. Her lips pressed against the second man's palm, and she parted them, breathing heavily on his skin.

The first man finished tying the blindfold, but the other let his hands linger. Who was he? Did she know him? The man did not move away from her, and in the haze brought by the incense, it took her a moment to realize Bartholomew's chanting had stopped. She felt him, or someone, by her feet, climbing atop the altar. Atop her.

One by one, the men's humming ended, and they took up Bartholomew's chant, rotating around the circle. One man uttered the strange commands, the others repeating him in lower voices. Hands — some soft and maintained with lotions and oils, some harsh like that of a laborer — began to stroke her body. She twisted, writhing in trepidation and anticipation.

Her legs were pushed apart. Bartholomew, or one of the others, scooted awkwardly between her thighs.

She opened her mouth to speak, to ask what would happen next, but the man beside her head put his fingers into her mouth, his palm on her jaw. She closed her lips around his fingers, silent as the other men circled and touched her, cupping her breasts, pulling her nipples, and closing fingers around her neck before releasing her.

The man between her legs entered her. She could feel his silk robes hiked up around his waist, and she could feel the trembling in his body as he pressed against her, in her.

The others groped her, teased her, and hurt her with their hands.

Between her legs, the man thrust vigorously, frantic with a need more primal than the ritual they were conducting. She let him take his pleasure and felt the moment when it was complete. Then, another took his place, eager with the same drive as the first man, the same drive that every man had. Out of pace with their slow, deliberate incantation, the men could not hold back, perhaps intoxicated by the same mixture in the incense that had overtaken her.

Despite herself, she felt her hips rising and falling with the second man's plunging thrusts. She felt her body responding, her need mirroring his. Blindfolded, the scent of the incense, the sound of the men's chanting, and the feel of their hands and bodies filled her mind with intense sensation.

When her second suitor finished, hands rolled her to her stomach, gently, insistent. She did not fight, and as a third man took his place behind her, she arched her back, accepting what was happening, swimming the current of the ritual along with them.

They kept their hands on her, kept joining her on the altar, and her pleasure and pain rose in cascading waves. As each man finished, she crested another wave, and her mind swirled with quivering ecstasy and harsh torment as the men's fever grew.

They spun her, turned her, and entered her again and again. They grew impatient and no longer waited their turn. They used her in every way that they could. Had it been seven? Had they begun anew? She thought they had, but she'd lost count. Lost track of time. Of where they were. Who they were. She only knew what she could feel them doing.

Then, she was rolled onto her back and held there with a hand around her neck. Other hands clamped down on her shoulders and legs. A man pushed his way between her legs, entering her quickly and violently. Her blindfold was torn away and she blinked in the stabbing light cast by the fires. She lay on her back, looking up at the masked face hovering above her.

She struggled, uncertain now what was happening, hearing guttural shouts instead of the low chanting. The humming had stopped. All of the men were holding her down and shouting. She tried to speak, to ask for acknowledgement that she was present, a participant as well as them, but a man's hand closed over her mouth, the tough callouses of a workman pressing hard against her lips.

Her heart hammered but no longer with passion, instead with fear.

Above her, the man rode her like a beast, releasing short, breathless grunts as he sped his attack, his eyes hard as his gaze met hers. They were the only thing she could see, the only thing not covered by his mask. He held her gaze, thrusting into her, his companions holding her down. Then, he glanced up and nodded at another man, his body tensing, a low cry escaping his hidden lips.

Steel flashed across her field of vision, and the hands moved away from her. Terrible pain bloomed across her neck. Her throat. They were cutting her throat.

Hot blood squirted. She felt it on her bare chest and shoulders. She tasted drops of it on her lips as she gasped futilely for air. She opened her mouth to scream, to shout, but she couldn't. She could only cough, liquid expelling from between her lips, her mouth filling with the taste of her own blood.

It spilled over her skin, dousing her upper body in bright crimson. Cold began to fill her, originating from between her legs, her most sacred place, where the men had spilled their seed. Cold crept through her slowly and then fast. Unable to speak, unable to shout, she watched as the men stood around her, silent now, as the cold spread from her core to her extremities.

A man, masked but otherwise naked, took his place at her head.

"By the blood of your daughter, we call to you!" he thundered.

"By the strength of her pleasure, we seek you! By the desecration of her body, we bind you!"

Cold. Bitter, painful cold. She felt herself slipping, sliding from her body, but to nowhere else. Nowhere she knew. She was dying. She was dying, and her soul was fleeing her body.

Fleeing but not gone.

Her soul, her spirit, was still there, not yet passed beyond the shroud, when her father arrived.

DETACHED, SLIPPING, VIEWING THE ROOM AS IF THROUGH A SMOKED pane of glass, she hung above herself. What had been her.

She saw Marquess Bartholomew Surrey stumble back from the altar. She could not hear, but she saw his mouth opening in panic and could imagine the high-pitched shrieks and demands he uttered.

It did him no good.

Her body, her corpse, curled into a kneeling crouch atop the altar. Then she, or what had been her, leapt at the marquess, grasping his skull with two hands and flinging him against the wall. He crumpled there, slumping to the floor in stunned terror.

What had been her turned, and the other six men, still masked and naked, bodies slick with sweat from the vigorous ritual, manhoods shriveling in fear, tried to run, but there was nowhere to go. They'd locked themselves into the circular stone chamber, and even if they'd had the presence of mind to find the key to the gate, what had been her was standing in the way.

What had been her sprang at them, reaching with unnaturally strong hands, rending their flesh into tattered strips like they were overcooked slabs of stewed beef. What had been her tore them apart, flinging pieces of them, chunks ripped from their bodies. In moments, the room was covered in hunks of flesh and sticky, dripping blood.

The fires had extinguished, the only movement the drip of

blood onto the floor. Even in the dark, she could see, and she saw a shadow rise from what had once been her. The shade of her father. She didn't dwell on the fact that she must be one as well. She didn't dwell on anything. She couldn't. She was dead.

Together, the two shades leaked from the room, flying fast into the cold, toward the unimaginable expanse of the shroud between their new world and the old one. The barrier parted, and the spirits flew through. Behind them, the shroud closed, and she felt nothing but cold.

THE CARTOGRAPHER I

"WHAT WILL YOU DO, OLIVER?" asked Duchess Matilda Wellesley. He sat down his heavy silver fork and picked up the crisp, white linen napkin from his lap. He dabbed at his lips and took a sip of dark red Ivallan wine before replying. "I'm not sure yet."

His brother John laughed. "Oliver, if you mean to have any choice at all, you had better decide soon. With Uncle William gone in such a terrible fashion, there's a vacancy in the ministry, a vacancy that has very few suitable candidates to fill it."

Oliver blinked at his brother.

"Father is considering naming you prime minister," continued John. "In fact, I think he'll do more than consider. Once the dust clears from this situation in Imbon, he'll want the ministry on stable footing. What better way to add stability than put another Wellesley in charge?"

"Me?" questioned Oliver, frowning at his brother across the candlelit table. "You think he'd name me as prime minister? That's absurd, John. I have no experience, first of all. Second, what about you or Franklin? Either of you would be better suited than I to bear the mantle."

John shook his head and grinned. "I've already told the old man I don't want it. Matilda fancies moving to the west coast. You recall her family is there? We have our eye on Westundon as soon as Philip vacates the seat. Can't very well handle the role of prime minister so far from the ministry, ey? And Franklin doesn't have any more desire than I to take on the ministry. Did you know that wife he found from Ivalla has him attending Church services four days a week? He's become rather serious about it and is even drafting plans for a new Church in Eastundon. He's attempting to shift the balance of Church power that way, I think. With that in mind, it's best he and Father have some separation. You know Father's thoughts on the Church. A prime minister with such close ties? I don't need to tell you Father wouldn't give it a second thought. And Philip himself? He has political duties as prince that none of the rest of us share. Management of the Congress of Lords and the ministry require separate positions and separate people."

"Well…" began Oliver, glancing between John and Matilda. "Father is in no rush to abdicate, which means Philip should be in Westundon for quite some time. You have no duties as a prince, and when he can be bothered, Father is quite capable of emerging from his study and leading. I have other responsibilities, John, and I don't see how it's necessary for me to become involved in governance."

"Perhaps," agreed John. "Stability, though, remember? Why name a prime minister we all know will only be temporary? It's best to put in someone who can serve in the role for an extended period."

Oliver shook his head. "I have other responsibilities. The Company, the Westlands… You know I'm meant to lead an expedition there."

"What of Imbon?" queried Matilda. "It was my understanding that both President Goldwater and Admiral Brach were counting on you to lead the action against the natives. You know the place better than anyone, don't you?"

Oliver's stomach soured and he took another long drink of wine. At his elbow, an attendant hurried forward to refill his glass.

"I'm told the Company's gaze has left the Westlands for the moment. At least until they clean up this mess in the tropics," said John, peering at his younger brother. "Imbon, is it? Do you want to lead the marines against the natives?"

"I don't want to do any of it," muttered Oliver. He picked his knife and fork back up but did not move to slice another bite from the seasoned hunk of roasted beef on his plate. "I'd sail to the Westlands still, if the choice was mine."

John tore a piece of bread in two and slathered a chunk of butter across one side. "If that's your desire, you'd best make it known. Once Father settles his mind on something, he doesn't change it." John raised his butter knife in the air. "Imbon and then prime minister. I suspect that's what the old fox is thinking. It makes sense, Oliver, even if that's not what you desire. Ever since Northundon fell, it's been likely the mantle of the ministry would rest on your shoulders one day. We've all expected it, sooner or later."

Gripping his fork tightly, Oliver shook his head, forcing away memories of his uncle. His uncle declaring that he'd never be able to live his own life. His uncle claiming the Crown would use him as it saw fit. His uncle had been right.

"What's wrong, Oliver?" asked Matilda.

He put down his fork and forced himself to relax his hand. "Still adjusting to William being gone, I guess."

"The time for play is over, brother," said John. "You had a better run than the rest of us, and while Philip is the one who will wear it, the weight of the Crown rests on all of our heads."

"I'd hardly call what I've been doing these last years as play," complained Oliver, retrieving his fork and digging it into the beef. Pink juices oozed from the rare cut of meat as he sliced off a bit. He stuck it into his mouth, chewing the tender flesh as much to give him an excuse to stop speaking as to sate his hunger.

"You've done good work for the Company," commended John. "Great work, really. Showed a real talent for mapmaking and for adventure. But those shares you've accumulated, the stacks of coins, the properties, all of that wealth, it is play. You spend it, yes, on luxuries and that ridiculous airship, but you could have spent just as freely without a single coin from the Company. Father has never been one to say no to his youngest, and he would have opened the treasury for you. While Matilda and I have been busy ensuring the succession, producing heirs to the throne along with Philip and Franklin, you've spent countless nights in the beds of every nubile young lady this nation has to offer, but not a one of them has produced a legitimate heir. Tell me that's not play."

Oliver grunted but did not respond. His brother had a point with that last bit. He ran his hand over his hair, checking the knot in the back.

"Will you settle down, Oliver?" asked Matilda.

Oliver thought she was asking innocently until he saw the wicked gleam in her eye.

"Aria, Isabella, some young thing I do not know?" continued his brother's wife. "I'm told Baron Child is ready for his daughters to assume their responsibilities — find a husband, produce grandchildren, that sort of thing. I imagine either girl would be thrilled at a chance to settle into King Edward's palace, or perhaps a home in the city would better suit? A man with your resources could give them whatever they wanted. The only problem, how to choose between the two? Maybe that is why you've had such a difficult time assuming a more, ah, traditional role for one in the royal family."

Grinning at Oliver, John chomped down on his bread.

"Of course," added Matilda, twirling her fork in her hand, "maybe you don't plan to choose. Generations ago, there was a Wellesley who orchestrated a similar feat. Raised his mistress to duchess, did he not, John? I cannot recall that old fellow's name."

"I was never good in history," admitted John.

"Will you tell me, Oliver, if you mean to court them both?" tittered Matilda. "The scandal would be delicious, and I can't tell you how much I'd enjoy watching all of the old hens lurking around these corridors when they heard the news."

"I'm not… I don't think the baronesses would agree to such an arrangement," mumbled Oliver, looking down at his plate.

"You never know," said John with a wink.

"Why are you two encouraging this?" complained Oliver, sitting back and waving a hand between his brother and his wife. "You might delight in the scandal, but it'd be of no help to the Crown."

"No, of course not," said John with a laugh. "You're right. We should not encourage it. It's just that you, little brother, have always had free reign to involve yourself in all manner of scandals and controversies. I can't say I haven't been jealous of your freedom, and I can't say that I won't enjoy seeing you trying to fight your way through the towers of paperwork and bureaucracy in the ministry, but I will miss hearing about your adventures. You've lived the life I could only dream about. You've seen places, done things that—"

Matilda harrumphed.

"Not the Child twins. I didn't mean them," said John with a grin. He winked at Oliver. Beside him, Matilda rolled her eyes. He turned to her. "You've spoken just as often as I of seeing the floating islands in the Archtan Atoll. You're just as curious about those pirate-infested waters off the coast of the Southlands. And to see the sunrise from the deck of an airship over the boundless sea! Why, we've only been to the United Territories half-a-dozen times, and each of those a diplomatic mission involving as much adventure as stumbling to the water closet in the middle of the night with no fae light."

"We have a good life, John," chided Matilda.

Gathering his wine, John raised his glass. "Yes, raising children, living in the palace, it's a grand adventure. It's no Archtan Atoll, though." Giving Oliver a conspiratorial look, he leaned closer and whispered, "And it's no Child twins."

Matilda clutched his arm and yanked him close, planting a kiss on his cheek. "I am only one, but follow me to bed, husband, and I'll make you remember that you couldn't handle two of me."

She stood and nodded at Oliver. "It's time for me to retire. Don't keep him up too late."

"With you waiting, my sweet, I won't be late at all," claimed John.

Flouncing out of the dining room, Matilda disappeared, and a gaggle of servants swooped in to clear her plate and refill the two dukes' drinks.

"She's a good woman," said John. "My advice is to find one like that, one who is willing to put up with you, and let her settle you down. It's not a bad life."

Not responding, Oliver took another bite of his meat.

"I meant what I said earlier," remarked John. "If you mean to have some say in what horizon you'll chase next, you'd best do it soon. My understanding is that once William's funeral has taken place, Father will instruct Admiral Brach to sail for Imbon. It's going to be difficult for you to avoid that assignment, if that's what you plan on."

Oliver grunted.

"I know it was painful for you," continued John. "It sounded... It sounded terrible."

"It wasn't pleasant," admitted Oliver.

"You had friends killed in the attack?" asked John.

Oliver drew a deep breath and answered, "Yes, some of the people we lost there were my friends. Good men I've known for ten years or more. None of them were my enemies. Not the officers of the Company and not the natives, either. I thought it would be different in Imbon. I really did."

"It was all over these figurines?" questioned John. "What was so special about them that made the natives revolt?"

Oliver shrugged. "I don't know. Father looked them over and then sent them to the museum. Church scholars are studying the items now. If there are any strange properties to the statues, no one has found them yet. The natives claimed they contained the spirits of their enemies. Reavers, they called them."

"Well, there must be something to it if the natives revolted," declared John. "They had to know they'd lose any conflict against Enhover."

Oliver nodded. He'd gone to see the figurines with Sam, and as his father had claimed, they all appeared to be there, tucked away in a back room of Southundon's Royal Museum. They were not on display, but they were available for study, the statues and nothing else. The tablets, the ones he'd recognized a sorcerous symbol on, were missing. If there was truth amongst the artifacts they'd found in Imbon, it was on those tablets, and those were still in his father's clutches. The old man was still transcribing the symbols, and he didn't want them displayed publicly until he was certain there was nothing dangerous about them.

John glanced at a tall clock that sat in the corner of the private dining room, then he looked to Oliver's wine glass. "If you mean to finish that while I'm here, you'd best hurry. Matilda is waiting…"

Oliver reached for his glass but paused as there was a knock on the door.

"Enter," called John. He frowned as their father's chief of staff cracked the door and leaned in. "Edgar, what can we do for you?"

"I'm afraid I have terrible news, m'lords," murmured the man. "You need to come with me to your father, immediately."

"What's the matter?" questioned Oliver, standing. "Shackles, you have to tell us, is the old man all right?"

"It's your cousin, m'lord, Lannia. She's… she's not all right."

THE PRIESTESS I

SAM TURNED THE PAGE, the ancient parchment crinkling with the motion.

"I can't believe you've been carrying that book around with you," muttered the red-haired man across the table from her. Timothy Adriance was looking distraught, staring at the book. "A tome like that, it should be secure, held safe in a library where it can be cared for. Books must be preserved..."

"A book is an object," she said, waving a hand at him. "Its value is the knowledge it imparts upon the reader. The knowledge should be cherished. The book should be used. I could make the argument that the Church's greedy secrecy around the information in books like this has caused far more problems than it's solved. Perhaps it'd be better if those restricted archives of yours were opened to the public. The tomes there could be copied, distributed—"

"You know not of what you speak!" snapped the man.

"I know the cost of sorcery when it's let loose in the world," argued Sam. "I've seen the horrors with my own eyes. I've been in front of a sorcerer without the knowledge to fight against what they summoned, and I've seen the deaths that have resulted. Have you?"

Adriance grunted. "You do not know what is contained within those books, the horrors that are still unleashed. The Church is guarding knowledge that is far more dangerous than what the mean conjurers you've faced were capable of."

"Bishop Gabriel Yates was one of those I faced," remarked Sam. "Did he not read the texts in your secret archives? What he learned, he learned from the Church! Where were you and the other scholars when he applied that knowledge and killed hundreds of people? If I'd had access, if you'd shared what you know, then perhaps I could have stopped him earlier."

Across from her, the priest winced. "Gabriel Yates did not understand what he had. He… Some of the texts were hidden from him by others in our order."

"I wonder how many lives could have been saved if everyone knew what to look for," said Sam. "How many hundreds, or thousands, would be alive today if the knowledge of such evil was not a secret?"

Adriance touched the silver pendant hanging on his chest. It was the one she'd stolen from him and placed underneath Bridget Cancio's corpse. Sam had recovered it from the ruins of Bishop Yates' mansion and returned it to Adriance before anyone else saw it. Just she and Raymond au Clair knew what she'd done with it, and Raymond wouldn't be talking.

The priest was suspicious of her, about the theft and for other reasons. Timothy Adriance wasn't a dumb man, and he must have known she'd taken the emblem for a purpose, but fortunately, the purpose was beyond him. He didn't know the details of what had happened in Westundon. He didn't know how Bishop Yates had fallen, and she hoped he never would. She hoped he understood enough, though, to agree with the importance of sharing his knowledge with her. She needed him to help her translate the leather-bound grimoire she'd found in Isisandra Dalyrimple's effects, the Book of Law. Prying the forbidden knowledge from between Adriance's lips was proving far more challenging than lifting the silver emblem from the table beside his bed, though.

"I saw the Imbonese statuettes, the uvaan," said Adriance, changing the subject, "the ones the king turned over to the museum. Thank you for interceding on my behalf and getting me access."

"And?" she asked. She'd seen them too but had been unable to determine any occult properties. Unable to determine anything at all, actually.

"A prison, yes, that's what they are supposed to be?" asked Adriance. "A prison for the enemies of the people of Imbon?"

"That's what the natives said to Duke before the fighting broke out," confirmed Sam. "I don't know if they were telling the truth."

"I think they might have been truthful," said Adriance. "If I'm right about the uvaan, they are a sort of prison, but one that is unique. The uvaan may access a place that's outside of both our world and the underworld. It's a true prison, then, for spirits. They're held outside of the circle. Do you understand?"

"I think so," muttered Sam. "They're no longer part of the cycle, then? They cannot die, but they cannot be reborn into life, either?"

"Correct," said Adriance.

"A prison, but not to trap an enemy for a moment or for years, but forever," said Sam, frowning.

"One meant to last for eternity," agreed Adriance. "Worse than a killing, I suppose. I cannot fathom what it must be like for a spirit trapped in such a thing. I don't think they would be happy about it."

"What would happen then, if they escaped?"

"I'm not sure they can escape," speculated Adriance. "The uvaan are a door to the prison, yes, and if the door is gone, it's quite possible the spirits are trapped there forever. While the uvaan remains whole, like any good prison, I believe a key is required to open it. With a key, then I think whatever is inside could be released, but only with the key."

"Interesting," said Sam. "Where is the key, then?"

The priest merely shrugged.

Sam opened her mouth to question him further, but a sharp rap on the door interrupted her.

Adriance stood and opened the door to reveal a man in Wellesley livery.

"Mistress Samantha?" asked the man, eyeing her. "Your presence is requested at the palace."

"My presence?" asked Sam. "Why?"

"To meet with the king," replied the messenger. "He requested you come immediately."

Timothy Adriance's mouth fell open, and Sam frowned.

The messenger stood in the doorway waiting.

"Well, I suppose I cannot say no to the king," she murmured. She stood and eyed the servant. "You'll take me to him?"

The messenger nodded, and she followed him out into the night.

THE CARTOGRAPHER II

THE MOMENT EDGAR SHACKLES led him into the room, Oliver could feel a palpable sense of unease. His father sat in front of the fire. Earl Gerrald Holgrave, the Chair of the Congress of Lords, sat on a couch across from him. A man Oliver did not know stood before them, his silhouette outlined by the light of the fire. When Oliver got closer, he saw an open notebook in the man's hand and a grim expression on his face.

John asked, "What is it, Father? Shackles said something happened to Lannia?"

"A moment," said the king, turning to his chief of staff. "The priestess?"

"I sent a messenger to fetch her," answered Shackles. "She should be here shortly."

"The priestess?" questioned Oliver. "Sam?"

His father nodded confirmation.

"What—" Oliver began, but a knock on the door signaled her arrival.

She slipped in and gave Oliver a questioning look. He could only shrug.

"Inspector Moncrief, if you please," said the king.

The man with the notebook cleared his throat. He looked

nervously around the room then began. "M'lords, m'lady, approximately six turns of the clock past, the magistrates received an anonymous tip that there had been a murder deep beneath Marquess Bartholomew Surrey's townhome. The marquess regularly resides in Southwatch, but his family has maintained a residence here in Southundon for—"

"Yes, yes," said John. "We know the Surreys. What of the murder?"

Blanching, the inspector continued, "It, ah, it's worse, m'lord. Myself and a pair of watchmen responded to the tip and found the house lit, but there was no response when we knocked on the door. We peered inside of the windows and saw nothing. Finding it rather unusual that the house was lit but there was no answer, and of course with the reason for our visit in mind, I authorized the breaching of the front door. Inside... At first, we found nothing, but on further inspection, we located a locked door, which led to the basement of the townhome. It was decorated with quite unusual and disturbing artifacts, but worse, through that basement room, we found the entrance to a stone chamber."

The inspector paused, and Oliver glanced between the man and his father. The king sat patiently, his fingers pulling gently on his thin goatee, not prodding the inspector to speak faster.

Duke John, though, was not willing to wait. "Well, out with it, man. What did you find?"

"Your cousin, m'lord. Lannia Wellesley," said the inspector. "She was surrounded by what we believe are several others. They died in a most violent manner."

"Sorcery," hissed Oliver.

The inspector, lips pressed tightly together, nodded.

King Edward added, "None of us could think of any other explanation."

"A failed ritual?" wondered Sam.

"No," said the king, "at least, not in the way you mean. When I heard it was Lannia, I immediately rushed to the site myself. I believe a ritual was successfully conducted, and they made contact with a spirit from the underworld. It appears as though they could not control it, and the spirit slaughtered them."

"How—" began Sam.

The king stopped her with a raised hand. "I am no expert in these matters. Unfortunately, neither is Inspector Moncrief. You, however, are. You are the only two in Enhover who've faced evil like this. You're the only two who have any chance of understanding what transpired in that chamber. I don't want to say too much and bias your findings. Oliver, Samantha, the Crown needs your assistance."

Uncomfortably, Oliver nodded. He looked to the inspector. "Moncrief, show us to the Surrey home, then?"

SITTING ALONE IN A BLACK INSPECTOR'S CARRIAGE, OLIVER AND SAM rumbled through the nighttime streets of Southundon. Yellow light from the gas lamps spaced along the street flashed by the window, illuminating the interior in regular intervals of pale color.

"Two days, Duke," stated Sam. He didn't respond. She prodded him. "Two days until your uncle's funeral and the end of our freedom."

"My freedom," corrected Oliver. "John thinks our father will name me prime minister."

"Your freedom," agreed Sam. "Congratulations on prime minister, I'm told it's a plum position." She leaned forward and jabbed a finger at him. "What I meant was, unless you're willing to loan me your airship and crew, I'm not very well traveling to the Darklands. I can't get there on my own. If your plans and freedom are curtailed, then so are mine."

"We'll leave," grumbled Oliver. "We'll leave."

Sam sat back, crossing her arms over her chest.

"What would you have us do?" questioned Oliver. "My cousin, my flesh and blood, was killed in a sorcerous ritual. I cannot turn my back on my family. And you, can you turn your back on your mission? For months, you've prattled on about how you and your mentor are the last line of defense against sorcery, the last guard against the dark arts. Well, the dark arts are being practiced right here in Southundon, less than a league from where we've been sleeping! How can we not investigate?"

"I'm here in the carriage with you," said Sam. She squeezed herself then continued, "And you're right. This is my role, my life now. Fighting sorcery is all that I am, but I don't have the tools, Duke. I don't have the knowledge to face the depth of what the dark arts are capable of. Another Isisandra, another Yates, perhaps we could prevail against them, but we both sensed what was loose atop the old druid fortress. Ca-Mi-He, the great spirit. I don't even know where to start on dealing with something like that. I don't know where else to turn, either, except south. In the Darklands, we can find what we need to know. You say I don't want to fight — I do! But I need to gather the right tools to do it."

Oliver grunted.

Sam sat silently, watching him.

"Let's see what happened to Lannia, and then we'll decide what to do next," suggested Oliver. "I have no plans to accept the position as prime minister. I have no plans to be in Southundon long enough for my father to even offer it. Ainsley has been quietly stocking the airship and preparing the crew. In two days, they'll be ready to depart. While the capital is busy with William's burial, we'll slip away unnoticed."

"Unnoticed?"

"Unnoticed for long enough," said Oliver, a grin starting to form. Then it wavered and fell.

Lannia. His only cousin. The only child of William, who had died by Oliver's hand. Now, she was dead as well, killed by the practice he'd sworn to root out of Enhover. He'd grown up with Lannia in his father's palace. They'd been true friends during their younger years, and while life carried them apart, he'd always enjoyed her company. He'd always shared things with her that he trusted to no one else. More than anyone in the family, she'd understood him. And now, she was dead. Killed by sorcery.

"WE FORCED THE GATE, M'LORD," EXPLAINED INSPECTOR MONCRIEF.

Oliver nodded and gestured for the man to lead them inside.

"I, ah, I'd rather not, m'lord," said the inspector, beads of sweat popping on his forehead in the chill, stone corridor. He offered weakly, "With fewer of us in there... ah, you can conduct a more thorough investigation, I think. We can compare notes when you come back out."

Oliver grunted and raised his globe of yellow fae light. The brilliant creatures were swarming frantically, and he pretended he didn't think it was because they could sense the bitter cold aura of sorcery ahead of them.

"You feel that?" he asked Sam.

"Feel what?" she wondered.

"Nothing," he said, ducking through the bent and twisted frame of the steel gate.

Even before they entered the circular stone chamber, he could see broad, crimson pools of blood that had spread into the mouth of the hallway. The blood covered the path wall-to-wall, and it was obvious from boot prints in the liquid where Moncrief and his partners had walked.

What they couldn't see until they entered the room and the fae light shone to illuminate it all was the grisly nature of the killing. Blood, gore, and bits of people were strewn around the room like wrapping and ribbon from a child's New Year gifts. The walls, the stone ceiling, the altar in the center of the room, the braziers still hot with embers from a fire, all of it was covered in viscera and splatter. The entire floor was coated in a thin layer of blood, and after a moment, Oliver gave up even looking to see if he could step around it. He couldn't. It was everywhere.

"There is a drain on the floor here," said Sam, her face pale, her voice tight. "This place was built for bloodshed, but it looks like it was, ah, stopped up with... flesh."

She covered her mouth with her hand and looked away, but there wasn't anywhere better in that charnel vault to rest her gaze. Oliver winced and stayed still a moment, forcing down the bile in his throat.

"Several others were killed, Moncrief said." Sam swallowed and shook herself.

Looking around, Oliver didn't think he could describe it any more accurately. How many bodies had provided the material for the mess strewn about the room? More than a few, less than a lot...

Cringing at the sounds of his boots lifting with each step from the sticky blood, he circled the altar, knowing that somewhere in the room, he would find Lannia.

Slumped against the wall on the opposite side of the altar from the entrance, he did. Her neck was opened to the bone with a vicious slash. It took little imagination to guess that was what killed her, but her entire naked body was covered in blood, like it had been painted on her. It was too much for it to be her own.

"Duke, look at her fingers," whispered Sam.

He did and frowned. Her hands were stained crimson, like the rest of her, and at least half of her fingernails had been torn off. Several fingers appeared broken, and her skin was ragged, liked she'd been digging. He stooped, looking closer. No, not digging. Skin and blood was trapped beneath her remaining fingernails. She'd been rending. Tearing.

"She did it," he said, his voice quiet but certain.

"How?" wondered Sam. "The strength it would take to... to do this..."

Both of them turned, surveying the room, not willing to touch anything except for what they had to. They found discarded piles of clothing, covered in ruined flesh but undamaged, as if it had been removed voluntarily. They found a knife, which could be the one that had been used to cut Lannia's throat. Wishing it wasn't necessary, they'd peeled off the silk sheet from the altar. Underneath the table was a variety of materials — wax candles, a thurible that was still warm from use hours earlier, incense, towels, and small jars that Sam warned him not to touch.

"Poppy?" he asked, peering at an amber glob of paste.

"That and others," she said. "Common intoxicants, I think. I recognize some of these from, well, they're used in pleasure houses. At least a few of those can be absorbed through the skin. The girls, ah… I couldn't tell you which substance is which. Best not to risk touching any of it."

He didn't bother to tease her about how she knew which substances were distributed in pleasure houses. Instead, he turned back to the body of his cousin. "The gate was locked, Moncrief said, and he confirmed there had been no footprints in the blood until he and the other inspectors arrived."

"Something invested Lannia and took out its rage on the others," surmised Sam. "They called a spirit and couldn't control it. It killed them and I suspect returned to the underworld once the bridge through the shroud was severed."

"You think there is no longer a risk?" he asked.

She raised an eyebrow and glanced around the blood-covered room.

"You know what I mean," he said.

"Outside of our experience atop the druid keep, spirits rarely linger in this world," responded Sam. "When the bridge they crossed to get here and the binding the sorcerer sets to control them are broken, they cannot stay. I don't believe there is any additional threat to us from what happened here. Of course, it's concerning that there are still sorcerers operating in Enhover who have the skill to contact underworld spirits, but it's a little comforting that they cannot do it well. Whatever happened in here, whoever was responsible, they did not have the skill of your uncle or Yates, not even of Isisandra. These were amateurs, and they paid a heavy price for their folly."

Oliver looked over the blood-splattered room and then back to Lannia.

"This was probably an isolated cabal," suggested Sam.

"And Lannia's involvement?" he asked.

Sam grimaced.

"Tell me what you're thinking," he instructed.

"Her father died two days ago," said Sam. "He was a sorcerer. Which spirit do you think they were calling upon? Lannia could have been useful to them, a way to call to her father and strengthen the bridge. A strong enough bridge would give a spirit great power when it arrived."

Oliver winced.

"It's not your fault," said Sam. "There's nothing you could have done to prevent this. It's probably not Lannia's fault, either, for what that is worth. They could have abducted her and forced her part in the ritual. See those manacles? These were sorcerers, Duke, and they got what was coming to them."

"I'm the one who killed William," said Oliver, forcing himself to look away from his dead cousin. "He was family, and I killed him. Lannia has paid the cost."

———

"Let the inspectors handle it?" questioned his father. "What do you mean let the inspectors handle it?"

Oliver cringed in the face of his father's calm interrogation. Other fathers might have yelled. They might have bellowed and stormed around the room. But not Edward. When the king was angry, he never showed it. Only Oliver's long history of irritating the man gave him any hint that he was venturing into dangerous waters.

"They're trained for this, Father."

The king snorted. "No they aren't. They made a muck of it up in Harwick, didn't they? The senior inspector there is dead. A brilliant investigative mind, wasn't he? So brilliant he didn't realize the society he professed allegiance to was at the heart of the conspiracy. So brilliant he didn't anticipate the Church coming with knives out and slitting his damned throat."

In the corner of the room, Inspector Moncrief shifted uncomfortably.

"The inspectors have no experience with this type of criminal behavior," insisted the king, glancing between Oliver and Sam. "Only you two do. Only you two can get to the bottom of what happened."

"We believe the threat is over," declared Oliver. "The perpetrators called upon a spirit but lost control of it and it killed them. We can safely assume that one of those men was Marquess Bartholomew Surrey, and there are no clues left to identify the others or even to determine how many they might be. The inspectors are perfectly capable of checking the reports for missing people and making the connections to this crime."

"Lannia is family," reminded the king. "We are Wellesleys, and we do not turn our backs on family."

"I am not turning my back on family, Father."

The old man's lips pressed together, and then he said, "Leave us, Moncrief." The inspector shuffled quickly out the door and shut it. King Edward guessed, "You're still thinking of your mother."

Oliver didn't respond. It hadn't been a question.

"It's a foolish quest, Oliver," said the king. "I know you believe she lives, despite all evidence to the contrary. It's been twenty years, son, and there's been no word, no rumored sightings, nothing! Even if you're right, if she did somehow escape Northundon when no one else did, if she did somehow find passage out of Enhover undetected, and she did find a place to hide outside of the notice of our empire for two decades, why do you think you'll find her? If she lives, which I do not believe she does, then she is well hidden. She does not want to be found, not by you, not by anyone. If she's avoided notice for this long, she will continue to do so."

"I have to try," stated Oliver.

The king's stare bored into him. "Why?"

"Family," responded Oliver. "You taught me that. We must never turn our backs on family. Lannia is dead. I wish she wasn't, but she is, and there is nothing I can do about that, but Mother is not. Lilibet lives, Father. Maybe she's hiding and will never be found, but maybe she needs our help. I have to find out."

"Your family is here, son."

He met his Father's gaze and shook his head. "Not all of it."

The king snorted. "Leave me, Oliver. I have no stomach for continuing this discussion right now."

Oliver turned to go, and as he was walking toward the door, he heard his father say to Sam, "Not you. I have something to show you."

THE PRIESTESS II

"I HAVE SOMETHING TO SHOW YOU," the king told her.

Her breath caught and she froze.

Oliver, looking back quizzically, left the room without comment.

She and the king were alone in his study.

"M'lord," she said quietly.

"You went to the museum and looked at the Imbonese figurines?" asked King Edward.

"I did," she acknowledged.

"What did you think of them?"

"I... I don't know, m'lord," she stammered. "I could not detect any supernatural properties. They have intriguing symbols etched into the wood, but perhaps that is it."

"That's not all," chided the king. "Do not act stupid, girl. You think Imbon buried and flooded these things and then rebelled over their discovery all because there are some carvings on the wood? Tell me what you suspect."

She shifted uncomfortably.

He waited, studying her.

Finally, she offered, "It could be these figurines, the uvaan, serve as a sort of prison. They may truly hold the spirits of

Imbon's enemies, as the natives told your son. If that's the case, they are relatively safe."

"A locked door remains a locked door until someone introduces a key," agreed the king. "I also believe these are prisons, locking spirits away from our world and the other. Safe, as you say, but surely the creatures inside are not."

She nodded, her hands balled into fists at her sides.

Stroking the hair on his chin, the king stood from his seat before the fire and walked to his desk. On top of it was a cloth-covered object. With a twitch of his hand, he removed the cloth, and she saw a dark clay tablet. One of the ones recovered in Imbon, she was certain.

Her gaze moved from the tablet up to the king's face.

"Sorcerers are operating within the boundaries of our empire, Samantha. They are the rot that may cause it all to crumble," the king told her. "Oliver is blinded by memories twenty years old, and he cannot see what is obvious. He yearns for the comfort of his mother's arms, the safety he felt there when he was a child, but the time for childhood fantasies is over. It is time for him to leave that in the past and to face what is in the future."

Sam stood stone still, unable to look away from the king, unable to respond.

"You were well trained by your mentor," continued the old man. "You suspect something about what happened in Northundon, don't you? Tell me what you suspect about Lilibet."

Sam shook her head slowly, unable to tell this man, the king of the empire, what was obvious. She could see the understanding in his eyes, but it was too much to voice it.

"You think Lilibet is the only one who could have performed the sorcery you found in Northundon's gardens," said the king as if reading her mind. "You think she was a sorceress and whatever ritual she performed was meant to facilitate her escape. You think she still lives. Is that why you want to go to the Darklands, to locate Lilibet?"

Sam swallowed.

"The threats I am concerned about are at home," said the king. "Let the Darklands do as they have done for centuries, for time long before we became a nation. They have no interest in us, and I have no interest in them. What happed here today, in our capital, is what worries me."

"I understand, m'lord," she whispered.

The king's finger tapped on the clay tablet on his desk. "I'm told there are few people these days who understand ancient Darklands script. With a mentor as wise and well respected as yours, I wonder, are you one of those few?"

She shifted. "I, ah, I know a few words, m'lord."

"Then perhaps you can do something with this," King Edward suggested. "Perhaps you can tease some meaning from it. Or maybe one of your allies can? Is what Oliver found in Imbon a threat that should be destroyed, or should it be hidden? Is this the missing key to something we can use? Did the natives hide it because they were afraid of it or because it is a weapon? I do not know, but if you find out, will you tell me?"

"Of course, m'lord," she said, finally able to break the iron lock of the man's gaze. She looked at the tablet in front of him, wondering why he was giving it to her, wondering what he'd done with the others. He was the king, though, and she wasn't about to ask.

"Samantha," warned King Edward, "if the people of Imbon locked their enemies within those figurines, if this gaol was meant to last for eternity, there might have been a good reason. Be careful with the key, will you?"

SHE SAT THE CLAY TABLET ON THE TABLE IN FRONT OF THE PRIEST.

Timothy Adriance looked up, startled.

"Can you read this?" she asked.

Frowning, he scooted the small stand with the hanging fae light globe closer. He stood up and leaned over the tablet.

"This is… this is one of the tablets recovered from Imbon?" he asked.

"It is," she confirmed. "Have you seen it? Have you… Did you speak to the king about what we discussed yesterday?"

"The king!" exclaimed Adriance. "Of course not. Why would I — What did he say?"

"What can you tell me of this tablet?" asked Sam, ignoring the priest's question.

He frowned at her but finally looked down at the tablet. "The language of origin is definitely the Darklands, but it's not a pure form of the tongue. I'd need time to plot the connections, decipher the syntax."

"Let me know what you find, will you?" she asked.

Not looking up, the scholar was already moving his notebook closer, licking the tip of his quill, and preparing to start diagraming the text of the tablet.

Smirking, Sam turned to go, confident the priest would do little other than try to unravel the secrets held within the tablet. He, at least, she understood. Timothy Adriance was scholar with little regard for anything other than uncovering the secrets of the ancients.

The king, she was unsure of. Why had he given her the tablet? Had it been a bribe to convince her to stay in Enhover? Had he truly sought her help in translating the symbols and script? If so, why was he still holding onto the other tablets instead of sharing them with her or with the scholars in the museum?

She walked outside of the room, peering around the darkened library. The Church's library, a place she was unsure if she was still welcome, but so far, no one had thrown her out. Timothy Adriance was known there, evidently, and the other priests scuttled out of his way, deferring to the red-haired man who wasn't any older than she.

She was learning that the Church, for all of its mystery and hidden motives, was nothing compared to the Crown. What did King Edward want? Why had he told her that Lilibet was not the woman Duke recalled from his youth? Did the king suspect that his wife had been walking the dark path? Did that explain why he was in no hurry to discover where she'd been for so many years?

THE CARTOGRAPHER III

OLIVER FLIPPED up the collar of his long coat and stuffed his hands deep inside his pockets. Winter was breaking in the south of Enhover, but near the sea, a damp mist blew in, causing him to shiver and increase his pace, his booted feet clomping across wet cobblestones. Beneath the street, the ground rumbled with the passage of cars rolling along Southundon's underground rail. Far above, a metal stack belched thick smoke, black flecked with red.

He kept moving, hoping to get away before the cloud descended upon the streets. Red saltpetre mixed with industrial coal provided dense, portable fuel that made Enhover's rail the envy of the world, but the stuff caused an awful mess. The city streets were layered in soot, the black powder piling around the stacks and then spreading as feet and wheels tracked it all over Southundon.

Most often, members of his family, other peers, and wealthy merchants traveled those streets on quick-moving mechanical carriages. They rarely had to step foot on a stretch of cobblestone that wasn't meticulously swept clean by liveried staff. They gave the accumulating filth in the lesser quarters of the city as much thought as they did the hard cases in the asylum, which is to say they gave it no thought at all.

This evening, Oliver had wanted fresh air. Chilly or not, he'd decided a stroll through the city would clear his head. It'd been years since he'd traversed the streets of Southundon freely, and he'd forgotten how far from fresh that air was. Briefly, he considered taking a carriage out of the city and walking through the woods, but a late jaunt into the environs he'd so recently confronted his uncle was the opposite of a respite. He needed somewhere quiet, if such a thing could be found in Southundon, but he also needed somewhere with light and people, people who he didn't know, who wouldn't ask him questions or make insinuations.

He walked down to the harbor and found a pub he was certain wasn't frequented by anyone he would know, the Sailor's Grief. The sign above the door showed a sailor returning home to his wife. Oliver snorted, his lips twisting in a wry smile, and he walked in.

Oliver made his way through a half-full room and ordered an ale from a dull-eyed barman. He settled down on a stool, sipping the mediocre brew and pondering what was next.

His father had accused him of ignoring the needs of the Crown by planning to find his mother. It wasn't illegal, yet, to leave against his father's wishes. Until the old man had it written up as a proper decree, no courts would punish Oliver for defying the monarch, but the magistrates were not the ones who gave him concern. What would King Edward do if Oliver fled in search of Lilibet? Would he do anything?

Finishing his ale, Oliver decided that there was little personal risk if he defied his father. The old man rarely issued any real punishment to his sons, and even direct defiance of an order would not lead to a stint in Sounthundon's gaol. No, the strongest reprimand King Edward would give to his youngest was to force him into the ministry, and it seemed that was already going to happen.

But while there was little personal risk, King Edward wouldn't stand for anyone outside of his own bloodline disobeying him.

Sam, Ainsley, and the rest of the Cloud Serpent's crew would face incredible consequences if Oliver left after his father issued an edict. They might do it, out of loyalty to Oliver, but could he let them take such a risk? Even if there wasn't a direct order, how would his father treat anyone who helped Oliver avoid his duties to the Crown?

He grunted and tossed a few coins onto the bar top. He needed to go find Captain Ainsley.

"WE LEAVE TOMORROW OR MAYBE NOT AT ALL," SAID OLIVER. "I have to warn you there's a risk my father may consider you a conspirator. If I'm not there to explain that I forced you to accompany me…"

"Mmm hmm," mumbled Captain Ainsley, inspecting a heavy brass cannon barrel. She poked at the portal door in front of it, ensuring it was shut tight, and then counted the neat stack of iron balls her crew had arranged beside the cannon.

Oliver blinked at her and then glanced at First Mate Pettybone.

"She thinks if we drop you off in the Darklands, you're almost certain to die there," explained Pettybone. "If you do, we won't be coming back to Enhover no matter the circumstances of our departure. The captain is a bit of a gambler, m'lord. If you die but we do not, she'll have an airship, m'lord."

Oliver crossed his arms over his chest. Ainsley scowled at her first mate but didn't meet the duke's glare. He cleared his throat and waited, watching her back.

Finally, the captain turned and faced him. "I'd rather serve you while you're living, m'lord. I'll be as loyal to you as a sister as long as you're alive and I'm your captain, but a girl's gotta hedge her bets, you know? Gotta keep an eye on the future, m'lord."

"What would you do with an airship if you had one?" wondered Oliver.

"Ah, private trade, I suppose," murmured Ainsley, stooping down and recounting the stack of iron cannon balls.

"Private trade… you aim to turn pirate?"

"I aim to keep you alive, m'lord," huffed Ainsley, standing and pointing a finger at him. "But if I fail that, what chances do you think I'll stand back in Enhover? You are right. There is no chance your father or the Company is going to welcome me back if I'm involved in your demise. No, if you die on this adventure, then we're outlaws. We've no choice in the matter but to stake out for ourselves."

"My death is far from certain," complained Oliver.

Ainsley shrugged.

"We had to tell the crew something, m'lord," added Pettybone. "We had to make sure they knew there were options if… if you didn't make it back home with us. You can't take men on a voyage like this without letting them know there is a plan."

"Wait!" cried Oliver. "You told the crew that if I died, you would turn pirate?"

Ainsley balled her fist as if to punch her first mate, but then admitted, "Pettybone is right. I had to tell them something."

"You don't think that might put ideas into their heads?" screeched Oliver. "You don't think that maybe some of those crew members could decide it would be a lot easier to settle matters while we're over the sea and avoid an onerous trip to the Darklands? Spirits forsake it, Captain! They could slit my throat and dump my body over the edge at any moment. If they're already planning to turn pirate, what's one more murder on the indictment? The royal marines can only hang them once, after all, no matter what they do on the way to the gibbet."

Ainsley frowned, and Pettybone scratched the back of his head beneath his knit cap.

"Perhaps some more pay, m'lord, would assure the crew that you're worth more to us alive than dead," suggested the captain.

"You also ought to lock the door to the captain's cabin when you're sleeping, m'lord," suggested Pettybone. "Just in case."

Oliver groaned and kicked a cannon in frustration.

"The crew is loyal to you, m'lord," assured Ainsley, a bit unconvincingly. "They're not going to turn on you. We'll be ready tomorrow to sail for the Darklands, or we'll take you off to the Westlands if that's what you'd prefer. Where you direct us, m'lord, we will go. The boys are going to need a bit more pay, though."

Oliver grunted.

Just then, a cannon ball thudded down on the stairs leading to the deck above. Step by step, it thumped down to the bottom and rolled across the floor of the cannon deck. They could see a pair of dirty feet standing in the doorway above.

"Frozen hell, Mister Samuels," growled Pettybone. He stalked toward the hapless sailor.

After the first mate passed from earshot, Ainsley quietly said, "The crew'll fly wherever you direct us, m'lord, but if it's the Darklands, might be best if I can get them proper drunk the night before. You think we'll sail tomorrow? Are you certain?"

"Just be ready, captain," he said. "Just be ready."

OLIVER STEPPED DOWN FROM THE MECHANICAL CARRIAGE AND tugged his coat tight in the chill air. Two turns of the clock before midnight, noise bubbled from the wood-and-glass fronted pub before him. A new establishment, arriving in the capital with a splash, the Juniper Goddess was packed full of wigged and suited patrons. Specializing in gin cocktails with exotic mixtures from the tropics, it'd caught the imagination of the wealthy citizens of Southundon.

Oliver wondered if Commander Brenden Ostrander had gotten a taste for tropical spices during his time in Archtan Atoll or if the man was simply chasing the latest trend like the other revelers inside.

"Wellesley," called a voice.

Oliver turned and saw the commander disembarking from his own carriage.

Ostrander smiled and gestured to the place, "A bit crowded in there, but I'm told it's the place to be seen by the right stripe of folks. I tried coming a few days back, and even in uniform, the attendant couldn't find me a place to stand, much less a place to sit."

"I think they'll find me a spot," remarked Oliver. He frowned. "When did you care about being seen by the right stripe of folk?"

"When Admiral Brach recalled me back to the capital," replied Ostrander, raising his hands in front of him. "There's more politicking than fighting around here. In Southundon, the royal marines say a sharp quill will get your farther than a sharp sword."

"That's what you wanted to meet about? Politics?" wondered Oliver, making a show of covering a yawn with a closed fist. "It's late, and I don't have the patience for it tonight, Ostrander."

"Not politics," assured the man, shaking his head. "I want to talk military maneuvers. I heard you're leading the retaliation against Imbon. Brach's assigned me to the mission as his second, and I thought it best if we spoke about it before we set sail. I've spent time in the tropics, and I flatter myself that I know how to run a campaign there, but you're the one with boots on the ground knowledge of Imbon."

Oliver grunted.

"I can't say I'm looking forward to this," continued Ostrander, "but if there's anyone I'd want by my side, it's you. You did right by us in the atoll, m'lord, and..."

The commander frowned, and Oliver glanced up the street.

Over the cacophony of the drunks in the pub, he heard the all too familiar shriek of panicked screams. It was coming from up the hill, closer to the palace than the harbor. Toward the Church's library. Why would there be a panic near the Church's—

"Fetch a company of marines," he instructed Ostrander. He frowned. "Make it two companies, if you can find enough of them awake and sober. Full arms, but speed is more important than preparedness."

"What?" questioned the commander, peering into the thick night air and looking for the source of the alarm.

"Go get them now," instructed Oliver. "When you've got them assembled, come to the Church. Ostrander, be ready for anything, and hurry."

THE SCHOLAR I

TIMOTHY ADRIANCE SET down his quill and rubbed his eyes. They were burning from exhaustion, and when he glanced at the half-dozen candles he'd placed on shelves around the room, he realized it must be several hours after dark now. On a table in front of him was a sheaf of parchment covered in his cramped notes, an ash-gray, clay tablet, and a half-yard tall wooden figurine.

The figurine, an uvaan, was roughly-hewn but with some skill, like a talented artisan had worked with primitive tools. It was enough that he could see it was a bald, portly man with a menacing scowl on his lips. The uvaan's face belied the jolly curve of his belly. Details were missing, but the figurine evoked a sense of uncomfortable familiarity, as if the bald man was a neighbor, one who constantly caused trouble.

Along the base of the figurine were crude symbols and letters. Adriance believed it was the tongue of Imbon, though he could find little information about the written form of the language. The tablet had the flavor of the Darklands. Ancient Darklands, bastardized and evolved. It was as if settlers had left that secretive land, and for generations, their speech had grown into something new. The thought brought him some comfort. It made sense, after all.

Had a group left the Darklands and found a home in Imbon? Darklanders seldom traveled, but he supposed they could have. Nothing was known of the Darklands' history prior to the accession of the Wellesleys and the initial spread of Enhover's commercial empire. Geography wasn't his field of study, but as far as he knew, it was entirely possible that the island of Imbon had been settled by refugees or explorers from the south.

It led him no closer to deciphering any messages the objects held, though. He was passing fair in ancient Darklands, as were any of the Sect of Sages scholars, but he did not know Imbonese at all. He wasn't sure if anyone in Enhover knew that tongue, but he knew no one in Romalla did. He preferred his books, but he wasn't completely unaware of what was happening in the world, and he certainly wasn't going to travel to Imbon and ask one of the rebels to help him. If a translation happened, it would be done by him alone.

Duke Wellesley had related that the natives claimed a reaver was held within the figurine. It was a generic term, either through poor translation or poor imagination, and it could have described any number of underworld creatures that had crossed the shroud over the years. Timothy Adriance estimated half of those tales may have some seed of truth, and the other half did not, but none of the creatures he'd read about seemed any more likely to be referred to as a reaver than any of the others.

For a while, he'd speculated whether the nature of the figurine was the reason for the term. Was anything imprisoned in such an object referred to as a reaver and hence the generic designation? Unfortunately, there was no way to know if that was the case.

He'd become sure, though, that there was something within the figurine. The tablets remained obstinate, but the figurine itself was curiously cool to the touch. He'd experimented and held a candle close to the wood, but no matter how long he'd held it, no matter how close he'd gotten, it didn't warm the statue. A vestige of contact with the underworld? It was a question written in his notes, along with many more.

Reavers. He frowned, twirling the quill in his hand. He hadn't heard the term used specifically before, had he? He shook his head, stretched his back, and then bent over the clay tablet again.

What if the script was read from the righthand side instead of the left? In the Vendatt Islands, some of the local languages were written as such. The characters on the tablet originated from the Darklands, but what if the way the tongue had been written had been influenced by a new locale?

His breath coming in quick, excited bursts, he tried to read backward, sounding out each letter and word. It was still foreign, but some of the roots of the words began to feel familiar. Yes, ancient Darklands, he was sure of it. The three symbols there, it was a common formation. And there, another that he recognized. It wasn't just a few stray characters that matched. The core of this language was founded on the same principles as Darklands script. It was just written backwards.

Whispering, he continued, working out words, unable to understand many of them initially but thinking he was getting the pronunciation close. Over and over, he repeated the phrases, most of them foreign to him, but a few began to feel correct, like they belonged on his lips. They were spelled differently, but he teased out meaningful sounds. The words began to spill out effortlessly.

Growing excited, he read faster, listening to the cadence of his voice as he repeated the script. He adjusted pieces, changed his pronunciation, and he organized his thoughts.

Ancient Darklands from six- or seven-hundred years ago he thought. Faster and faster, he repeated the phrases, his deft ears picking out common elements. The meaning was drivel, nothing that he could understand—

In the center of the table, the wooden figurine caught fire.

He blinked at it. The flame burned bright purple. Purple flame. Where had he read about purple flame?

It danced merrily, but he felt no heat from it, and he saw it was leaving no mark upon the wooden table. He picked up a scrap of paper and tentatively held it to the growing fire. Nothing happened. He frowned and moved his fingers back and forth through the odd flame, feeling nothing. How long had he been studying the text? Was he having visions?

Despite the lack of heat, the exterior of the figurine burned quickly. In moments, the entire object was charred black, and the flame sputtered out. Then suddenly, it split, like a fire-roasted chestnut, and bitter cold exhaled from the hollow interior of the statue.

Adriance peered at the opening and saw it went deeper than just the shallow indention he expected. Even in the light of the candles, it was dark, like a tunnel. He leaned forward, staring into the black beyond, squinting his eyes to see into the darkness.

Then, he regretted doing that.

Scrambling from far away was the skittering sound of claws against stone. Dozens then hundreds of fat, black beetles flooded from the interior of the figurine.

Adriance staggered back, knocking over his chair, staring open-mouthed as the things burst into the light and took flight, purple bodies shimmering in the candlelight beneath black wings. They buzzed around him, their wings making a high-pitched whistle. He swung his hands violently, trying to keep them from his face, backing against the wall to avoid the worst of the swarm, but they showed no interest in him.

The cloud of beetles poured into the room and then vanished outside into the hall of the library, their buzzing wings causing a hideous drone that nearly covered the shouts of surprise and alarm from other library patrons outside. Beneath that, Adriance heard something else. A scrape and a drag, like furniture being moved.

Timothy Adriance glanced back at the figurine and screamed.

Standing before the open container, too large to have been inside it, was a desiccated corpse. Echoing the flame, its eyes burned a malevolent purple, and its flesh was pallid gray. Its body was wrapped in tattered, decaying remnants of a burial shroud. It opened its mouth, showing jagged, yellowed teeth but no tongue.

It was laughing or crying out maybe, but it made no sound until it staggered toward him.

Adriance could only stare in horror as the thing closed on him. A reaver. A corpse preserved and then animated. That was where he'd heard the term before. Like a violent slap, the knowledge crashed into his memory, but it was too late. He recalled a depiction of the creatures just like this one. He knew what they were.

It was his last thought before the creature reached out with supernaturally powerful arms and gripped his shoulders. Suddenly, a terrifying urge to live cut through the fog of his fear. Adriance began to struggle, but it was too late. The thing had him, and it pulled him closer toward its open mouth. It smelled like dust and old parchment.

The yellowed teeth closed on his forehead and cheek, and with a turn of its head, the reaver ripped a strip of flesh away. Red blood covered his vision. The reaver's broken teeth closed on him again. Unable to free himself from its iron-grip, he jerked his head. With the movement, his skin tugged, tearing away from his skull. Blood poured like a waterfall down his chest as the monster ate him, one bite at a time, ripping off the skin of his face in ragged flaps.

Finally, its bone-crushing grip on one of his shoulders relaxed, and he thrashed with his arm, beating at the thing helplessly. His eyes were covered in blood, and he could no longer see, but he could feel.

He felt cold, bony fingers grip the collar of his priest's robe and the thin chain of the Sect of Sages. With a powerful yank, the reaver tore the fabric and broke the chain, exposing more of his skin. The reaver chomped down on his neck, pulling with its teeth, ripping away his flesh, chewing and biting until everything went mercifully black.

THE CARTOGRAPHER IV

HE RAN through the soot-covered streets of Southundon, dodging around mechanical carriages and pedestrians, most of whom were walking with the queer, shuffling gait of those who'd had too much to drink, stumbling home long after they ought to have been abed. As he ran, even those glassy-eyed night stalkers began to get odd looks on their faces, and Oliver wasn't the only one staring toward the Church.

From two blocks away, he could already see a bright orange glow emanating from the windows of the library. The clang of the fire brigade's bells filled the space between the panicked wails of… something.

Oliver skidded to a stop on the broad avenue that led to the double-height doors of the Church's library. The doors were open, and there was fire inside, but that couldn't have caused the panic he was hearing.

Few people were out in the courtyard before the Church, as it had been closed to the public for hours, but Oliver saw one man staggering across the cobblestones. He strode toward the man and caught his sleeve. "Hold on. What happ—"

A face turned to him, glistening in the yellow light from the gas lamps that circled the plaza. One eye, quivering in pain, was all that was recognizable of what had once been a man. The skin of his face had been torn away, showing red muscle coated in crimson blood. The man's teeth gleamed white in the night jutting from bare gums, while his second eye socket looked back at Oliver, empty and black.

Oliver backpedaled, shaking his hand, sticky from the blood that covered the man's dark coat.

The man opened his mouth as if to scream, but his tongue was missing, and only a pathetic whimper escaped where his lips had been. His lone eye stared at Oliver, pleading.

Glancing around wildly, Oliver saw more victims lying prostrate on the cobblestones, slumping against the walls of the buildings around the library, or staggering lost and confused like the man.

"Spirits forsake it," whispered Oliver. "What happened?"

The racket of the fire brigade chased him to the side of the avenue, and he watched the giant mechanical carriages, totting huge tanks of water and long canvass hoses, rumble past. Men dressed in treated long coats, wearing thick helmets, and carrying gleaming axes began to spill off of the carriages, racing toward the door of the library. A voice cried out, and Oliver saw Sam dart in front of the men, her arms outstretched, trying to block their way. Cursing, Oliver ran after the brigade.

"You cannot go in there!" shrieked Sam.

"We have to, ma'am," growled a man who must have been the leader of the brigade. "We have to get to the fire. That's the spirits-blessed Church, woman! Move aside, or we'll move you."

"Hold," demanded Oliver, skidding to a stop beside Sam. "I am Duke Oliver Wellesley. If this woman says stay outside, then stay outside. It's for your own safety."

"Wait a—"

"Sergeant, look at these people around the square," said Oliver, pointing at a few of the victims. "Look at them hard before you decide you want to rush in and face what did that to them."

"Sir…" mumbled one of the fire brigade, standing several

paces behind his sergeant. Pale faced, the man watched as a blood-soaked woman stumbled into their carriage and fell, her hands gripping her face where her skin had been stripped away. A low moan escaped her lips, and the entire fire brigade stared at her wordlessly.

Oliver turned to Sam. "What's in there?"

"I don't know," she admitted. "It was out here attacking people and ran inside when I arrived."

"You didn't go after it?" he asked.

She blinked at him then pointedly looked at the burning library. "It killed a score of people out here in moments and then ran into a burning building. Duke, I don't know what the frozen hell it is. I don't know how the fire got started. All I know is— Ah hells, I do know."

"What?" he demanded.

"The uvaan," said Sam. "The figurines you recovered from Imbon. A priest, a scholar I'd found, was in there studying an uvaan along with an Imbonese tablet I'd collected from your father. The prison and the key. Spirits forsake it, that fool Adriance let out a reaver!"

"Who let— A reaver? Someone let out a reaver?" questioned Oliver. He paused. "What's a reaver?"

"I don't know," snarled Sam, glancing through the open library door at the flames dancing along the stacks of books.

"What do we do, m'lord?" asked the sergeant of the fire brigade.

"Smash the windows and put what water you can through them. Douse the nearby buildings so it doesn't spread," instructed Oliver. "Sergeant, make sure no one enters that building. If they do, they'll die. Spread the word. Commander Branden Ostrander is coming with two companies of royal marines. Tell him... tell him it's like what we faced in Farawk, off the atoll."

"And what are we going to do?" questioned Sam.

Oliver drew his broadsword. "We're going in."

"Are you spirits-forsaken crazy!" cried Sam, pointing at the flames licking at the books and parchment inside the open doors. "We cannot follow whatever did this inside of there. It'll... It'll burn up in there, I'm pretty sure."

"Do you know what's on the other side of the Church's library?" asked Oliver.

"The palace," snapped Sam. She winced. "Oh."

"My cousin died yesterday, and I'm not ready to lose another family member," said Oliver. "Come on. We're wasting time."

HE DASHED UP THE MARBLE STAIRS OF THE LIBRARY TO THE MASSIVE, double height doors. He could feel the heat radiating from the growing fire. Stacks of books and shelves of rolled parchment were all flaring alight. The crackling of burning paper filled the room, and the flames cast an orange and red glow across all that he could see. Smoke billowed up, clouding the soaring, frescoed ceiling. Dancing embers floated through the air like fireflies on a warm spring evening.

"Hells," muttered Sam, glancing behind them at the gawking people beginning to fill the square.

Oliver strode inside, holding a hand in front of his face in a vain attempt to keep the heat away and to shield his eyes from the flying embers. He ignored the bodies of priests that were scattered amongst the aisles and followed the wide pathway between the open stacks of books.

The core of the library, the grand hall, was filled with text after text of religious work — the Church's doctrine, treatises on that doctrine, and critiques of anything ever written critical of the doctrine. Very little of it was ever read. It burned though, hot and fast, and Oliver broke into a run, racing between the shelves and feeling the heat of the fire sear his face.

At the far end of the hall was the opening to a passageway that led through a private section of the library and eventually to a courtyard, across which was the back entrance to the king's palace.

Bodies littered the thick carpet they ran down. Throats were torn open, bones crushed, faces bashed in by sheer blunt force. Whatever he and Sam were chasing, it was no longer taking time to flay its victims. It was in a hurry, and as it'd run through, it had caused havoc amongst the people attempting to flee the burning building.

At the opposite end of the hall, Oliver could see several prone figures wearing the livery of the household guard. Halberds and swords lay scattered beside them, gleaming with polish, drawn but unbloodied.

"That thing could be in the palace by now!" cried Sam.

"I know," he growled.

Then, he was flung like a child's doll and tumbled across the floor, crashing into a shelf of burning scrolls.

"What the—" cried Sam. Then her voice was lost in a stream of unintelligible curses.

Oliver sprang to his feet, shaking off the ash and flames from a dozen burning manuscripts that had fallen on him, and his jaw dropped to his chest.

Sam was scrambling back, sliding away from the questing grip of a corpse. Clad in the tattered remnants of a burial shroud, the thing looked ten years dead.

Gripping his broadsword, Oliver charged, taking advantage of the grotesque creature's focus on Sam. He thrust his blade into the reaver's back. Moaning, low and angry, the monster twisted, the steel of Oliver's blade gouging flesh. He jerked his sword out moments before he lost his grip and retreated, watching in horror as the animated corpse turned on him.

Its mouth opened in silent laughter. Yellowed teeth, flecked with red, filled its maw. Its front was covered in the fresh blood of its victims. He could see through the gaping hole in its hollow chest where he'd slammed his broadsword into it.

"Frozen hell," he muttered.

It shuffled closer to him.

"It's faster than it looks," warned Sam. Then she darted at its back, lashing the reaver with her kris daggers.

The creature ignored her blows, not feeling or not caring about the damage, and kept after Oliver, picking up its pace. He fell away, staring in horror. It lurched after him, its eyes burning malevolent purple, its mouth open, a hungry moan chasing him backward.

He could see flesh stuck in its ancient, broken teeth. Those people, missing their skin — it was because the damned thing was eating them!

Feeling the heat of the burning books at his back, Oliver switched tactics and attacked, swinging furiously, bringing his blade against the creature's wrist and severing it, striking at its chest and smashing ribs hidden beneath desiccated flesh. He disemboweled it, opening its stomach and showing an empty cavity where its entrails should have been.

Behind it, Sam continued her attack, coming close and stabbing her daggers into it, yanking on them and tearing away hunks of dry meat that rained down to the carpet. The creature spun and swept a hand at her face. Panic in her eyes, she ducked.

Oliver leapt at the opportunity and slashed his broadsword against the reaver's neck, feeling the blade crash through tough muscle and crunch into the brittle bone of its spine. Its head was severed from the strike and spun free, thumping down and rolling across the ash and embers on the carpet.

The reaver kept going, punching its arm against Sam's head. Only the fact that Oliver had cut off the appendage at the wrist keeping it from grabbing her. Sam fell back and rolled away. Headless, the creature pursued her.

Staring helplessly at its back where Sam had riven devastating blows, Oliver cursed. He'd cut the thing open. There were no organs inside. There was nothing they could strike to kill the monster. They might be able to chop it to pieces, but...

He glanced at its head, a pace away from him on the carpet.

Hate-filled eyes stared back at him. Its jaw snapped helplessly.

Grimacing, he kicked the head, sending it flying like a sports ball into the burning stacks of books around them. With a whoosh, the dried flesh, fabric, and bone caught fire, and he saw its mouth open in a wordless scream as the flame consumed it. A clatter of bone drew his attention, and he looked to see the motionless body of the reaver laying a few paces from Sam.

"Thanks," she gasped, staring in horror at the fallen creature.

"That was a reaver?" he asked, moving to help her up. "What... what is it?"

"Dangerous, it seems," she said, taking his hand and standing. "A corpse with the spirit still bound to it, I think. It must have escaped from its prison, the figurine Adriance was studying. The tablet your father— Duke, we've got a problem."

He turned, following her gaze, and saw that behind him, one of the fallen guards had risen. The man's eyes burned with the same glowing purple hatred that the reaver's had. His neck was a bloody mess of torn flesh where the creature had bitten out his throat, but that didn't stop him.

"It will keep coming," whispered Oliver. "The old man in Imbon said it would just keep coming... It's not just a spirit bound to a body, it's... Hells. What is it?"

The guard picked up a gleaming steel sword and started toward them.

"Duke, we've got to get out of here," hissed Sam.

"And leave that thing to roam freely?" he cried. "We have to kill it. Again, I mean!"

"How?" barked Sam as they both retreated down the main aisle of the library.

All around them, books and papers burned, filling the room with heat and smoke. They coughed on the suffocating ash and struggled to breathe in the stifling hot air. The guardsman pursued them with the same shuffling gait as the previous corpse, a bubbling gurgle escaping its ruined throat.

"Fire," declared Oliver. "Flames killed the first one. We can shove it into the fire."

"And another will rise right behind it," snapped Sam. "We can keep tossing these things into the flame, but they'll keep coming as long as there is a dead body nearby to inhabit. You can't kill them. That's why the Imbonese locked them in the uvaan. That's why they were buried and flooded. Duke, you have to understand. We cannot kill this thing!"

"Can we... can we put it back in the statue?"

"The way to the room Adriance was in is blocked by flame," snarled Sam, shuffling back quickly toward the door they'd entered. "If the figurine is still there, it's almost certain to have been burnt to nothing by now. Besides, I have no idea how to put the thing back in. We need... we need an opening in the shroud. A sacrifice we can tie the soul to and send it—"

"What are you saying?" shouted Oliver, walking backward beside Sam, his eyes fixed on the approaching reaver.

"I'm saying we've got to form a bridge to the underworld to send this thing back to hell," she growled. "It's the only way."

"That's—"

"Oliver!" cried a voice.

Oliver spared a look over his shoulder and saw his brother John entering the burning library. He gripped a broadsword in one hand, and in the other, he carried a golden circlet.

"We must put this on the creature's skull," he said, striding boldly to stand beside Oliver and Sam. Only the trembling of his broadsword gave away how terrified he was.

Oliver, not bothering to ask how his brother knew such a thing, warned, "It's far stronger than us but clumsy. Keep out of reach, John. I'll take off its arms, and you two get that circlet on it."

Not waiting for a response, Oliver charged, counting on the creature's jerky movement to give him a chance.

The animated guard slashed at Oliver with its blade, the attack awkward and stilted.

Oliver parried, letting the powerful blow slide off the edge of his steel. Then he counterattacked, not bothering with a feint at its body or head, knowing neither would slow it. Instead, he whipped his blade into the creature's arm. He fell back, letting it strike at him then countering again and again with blows to its limbs. The reaver had immense strength, and it could be quick, but it had no skill.

Oliver gritted his teeth as he fought it, forcing himself to ignore the bloodstained Wellesley livery that it wore. The man who'd once been part of his family's guard was dead, thinking of him would do neither of them any good.

Acting frustrated, the reaver struck wildly, disregarding potential injury, attacking relentlessly.

Oliver ducked a slash and swept his blade down on the thing's leg, severing it at the knee. Toppling over, the reaver kept coming, dropping its sword and crawling on its belly. Taking his time, Oliver aimed a blow and severed one of its arms and then the other.

Slipping by him, trying to avoid the flames in the stacks of books around them, Sam and John approached. She sat down on the back of the reaver and gripped its head, keeping her fingers wide of its gnashing teeth.

John knelt, stuck the circlet on its head, shoved it down hard, and then leapt away.

The three of them watched as the glowing purple eyes faded white and then went dark. The guard's head fell to the carpet. They turned to run, racing out of the burning library into the streets where a massive crowd had gathered.

Shouting to the fire brigades clustered in the plaza, Oliver called, "The books and manuscripts are lost already! Do what you can to make sure the fire doesn't spread to other structures."

"Doesn't spread," muttered Sam quietly, looking at the surrounding crowd. "I'm afraid we're too late for that."

THE PRIESTESS III

"WELL, at least we know what's in the figurines," remarked King Edward Wellesley.

"Yes, it seems we know," agreed Sam.

The man was seated in a comfortable-looking chair in front of the fireplace in his study. He gestured for her to take the seat opposite of him.

"I, ah…"

"You're nervous about having a drink with me?" asked Edward.

"It always starts with a drink," she mumbled, looking away.

He grinned at her.

Looking into his fire, shifting uncomfortably as he studied her, she wondered, would it be such a bad thing? The king was a spry man, and he had an air of confidence and experience that was magnetic. Confidence was always a good sign, she'd found. Duke wouldn't approve, of course. She frowned when she realized that would bother her.

"I'm not trying to sleep with you, Samantha," assured the king. "You're a beautiful woman, but you're more useful to me for your skills rather than your looks. No, when that desire strikes me, I find there are plenty of servants around who require little convincing. That's not why I'd like to speak with you tonight."

Somewhat reassured, she settled into a chair across from the older man, feeling as if she was moving through a strange, fanciful dream. It was closer to dawn than to midnight, and she'd just fought a corpse in a burning library. She was sharing a drink with the king of the largest empire the world had ever known. She needed that drink.

"How did the reaver escape?" wondered the king.

She shrugged. She hadn't been there.

"The man who was studying the uvaan," pressed the king, "did you give him the tablet that you got from me?"

She coughed into her fist and admitted, "I did."

Taking a sip of his drink and then sitting back, tugging on his goatee with his free hand, King Edward did not comment.

"I didn't think… You must understand, m'lord, I had no idea—"

"No idea it would work?" he asked her.

She blinked at him.

"You've seen enough to know that sorcery is real," chided the king. "It's very real, and it's a threat that lays all around us, sitting there in ancient documents and artifacts, waiting to be discovered anew. My ancestors spent their lives destroying what evidence they could find, as have I, but it's never enough, is it? One must always be prepared to battle the darkness. It's the role of your Church, the Council of Seven, though I've been sorely disappointed in them of late. This latest attack actually happened on the grounds of the Church, the one place it should be least likely!"

"Prepared to battle," she repeated. "Yes, we must be. I will admit I was not prepared for what happened earlier this evening. It seemed no one was, except…"

King Edward raised an eyebrow, waiting.

"Did you give Duke John the circlet we used to banish the reaver?" she questioned.

"He told me a churchman gave it to him along with instructions of what to do," responded the king, smiling at her. "We've inquired with the Church as to the identity of this man, but it seems no one can find him. Whoever it was, it's clear they were wearing a disguise. No one is who they seem, are they?"

She shifted.

"Why do you ask if I was the one who gave it to John?" wondered the king. "Surely you don't mean that to sound like an accusation."

She swallowed, realizing he had not answered her question and also hearing his warning. "You kept the tablets. I thought that maybe…"

He kept pulling on his goatee, watching her.

She glanced at the door to his study, the back of it visible from their seats by the fire. It was studded with stout locks and chains. She wondered if there were other defenses as well. It made sense for the king's study to be secure, but she couldn't help thinking that kings were not the only ones who guarded their secrets closely.

"I want to tell you something, though perhaps it is something you already know," said the king, interrupting her thought. "Lilibet Wellesley was walking the dark path. No one understood how far she'd progressed, the depths of her knowledge, until it was too late. She, like many of the capital's peers, spent time in the secret societies, learning their strange rituals, perusing their libraries, hoping to find knowledge the rest of them had overlooked. She surpassed those fools. She began her own study, her own, ah, research. It wasn't until Northundon that it became obvious how far she had traveled."

Sam sat, watching the old man closely.

He offered a wan smile and continued, "When the shades attacked that place, we responded. We carpeted the city in explosions and fire but not the keep. Not my wife's place. Even now, I am not sure why. Why did we avoid it? Was it because deep down, we suspected? We knew? Days and weeks later, after the dust settled and the smoke cleared, the structures in the garden were plain for anyone with an airship to see. It was obvious someone had performed sorcery, but again, we did nothing."

Sam nodded. The king was saying what she'd thought, what she'd been too afraid to articulate to Duke. She shivered, realizing that her suspicions were not just wild guesses but the hard truth. She knew the king was telling her the truth. It was beyond doubt that Lilibet Wellesley had survived the fall of Northundon.

"We had correspondence from the city the morning of the attack, you know?" continued the king. "It described Lilibet's actions in court the previous day, decisions she'd made in her role as queen. All seemed well. Just the boring hum drum of running a kingdom. The next message we had was from Glanhow."

"The pattern that was erected in the garden would have taken half a day to assemble," suggested Sam.

The king, his fingers on his chin, nodded.

"If... if you believe your wife was a sorceress, what do you think she intended to accomplish?" wondered Sam.

King Edward sipped his drink and replied, "Escape."

Sam frowned.

"It is uncomfortable to say, but Lilibet felt smothered in her role as my wife," explained King Edward. "Our relationship and her responsibilities as queen were a burden to her, a drain on time she would rather spend in other pursuits. She loved her children, but she also loved the forbidden knowledge that the dark path offered. She kept it secret, how far she'd come, but it consumed her. Consumed her until she could think of nothing else. It consumed her to the point that she knew she could not continue as my wife and queen. She had to leave that life behind to take up a new one. A life where no one would question her, where she was free from expectations except those she set herself."

"Escape to where?" wondered Sam.

"Where do you think?" asked the king, smiling at her slyly.

"The Darklands," whispered Sam.

The king nodded. "The Darklands is the one place in the known world Enhover does not send emissaries, and of course, such a place would be a tempting location for a sorceress. Did you know that during the fight over Northundon, we lost an airship? Just one. It vanished without a trace. No one saw what happened, whether it chased the Coldlands raiders over the water and was taken down or if it crashed in some forest and has remained hidden. In the heat of war, it was ignored, and we lost additional airships once we began the campaign against the Coldlands. That first one was forgotten, just another statistic in the sum of war, but we must consider the possibility it did not go down."

"You think she boarded that airship and flew south?"

The king looked back at her.

"It is possible," said Sam, her mind swirling. She took a sip of her drink, wondering.

"That is why I want you to stay here," said the king, suddenly sitting forward. "I want you, and my son, to remain within the empire of Enhover. It would not be good for him, Samantha, to learn the truth."

"But, he already—"

"He does not know," said the king, shaking his head. "The evidence is there, plain to you and I, but he does not believe it. He remembers his mother fondly, and that is best. What would it do to Oliver if he were to find the truth? What would it do to him if he was forced to confront the fact that his mother was involved in Northundon, that she left her family to walk the dark path? After his uncle… Would the boy survive? He is strong, but I worry he is not strong enough for that."

"Why are you telling me all of this?" asked Sam suddenly.

"Because I sense you understand," responded the king. "You understand the burning hunger to learn more, to walk farther. You, more than anyone, may understand Lilibet and her choice. Because you understand, you can help me. You can help Oliver."

"You want me to convince him to stay here?" guessed Sam.

"I do," confirmed the king.

"I don't know if I can," she replied.

King Edward sat back. "You are a strong woman, Samantha. If

you want to convince him, you can. That creature, the reaver, it was headed to the palace, correct? Oliver has little care for his personal safety, but for me, for his nieces and nephews who were asleep under this roof, he cares a great deal. For his brother who had to plunge into the burning building to save you both? Oliver seeks his mother, but with proper encouragement, he will understand that his family is here. His place is here in Enhover."

"He's my… my friend," stammered Samantha.

"Keep your friend safe," suggested the king. "Spare him what he would find in the Darklands."

She gapped at the king, struggling for a response, struggling to decide if her loyalty to Duke required an angry refusal or if her loyalty demanded compliance with the king's wishes. A trip to the Darklands was certain to be fraught with danger, and it was no lie that Duke may not return, that she may not return. How would he react if he learned what she just had, that Lilibet was alive, she was a sorceress, and the king had always known?

"I told you my wife studied the occult for years," continued King Edward. "She had a secret chamber here, a nest as it is called. She collected artifacts and documents there. Whatever she kept in Northundon is lost to the shades, but what she left in this palace remains undisturbed. These artifacts are of no use to me, just reminders of a terrible truth I would rather forget. If you stay in Southundon, Samantha, perhaps you could evaluate these objects? See if they are dangerous, like the uvaan was, or if it is something you can use in your own pursuits. We must always be prepared to battle sorcery, Samantha. If you stay here in Enhover, and keep my son here as well, I can help you prepare for that battle. The Council of Seven has been of no use to me, but that does not mean no one from the Church is useful. Help me, Samantha. Help me keep your friend and my son safe. Do that, and I will be your ally."

THE CARTOGRAPHER V

"You're used to all of this adventure, Oliver, but I cannot tell you how worried I was for John," breathed Matilda.

John rolled his eyes, fiddling with his fork and stuffing peas into a pile of mashed potatoes. "It was nothing, Matilda. Oliver cut the thing down to size. All I had to do was stick the circlet on its head. Really, there was hardly any danger."

"Weren't dozens of people killed?" asked the duchess.

"Ah..." stammered John, glancing to Oliver for help.

"Did you not tell me the building was on fire?" demanded Matilda, thrusting at her husband with her own fork. "Your clothes were covered in soot, and you had those little marks where the embers had scorched you."

Shifting uncomfortably, John admitted, "There may have been some small danger, but we had to stop the thing. Like you said, my love, dozens had already been killed."

"And it was coming for us in the palace!" exclaimed the duchess. "We all could have been slaughtered by that monster."

"I'm certain the guards would have stopped it," assured the king, glancing between his sons. "They're trained for this type of thing. It just happened so fast they did not have time to get there."

"It was over before I even knew what was going on," agreed

John.

Oliver guessed his older brother was telling the truth, though his father was not. He asked John, "This priest who gave you the circlet, no luck finding who it was?"

"None," replied the Duke of Southundon. "To be honest, I'm no longer even sure it was a priest, though he was dressed as one. What about the priestess, the one who's been following you around, do you think she might know anything? I could have someone sketch the face of the man who handed me the circlet. I recall it quite clearly. Maybe it was another one of the Knives of the Council. Would she recognize them? They are the ones who should be looking after these matters, though why a Knife would not simply put the device on the creature's head themselves is beyond me."

"There are no other Knives in Enhover that she's aware of," said Oliver. "Besides, if this man took such pains to hide his identity, I am certain he would have been wearing a mask or some other disguise."

"Between this and Bartholomew Surrey, I'm beginning to believe that no one is who they seem," complained John.

Oliver frowned. His brother was right, but he had no idea how right. Both the king and Oliver had decided it was best not to share the full story of their Uncle William and the rest of his cabal. There was enough turmoil and unease as it was without everyone suspecting each other as secret sorcerers.

"Have you spoken to the priestess?" asked King Edward, glancing at Oliver.

"For a brief moment," replied Oliver. "Shortly after I broke fast."

"Did she have any new theories?" wondered the old man.

"She claimed she found some leads here in Southundon that she could pursue," said Oliver, frowning. "Evidently, there may have been some artifacts and documents left behind by the priest who unleashed the reaver. With time, she told me that she might uncover the nature of the creature."

"Interesting," murmured the king.

"Well," trilled Matilda, reaching over and gripping her husband's arm, "we are glad you are here, Oliver, and not gallivanting off on another voyage for the Company. In times like these, it is best for family to stay close. With both William and Lannia gone... I'm glad you're with us."

Oliver winced. At midnight, he had an appointment with Captain Ainsley. They planned to set sail for the Darklands. But now Sam was asking for more time, he knew his father might decree that he stay, and there were attacks within a stone's throw of the royal family...

"Oliver is a loyal servant of the Crown, Matilda," assured King Edward. "He would never turn his back when his family needed him."

Oliver stuffed a strip of roast pork in his mouth and chewed.

A BRISK BREEZE GREETED HIM AS HE HOPPED DOWN FROM THE mechanical carriage.

"You're going in there, m'lord?" asked the livery-clad driver.

"I am," confirmed Oliver. "The carriage can't make it through. Can you wait here for me?"

"Of course, m'lord," said the man, doffing his cap and pulling his scarf tight.

"Sit inside," suggested Oliver, talking over the man's protests. "Take a nip of that brandy to keep warm. That's an order. I'll be back in a few turns."

The driver, one of his father's personal staff, babbled thanks as Oliver turned and studied the wall of foliage in front of him, the forest that surround the old druid keep, his uncle William's sorcerous nest. It was passed down to Lannia, Oliver supposed, but now most likely in the hands of the Crown. William wouldn't have had any debts to settle, and with such a history, no one else would want the obelisk of menacing, living stone.

Menacing. Oliver could see why everyone thought that. It was tall and dark, and the inside was strange and discomforting. It had a grim history, capped with the death of his uncle. Not that anyone knew the keep was where the man had died, of course. They all thought it was a simple hunting accident in the surrounding woods. Still, it was enough that no respectable peer would be interested in acquiring such a useless structure, even if it was close to Southundon.

Ducking beneath a branch, Oliver entered the trackless forest and headed toward the ancient druid keep. There were no established paths to follow, not anymore, but there was little risk of becoming lost. The keep rose high above the surrounding forest, and any time there was a break in the canopy, the walls were easy to spot. More so, Oliver felt a tug, like he was following the pull of the furcula. Inexorably, he felt compelled to visit the keep, to walk its strange tunnels, to explore those twisting passageways.

Brushing aside a low branch, he resolved that if he began to visit the keep regularly, he'd have to get some men to clear a road to it. It wasn't a long walk, and at the moment, it felt good to stretch his legs, but a proper passageway through the trees would shave two hours off the journey to and from.

He breathed deeply, inhaling the clean scent of the wooded area, and exhaled. Ahead, the presence of the keep drew him like iron to a lodestone. The warmth he'd felt that night atop the roof called to him, the warmth that had coursed through him in defiance of the deathly cold of the spirit Ca-Mi-He. He remembered it vividly, like he'd experienced it just moments ago. He could feel it pouring through his body and into Sam's. He could feel how it had welled up from the stone of the fortress, passing through the barrier of his skin.

He had no idea what it meant.

The forest around the keep was quiet, though he heard the sounds of small wildlife scampering about, staying out of sight. There was no sense of danger beneath the pine boughs, just comfort. He felt no fear this brisk late-winter evening. It was a stark contrast to the last time he'd visited the fortress.

In an hour, he'd weaved his way through the trees and stood before the main entrance to the keep, a dark circle, the interior deep black where the rising moon lost its reach. From inside of his jacket, he produced a vial of fae light and shook the little spirits awake. Half-a-dozen of the tiny orange fae flared alight, illuminating the way. He began to walk up the tunnel, his booted footsteps echoing on the stone. A hundred yards into the keep, he stopped.

Ahead of him, a green glow was growing, like someone else was approaching with a flaring globe of fae light. From around the bend, he saw a swirling cloud of the creatures. He gasped. They must be the ones that had been released while he had been fighting his way into the keep. They were still there, somehow still alive. In Enhover's air, the delicate spirits never survived, but now, days after the confrontation with his uncle, they were alive and vigorous. They swirled around him and then condensed into a tight formation in front of him as he began to walk again. It was as if they were lighting the way for him, welcoming him home.

He shook his head. Fae, as far as he knew, had no thoughts. They flew around and slept, and that was it. They did not eat, did not produce waste, did nothing but get woken and spill light from their minuscule bodies. The little creatures could be sustained indefinitely if kept sealed in air collected in the Southlands. They were safe and steady sources of light, but no one had ever speculated that they were sentient. He wondered, could they think? And why had these particular ones not been extinguished by Enhover's air? He'd never heard of any of them staying alive for more than a few moments after their glass prisons were opened. Of course, as far as he knew, no one had experimented with such a thing inside of an old druid keep.

He opened his palm, hoping to coax one of the fae to land upon it, but instead, they just swirled around him, as if waiting for him to walk again. He sighed, and with little thought given to it, he passed through the twisting tunnels higher into the keep. He didn't consciously think about where he was walking, but he ended up ascending to the rooftop of the fortress. The green fae stayed clustered inside of the keep, reluctant to fly out into the open.

Ignoring them, he breathed the cool air and moved to the macabre iron crosses his uncle had installed near the edge. Between the grim metal, he could see Southundon. Thin plumes of black smoke rose above the city, as they always did, lit by the glow of the factories and the gas lamps. Dirty, industrial, powerful, Southundon was the seat of the world's greatest empire. When he saw it from afar, it was difficult sometimes to reconcile that it was his family who sat upon the throne, who ruled that empire.

Powerful, yes, they were that, but they were vulnerable, too. What would have happened had he and Sam not been there the night before when the reaver had attacked? Would John have still been approached by a mysterious priest with the means to subdue the monster? Without Oliver's and Sam's help, would John have been able to do it?

What would have happened had Oliver not fought Isisandra, Raffles, Yates, and William? Had the cabal bound the dark trinity, there was little question the rest of the Wellesleys would have fared poorly. His father, his brothers, their wives, their children, they all would have been killed through sorcerous means.

Oliver placed his hands on the stone of the fortress, feeling its smooth, seamless construction. For hundreds of years, perhaps even longer, the fortress had stood there. It'd been there when Southundon had been a tiny fishing village. It'd been there long before Enhover became Enhover. Long before the Wellesleys gained the Crown.

All empires fall.

He'd been taught that from birth. The druids had fallen, but he wasn't sure they'd ever been a proper empire. Their construction had remained, though. Their legacy was intact. Was his family strong enough to maintain their grip on the empire? Would they leave anything behind when they inevitably lost that hold?

He pounded his fist against the stone.

Philip, John, Franklin... they wouldn't have thought to look for the sorcerers had Oliver not been there. Had it been up to them, after Harwick, they would have merely written a stern letter to the Church. His brothers had skills that Oliver did not, and they were fulfilling their roles better than he ever could, but what if the strength of their family, of the Crown, was not on the back of an individual but on the group? His brothers had their roles, and he had his.

He put his palms down on the cool stone, searching for the warmth he'd absorbed the night of the fight with his uncle. It was there, he thought, but faint. Not as if it had fled, but as if it was slumbering. It couldn't have fled, that warmth, he realized. It was a part of this keep, integral to it. The warmth, a life spirit, was what kept the keep together. Without it, the keep would collapse, like a fae blinking out or a levitating stone falling from the sky. Oliver grimaced, shaking his head at the comparison.

The keep was stone, he told himself. Nothing more. Stone that had stood sentinel over the forest, over Southundon, for ages. Stone that had not failed in that time. Stone that had proven its strength by simply being there. Like his home in Northundon, the stone outlasted the brief lives of man. It outlasted because it was strong and reliable.

He sighed. Perhaps it was time for him to be that as well.

He looked across the river to Southundon. It was dirty, loud, and far from the wild parts of the world that called to him, but it was home. He took his hands off the stone of the keep and fought the urge to put them back, to stay there. It was comforting to be there, and he would come again. The fortress was calling to him, the spirit comforted by him as he was by it, but his home was across the river. His home was in Southundon.

"How'd the crew take it?" asked Oliver.

"Pettybone breached a keg of grog. The men who could play a bit of music did, and last I heard, they were ordering enough girls to the airship to have two or three of the lasses for every able-bodied crewman. You're going to have a bill from the brothel that I shudder to think of, m'lord. I only hope they don't get so drunk on the grog that they try and impress the fallen women by giving them a spin around Southundon on an airship."

Oliver blinked at her.

"You were the only one who actually wanted to sail to the Darklands, m'lord," she mentioned. "The men are content to receive the extra pay and stay tied to the bridge here in the city."

"I think he's more worried about the drunken crew piloting the airship," mentioned Sam.

"Ah, yes," said Ainsley, nodding confidently. "After a few more drinks, I'll head on back and make sure things don't get out of hand."

"Kick them off the airship," suggested Oliver. "I can bail the lot of them out of gaol, but I can't fix it if they crash the Cloud Serpent into a building."

The captain nodded and turned. She circled three fingers in the air toward the barman, ordering another round.

Oliver frowned at the back of her head.

"If she's in the Darklands, Duke, she'll still be there when you have time to go looking," said Sam quietly.

"If I ever have the time," muttered Oliver.

"What'd your father say?" asked Sam.

"He offered me the role of prime minister," replied Oliver. "He doesn't want to grant it so soon after William's and Lannia's burials, of course. There should be a period of mourning, but he means to do it soon. My father wants me to do something that shows the people I deserve the position."

"Find the sorcerers—" began Sam.

Ainsley interrupted, "Nah, Imbon."

Oliver nodded to her. "Imbon. He wants me to lead the assault on Imbon and ensure it's resettled. Upon my return, he'll reward me with the prime minister appointment." Oliver snorted. "Some reward."

"Well, it is a rather lucrative post, is it not?" inquired Ainsley.

"I don't need any of my father's sterling, Captain."

She grunted, disbelieving. "You can always use more silver."

"And what of the rest?" asked Sam.

Oliver smiled grimly. "The other uvaan, whoever was responsible for Lannia's death, William's acolytes, Ca-Mi-He? I suppose we've got a little time to find them, if you're interested. I've been thinking... Bartholomew Surrey visited Southundon frequently. Who did he socialize with when he was here? Were any of those friends also associated with those who are missing? With Lannia's involvement, I think you were right that Surrey was attempting to contact William, and it stands to reason those in the room were my uncle's acolytes. I think first, we ought to make sure the ones who perished in that chamber were the only ones."

Sam nodded. "That's logical."

"You're with me, then?" he asked.

"Of course."

"What about me?" asked Ainsley.

"Tonight, make sure the crew doesn't kill themselves, or worse, someone else," instructed Oliver. "Then, prepare to sail to Imbon. I have no desire to go back there and see the reprisal for the uprising, but it is my duty to the Crown, and it's time I stopped running from that duty."

Three mugs thumped down on the table in front of them.

Ainsley grabbed hers and raised it. "To the Crown and the empire, then."

"To the Crown and the empire," said Oliver and Sam, raising their mugs as well.

An empire bought in blood, built for one purpose, expanding the wealth and power of those that led it. The Crown, his family. They had it all, but the price had been high.

THE PRIESTESS IV

SHE ROLLED OVER, the silk sheets sliding across her bare skin. She tugged the covers tight around her, more for the pleasant feeling of the smooth fabric than the warmth it provided. At the far side of the room, her fire glowed with bright red embers, providing the only light to the chamber. Two stories below ground level, no sunlight ever breached that darkness.

It was quiet, too, and would remain so until she started moving about or until the king came to visit. He was the only other with a key to the locked gate that barred entry to the tower's basement.

In Lilibet's old chambers, the world passed by unnoticed.

Sam finally left the comfort of the silk sheets and found a candle beside the bed. She struck a striker and flicked a spark at the wick. The candle caught, and the low light bled out across the room. She lit a few more candles, shook awake the fae in her solitary globe, and then prodded at the embers in the fire with an iron poker. She put two more logs on, and they caught quickly from the heat of the coals. The growing flame bathed her bare skin in warmth.

She looked down at her naked body, turning her wrists to study the tattoos there, following the lines of black ink up her arms, across her collarbone, and coming to a stop in the center of her chest. Tilting her head down, she couldn't quite see where the two bands of tattoos met. She couldn't see the markings on her back either, but she could feel them. It made no sense, but all the same, she thought she could. The ink had been injected months ago, and the small wounds were long since healed. Still, the designs felt clear and distinct on her skin, like snakes writhing sinuously across her shoulder blades.

She turned to study the room, feeling the fire warm her backside as she did. A massive, comfortable bed. Embroidered, stuffed chairs with small tables beside them. A huge table set against one wall with a series of parchment-stuffed cubbies looming over it. A black slate board that took up the entirety of the far wall. Sticks of white chalk sat in front of it, but the board had been blank when she'd first seen the room, and she'd left it that way.

Had the king wiped the board decades ago when his wife had gone missing? Had Lilibet herself hidden whatever patterns she'd been practicing on that black surface?

Whatever had happened, it'd been years before, Sam was certain of that. When King Edward had showed her into the subterranean chamber, the floor and furniture had been thick with dust. He'd suggested she tidy it up before starting her study, but after seeing her expression, he'd dispatched a servant to handle the cleaning. Sam had let the woman inside and then ignored her until the woman finished, and when Sam attempted to thank her, Sam realized the woman was deaf mute. She'd commented on it to Edward, and the king had told her the woman was illiterate as well. He used her to tidy his own chamber. She was a servant accustomed to traipsing through the most sacred places of the empire, but without the means to tell anyone about it.

But even the servant did not have a key to Lilibet's old room. Only Sam and the king.

Shaking her head, Sam walked to the table, glancing over the papers she'd scattered there the night before. Thin, elegant handwriting covered the documents in neat rows. Lilibet's assured script, she'd learned. These papers contained no secrets of the occult, except for one. Lilibet Wellesley had been studying the dark path. That, in addition to whatever else Sam may find in the hidden chamber, was a deadly secret. The Queen of Enhover had been a practicing sorceress. Documents written in her own hand proved it. It was the kind of secret that could bring down an empire.

Why had King Edward shared this place with Sam? Why had he not destroyed everything inside decades ago?

Frowning, Sam looked to the clock above the fireplace mantle. Mid-morning. In a few hours, she was to meet Duke. It was time to get to work. They had sorcerers to hunt.

But before she began her morning ablutions, she pushed aside some of the loose papers to reveal a pair of gleaming, gold-engraved push daggers. Katars, they were called, though she had little familiarity with the weapons. The king had told her they were common in the Darklands when he'd shown them to her. Lilibet's own weapons, it seemed, though Edward had no answer when Sam asked why they'd been left in Southundon. The short blades were inscribed similar to her kris daggers, delicate etchings arranged in careful patterns. In the center of each steel blade, inlaid in gold, was Ca-Mi-He's symbol. Had Lilibet herself commissioned the etching, or had she found the weapons already inscribed? Were they blessed by the great spirit, or had its symbol been placed there for some other reason? Sam did not know, and the king claimed ignorance.

She could read enough of the patterns to know, though, the weapons would banish a spirit as easily as they would pass through a puddle of water. They would do a decent job on flesh as well. Their edges gleamed as if someone had sharpened them the day before.

Sam shivered for a moment, forcing away the obvious similarity to her own weapons. King Edward had claimed that Sam, more than anyone, would understand Lilibet's choice to follow the dark path. Two floors beneath the earth, sleeping in Lilibet's old bed, Sam felt like she'd come home.

SHE TROTTED UP THE STONE STAIRWELL AND OUT ONTO THE CITY streets of Southundon. The underground rail had brought her within three blocks of Bartholomew Surrey's townhouse, and as she walked along the streets, dodging through the teeming crowd, she decided the bustling city was nearly as claustrophobia-inducing as the narrow tunnels the rail passed through.

Buildings rose sharply around her, and the sky was clouded with smoke from the rail and the factories clustered in ranks outside of the city. Tightly bundled citizens covered every cobblestone near the entrance to the underground.

When she finally broke free from the throng and entered the calmer streets lined by homes of wealthy peers and merchants, she breathed a sigh of relief. She'd never thought the day would come when she felt relaxed in such a posh setting, but she'd never thought she'd spend so much time shoving her way through the citizens of Southundon, either.

The capital of Enhover's empire had the wealth and population that came with the title, but it didn't have any more space than its quieter sister in the west. All four provincial capitals had been established before the nation was united under the Wellesley's banner, and it seemed that since that time, they'd only been built higher, not wider.

In Southundon, people and buildings were stacked atop each other like worms trying to crawl out of a bucket. They wriggled and squirmed, constantly battling to be on top only to be forced back down as another climbed atop them.

Walking quickly, Sam found the townhouse of the late Bartholomew Surrey and paused in front of it, a scowl on her face.

Flanking the front door, a pair of city watchmen stood guard. The door was wide open, and she could see a legion of inspectors bustling about inside. Two mechanical carriages, embossed with the sigil of the ministry, sat puttering out front.

If Bartholomew Surrey had any friends associated with his dark craft, they would certainly know the man was being investigated now.

Grumbling under her breath, Sam ascended the marble stairs and presented herself to the watchmen at the top.

"Investigation underway, miss, move on," advised one of the men, speaking through a prodigious mustache that made her wonder how the man managed to ingest food without a mouthful of hairs coming along for the journey.

"Shouldn't you ask me why I'm here?" she responded.

"You're not an inspector, and they're the only ones allowed inside," remarked the other guard, leaning forward to leer at her.

"What if I am Bartholomew Surrey's secret lover or his partner in a criminal enterprise? Don't you think the men inside would like to hear from me?"

Both of the men stared at her in surprise.

Finally, the mustached one asked, "Are you?"

"Sorry. That information is only for the inspectors," she lilted, sharing a conspiratorial wink.

"I—"

"Sam, the priestess?" called an inspector from inside the townhouse.

She nodded.

"Duke Wellesley is upstairs in the marquess' study. He said to send you right in."

"My thanks, Inspector," said Sam. Then she flounced inside, batting her eyelashes at the watchmen and blowing the mustached one a kiss.

"You're the strangest priestesses I've ever laid eyes on," said the inspector quietly, shaking his head as he led her to the stairwell.

"You have no idea, sir," she replied. "No idea."

The inspector took her straight to Bartholomew's study and left her there without further comment.

Duke was inside, standing behind the man's desk and leafing through the papers there. He told her, "The basement has been cleaned out, both the room Lannia was killed in and the antechamber."

"Cleaned out by whom?" she wondered.

"Inspector Moncrief," he replied once Sam's escort had descended back down the stairs. "Evidently, the man did not just pull a random assignment the night of the murder. He's part of a task force that my father implemented some years ago. They hunt sorcerers, though Moncrief confided they've never actually found one. Still, they have some familiarity with the material and have been trained to handle it carefully. Mostly trained to not look at it, I suppose."

"Your father confiscated everything that was below?" asked Sam slowly.

"Well, it couldn't be left for anyone to find, could it?" questioned Duke, looking up from his papers. "You'd already looked over the items. I'm sure if you ask for further examination, my father will make the cache available to you."

"Yes," she replied, "I'm sure he will."

She wondered just what Duke knew of his father's interest in sorcery and if he knew how much of it was being shared with her. Certainly, Duke did not know that King Edward maintained Lilibet's old lair at the bottom of the king's tower. If Duke knew that, he would be beating down the steel gate to get inside, to understand his mother better and what had happened to her. There was nowhere he would find more clues, but Sam didn't think the answers would give him any peace.

She asked him, "Did you find anything here?"

"Maybe," he said. "It seems the marquess was a bit less careful than my uncle. This parchment has a list of names. Several of them have been recently identified as missing, and I assume they were the bodies found below."

"And the others?"

"I thought we'd go have a chat with them," he said. He gestured around the room. "We'll finish tossing Surrey's study and then go call upon the other names. Perhaps this list is planning for a benign social engagement. Perhaps it's about a business venture. Perhaps it is more."

Sam nodded, glancing at the list. "Who shall we visit first?"

"Two of them will be together this evening," responded the peer.

Sam frowned.

"We're going to crash their party," explained Duke.

THE CARTOGRAPHER VI

OLIVER DREW a deep breath and then adjusted his neckerchief, pulling it snug around his collar and tucking down in front. He smoothed the lapels of his jacket and shifted, muttering at the thick starch on his shirt.

Sam, sitting across from him, merely shook her head. She was dressed as she always was — tight leather trousers, a simple shirt, and a buttoned, tailored vest. She'd arrived in the carriage court with a thick woolen cloak, but she'd discarded it so she could be ready for action. Then, Sam had made some rather rude comments about his attire.

"This is how peers dress for a dinner party?" she'd asked him. "I was afraid you'd gone a bit daft."

"I don't want to give us away until the last moment," he'd claimed.

Rolling her eyes, Sam had not made further comment, but she'd made plenty of looks.

"You're sure this Inspector Moncrief can be trusted?" Sam asked him.

Oliver shrugged. "He's trusted by my father. I see no reason we should treat him differently."

"He failed to spot your uncle," mentioned Sam. "For a man

assigned to a special task force looking for sorcerers and reporting directly to William Wellesley, that seems a rather large oversight, does it not?"

"No one suspected my uncle," reminded Oliver. "Not even us."

Sam grumbled to herself and settled back in the carriage. They were quiet until a sharp rap sounded on the wall of the vehicle from the driver's seat outside. Sam stood, crouching to avoid the ceiling of the carriage, and offered a curt nod to Oliver.

"Good luck," she whispered.

"Spirits bless you," he replied as she opened the door and leapt out of the moving carriage into the dark night.

With the blast of cool air from outside, he tugged on his neckerchief again and then patted his sides, feeling beneath his long coat and dress coat where he'd secreted two gold-engraved katars. The short push daggers, with their H-shaped hilts, had been provided by Sam earlier that evening. They were formal-looking weapons, as if for display rather than use, but as he'd hefted the blades, he decided their sharp steel edges would get the job done, even if the gold filigree on the handles and the intricate designs on the blade made him feel a complete fool. Those designs, Sam had assured him, had the power to banish a lesser shade much the way her kris daggers did.

Eminently more practical than his broadsword, given their quarry. Not to mention, walking into the dinner party with the long blade of a broadsword swinging from his hip was crass, and this evening, he had a part to play.

The carriage slowed to a gentle stop, the brakes squealing in protest as they rubbed against the axles, and the door was opened by a uniformed footman, one of Inspector Moncrief's men. The man should have waited until the contraption rocked to a complete stop, but Oliver shrugged and disembarked, nodding at the man. Two dozen more of the elite inspectors were scattered around the block wearing a variety of disguises, watching and waiting.

Sam would scuttle around to the back alley where the carriages were parked while their owners frolicked. She'd search the ones they suspected. Then she'd slip inside and begin to reconnoiter the house.

All they had was a list of names. One was a minor peer, one was a common, and after a frustrating attempt at research, one appeared to be a pseudonym. There was nothing to tie these people to sorcery except their tenuous association with Bartholomew Surrey and his missing companions. There could be plenty of innocent reasons one's name might be on a list, so he and Sam would find what they could find, and if they proved any association with Surrey or sorcery, they would call Moncrief and his men to take the suspects into custody.

For once, Oliver had insisted they capture the suspected sorcerers and question them. Sam, always ready to draw her blades, had dropped her objections when he'd explained that questioning the suspected parties would be, by far, the most efficient way to determine if they had any other colleagues in the wind. If they killed them, they would never know, and both he and the priestess were tired of flailing about with no leads.

Leaving the carriage to the inspectors, Oliver ascended the wide stone stairs to the brightly lit front door of the townhouse. Inside, an attendant had evidently been watching for the arrival of the carriage, and the door was swept open before Oliver was three steps from it.

"Duke Oliver Wellesley?" asked the attendant, though there was little question in his voice.

Oliver nodded. "Care to announce me?"

The attendant performed his duties, and a titter of conversation rose as the gowned and suited peers turned to welcome the duke. A shiver of minor lordlings and ladies offered shallow bows and curtsies. He smiled broadly, forcing his lips open, and offered greetings to all, though he could not have named a single one of them. Finally, his host made his way through the herd and proffered his hand.

Oliver took it. "Avery Thornbush, it's been… years, no?"

"Years, m'lord," agreed the gaily dressed man. He wore a bright blue suit with a startling orange neckerchief. He had tall, gleaming black leather boots and a powdered wig that was pulled into a tail at the nape of his neck.

Oliver frowned for a brief moment, fighting the urge to run his hand back over his own hair, to feel the leather knot that held it back. Was Baron Thornbush aping his style in jest, or had Oliver inadvertently set off a trend amongst the young, stylish set of peers in Southundon? He shuddered at the thought.

"Something wrong, m'lord?" inquired Baron Thornbush.

"No, not at all," assured Oliver, "and please, call me Oliver. M'lord makes me think I'm standing in my father's throne room. I was merely trying to recall the occasion we last met."

"Ah," said the baron, touching a finger to his chin. "One of Lannia's legendary fetes after the final curtain of the theatre season?"

"Of course," said Oliver with a pained smile.

The baron either didn't notice the effect that Lannia's name had on Oliver, or he chose to ignore it. He gestured Oliver deeper into the room, through the thin line of minor peers, toward the center of the space where the more august party guests had gathered. The names poured over Oliver like a pitcher of water over a rock. He heard them, but he didn't absorb any information about the introductions until Baron Thornbush got to Janson Cabineau.

"Cabineau?" asked Oliver.

"I hail from Finavia, m'lord," said the man with a slight bend at his waist.

He gave Oliver an oily smile and drew himself up, preening like a peacock at the royal zoo. His suit was even more garish than Thornbush's, and he'd adorned it with a silver lapel pin sparkling with diamond studs. Three interlocking triangles, a valknut, Oliver thought.

"An unusual item of jewelry," remarked Oliver, staring at the man's pin. Cabineau was a name on the list, but surely he wouldn't be so obvious. "I don't believe I've seen anything like it."

"A bit of a personal sigil, m'lord," explained Cabineau, showing a dazzling array of bright white teeth. "I'm afraid I've no claim to title, just what sharp dealing and a bold approach to opportunity have brought me. I've purchased land in Finavia, though, near where I was born. To commemorate the occasion, I had an artist render this design, and a jeweler set it with all of the sparkling stones I could afford at the time. It's a statement, m'lord, though it may appear meagre by your own standards. It's a reminder of how far I've come and how far I intend to go."

"A merchant, then," said Oliver. "What is your business, Mister Cabineau?"

"Salted hams, m'lord," said the man, his smile faltering just slightly. "I'm the President of The Exalted Tounnes Company. We make our trade ferrying items between western Finavia and Southundon. A shadow of your mercantile enterprises, I am certain, but it's provided a healthy enough income for my purposes."

"Of course," said Oliver, nodding, recalling nothing he'd ever heard about The Exalted Tounnes Company.

Salted hams. Not worth the Company's time. There were dozens of smaller enterprises in existence now, modeling themselves after the Company, trying to establish regular trade routes that didn't have volume to attract the interests of serious players. They weren't doing anything different than what merchants had always done, but such organization allowed those of smaller means to pool resources and find a seat at the table. Men like Cabineau, it seemed. And evidently, the man had done well enough with his hams to gain an invitation to the party and well enough that his name had found its way onto Bartholomew Surrey's list. Was the man listed there because he was an acquaintance or because he was involved in Surrey's nefarious activities?

Oliver offered his hand and his congratulations, feeling the strain of his forced smile. "Well done, Cabineau, and I hope someday I can try one of these hams of yours."

"Certainly, m'lord!" exclaimed the man. "Perhaps I can—"

"Save us, spirits, from this talk of swine and sterling!" cried a young woman, pushing herself in between Oliver and Cabineau.

"My sister, Baroness Victoria Thornbush," introduced Avery. "She's been eager to meet you from the moment we received your reply to the invitation."

Victoria Thornbush, rogue and paint covering her cheeks and lips, her dress covering very little of her shoulders and cleavage, leaned forward and held up her hand.

Oliver took it, dipping to kiss the smooth material of her silk glove, trying to keep his gaze somewhere safe, which didn't end up happening. When he rose, the baroness twitched, letting the skirts of her dress whisper around her ankles.

"Do you like it, m'lord?" she asked, pulling on the dress. "I had the seamstress make it special for this evening."

Billowing and frilly was how he'd describe the bit below her waist. Clinging precariously was how he evaluated the top half. The dress was a startling white.

"A bold shade for this time of year," he murmured, trying to find something polite to say.

"It is, isn't it?" replied the woman with a smile. "It's been such a dark time in the capital that I thought it worth bringing a little light into our lives. I was close friends with Lannia, you know? I cannot tell you how horrified I was to learn of what happened to her. Please know, m'lord, the Thornbushes share your loss."

Oliver swallowed.

"Dispense with the formality, sister!" exclaimed Avery. "Oliver has come to us this evening to have his heart raised. Let us not add a pall of gloom to the occasion."

"Yes," said Oliver to the baroness. "Please, call me Oliver."

"Oliver," breathed Victoria Thornbush, offering him her hooked arm. "I cannot recall ever being so intimate with royalty.

It's making me quite breathless. Please, let me show you around our humble home."

The baroness took him by a small bar in the back of the room where a sharply dressed fellow was emptying bottles of sparkling Finavian wine into a seemingly endless array of crystal glasses. Then, she tried to take Oliver upstairs.

She was a beautiful woman, and he had no doubt she was well experienced, but Sam was supposed to be up there snooping through the Thornbush's private chambers. Flushing, Oliver declined the young woman's invitation. The sacrifices a loyal servant of the Crown must make.

Victoria, however, was not yet ready to release him to the other hounds, and she kept her arm linked with his. Shooting angry scowls at any other woman who dared to approach, she kept him moving on a circuit around the room.

Oliver smiled politely, sipped his wine slowly, and kept his eyes open. He tried to make use of his newfound acquaintance. Her brother, after all, had been the first name on Bartholomew's list. Avery Thornbush and Janson Cabineau were the reasons Oliver had decided to attend the party. He'd seen little sign of it so far, but it was quite possible the two men were involved in sorcery. Sorcery and hams. He supposed it could be the case.

Oliver questioned the baroness about her family's history, their current business, and their favored entertainments. It was a story he heard every time he was in Southundon and visited with the minor peers. They had everything they needed, but they constantly quested for more, endlessly jockeying for commercial prospects, standing amongst the others, and access to the finest the city had to offer.

Ruefully, Oliver admitted there was no greater prize in that chase than himself, and he led the baroness along so that she kept spilling information about her family. Letting her hang on his arm while they paraded around the party was a small price for the information he sought.

Did her brother Avery know Bartholomew Surrey? Yes, he

did, though the marquess spent many of his days in the city of Southwatch. What had her brother studied at university? Ancient languages and commerce. He'd attempted to turn it into a business locating and selling rarities and had even taken a share of an auction house, but she believed he'd sold that business. Did Avery keep odd hours, or was he a regular at the usual haunts of the lesser peerage? Odd hours, Victoria shared incuriously.

Finally, she pulled Oliver close and whispered, "I worry, m'lord, that you're more interested in my brother than you are in me."

He smiled at her. "No, of course not. I'm just fascinated. Your brother seems to keep such strange acquaintances."

"Strange?"

"Janson Cabineau," prodded Oliver. "An odd character for a social gathering such as this, is he not?"

"My brother has many peculiar interests, m'lord," said Victoria quietly. She looked around the room, licked her lips, and then continued, "Cabineau is not the first well-built young man who's caught my brother's eye. It is no secret, I suppose, but I do not believe our parents know. Their generation... you understand?"

"Your parents... Your brother prefers men?"

Victoria nodded, biting her lip with sparkling white teeth and eyeing him nervously.

"Oh," said Oliver, startled, blinking. "Surrey, Thornbush, Cabineau... they are all single men. That... that explains it."

"Surrey, you mean Bartholomew Surrey?" asked Victoria. "Explains what?"

He smiled down at her, holding his arm close so she stood right by his side. Softly, he said, "I'm glad I accepted your brother's invitation this evening. It's been a delight to meet you, m'lady."

"My brother is not the only one of us who enjoys the company of a vigorous man," remarked Victoria.

She allowed herself to be pulled close to him, arching her back so he was nearly forced to stare down the front of her dress.

"It's clear you want to learn more about my brother," continued the baroness. "On business for the Crown or the Company, no doubt. We Thornbushes have no secrets, m'lord. If it pleases you, I'll answer any question you have, tell you anything you'd like to know, but I think it a bit unfair if you are the only one who gets what pleases you."

He opened and closed his mouth, unsure of what to say.

"Come to the back rooms with me, m'lord, and everything the Thornbushes can offer will be yours," she pleaded. "If I am not to your taste, then you never need call upon me again, but I think you will, m'lord. I can be very generous. Please, m'lord, allow me to show you?"

Oliver swallowed, his throat suddenly dry. The girl was beautiful, but he was meant to be investigating her brother. Of course, she claimed she'd tell him everything. If he was no longer interested in her charms, that may not be the case. A pleasant bargain, he decided, and anyway, it seemed that perhaps the secret Avery Thornbush was hiding was not what they had suspected.

Oliver told her, "M'lady, I admit I've a keen interest in your family. Perhaps we can find somewhere private to discuss it?"

She smiled at him. "My brother's study is on the first floor. We can duck in without taking the stairwell in front of so many prying eyes. I'm sure none of the guests will miss us if we're quick, and if we're not, I don't care what any of them think."

Grinning down at her, struggling to keep his eyes on her face, Oliver gestured for her to lead the way.

She hugged his arm tight and pulled him toward a narrow hallway that led to the back of the house. "Stay behind me, if it pleases you, m'lord."

"Oliver, just Oliver," he murmured, allowing the young woman to guide him away from the party toward a quieter part of the building.

They walked down a narrow but well-appointed corridor to a polished, steel-bound wooden door.

"My brother's study," said Victoria. Then she turned and swept open the door.

Oliver stepped inside and paused.

On the desk in the center of the room, facing away from the door, sat Janson Cabineau. He was shirtless, and Avery Thornbush, also shirtless, stood on the opposite side of the desk. Avery lifted his head from where he'd been nuzzling Janson's neck. His startled gaze met theirs.

"Oh my," said Victoria, covering her mouth with her hand. "I thought you were out with the guests…"

"It's not what it looks like," claimed Avery, standing straight and reaching to adjust a coat he wasn't wearing. The young peer shifted uncomfortably. "I, ah…"

Oliver, ignoring both of the siblings, stared at the bare back of Janson Cabineau. The man's shoulders were corded with taut muscle and traced with finger-width black lines of intricate tattoos.

Oliver, recognizing a symbol in the center, mumbled, "The Hands of Seshim."

"What?" asked Victoria.

Her brother and Janson Cabineau sprang into action.

The merchant spun his legs and leapt off the table. The peer jerked open a drawer in the desk and removed a stick of bone-white chalk. Cabineau charged, and Avery bent, scrawling on the surface of the desk with the chalk.

Oliver dipped his hands into his dress coat and gripped the two katars he'd secreted there. He yanked them out in time to meet Cabineau's charge. He slashed at the man with one of the blades and pulled back with the other, preparing to punch the razor-sharp tip into Cabineau's face.

Crying and gripping an arm sporting a bloody gash, Cabineau stumbled out of reach. Avery cursed and threw his chalk down, only a few unsteady lines scrawled on the table. He darted to the side of the room where he picked up a leather rucksack and then rushed to the window, kicking it open.

Behind Oliver, Victoria was shrieking in panic.

Oliver advanced on Cabineau, gripping the two katars, feinting blows which forced the shirtless merchant to retreat.

Avery scrambled out of the window, and moments later, Oliver heard a strangled cry of surprise. He grinned. Sam must have been drawn by the shouting. Cabineau, apparently realizing that, weaponless, he was certain to lose the fight, turned and sprinted toward the open window, diving out of it without pause.

Oliver ran after him, Victoria Thornbush following close behind. She was shouting and wailing in confused fear. Clambering out of the window, Oliver saw Sam leaping to her feet, glaring at the stunned form of Cabineau who lay on the cobblestones of the back alley.

"Where the frozen hell did you come from?" she shouted at the prone man, rubbing the back of her head.

"The window," mentioned Oliver as he jumped down.

"I saw a different man in the alley and started after him. Then this one came out of nowhere," complained Sam. "Are these... How come neither of them is wearing a shirt? What's going on inside of that party?

Oliver pointed a blood-stained katar down at the merchant. "He's got the markings of sorcery on his back. The other one—"

He turned to look where Avery had fled around a corner of the building. Suddenly, the man came pelting back, the rising shouts of the inspectors chasing him. Moncrief's men were doing their part, and with the inspectors already in position surrounding the townhouse, there was nowhere for Avery Thornbush to run.

"I've got this one— Oh hells," muttered Sam.

Avery, skidding to a stop in the center of the alleyway, plunged a hand into his leather bag and removed a fistful of what appeared to be thin copper chain. He tossed it smoothly, and the chain fanned out, forming a circle and then falling silently onto the cobblestones where it flashed with brilliant blue flame.

Oliver gapped at the pattern the delicately linked chain had formed, a perfect circle inset with a five-pointed star. The baron stepped inside of the circle as a group of Moncrief's inspectors came racing around the corner.

"Hells," muttered Sam. She jabbed a finger down at Cabineau and turned to Oliver. "Watch him."

Grunting, Oliver strode forward and kicked as hard as he could, catching Cabineau in the ribs and lifting him from the cobbles with a terrible thump.

Sam, her kris daggers held wide, leapt at Avery Thornbush.

The man was pinching his thumb and middle finger together on both hands, muttering a strange incantation. Around him, springing from the links of the chain, sparks of incandescent white-blue flame rose into the air in a twisting column.

Oliver could feel a wave of cold air rush past him from the growing barrier. The alleyway was filled with a sound like cracking ice. He raised his katars, prepared to charge after Sam, but she burst through the wall of blue sparks like she was striding through a sheet of falling water.

The sparks fell away from her, running off her shoulders and back, and her daggers found the panicked peer, stabbing deep into his chest, piercing his heart. The man's hurried chanting stalled as his breath left his lungs and his soul his body. Avery Thornbush slumped to the ground in the center of his pentagram.

Sam turned to look back at Oliver. She cried, "What is she doing?"

Oliver glanced down and saw Baroness Victoria Thornbush kneeling beside Janson Cabineau, two fingers pressed against the man's neck.

She looked up to Oliver. "He's dead, m'lord. Your kick killed him. What—"

"Spirits forsake it, Duke," growled Sam. "We needed one alive. There's another name on that list."

"I just kicked him!" complained Oliver, looking from his boot to the motionless Cabineau. "Frozen hell, I've kicked my brothers twice as hard, and they're still alive."

Muttering, Sam knelt within the circle, the flickering white-blue sparks still rising around her. To Oliver's shock, she drew the edge of one of her kris daggers across her palm and then sheathed the blade. She used her good hand to force open Baron Thornbush's mouth, and she let her blood drip down onto his tongue.

"Sam," worried Oliver. "What are you…"

"You can't!" screamed Victoria Thornbush.

She lunged forward, trying to intervene. Oliver caught her and pulled her close.

"It's all right. She's not hurting him," he whispered into the ear of the struggling woman. He almost clarified, not hurting the dead man anymore.

The frantic woman's nails dug into his arm, and she kicked back at him, but he only held her tighter, feeling her hard muscles beneath soft flesh, whispering into her ear but failing to calm her.

Over shouts of protest from Victoria, Oliver heard Sam demanding of the dead body, "By my blood, I command you. Avery Thornbush, who are the other members of your cabal?"

Sam bent over the body, whispering closely.

"Who amongst you lives!" she cried, blood from her wounded hand still dripping into the corpse's mouth.

Oliver could hear no response, see no motion, but evidently Sam did. She kept pressing the spirit, demanding answers.

"Who—"

Then, she stopped and looked to Oliver and Victoria Thornbush.

"Frozen hell," muttered Oliver.

Victoria stomped on the bridge of his foot with the sharp spike of a high heel and then she swung her head back at him, a pile of intricately pinned and upswept hair bouncing off of his face. Her small white teeth clamped down on his arm, and he cried out in pain, instinctively releasing her. She spun, drawing a steel pin from her hair and swinging it at him.

He raised a forearm to meet hers, blocking the attack, and then he punched her in the face.

The baroness staggered back, one hand still holding the steel pin, the other clutching her face where blood poured from a broken nose. Crimson liquid painted her full lips and chin, splattering on the stark white of her dress.

"I'm sorry. I—" babbled Oliver.

Sam reached around the woman's neck and slashed her sinuous dagger across Victoria's throat, opening the flesh wide and sending a prodigious waterfall of blood cascading from the open wound.

Oliver looked away, grimacing.

Moncrief's men scrambled around, shouting commands, rushing inside to corral the confused peers that had been at the party, but steering clear of the bodies and the copper pentagram Avery Thornbush had laid out.

Oliver, taking deep breaths, finally got a hold of himself.

Sam cleaned her weapons and put them away. "I didn't find anything in the carriages or upstairs. How did you know it was them?"

"Male intuition," groused Oliver.

"Yes, m'lord, we can have them removed tomorrow. The contraption below, the one with the, ah, the wings, will be placed in the throne room by the end of today."

Oliver nodded and waved the work foreman away.

The man placed his floppy cap back on his head and disappeared inside.

Oliver resumed pacing the rooftop of the ancient druid keep, trying to ignore the three iron crosses his uncle had used as sacrificial altars and also the itchy feeling that, if he wanted to, he could know what work was happening deep within the keep without the foreman's input. Dozens of men with hammers, saws, and other heavy tools were removing all traces of his uncle's occupation. The gates and manacles William and his minions had installed would be gone. The scraps of bindings, the bones of those bodies who'd not been removed yet, it would all be gone. The only remaining tie to his uncle's terrible use of the place would be the blood still splattered on the floors and the walls.

Oliver would leave the blood there. It was a silent reminder of the horrific cost of sorcery, of why it must be stopped, eradicated from human knowledge.

He sighed.

Eradicated from human knowledge. It sounded like something Sam would say. She had a point, but it was easier said than done. The little show they'd put on behind Avery Thornbush's townhouse would be impossible to cover up. Dozens of peers had been inside the building. Just as many of Moncrief's inspectors had been into the back alley before the signs were obscured. Could they ever be sure that none of those people had seen a secret they could use as an entrance to the dark path? The peers had access to nearly limitless funds, and Moncrief's men had the regular duty of handling occult artifacts that no one was supposed to know about. Could he and Sam trust any of them?

Shaking his head, Oliver continued to pace, feeling the bubbling tension as the work continued below. He felt that work. How could he feel it?

There were no answers and no one he could ask. Somehow, his body responded to the old druid fortress, or perhaps it was the other way around? Was the fortress responding to him? He wondered if it was because he'd spent so much time in a similar structure in Northundon. He could have gained an affinity there for the ancient construction, or he could simply be imagining the feelings. His unconscious mind might be making clumsy attempts to grapple with his turmoil, both in the past and over the last several months.

Simply imagination. He wanted it to be true, but he knew it was not.

He could feel the men removing a stubborn steel gate. He thought he could hear their cursing as they banged on the stubborn hunk of metal. He knew when they lowered one of the odd constructions from the ceiling and sensed as they moved it through wide circular tunnels, tilting it so the broad spans of wood and hide that stretched from it didn't bang against the tunnel walls. He could feel them set the contraption down in the center of the throne room.

That odd device, a two-yard wide tube braced by long, stiff panels on either side of it, rested on skids that turned on hidden axels, and despite the light construction, Oliver knew the frame of the thing was remarkably strong. The contraption and the other bizarre artifacts left in the fortress had been a mystery to him years before, but they no longer were. He knew what the thing was built for, what it could do. He knew, but he couldn't explain how he knew.

The warm presence he felt when he walked into the keep was sharing with him. The spirit, tied indelibly to the stone of the fortress, was aware of all that happened within. He felt it reaching for him, and he did not push it away, but he did not reach back, either. He was not ready, not yet.

He held his hand above the stone of the battlement, but he did not touch it. He didn't need to any longer. The more time he spent within the ancient keep, the more he felt the connection, the more the place felt like home. He balled his fist and let it hang by his side, looking across the forest and the river at Southundon.

He was still on top of the roof when the workmen finished their day. He could feel as they walked down the tunnels, approaching the exit. He peeked between the crenellations of the battlement and saw them below. Just as he felt, one by one, they exited the keep and started down the rough road they'd hewn from the forest.

How. How was it possible he could feel it?

THE PRIESTESS V

"You summoned and bound a man's spirit?"

She jerked, springing up from the table and cursing.

In the doorway, King Edward Wellesley watched her with a smug grin on his face.

"I'm sorry, m'lord. I-I didn't hear you knocking," she stammered, tugging on her vest to right it, looking down at the table where she'd been studying Lilibet Wellesley's notes.

"I didn't knock," admitted the king, stepping into the room and walking over to look at the documents on the table. He tugged on his goatee, frowning. "This is ancient Darklands script, is it not? How much of it can you read?"

"Not much," she admitted. "With what I know, what Lilibet wrote down, I've been able to piece together a few phrases here and there. Not enough to—"

"To summon a spirit and bind it?" questioned the king, raising his eyebrows as he met her gaze.

She crossed her arms over her chest.

"That is what you did, is it not?" asked King Edward.

"I, ah, I did not summon it," she explained. "I merely prevented it from departing."

"And with your blood you bound it?" he pressed her.

She felt prickles of apprehension on her back and had trouble meeting the king's steely gaze. He'd shown her kindness. He'd allowed her into Lilibet's old sanctum, and he'd frequently expressed an abiding hatred for sorcery. There was no question that what she'd done had crossed the line. It was a line she knew had to be crossed if they wanted to keep the dark art from Enhover, but would the king see it that way?

She had to do it. What other way was there to ensure the cabal had no additional members? That had been the only way she'd learned Victoria Thornbush was involved. Had that woman done what Sam suspected she'd been meaning to do with Duke, she could have taken material from him. The blood and the seed of kings had incredible potency, and Sam imagined the woman had plans for Duke's.

She thought all of that but said none of it.

The king waited patiently.

"I did not intend to…" she mumbled. "I only meant… I knew that if we let his spirit slip away, we'd never have confidence that we got them all. We only had the one chance and no other clues."

"The Knives of the Council of Seven have always made compromises to right the scourge of sorcery," responded the king. "They've always taken steps that would otherwise, well, would otherwise earn a death sentence from both the Church and the Crown."

She swallowed. He was right. They both knew he was right.

The king leaned forward, shuffling the papers on the table and looking at what she'd been studying.

Her belt and daggers were on the corner of the table. In the blink of an eye, she could lunge and grab them. The king was unarmed. She would have little difficulty with him. But then what? She'd killed before, and it had rarely bothered her. When she killed, it was for a noble cause, a necessary evil to prevent worse atrocities. If the king turned her into the Church for sorcery, it would mean her execution. How far would she go to save herself?

At her side, her fingers twitched.

If she killed this man, could she get away? His chief of staff, Edgar Shackles, knew she'd been given access to the room. She could move the body to somewhere public, somewhere she wouldn't be a suspect. She could track down Shackles and ensure he would not talk. Would anyone else suspect what had happened? Would Duke?

Duke. She grimaced.

"Are you done considering it?" asked the king, interrupting her thoughts.

She looked up to meet his steady gaze. His eyes flicked toward her daggers. He knew what she was thinking.

"What do you want of me?" she asked.

"Like the Church, I want to eliminate sorcery in Enhover," said the king. "Unlike the Church, I understand this is a job that will never be finished. You did well, killing the Thornbush boy and his sister. You did well, tracking down the Dalyrimple girl, Bishop Yates, Raffles, even my brother. It was good work, but it was not the end. I think you and I both understand that."

She nodded slowly.

The king tapped a finger on the paper-covered table. "Knowledge like this exists in the world. We can search for it, confiscate it, quarantine it, but we'll never get it all. There's always another hidden cave like the one my son found in Imbon, a secret hoard some ancient family member began that the heirs discover anew. Aside from all of that, there's always someone willing to experiment, to chart their own maps, to create new ways to walk the dark path. Many of those will die on their walk, but some will not. The underworld exists, and like all potential knowledge, the means to reach it are there to be discovered." The king smirked. "When either man or the underworld ceases to exist, then I will no longer care about the plague of sorcery. Until then, I care very much."

"I didn't... With Thornbush, I had to—"

The king held up a hand. "The Church, in its wisdom, decided that there must be those allowed knowledge of the dark path to hunt the dangerous foes who walk it. They sanctioned a certain, ah, flexible relationship with the rules for their Council and its Knives. For everyone else, both the Church and the Crown have made sorcery a crime punishable by death."

"Yes, as a Knife of the—"

"You are no longer sanctioned by the Church," interrupted the king.

She closed her mouth.

"The Church is ineffective and foolish," continued King Edward. "Losing their support is no great loss, but if you plan to continue this pursuit, if you plan to continue eradicating sorcery from Enhover, then you need a new patron. I ask you, Samantha, will you be my hunter? Will you work on behalf of the Crown to protect our shores from the shadow of the underworld?"

"Of course," she breathed, air leaving her body, relief washing over her.

"You won't have protection from the Church or from the other Knives of the Council," warned King Edward. "You understand, I hope, how the Crown cannot be publicly involved in these types of things. You will, however, have access to what assistance I can provide. Lilibet's effects, for one, the sterling in my treasury, my inspectors… my son."

"I would be honored, m'lord," she said quietly.

"Oliver is bull-headed, sometimes," said the king. "I'm afraid no matter what I say to him, he'll do as he pleases. He'll pursue these matters regardless of what his old father thinks. On this journey, while you hunt, will you watch out for him? When you can, stay by his side, keep him out of trouble. To me, that is equally as important as the other work I ask of you."

"I'll do anything that you need, m'lord," she replied, bowing to the man.

"If he tries to slip away, you'll go with him and watch his back?"

She nodded.

"Good," replied King Edward, "In the meantime, I have something I need you to do."

———————

SHE STOOD ATOP THE ANCIENT DRUID KEEP, LOOKING OUT OVER THE dark forest, the black band of river reflecting the silver light of the moon, and the sparkling city of Southundon beyond it. Above, clouds whipped through the sky, obscuring and revealing the moon in turns, casting the landscape below in ever-changing patterns of dark and silver.

A cool breeze, heavy with moisture and the scent of the sea, gusted over the battlements, chilling her and making her shudder at the memory of the last time she had been on this rooftop, the last time she'd felt so cold.

From a pouch on her belt, she removed a roughly carved wooden symbol and a canteen of water. She drank but did not swallow. She swished the water in her mouth, letting each drop of it swirl, touching the sides of her cheeks, her tongue. Then, she knelt, turning the simple carving over to where she could see the back of it. It was stained dark from a dubious-smelling preparation.

She bent and dribbled water from her mouth onto the back of the emblem. It bubbled and popped, quietly hissing where the water touched the solution painted onto the wood.

When she was confident that she'd covered each bit of it with water from her mouth, she spit the rest of the liquid out to the side and drew Ca-Mi-He's tainted dagger from behind her back. She used the tip of the blade to flip the wooden carving over and the hilt to press down on it.

The solution on the back of the wood should bind the carving to the stone of the fortress. The design was Imbonese, and the wood was from that island. Ca-Mi-He's dagger invoked the power of the great spirit, and her saliva, tainted by the spirit's touch, activated the binding. Repetition and symmetry, the tools of a sorcerer.

King Edward had told her that the symbol would draw the reavers to it should any more of them escape. Not a binding, exactly, but an irresistible call. It was a precaution, a safety measure, as they still did not fully understand the nature of the creatures. Best to draw them as far from the city of Southundon as possible, which she could find no argument against.

She'd been stunned when the king had suggested it. Shocked that the man had knowledge to design and craft the emblem, but he'd had access to his wife's grimoires for years. He said he'd been unable to read much of it, as he professed complete ignorance of the ancient Darklands tongue, but he showed her Lilibet's notes describing such a ritual. They'd been stashed in a small cubby in the room that Sam had not yet sorted through and were written in the same, clear hand as the rest of the queen's notes. They'd modified the ritual to account for Sam's performance of it and the specific nature of Imbon, but otherwise, it was spelled out with remarkable precision.

An odd and fortunate coincidence that Lilibet had studied the attraction of creatures like the reaver, but the notes were there, written in the same script that covered every page in the chamber. If Sam had held any doubt about Lilibet's proficiency as a sorceress, reading the detailed instructions erased them. Not everything in the room hinted at such skill, but it was enough. Sam suspected the queen had taken much of her research with her when she fled, but the king could only shrug when she'd mentioned it. As Sam had read the note about attracting spirits drawn fully from the underworld but unbound, King Edward had looked on, quiet understanding in his eyes.

Sam had suggested that instead of her saliva, she use blood, but the king insisted they do it the way Lilibet had outlined. He demanded Sam not open her skin. With Ca-Mi-He's influence, not to mention the reavers, he claimed they would do what was necessary and nothing more. Any more would be dangerous.

He'd told her, "You don't want the reavers acquiring a taste for your blood, do you?"

Thinking back to the encounter with the reaver, she agreed. She was glad he'd talked her out of taking the ritual farther but confused how the man seemed so knowledgeable about the dark arts. How much of his wife's material had he read? How much had he understood?

Hoping it'd been long enough that the preparation had time to bind spirit to wood to stone, she stood. She waited, wondering if she'd feel the touch of Ca-Mi-He as the power of the spirit was used in the binding, but she felt nothing except the cold breeze.

The breeze. Was it the breeze or something else? Grunting and hugging herself nervously, she turned and left.

THE CARTOGRAPHER VII

"Admiral," he said.

"Duke Wellesley," replied the man, offering a shallow bow. "I am glad you agreed to accompany us."

Oliver snorted. "Agreed, was forced by my father... It is all semantics, no?"

The admiral shifted uncomfortably. "I'm glad you'll be with us regardless of how it happened. My men are no stranger to this type of campaign except..."

"Except for the giant lizards," Oliver finished.

"Exactly," responded Admiral Richard Brach, straightening his immaculate navy-blue coat. "We'll have the usual armaments and a strong contingent of marines. With the Cloud Serpent's artillery, I'd say close to four-score good brass cannon, holds filled with red saltpetre bombs, and the new rockets your father's men have been developing. I'm bringing three companies of royal marines with standard tropical kit, your sailors if they care to engage, and instructions to clear the island for rehabilitation. The Company will have seagoing vessels departing at approximately the same time we do, and I expect their arrival one week after we've finished our campaign. There will be additional marines with the seagoing fleet with a long-term assignment to provide security for the colony."

"Tell me of the rockets," said Oliver. "It was my understanding they were determined too dangerous for use on airships."

Admiral Brach brushed an imaginary piece of lint from the epaulets on his shoulder. "Well, that is true. A combination of red saltpetre-infused gunpowder and the conventional sort makes for substantial ignition along with a rather large pop at the end. If it fails to clear the decks... We've used the munitions in land combat and tested them at sea. This will be the first campaign they're authorized for deployment in the air. I'm still uncertain they will be necessary, but they're as safe to transport as any explosive. If we light them, of course, the men need be careful."

"Of course," agreed Oliver, running a hand over his hair and checking the knot at the back. "I will accompany your expedition as agreed. I will offer my serves as a cartographer familiar with the terrain as well as a man who has spent some time with the natives. I'll do my best to ensure the campaign proceeds as smoothly as possible, but neither I nor my men will engage in combat unless we're threatened. On those terms, I'll accept the voyage."

"It's rare a Wellesley is reluctant to bloody his blade," complained Admiral Brach.

Oliver put a hand on his broadsword and leaned toward the admiral. "When I was last in Imbon, I killed half-a-dozen natives with this very weapon. I wounded as many more, though I cannot account for them after they fell from the battlement I was defending. I fired a cannon that took one of those lizards in the gut, and I held the wall until the corpse of the thing came crashing through it. I stood my ground in the compound until one of our own men knocked me on the head from behind and hoisted me onto the airship. Admiral Brach, if I ever hear you doubt my valor again, I'll be seeing you on the dueling grounds."

"M'lord, I-I meant no offense."

"What did you mean, then, Admiral?"

"It's just... I expected you'd want to, ah, a misunderstanding, m'lord," stammered the admiral. "Of course your assistance is appreciated in whatever way you see best to provide it, and not a man in the royal marines could question your bravery."

"It's easy to float above an island filled with poorly armed natives and roll bombs from the deck of an airship," said Oliver. "It's more difficult, Admiral, to face a man blade to blade, to look into his eyes and understand that one of you will die. When you've done that, it changes the cost of battle. The economics are different when you're standing in a puddle of blood, unsure if it's a friend's or a foe's. It's worth remembering that not long ago, these people were part of our empire. They worked with the Company hand-in-hand. Technology has given Enhover much, Admiral, but it's taken from us as well. I worry we've forgotten what it is to wade into the mud."

"I speak the truth when I say I meant no offense," claimed the general, "but I must say, m'lord, you are in a rather odd mood today. I'd thought you'd leap at the opportunity to avenge your friends in the Company who fell during the uprising."

Oliver's lips twisted and he nodded. "You're right, Admiral Brach. I am in an odd mood. Shall we get a drink?"

"Yes, yes," said the admiral with a slow release of breath. "That would be much appreciated."

Oliver poured them drinks, and then they settled down around his map table in the center of his study. Spread out on the surface were all of the maps he could find depicting Imbon. It was a small place compared to Enhover, but several times larger than a typical island in the tropics, which was giving them some strategic concerns. For one, it was evidently large enough to hide lizards the size of an airship. They worried what else could be lurking beneath that jungle canopy.

Oliver had begun fashioning an amalgamation of the old maps of Imbon, the updates he'd made recently when discovering the sunken pool there, and his best guess of what it may look like now after the uprising. It wasn't perfect, but it was the best intelligence they had.

"You understand they've had several weeks to fortify the place," he explained to Admiral Brach. "Construction in the tropics is quick if they're organized. It's bamboo and dirt for the most part. I have no way of knowing what we might find."

"Fortifications are no bother," responded the admiral. "Anything constructed of wood can be flattened within a turn of the clock. Earthen structures pose a bit of more difficulty, but the marines have faced such before. If you recall, Rhensar tried to dig in. They built bulwarks, tunnels, all of it. We found it was difficult to destroy the structures from above, but we could destroy anything on the surface and create a safe landing for the men. Once on the ground, they poured fuel down the tunnels and lit it. If the fire didn't kill those inside, the smoke did. In Rhensar, we took a gamble and let some of the opposition go to warn the others. We risked them crafting more intricate defenses, but in the end, they understood they could not stand against us and surrendered. Of course, in Imbon, we'll have no opportunity to grant quarter."

Oliver winced, uncomfortable with the grisly thought of destroying a people.

The admiral studied the maps, evidently unaware of the discomfort his comments had caused.

"I agree, Admiral. It's unlikely that the natives will be able to build anything that gives us trouble," said Oliver, "but we should consider what capabilities they may have which Rhensar and our historical opponents do not. Pouring fuel into a tunnel system won't be easy if we're being harried by those lizards. Also, Brach, we must carefully guard against trickery. It's my belief that above all, the natives will try to capture one of our airships."

"Capture an airship?" questioned Brach dubiously.

Oliver nodded. "I believe it's why they did not immediately kill Governor Towerson during the uprising. It's why they didn't overrun the compound in the days after the initial clash. When they attacked us, I think their purpose was to capture the Cloud Serpent."

"To what end?" wondered the admiral. "An airship is a formidable weapon, but a single one flown by an inexperienced crew would cause little difficulty. You know as well as I that there's more to it than raising a sail and pointing a cannon. I don't imagine the natives know of our new rockets, but with such weapons, taking down another enemy in the air will be short work. Even without the rockets, we've drilled the royal marines on air-to-air combat. We can't think of every possibility under the sun, but our men are better prepared for such things than anyone else could be."

"That's what worries me," acknowledged Oliver. "Attacking our fleet would be futile, and if simple escape was their only goal, why not do it upon the sea right after the uprising? I've spent weeks mulling it over, and I have no answer. If I was a native on Imbon, what reason would I have to risk the very existence of my people in exchange for a single airship?"

Admiral Brach frowned, evidently not convinced, but he was a careful man, and Oliver knew his father had put the admiral in charge of the royal marines specifically because Brach considered every possibility. The admiral sipped his drink and thought.

Oliver stood and refilled his own glass, walking around the table and studying the maps of Imbon.

"We'll be at the greatest risk while the marines are disembarking," said Admiral Brach. "From hundreds of yards above the ground, there's nothing they can do to board us. When we're low, a savvy commander may put us at risk with a creative plan. Boarding us would be difficult even then, but we're not invulnerable."

"Is there precedent?" wondered Oliver.

Brach nodded. "In the final days of the war against the United Territories, Pierre de Bussy lured us into a trap. We came low, chasing the general himself, and he led us close to a nearby hill where he'd secreted a cannon emplacement. Dozens of the things fired before our airship realized the enemy was there. Under that kind of barrage, the vessel broke up, and… well, you can imagine what it'd be like on an airship that was splintering beneath your feet. We lost the airship and a good crew that day."

"Pierre de Bussy, Governor of Finavia's colony in the Vendatts?" asked Oliver.

Brach nodded. "He was the general of Finavia's army back then. After the war, your family bought his allegiance with the posting to the Vendatts, and for the last twenty years, he's been advocating for Crown control of the United Territories — and making himself a fortune in the bargain. I daresay, de Bussy's wealth may rival that of our merchant princes here in Enhover."

"I suppose I knew something about his past but not the details," responded Oliver, checking the knot that kept his hair tied back. "I've met his son, but not the governor."

"When the one man who had discovered a way to fight back against us bent the knee, it sucked the wind out of the sails for the rest of that continent," continued Brach. "If de Bussy bowed, then who else had the courage to fight back? Pierre de Bussy understood more than the rest of them. He still does. He tricked us and brought down one airship, but we had plenty more. He knew there was no way to win against us in the field, so he proved his worth and then negotiated a fat prize. It set the tone for the last twenty years, you know? Don't fight the Crown, join it. There are worse things than managing Finavia's colonies in the Vendatts, and he's harvested an income that could support his family indefinitely. He's a living example of how the bargain does not have to be a terrible one."

Looking down at the maps of Imbon, Oliver nodded. "There are far worse things than a posting in the Vendatts, Admiral."

THE CAPTAIN I

"Look sharp, lads!" Captain Catherine Ainsley barked. She strode the deck of the Cloud Serpent, her tall black boots banging hard on the wooden deck of the forecastle. She clasped her hands behind her back, feeling the hilts of her paired pistols bouncing against her elbows as she walked. On her back, she wore her two cutlasses, the leather sheaths high on her shoulders. Wooden-handled dirks poked from her boots, and she could feel their length as she walked. She drew a deep breath and then released it. She was ready for what was to come, though if all went to plan, it wouldn't be much.

She reached the front of the airship and adjusted the brim of her tri-cornered hat, blocking out the morning sun. By the time they sighted Imbon, the sun would be a bit higher, almost directly overhead. Great light for coming upon land. Great light for bombing a place, she supposed.

Looking around the sailors stationed on the forecastle, she noticed with pleasure they'd already settled the two forward deck guns on their stands and had cleaned and polished the weapons. Two buckets of apple-sized shot sat nearby where they wouldn't be stumbled over, and a canvass sack of powder was there and ready for use.

All was in order. The only thing that was left was moving the tins of red-hot embers into place. Those would be used to light the tapers, which would light the wicks, which would ignite the powder in the cannon. No sense setting that out too early, not on a wooden airship floating a thousand yards above the sea.

A quarter league ahead of them, five hundred yards lower, were the three airships under Admiral Brach's command. They were packed full of artillery and marines. Three hundred of the well-dressed lads if what she'd been told was accurate. Good-looking fellows, for the most part, though she preferred a man with a bit of scruff on his chin and some scars on his skin. The kind of man you didn't have to tell where to go and what to do.

Sighing, she glanced back behind her.

Her crew was working diligently. Mostly men, a few women. None of whom it'd be proper to tumble. Wouldn't have been such a bad thing to have a marine captain onboard. Better a man who required a bit of training than no man at all, and she'd found there were some advantages to a man who'd built his life around dutifully following orders.

She frowned.

Climbing up the ladder to the forecastle was a sailor hauling two heavy buckets of water. It would be stationed around the deck for when the fighting started and the crew began frantically lighting wicks. The men were trained to be careful, but no one was fully prepared for a battle. Best to have the water nearby. But that wasn't why she was frowning.

"Mister Samuels!" she cried.

The sailor set down his buckets and offered a sloppy salute. She wondered if the man was even capable of a smart one. Before this voyage, she'd never seen him try. Samuels, like many of the crew, was impressed by the rigid discipline of the royal marine airships they were sailing with. They were impressed, but her crew was not quite to royal marine standards of discipline.

"Mister Samuels, where are your shoes?" she questioned.

He scratched under his arm and glanced down at his feet. "Lost 'em, Captain."

"You lost your shoes on an airship?" she demanded incredulously. "How is that possible?"

Samuels kept scratching and shifted uncomfortably, his toes flexing and squirming on the wood.

"Mister Samuels," she continued, "If we have need of those buckets you're carrying, it's because sparks and flame are threatening our deck. If we're taking fire, in the heat of battle, do you really think it wise to run around barefoot?"

"Been working barefoot since I set to sea ten years ago, Captain," claimed the sailor.

"Aye, and have you been in combat during those years?"

"Ah, not really…"

"Mister Samuels, go find First Mate Pettybone and ask him to find you shoes," she instructed. "Whatever hell the first mate gives you is a small price to pay for losing the first pair."

The sailor offered another salute, this one even worse than the first, and scampered back down the ladder.

From behind her, a voice remarked, "I don't know if I'd have the temperance to keep men such as these in line. You're a natural, though, Captain."

Ainsley turned to see the strange priestess that accompanied Duke Wellesley standing behind her. She asked the woman, "How long have you been there?"

The priestess gave her a sly smile.

Grumbling to herself, Captain Ainsley resumed her position at the front of the airship, staring out at the sea and sky before them. The priestess joined her.

Finally, Ainsley asked, "The duke is pleased with my captaining, then?"

The priestess shrugged. "You've still got the position, don't you?"

"Aye," she said, waving behind her, "but what's he going to do? Promote Pettybone or Samuels?"

Laughing, the priestess admitted. "That's true."

After a moment, Ainsley asked, "What is it you're doing here?"

The priestess turned and blinked at her.

"Sorry if that was impolite," said the captain. "I mean… I mean what I said. Your job is the fight against sorcery, is it not? Is that what you think is happening in Imbon? You think these lizards are spirits or something? Are we going to be facing anything like what happened with the sorcerers you hunted?"

"That was a bit impolite," remarked the priestess, "but you're the captain, and it's your airship. It's natural you feel concerned about what you're sailing toward. As to why I'm here, it's only a precaution. The truth? I don't know if those lizards have anything to do with sorcery at all. If so, they're nothing like any sorcery I've heard of, but last time you and Duke were in Imbon, there were artifacts recovered that were dangerous, things that need educated, experienced evaluation. You heard about the fire in the Church's library?"

Ainsley nodded.

"That was from one of the figurines you brought back with you."

"Spirits forsake it!" cried Ainsley. "We had several dozen of those things aboard the Cloud Serpent. What if—"

The priestess held up a hand. "Quiet, please. Both the Crown and the Church would appreciate that information being held by as few people as possible. There was little danger while you were flying back to Enhover. Unlocking the statue would not have been possible by someone ignorant of certain rituals and ancient languages. I don't know that we'll encounter similar items, but if so, it's best someone who knows what they are doing is there to manage it."

"Someone educated and experienced?" guffawed the captain. "Seems like that was sort of the problem, ey?"

The priestess grinned and flicked the brim of Ainsley's hat with one finger. "You're wiser than you look, Captain. Have no fear. I do not intend to do anything with any objects we find except sequester them in your hold. In truth, I suspect we'll find nothing, but if we do, my intention is that it's packed away safely and no one takes a look until it's on the ground back in Enhover."

"Sounds good to me, Priestess."

"Sam," replied the priestess. "You may call me Sam. Catherine, is that your given name?"

"I prefer Ainsley," she replied, "or Captain."

"I'm always willing to respect another woman's preferences," claimed the priestess. She waved at the men working behind them. "Let me know if you'd like some company while we're traveling, Captain."

The priestess walked away, and Ainsley stared at her back, wondering what the frozen hell the strange woman was talking about.

THE CARTOGRAPHER VIII

THE VERDANT green hump rose like an emerald from the shimmering blue water all around it. As far as they could see, there was nothing but the bright blue sea, Imbon's tropical forest, and a column of thick white smoke trailing from the peak of the island's mountain. For a moment, it gave Oliver an uncomfortable reminder of what the island had looked like the last time they'd visited. He quickly saw this smoke wasn't from burning structures but from the cap of the volcano that formed the island. Venting was common on tropical formations, but the echo of the smoke from before was difficult to ignore.

As they sailed closer, Oliver began to pick out the brown bodies and white sails of ships anchored in the colony's harbor. It wasn't until they were just a few leagues away that he saw over a sharply sloped ridge to the colony itself.

It looked much the same as it had the last time he'd arrived, except this time, there was no column of thick black smoke. The buildings showed little evidence of repair, though, and several walls around the Company's compound were still flattened.

"They moved the lizards," remarked Captain Ainsley.

He nodded. He was looking at the corner of the compound where a cannon platform had once been. He'd been standing there when one of the giant lizards had collapsed on it. The bamboo walls were demolished, clear evidence of what had happened, but there was no trace of the massive green creature that had fallen. There was no trace of anyone.

"Looks quiet," remarked Sam.

"They must have known we were coming," said Captain Ainsley. "A lookout on top of that ridge with a spyglass could see us fifteen leagues away. Plenty of time to signal the settlement and get everyone into hiding."

"But why?" wondered Oliver. "You think they mean to wage war from the jungle?"

"I'm not tactician," replied Ainsley, "but I wouldn't be standing in the middle of the compound when a bunch of airships from Enhover came seeking vengeance. Whether or not they mean to fight, only a fool would be standing in the open when we drift overhead."

Oliver grunted. She had a point.

He ran a hand over his hair, feeling the leather thong that tied it back. He told Ainsley, "Let's pick up speed and fly in above the marines. Admiral Brach is going to see this and think nothing is amiss, but something is. I can feel it. It's not right."

Ainsley turned and barked out orders.

Oliver leaned forward, his forearms resting on the gunwale, studying the quiet village as they approached. Signals were passing between the royal marine's airships, and they began to descend, spreading out as they did. The center vessel headed directly toward Imbon's settlement, the other two floating out to the flanks.

"He's too low," muttered Oliver, watching Brach's command vessel as it coasted one hundred yards above the harbor and then the village.

The airship slowed to walking speed as its shadow passed over the village and crept up the ramp to the Company's compound. The gate hung open where the natives must have left after overrunning the place. There was no movement.

"Frozen hell, he's too low!" snapped Oliver.

"There's nothing there, Duke," said Sam, studying the huts in the village. "They've fled into the jungle or maybe even escaped off the island. What would they accomplish by staying within that compound other than making an easy target for bombardment?"

Gripping the hilt of his broadsword, Oliver scowled but had no response. Something wasn't right, but all he had was a feeling. If they signaled Brach, what would he even tell the man? Be cautious? He'd voiced that half-a-dozen times before they had boarded the airships and set sail for Imbon. The admiral knew it, but he had his orders from the king. No matter what, Brach was going to put men down on the island, and they were going to clear it out for resettlement. It would have been easier had the Imbonese lined up on the shore, but even if Brach had to hunt them one by one through the jungle, he wasn't going back to Enhover until he'd done it.

"What'd they do with the lizards?" wondered Oliver, half-expecting the giant beasts to come bursting out of the governor's mansion, snapping their teeth at Brach's airship.

"Look at that," said Sam, pointing to the center of the compound where the dirt yard was just coming into view. "Looks like a burial mound to me. Do you think they'd bury a lizard?"

Oliver frowned. It did look like a burial mound. For lizards, though? Perhaps they'd buried the dead Company men there to avoid sickness. It wasn't uncommon for illnesses to breakout and spread quickly on the small islands in the tropics. He wasn't a physician, but leaving dead bodies out in the open on a contained landmass did not seem wise.

"It could—"

The mound exploded.

Thunderous rumbles burst from the center of the compound, and a giant plume of fire and smoke rose toward Brach's airship. Brown dirt and black iron bounced off the hull of the airship, shattering some of the boards on the keel and rocking the vessel like it was in the midst of a severe summer storm. A man, screaming in terror, fell from the side of the airship into the billowing dust and fire below. The airship jerked higher, water trailing like blood as they emptied the bilge, dumping the water that must have been soaking their levitating stones so they could swoop in low.

"They were ready," murmured Ainsley, watching the action ahead of them. "Someone had a hand on the emergency lever."

One hundred fifty, two hundred, three hundred yards higher, the airship rose and then slowed and hung steady. A rain of broken wood, dirt, and iron fell from the bottom to vanish into the dust below. From what Oliver could see of the aft side of the airship, quite a few planks had taken heavy damage, and several were missing. At least one man was killed when the violence of the impact knocked him overboard. Other men were scrambling about in a panic, but Oliver saw no additional casualties. The tender bodies of the crew had been protected from the blast by the hull of the vessel.

"Integrity of the stones and the superstructure around them looks good," murmured Ainsley, lowering a spyglass and slapping it against her palm. She shouted back to Pettybone. "Signal a report to 'em about what we can see. Brach and his captain are probably sweating, wondering what the underside looks like."

Pettybone turned to the Cloud Serpent's flag man, and the young sailor began raising and lowering his flags in a swift pattern, communicating with Brach's airship, Enhover's Slayer, though Oliver wasn't sure anyone would bother to look back at them.

In the compound, the smoke and dust drifted away, and a few individuals could be seen racing out of buildings and then running down the ramp into the village.

"A trap," muttered Oliver, watching the fleeing natives.

"Clever," acknowledge Sam, her eyes darting between the damaged airship and the perpetrators, "though it didn't do much."

To punctuate her statement, Enhover's Slayer rolled their first barrel of red saltpetre munitions over the edge. The thing fell straight down and landed in the huge crater in the center of the courtyard below them. It burst, sending flame and balls of screaming lead pelting into the wood around it. The artillery men on Enhover's Slayer adjusted their aim, and buildings in the compound began to explode. Concussive blasts, like drums on parade day, rocked the midday air.

Oliver watched as Brach's sailors strategically began to demolish the Company's compound, placing barrels where they could blow open walls and then a second barrage to shred anything remaining inside with flying lead.

"Signal them to conserve their munitions," instructed Oliver. "There's no one alive down there."

Ainsley nodded and relayed the orders.

Several more barrels dropped from Enhover's Slayer before the bombardment stilled. It was evident that Brach had ordered the barrage as retaliation for the blast against his airship, but like Oliver, he knew that no one would be stupid enough to trigger the trap and then wait in the compound for the response. Even if they'd taken down the Slayer, the three other airships could easily mop up anyone caught in the open.

"They meant to bring the thing down and failed," mused Oliver. "Had they been successful, what would they have done?"

Sam frowned at him.

He pointed at the line of jungle near the compound. "Captain Ainsley, take us a little closer. My guess is that there's a couple hundred natives crouched in waiting to rush out and scramble over the Slayer had they managed to down her."

Nodding, Ainsley adjusted course, but before they got close, one of the airships on Brach's flank must have had the same thought, and suddenly, the starboard bank of their cannon erupted into life.

Between the thumps of the cannon blasts and the whistling of the heavy balls of iron flying through the air, Oliver heard screams of pain and panic. As he'd guessed, the natives were clustered along the tree line of the jungle, and they hadn't fled when they should have after their initial trap failed.

The second flanking vessel turned, and soon, they began a fusillade as well, the two airships punching giant holes in the jungle canopy. Broken trees, torn leaves, and smashed bodies. Through the holes in the jungle, Oliver could see flashes of movement as people fled deeper into the trees.

Admiral Brach, his airship back under control after the attack, drifted overhead, letting the other two airships blast the edge of the foliage with cannon. Brach appeared to be tracking the progress of the natives' flight.

"Hells," muttered Oliver.

"What?" asked Sam.

"He's going to drop on them."

"That's what we're here for," she said, placing a hand on his arm.

He shook his head. "No, I mean... Yes, I don't want to see this, but all of those people look to be running in the same direction, don't they? They're going somewhere. It's a small island. In a few turns of the clock, we could know where they're headed."

They, and the people below, did not get a turn of the clock. Brach waited until the stream of humanity began to cross a narrow creek, and then his men started to drop their bombs again.

The barrels rolled over the edges of the airship and fell into the open space below, exploding on impact, launching buckets of lead pellets into anyone within twenty yards of each blast.

Snipers on the airship shouldered rifles and began taking cracks at those who crossed above or below the airship's range. Over and over, Oliver heard the sharp retorts of the firearms and the thunderous concussions of the barrel bombs.

Behind them, the first flanking airship maintained its assault on the edge of the jungle, slowly moving inland, creeping deeper with its hail of cannon fire. The second airship drifted across the jungle, periodically rolling barrels where the crew must have seen clusters of people running from the cannon, afraid to cross the barrier which Enhover's Slayer maintained along the creek.

For the rest of the day, Enhover's airships fired cannon and dropped bombs. By nightfall, a square league of jungle was completely devastated. It looked like the trampled grass of the lawn after one of Philip's galas, though instead of dropped and broken wine flutes, it was bodies Oliver could see peeking from underneath downed trees.

He couldn't estimate how many natives had been killed in the action, but by the time the sun touched the horizon, the cracks of the firearms had grown rare. The snipers saw nothing below worth shooting.

Knowing that on the morrow, they would lower the marines to continue the campaign through the jungle, Oliver couldn't decide how he felt about the annihilation. He hated to see the bloodshed, but the next day, Enhover's people, his people, would be at risk.

He needed a drink.

HIS BOOTS THUMPED ONTO THE GROUND, THE PACKED SAND SOFTENED by ash fallen from fires set during the uprising and the retaliation the day before. A quarter league from them was the village of Imbon and the Company compound that oversaw it. Both areas were crawling with blue-coated royal marines.

Oliver held a hand up to his brow, blocking the sun from his eyes, and looked at the verdant mountain that rose behind the settlement. The top of that mountain was belching a steady stream of thick, white smoke. The ash beneath his boots wasn't just from the conflicts of man, he realized. The mountain itself was discharging a thin layer of the stuff all across the island.

"Duke Wellesley," said a well-dressed royal marine officer, walking briskly to join them.

"Commander Ostrander," acknowledged Oliver.

The commander nodded to Oliver and then doffed his hat and

bowed to Sam and Captain Ainsley. "I recognize you both, do I not?"

"My captain, Catherine Ainsley, and my priestess, Sam," introduced Oliver.

Ostrander wiped the back of his hand across his sweaty brow and settled his hat back on top of his powered wig.

"A bit hot in the tropics for that, is it not?" questioned Oliver.

"Admiral Brach's a traditionalist," explained the commander. "You should see him at officer's supper each evening. Full suits and wigs for all of us. You'll never find a smarter dressed group eating beans, salted pork, and stale ship's biscuits. That man's back couldn't be straighter if you rammed a flagpole up his arse." He glanced at the two women. "Apologies."

"They've done worse," said Oliver, gesturing for the commander to lead them toward the village.

"We've done what?" asked Sam, raising an eyebrow.

"I didn't mean it like that," muttered Oliver. "I meant you've said worse in front of me... fouler language."

Sam shrugged. "I thought you were speaking of that time I rammed a ship's mast up a man's arse."

"Hells," muttered Oliver, turning from her.

"You boys are cute," said Captain Ainsley, clapping Oliver and Commander Ostrander on the shoulders. "Come on. I think I know the way."

She started off toward the village, and Ostrander hurried to walk beside her.

Sam fell in next to Oliver and playfully elbowed him in the ribcage. She whispered, "He reminds me of you the first time we met."

Oliver tried to ignore her.

"Looks like they've run Enhover's flag back up the pole at the compound," Sam called ahead to Ostrander.

The commander's stride lengthened, but he didn't turn.

Despite the grim work they were embarking on, Oliver couldn't stop a smile. He still admonished Sam, "Let's be serious.

I can't imagine any of the natives have stuck around in the village or the compound after that bombardment, but I couldn't have imagined those lizards attacking, either. I'm certain we haven't seen the last surprise from Imbon."

THEY HUDDLED AROUND A TABLE, A CANVASS TENT HANGING listlessly above them. The flaps had been pulled wide open and tied back, but the marines had erected the tent on the beach down near the surf where it was protected by sharp ridges of jungle rising on either side. The wind barely stirred the air beneath the canvass.

Across the table from Oliver, Admiral Brach slapped the back of his neck.

"Will these bugs be plaguing us constantly?" questioned Commander Ostrander, scratching at an angry red bump on his hand.

"There are some herbs the natives grind down to oil. They rub it on their skin, and it's quite effective," replied Oliver. "It smells funny, but I found it was worth it. Of course, I don't expect we'll find many natives who are willing to share which herbs they use to create the mixture. Perhaps one of the shipboard physicians is an herbalist? They could scout the Company's herb gardens and see if they can find something. The best solution, though, is to find somewhere with a constant breeze. If we can clear the compound, that would suit. Or you could sleep aboard the airships. I don't relish the idea of getting hauled up and down every time I want to talk to someone, though. Aside from relocating camp to higher ground, my best piece of advice, Commander, is to close the tent flaps when you retire and sleep in your sleeves and trousers."

The man grunted, and Oliver saw Admiral Brach glancing at the raised tent flaps. Lowering the flaps would stave off some of the insects, but during the day, it wasn't worth blocking the little bit of wind that reached them. Worse, though, would be meeting outside of the tent where the tropical sun blazed like forge fire. During his travels, Oliver had found that the middle of the day in the tropics was best for a cool, stiff drink followed by a nap in the shade. Unfortunately, they had work to be about.

"Right here, this depression is where the artifacts were recovered," said Oliver, stabbing a finger down onto the map on the table. "There are warehouses and a small pier over here for loading spices. These lines, those are the largest plantations. Here, at the base of the mountain, that's where the Company found a series of caves that Towerson began using for spice storage. The caves are quite deep. If I was afraid of fire from above, inside there is where I'd hide. The only other structures that could conceivably hide so many people are the warehouses. If they're not gathered in either of those places, I'm afraid they've scattered in the jungle, and we've got some work ahead of us."

Brach, rubbing his chin, suggested, "We could send half the men through the jungle and transport the other half down here to the plantations. They could both close in and meet at the caverns. That way, if they're in there, they won't have a chance to escape."

"That's a rough trek through the jungle," warned Oliver. "Hot, humid, and little in the way of pathways. At least, few that you're likely to be able to locate."

"You didn't map them?" wondered Ostrander.

"The jungle will grow over a footpath in two or three cycles of the moon," explained Oliver. "The natives' traffic patterns changed seasonally, depending on where they were finding the easiest sources of sustenance. When we arrived, there weren't any permanent paths, just temporary tracks that might disappear by the time my ink was dry. Instead of trying to maintain roads through the undergrowth, Towerson found it much easier to sail around. Even on a small ketch, the journey isn't more than a few turns of the clock. Hacking your way through the foliage will take two or three days."

"Hells," muttered Ostrander.

"The coast belonged to the Company," explained Oliver, "the interior to the natives."

"It must be done," commanded Admiral Brach. "If we don't move through the jungle, we can't assure it's clear of the enemy. We'll do it for the Crown."

"For the Crown," responded Commander Ostrander grimly

Oliver decided he'd recommend the man for a promotion if they both returned to Enhover hale. Competent, loyal, and, unlike Brach, a realist. The empire needed more men like Brendan Ostrander.

"Don't suppose you fancy leading the way?" the commander asked, turning to Oliver.

Oliver shook his head. "I'm planning to go up here, to the pond we found that started this mess. Cleaning out this island for resettlement is all well and good, but I want to understand how this began."

Admiral Brach grunted but did not voice his disagreement. He was the senior military official, but Oliver was a son of the king.

Frowning, Oliver studied the map. Brach understood the mission, but he hadn't been fully briefed on the rest of it. He didn't know that the pool had hidden a trove of artifacts, and it was study of those artifacts that led to the release of a reaver in Southundon, the deaths of dozens, and the loss of the Church's library. There was more to accomplish in Imbon than simply spilling the blood of all its people.

Finally, Brach mustered the courage to ask, "Do you think splitting from the war parties and traipsing through the jungle alone is wise, Oliver? I'd rather not compromise the effectiveness of our forces by spreading too thin."

Oliver waved a hand to placate the man. "I'm not asking for an escort, Brach. I'll have a contingent from the Cloud Serpent, and I think that will be sufficient."

"Not if you run into serious resistance," warned Ostrander. "In this foliage, even if we hear combat, no one will be able to come to your aid quickly."

"The Cloud Serpent will provide overhead support and a platform for rescue if we need it," assured Oliver. "And there won't be much traipsing. I'm not looking to dig out nests of rebels. I'll be finding the shortest route to this pool. We'll drop in the closest spot we can find an opening in the canopy and do a quick hike in and out. We should have time to catch up to your forces before the engagement begins at the caverns."

The two military man eyed each other, and Brach remarked, "If something happens, your father will kill me."

"I'm not asking, Admiral," mentioned Oliver.

The admiral nodded crisply and then turned back to the maps. "All right, then. I'll take half the forces around to the warehouses and the pier. Ostrander, you'll take the men through here and come up behind the warehouses. We'll plan for a two-day overland journey, which means my forces will depart a day and a half after you. Let's see… If you leave this afternoon, then midday two days from now, we'll reunite here…"

Seeing Brach was merely repeating the path Oliver had already inked on the parchment, he let the admiral drone on. The pool, a prison designed to house the reavers, an inspiration for the natives to rebel, risking everything that they had. Something inside of there could be a clue. He worried what it would be.

LOOSENING THE TIES ON HIS SHIRT, OLIVER REGRETTED BRINGING HIS coat. The attire was proper for a gentleman, but it was spirits-forsaken hot. Admiral Brach's stifling formality had gotten to him, he admitted. When they'd parted, the man was dressed in a full suit, his powdered wig, and, Oliver suspected, a dusting of rogue across his cheeks, though it could have been that the man's face had achieved a natural redness dressed like that in such a warm clime. Regardless, the admiral's ostentatious decorum had been enough to guilt Oliver into donning his own coat.

"Is it always this hot in Imbon?" complained Mister Samuels.

Oliver glanced at the sailor and acknowledged, "Hotter, usually. It's the humidity. Makes it feel warmer than it is. The same reason Enhover feels so cold in the winter, actually."

The man grunted and adjusted a pile of empty sacks on his back. He was serving as their porter on the expedition. Sam was there for her knowledge of the supernatural and Captain Ainsley because she relished any opportunity to strap on her pistols.

Folding a small map he'd sketched to take with them, Oliver pointed uphill. "Just four hundred yards farther. We can't see it because of the canopy, but I'm fairly confident that's where we'll find the pool."

"Why couldn't we see it when we flew over, then?" muttered Mister Samuels.

"They drained the pool when they were looking for the star-iron and found the tomb," explained Oliver. "That was months ago. In the tropics, that's plenty of time for vegetation to grow over any open ground. Besides, we needed to approach on foot and do a bit of scouting to ensure the area is clear of natives before we go barging in."

"Lead on, then," suggested Sam, her fingers nervously tracing the hilts of her kris daggers.

Oliver nodded and glanced over the party's kit one last time. He frowned. "Samuels, why are you not wearing shoes?"

"Frozen hell!" barked Ainsley, turning on her crewman.

"Lost 'em," muttered the sailor, looking down at his feet.

Ainsley rubbed her hands over her eyes, cursing beneath her breath.

"Watch out for snakes, then," advised Oliver, turning and leading the party into the thick foliage that surrounded the clearing they'd dropped into. "Underneath the ferns, there are small green ones. They blend into the leaves of the jungle. Small teeth, but if the fangs break your skin, you've got two, maybe three turns of the clock before you succumb."

"Succumb to what?" asked Samuels, falling into the rear of the line.

Oliver, slashing through fronds and branches with a cutlass he'd borrowed from the Cloud Serpent, called back over his shoulder, "You should have worn shoes, sailor."

Hacking and grunting as he carved a tunnel through the jungle, Oliver realized four hundred yards was going to be a very long way in such thick vegetation. Cursing as invisible insects feasted on the bare skin of his neck, he sped up, sharing his rage at the small bugs with the plant life in front of him.

For a turn of the clock, he chopped and slashed their way through the jungle. Sam was right behind him, Ainsley behind her, and Mister Samuels brought up the rear. The sailor regularly asked if anyone had seen any snakes, and the rest of them regularly offered vile curses and muttered complaints as they forced their way ahead. Finally, arms aching, Oliver burst through the wall of vegetation and stumbled into the clear.

In front of him, a slope led down into a giant, grass-covered bowl. Trees towered around the rim of the bowl, obscuring it from above. Waist-high fronds of jungle plants were already rising near the bottom of the drained pool, but for now, it was mostly covered in calf-high grasses. It wouldn't be long before the entire spot was overgrown, and by then, it would be nearly impossible to find again.

"Down there," said Sam.

Oliver nodded. At the bottom of the bowl was a two-yard-wide black hole that led into the earth. Beside it was a dark metal disc that was already half-obscured by plant growth.

"That's what I felt when I swam down," he said, pointing at the big metal disk gleaming smoothly in the bright sun.

Without further comment, he walked and slid down the steep, muddy slope. At the bottom, he crouched beside the cap to the hole and ran his hands over it.

"It's not star-iron, but what is this? It's not iron or steel, I don't think. You know, I'm not even sure if this is metal. Could it be fired clay?"

Ainsley put a boot on the disk and tried to move it, but she couldn't budge the heavy object. "Capped with this and then flooded? They didn't want anyone finding what was down here."

Oliver nodded, looking up the slope where the royal marines and Company men had left a large, manual pump. A thick canvass tube lay like a dead serpent, stretched to the bottom of the pool where they'd pumped out the water.

A huge effort by scores of men applying technology that, as far as he knew, the natives did not have. When they'd built whatever tomb was down below, dug out the huge pool above it, and dammed it so it filled with water, they'd never intended this site to be located. They'd marked the location instead of hiding the artifacts in the jungle, but he didn't think anyone was ever meant to go inside. The only giveaway had been the false totems they'd scattered around the edge. Oliver guessed that would be more than sufficient to keep any locals from diving into the pool. It was pure chance he'd happened by the site, ignored the warnings they'd set, and taken the initiative to dive down to the bottom. Outside of his unique circumstances, he doubted anyone else would have had the wherewithal to locate the tomb and also have the resources to open it.

"Shall we?" asked Sam.

"That's what we're here for," said Oliver. "You'll lead from here?"

Sam nodded, shook a vial of fae light that was hanging around her neck, and then peeked into the gaping, black hole. She climbed inside and descended a ladder Oliver suspected had been left there by the marines and the Company men.

He wakened his own fae and followed her down.

THE PRIESTESS VI

SHE CAREFULLY SCALED down the rickety ladder, turning her body so the light of the fae shone on the small circular chamber and the opening that led to a narrow tunnel. Ten yards down, she made it to the floor and moved out of the way for Duke, Ainsley, and Samuels to come behind her.

Looking into the tunnel, she saw it was formed of black volcanic rock and led into the mountain. Her light didn't reach the end of the passageway, but she saw nothing menacing. It was warm, like the rocks had absorbed the brilliant heat of the sun and contained it deep underground. A thick scent of recently rotten eggs accompanied gusts of hot, heavy air, as if the mountain itself was breathing in and out.

When the rest of the party was on the floor, she crept down the tunnel, one hand on a dagger, the other on the glowing vial of fae light around her neck. With each step, the temperature rose. It was unpleasant, and when she let her hand brush against the rock wall, it was like touching the side of a mug of freshly poured tea. Not a dangerous heat, but within moments, sweat was pouring down her face. She walked fifty paces until the tunnel opened into a chamber the size of the Cloud Serpent's hold.

"It is a tomb," she muttered, stepping cautiously into the room.

The walls rose in a dome far above her head. They were lined with empty shelves that she imagined recently held the uvaan and the dark clay tablets the Company had recovered. In the center of the room was a large sarcophagus carved with the likeness of a man. The heavy stone lid of the container was opened but still resting atop the sarcophagus.

Duke walked past her and held his light so it shone inside.

"Bones," he muttered. "Bones wrapped in cloth. It looks just like the reaver we fought in Southundon."

There was a pause, as if they were all waiting for it to move, but it did not.

Sam joined him and peered inside. He was right. Except for the missing malevolent purple glow in its eyes, it looked nearly identical to the one they'd battled in the Church's library. "Not invested with a spirit, maybe?"

"What are we looking for in here?" questioned Samuels, walking a circuit around the chamber and glancing at the empty shelves. "The marines cleaned this place out, it looks like. Nothing but dust and bones. And this thing."

Sam looked at what the sailor was referring to and saw a huge stone carving above his head. A serpent, eating its tail, circled the room above the shelves.

"An ouroboros," she said. "Curious."

"Ey, and look at this," said Ainsley, scratching the toe of her boot along the dusty floor. "These seams look rather regular, given how natural the rest of the cave is. They dig this out and then lay blocks in the floor? Makes no sense."

Sam knelt near Ainsley, feeling a perfectly straight line. She told the rest of the group, "Help dust this off. Let's see what it looks like."

Moments later, they were standing atop the sarcophagus, which seemed a bit morbid, but it was the best point of view to study what they'd uncovered on the floor.

"Are those letters?" wondered Duke.

"Horuca," answered Sam, a tingle running down her spine. "It's Darklands tongue. A traditional beginning to an incantation. A prayer to the spirits, of sorts, for success in an endeavor."

"The lines are filled with ash," remarked Ainsley. She hoped down and wet a finger, which she touched to the dust on the floor. She sniffed it. "Not gunpowder, but it ain't rock dust, either. Did the marines that cleared this place out mention a fire?"

Sam glanced at Duke, but he could only shake his head. He said, "We didn't get much of a chance to talk to them, remember? Giles and the rest of the bunch who found this place all fell when the compound was overrun. It was women and children we rescued, and none of them were in the party that came up here."

Ainsley rubbed the dust between her fingers and then brushed it off.

Getting an uncomfortable feeling, Sam shifted her feet, glancing between her boots at the face on the lid of the sarcophagus. "Duke, does this face look Imbonese to you?"

He jumped down onto the floor beside the captain and peered at the face between Sam's boots.

"Could be," he mused, running his hand over his hair. "Looks more Southlands, though." He leaned closer and brushed a finger across the stone. "These pocks, here, see? It reminds me of the ceremonial scarring you see on the faces of the Darklanders. I was never able to figure out what the scarring meant, but Company men who'd been on the continent longer than I think it signifies rank."

"What would those marks mean, then?" questioned Sam, tilting her head to look at the face.

"Nothing, except whoever's face this is, they were probably from the Darklands," replied Duke. "The Imbonese have a similar look, but their cheek bones aren't quite as distinct, and they're darker… Spirits."

Sam crouched down, straddling the stone face, a tremor of suspicion running down her spine. "The scholar who was studying the uvaan in the Church's library believed the text on the tablets could have originated in the Darklands. The people of Imbon came from somewhere. This face, the language on those tablets..."

"It fits together, doesn't it?" muttered Duke. "It's not just their sorcery they got from that forbidden land. They themselves..."

"What are you two talking about?" questioned Mister Samuels.

"They were trying to steal an airship you thought, right?" mused Ainsley, ignoring the crewman. "Why? That's the question that will solve this mystery. Airship travel is quite easy, but there are seaworthy ships in the harbor that could make the journey. Hells, that's the only way anyone has made the journey, right? No one has visited that place in twenty years. Why would the natives need an airship to do it now?"

"You're right," agreed Sam. "Why an airship?"

"I don't think the answer is in this room," muttered Oliver.

Sam eyed him. She knew what he was thinking. The answer wasn't here, but was it there? Imbon was halfway to the Darklands. He'd promised his father he would not go, but if the uvaan came from there, then it was a choice between finding the source of the mystery or ignoring it. Ignoring the mystery and his mother. Sam grimaced and clambered down off the lid of the sarcophagus.

"Spirits forsake it, it's hot in here, ain't it?" complained Mister Samuels.

"Imbon is volcanic," said Duke. "There's been no active lava flow since the Company's arrival, but it stands to reason there could still be hot spots beneath the ground. We're, what, fifty yards below the surface? That's deep enough we could be close to a hidden flow."

"Shouldn't that have heated the pool the first time we were here?" questioned Sam. "If I recall, it was quite cool. That's why you jumped in, right?"

Duke frowned but did not reply. Evidently, he had no answer to that.

Mister Samuels walked across the figure carved into the sarcophagus, moving edge to edge while looking up at the ouroboros that circled the room above them.

"Get down from there," instructed Ainsley. "There's a person inside of that box, sailor."

Samuels scowled at her. "You was up here too."

"Get down," repeated Ainsley.

Samuels walked to the corner and made to jump down, but the heavy stone lid shifted under his feet, toppling off the box and crashing to the floor, the sailor coming down hard on it and rolling away.

"Hells, man!" cried Ainsley.

"I'm all right," grumbled Samuels, sitting up and clutching his elbow. "I think."

Sam walked around the burial box to check on Samuels but stopped. The sarcophagus lid had flipped over when it had fallen, and the underside of it was filled with an intricate mechanism. Gears and wires were covered in dust, gleaming where they'd recently moved.

"What is this?" mumbled Duke, crouching beside the lid to look at it.

"I have no idea," replied Sam. She pointed to one of the gears. "Look, it's moved recently. Do you think..."

"A trap," said Ainsley. The captain was standing beside the sarcophagus and holding up a wire cord that had been snapped. "When that lid was first moved, it musta pulled on this and triggered, ah... something."

"Triggered what?" questioned Duke.

"Spirits, it's hot," grumbled Samuels, stepping onto the edge of the lid and keeping his dirty toes away from the mechanism. "I swear that floor is getting warmer the longer we're in here. It's burning up my poor feet."

Captain Ainsley's fists clenched convulsively, as if she meant to strangle the sailor, but Sam put a hand on her shoulder.

"There's been no volcanic activity since Enhover discovered this island, but now, the mountain is active," she said. "That activity coincides with the breaching of this tomb, does it not? The tomb is opened. The volcano is active. The lizards appear, and the Imbonese try to steal an airship."

"It's all related," acknowledged Duke. "Is it… is it possible that little cord could have triggered the activity in the mountain?"

"You're the cartographer," said Sam.

He shook his head. "A cartographer, not a geologist. A spiritual trap, maybe?"

Sam shrugged. "The uvaan were a higher form of sorcery than I'm familiar with, and of course we don't even know what those lizards are. Could they have bound a spirit to the mountain, somehow? It is possible, I suppose. If spirits can live within the stones that float our airships, then why not within this island?"

"It still doesn't explain why they'd need an airship," reminded Ainsley. "If they were worried about the volcano alone, escape on the sea would still be an option."

"Long ago, someone fled the Darklands with the uvaan," said Sam, pursing her lips in thought. "They buried them here and sealed the tomb. They might have set a trap and then settled down on this island for generations, but why?"

"The natives used sorcery similar to what Isisandra and Raffles used to take over the footmen in Philip's palace," added Duke. "They used it on Governor Towerson. That symbol on the back of the footmen's necks, it's what tipped me off that something was amiss here."

Sam nodded grimly. "It's all connected, but spirits forsake it, I can't see how."

"I don't know what we're talking about," grumbled Mister Samuels, glaring at the stone of the floor. "I just know I can't stand it in here much longer. The soles of my feet are going to be cooked through."

"Why'd they come here? Why'd they want an airship?" growled Duke, slapping the back of his hand into the other.

"Is that thunder?" asked Samuels.

Sam glared at him and then blinked. It was thunder, though the sky had been bright blue when they'd entered the tomb.

"Cannon fire!" exclaimed Duke. He looked around the tomb and then to her. "They must have found where everyone was running. Sam, is there anything else we can learn from here?"

"This place isn't going away," she said, shaking her head. "Whoever is in that sarcophagus hasn't moved in centuries. Right now, I'm more interested in speaking to someone alive, someone who may have answers. Do you think it's possible we could capture a native and question them?"

Duke shrugged. "We can try."

"Let's go do it," she said.

Mister Samuels, stepping lightly on the hot volcanic stone, led the way back up the tunnel to the light of day.

Sam raised her fae light high, turning and studying the ouroboros carved above, the letters embedded in the raw stone of the floor, and the mechanism on the underside of the sarcophagus lid. Darklands artifacts buried in a lone island in the tropics. Who had done it, and had it all been to hide the uvaan?

THE COMMANDER I

SWEATING and itching like a madman from innumerable insect stings, Commander Brendan Ostrander shuffled along, offering a hope to the spirits it would be over soon. Hells, the things he was doing for the Crown. For his family, too, he supposed, but he couldn't help wondering whether they would rather he be sitting behind a desk in Southundon, coming home to them every evening, instead of risking his life and sanity for a promotion. Or better yet, he could be involved in a proper trade like his wife's brother.

She'd smiled when he told her of the Imbon campaign, hadn't she? He thought she understood the sacrifice would be worth it. A record of steady service in Archtan Atoll, leading a successful campaign in Imbon, a friendship with the duke... it could lead to a promotion and a title with a bit of luck. He thought she'd understood.

He waved his hand in front of his face in a vain attempt to stir the air, to make his own breeze, to dissipate the cloud of insects which swarmed around the exposed skin of his face.

His children would enjoy the royal school, he hoped. A bit stricter than their tutors had been in Archtan Atoll, but they would have others around of their age and station. Surely, that would be good for them. Besides, whether they decided to follow in his footsteps into the armed services or perhaps take a commercial tact, the royal school was where they could make the necessary connections. That was, if he made it out of this spirits-forsaken place.

Under Brach's stiff wing, on speaking terms with Duke Oliver Wellesley, he was doing his part. He was doing all that a man of his station could do. Frozen hell, he'd gotten the runs and guessed he'd lost half a stone of weight already! They certainly hadn't discussed that bit when he'd been recruited into the marines. He would be a changed man in more ways than one, if he made it home.

Maybe a few years behind a desk and stopping at the pub for a tipple on the way home each evening wouldn't have been such a sour fate. He'd earned his station, and his children could as well. At least they'd have a better start of it than he had.

"Commander," mumbled a man holding up a round canteen. "Have a drink, sir. You're looking a bit red in the face. Duke Wellesley told us to drink. Said we'd pass out if we didn't. I just refilled this at the last stream. Got it deep enough that none of the ash fouled the water. It's good, sir."

"Drinking that water is why I was crouched over cursing for half a turn of the clock this morning," Ostrander complained. "It's not the falling ash that's making us sick. It's whatever animal pissed in the water upstream."

"We've got to drink, sir."

"I know, Captain," grumbled Commander Ostrander, accepting the canteen. "I was in the atoll before this, you know? I know how to survive in the tropics."

"Of course, sir," replied the captain, cursing and slapping a stray branch out of the way. "I suspect you never had to hike across country like this, though."

The commander grunted. The captain had a point. Several years in the atoll, and he'd never had to spend the night out in the open. Never had to spend the day hacking his way through the jungle. They would just sail around to the other side of the island when they needed to get there or, if they had an airship, sail right over it. Hells, they were in the atoll to mine the levitating stones that made the airships possible. With Enhover's technology, it was rare a man in his position had to thrash about in the field like this anymore.

Brach. He swished the water in his mouth and spit, thinking of that pompous bastard. The admiral had probably been having a good laugh about it along with his evening sherry.

Ostrander took another sip of water and swallowed this one before pouring a little into his hand and smearing it on his neck and face. Grimacing, he tore off his wig and tossed the thing into the foliage beside him, ignoring the grin on his captain's lips. He scrubbed his face, the white ash that had been falling like snow and the talc powder from the wig blending with his sweat to form a muddy mess that covered his fingers and brow. He thought maybe it would keep some of the insects away.

He promised himself if he managed to make it off this spirit-forsaken island, he was going to apply for a job at a desk back in Enhover, no matter what the admiral claimed it would do to his career.

He tilted up the canteen one last time, sloshing water into his mouth and no small amount down the front of his royal blue coat. He handed the container back to the officer and craned his neck at the men ahead. Five of them were hacking and slashing with curved sabers to carve a path through the jungle. Useless weapons in a modern military, he'd always thought, but they were damned effective at carving a hole in the jungle. In rotating teams, the men had been burrowing their way across the island, coming up over the ridges around the village of Imbon and progressing toward the warehouses and plantations on the other side.

The plan had been to harry any natives ahead of them and force them through the jungle and into the open where Brach was waiting with more men and the airships. Down around the warehouses and in the open fields of the plantations, Enhover's superior weaponry would be insurmountable. It was only in the jungle that the natives could make it a square fight. Though, since he'd led the column of men out of the ruins of the village and into the battle-scarred terrain nearby, they'd yet to see a living enemy.

They'd stepped over plenty of dead ones in the immediate vicinity of the village, but a league and a half from there, it was just flora and fauna. The jungle, grown into a nearly solid wall of green, was populated by a dazzling array of screeching monkeys, screaming birds, and vicious insects.

If there were natives hiding out there, they were easily avoiding the column of grumbling, sweating, noisy marines from Enhover. There could have been a hundred native warriors waiting just a dozen paces away to ambush them, and Commander Ostrander would have no idea. Except for where they'd cleared a pathway with swinging sabers and stomping boots, he couldn't see more than a few paces in any direction.

More than ambush, though, he feared them not making it as quickly as they'd planned. It was impossible to assess their progress in the thick undergrowth, and he'd started to lose men — one to a snake bite and four to the runs and the resulting dehydration. More and more often, the men were complaining of cramping stomachs and rising fevers. His own belly growled in sympathy. It was disease from the insect bites and bad water, but there was little they could do except press on. Brach had all of the physicians with him on the airships, and Ostrander's men needed to get to them quickly, or there wouldn't be much fight left in the company.

He glanced behind at the red-faced, slow-moving column. They were standing there, sweating, waiting on the men ahead to cut a path. He barked, "Switch the men."

The five in front sheathed their sabers and stood gratefully to the side. Grim-faced, the next five men passed him by, drawing blades. Without need for further instruction, they started to attack the jungle in front of them.

Just half an hour later, a distinct rumble crashed through the trees and branches.

"Brach's airships!" cried Commander Ostrander. "That can't be more than a few leagues away, and we've got the plantations in between us. Hurry up men, double time. We're getting close to the end of this nightmare."

He waved behind to call up a fresh set of soldiers to hack their way through the vegetation. The men, just as eager as him to be free of the smothering jungle, charged ahead. Sabers flashed, and the men pressed onward. The boom of the cannon sounded as a counterpoint of their grunts of exertion.

It took another hour, but finally, they broke free of the jungle and emerged into the relatively clear space of the spice plantations. Trellis after trellis of bamboo racks supporting rows of flowering vines spread out in front of them. The ways between the trellises were narrow but clear, and through the length of the fields, he could see the three royal marine airships hovering over the long buildings of the colony's warehouses.

"What are they shooting at?" wondered the captain.

Ostrander shook his head, not sure. Thick smoke roiled around the airships, slowly dissipating in a steady breeze, but the guns continued to thunder. He couldn't see anything on the ground.

"We'll circle the fields," he instructed, the order getting relayed back to the bulk of the men by the officers. "If we move around there to the west, we can come up behind whatever it is they're firing on. A quarter turn, men. Run a whetstone over those sabers, check your firearms and your powder, and empty your bladders. This is what we came for."

AN HOUR LATER, THEY MADE IT AROUND THE EDGE OF THE peppercorn plantings, and Ostrander saw what Brach was up to. Tied to the spice piers, two dozen small vessels were sinking in the shallow water, ketches and cutters that must have been seized by the natives when unknowing merchants from the Vendatts came to trade. Brach had blown gaping holes in the hulls of the vessels, and even from half a league away, Commander Ostrander could see the boats would never be seaworthy again.

Between the piers and the orderly rows of the warehouses, they could see individuals running back and forth, dodging to and fro to avoid the snipers on the decks of the airships.

"Must be holed up in the warehouses," muttered the captain, watching the fracas with a hand over his eyes.

Commander Ostrander nodded. "I thought they would've been back in the caves, but perhaps they were staging to flee on the water. Well, makes it easier for us." He turned to the men. "Form up, boys! We'll hit 'em hard from behind while they're worried about the attack from above."

The men, professional soldiers all, hoisted their weapons, checked over their kit, and then fell in behind Commander Ostrander as he set a quick, ground-eating pace. These men had spent the last two days forcing their way through the jungle, hacking and fighting for every step. Now, in the open, a new energy surged through their legs. He could feel the mood rising behind him as he marched. It wasn't the first native population they'd had to quell, and they knew it wouldn't be the last, but the end of this campaign was in sight. The men would do their job, but every one of them was ready to get back on the airships and go home to spend their action pay in the flesh markets and ale sinks of Southundon. The best of them might even save a little bit of that coin for the missus and the children, if they had any that they acknowledged.

The royal marines drew a certain type, particularly those who were selected for service in the tropics. Some might call them bloodthirsty. Ostrander thought of them as practical. For Crown and Company, they would do what was necessary. Hard men for a hard job.

Quickly, they covered the ground between the jungle and the

warehouses, unnoticed until they were several hundred yards from the structures. Then, some of the native men who were racing about started to point at them and yell.

Soon, dozens of shirtless men and a few women were pouring out of the giant structures, wielding crude knives, bows, and spears. Ostrander also saw a handful of blunderbusses that must have been scrounged from the wreckage of the compound. Deadly weapons, if the natives had trained how to use them and had managed to keep their powder dry in the stifling humidity.

But Ostrander and his men did not pause at the sight of the opposition. They kept marching.

The natives began assembling in a bunch. First dozens then fifty and then a hundred. When they'd gotten three-quarters of the way to the group, Ostrander estimated there were two hundred of the natives, outnumbering his own men, with more still coming. In front of the native force, a giant of a man with wicked-looking scarring on his torso was raising a massive club and shouting exhortations to his warriors. He was stirring them up, trying to whip them into a frenzy.

In contrast, the marines marched on quietly, saving their breath for the fight.

Fifty yards away, the giant native started spinning the club above his head, screaming at the top of his lungs in a strange language that Commander Ostrander did not understand. Two hundred and fifty of them now, and the commander could sense that in moments, they would charge.

Ostrander held up a hand, stopping his men.

They fanned out around him with no need for instruction, forming ranks of three perfectly straight lines. This was what they drilled every day for. This was what they did. Without a word, they waited.

The natives, all shouting and hollering now, waved their weapons and stared death at the royal marines. Then, they broke into a frantic run when the huge leader pointed his club at Ostrander's line. Three hundred of them, the flow from the warehouse finally trickling to a stop. The natives raced directly at Commander Ostrander and his men.

The commander held a fist in the air and waited. The eyes of his captains and sergeants were on him. Everyone else looked ahead calmly. A group twice their number, weapons held high, was rushing directly at them. To their credit, not a man broke formation.

At twenty-five yards, Ostrander dropped his fist. His captains shouted orders, and the first rank pulled the triggers of their blunderbusses. Fifty of the weapons erupted at the same moment, flinging lead at their charging enemies.

A breath later, the captains shouted again, and the first rank knelt, digging into pouches for another wad of powder and another load of shot. Another call from the captains, and the second rank fired, fifty more barrels barking with flame and smoke.

The second rank knelt, and the third fired.

The natives were just five yards away when, still on their knees, the first rank got off a second volley at point blank range, ripping through the tattered line of attacking natives. Then, the marines dropped their firearms and, as a unit, drew their sabers while the second rank stepped around them, ready to take the charge.

Two hundred discharges from the blunderbusses had devastated the attackers. Bunched in a tight mass, as untrained warriors always came, it'd been impossible for the marines to miss even at twenty-five yards on the first volley. Half of the natives had fallen, and most of those still coming had blood streaming from where shot had ripped into their unarmored bodies. Even the uninjured survivors showed the terror of those who'd lost most of their companions in the span of a few breaths. When they hit the line of royal marines, they were wild and panicked.

The slaughter continued.

Trained for just such an attack, the second rank of marines had stepped around the first and hefted their firearms, now fixed with bayonets. They stabbed into the oncoming wave of the attackers, skewering several, shoving the bodies to foul the path of others, or simply deflecting the charge with their firearms. Their purpose was to absorb the first swings and push attackers off balance, and then the men who'd been in the first rank attacked, swinging sabers at men and women who'd been thrown from their lines of approach. That rank struck ruinous blows, swiping at arms and legs, maiming their opponents, and knocking them to the ground. The third rank advanced, slashing and stabbing down at injured natives, cleaving into necks or heads, and stabbing into their chests.

Three ranks, each with a different purpose, operated flawlessly as one cohesive unit. Most of these men were experienced. They'd been in the royal marines for years. They'd trained on these maneuvers thousands of times. At least half the marines had used these exact same tactics in combat, and those who had not were bolstered by the confidence of their peers. The training was embedded in every motion, one unit defending, one injuring, and one finishing the task. It wasn't just the airships and the bombs that made them royal marines. They were the best disciplined fighting force in the known world.

Commander Ostrander watched with pride as the lines moved out in front of him, decimating the charge of the natives, butchering those who'd thought to raise blades against them.

Half-a-dozen paces from him, a man crawled on the ground, a short-handled axe in his hand. A deep laceration split his thigh, but he kept coming, dragging himself closer. Ostrander stepped forward and brought his blade down, ending the man's struggles. By the time he looked up from the kill, his men had won the day. All around them, dead natives littered the battlefield like a carpet.

"Reload!" he bellowed into the suddenly quiet space. "Prepare to breach the warehouses." He observed for a moment as the men prepared for another bout and then turned to his captains. "Report."

"One man dead, sir, four grievously injured. Several others

with minor wounds, but they're in condition to fight until we can get them to the infirmary on the airships."

Ostrander nodded, "Assign two men for each of the seriously injured. Have them move toward the docks and prepare for evacuation. Two more to carry the casualty. If that's all…"

The captains nodded and assigned the necessary men. Then one of them gripped his saber, arranged a squad of marines around him, and approached the open doors of the warehouse.

Ostrander watched as the men spread out on either side to rush in, creating a pattern of cover for each other. The marines were not as well trained in this style of close combat, and he considered whether they should wait for Brach to fly over and simply bomb the buildings, but there'd been a reason so many natives were gathered here instead of fleeing for the jungle or the caves. Either option would have been a safer choice for them than the shoddily constructed warehouses. Ostrander observed as his captain dropped a fist, and royal marines started to pour inside the warehouse.

There were several scattered shots, the clash of close combat, but nothing like the cacophony of the first engagement. He guessed only a few combatants had been left inside or perhaps the injured. It was just a few short minutes until his captain reemerged.

Commander Ostrander frowned. The man's face was chalk white, but he bore a broad grin. He asked the man, "What is it?"

"Captives, sir," explained the captain. "They had hostages. Enhoverians. People from the compound. Sir, there are women and children."

Ostrander dashed to the door, darting inside and feeling his jaw drop open. Forty people were clustered in the center of the open warehouse floor. Bodies of natives were littered around where his men had felled them, but there was no doubt who was local to Imbon and who had come from Enhover. Already, royal marines were kneeling beside the captives, offering them food and blankets. Women and children cried. Men looked on stoically, as if they couldn't believe it, couldn't comprehend that over a month after the initial rebellion, they'd been rescued. None of the captives spoke. They merely nodded or opened their hands to accept his men's offerings. They were scared, still, shocked. He didn't blame them.

Beaming, Commander Ostrander stepped back outside and called, "Signal the airships. Tell them to drop down for immediate evacuation. Signal victory."

A sergeant, eyes bulging with the excitement of finding living captives, rushed off to instruct the signalman. The fire from Admiral Brach's cannons had ceased, and Ostrander knew the men on the airships must have seen the skirmish. Anyone with a spyglass would already know the results. Even without the signals, Brach would be on the way.

Their campaign was not over. Between the initial barrage and the natives his men had just killed, he guessed a thousand had fallen. There would be thousands more hiding somewhere on the island, but they could be rooted out in time. However long that took, whatever other results they found, the mission was now an unabashed success. They'd found women and children who'd survived the uprising! It was unexpected, unprecedented. Admiral Brach, Duke Wellesley, they'd be named in Enhover's papers as heroes. They and Commander Brendan Ostrander.

"WE DID GOOD WORK TODAY, SIR," SAID HIS CAPTAIN, WATCHING AS the first group of captives were strapped into harnesses that would be used to lift them to the decks of the airship Franklin's Luck. "Right good work."

"What was it Duke Wellesley said?" asked Ostrander. "Some bit about tattoos? That woman over there, she has one?"

The captain glanced at the woman who was clutching two small children in her arms. "I talked to her, sir. Bit of a sad story. She had a rough go back in Enhover and fled with the two children. No father, sir, and she made what life she could for them in the tropics. You ever met a fallen woman without a bit of ink on her, sir? It's nice to think we're rescuing the wives and children of proper citizens, but most of these women worked the pleasure houses, and I'd bet my action pay that a few of those men were liberated from the Company's gaol. People like that, they're survivors, sir. They aren't like you and me, but they still deserve rescue. Let's just hope the papers leave those details out, ey?"

Commander Ostrander smirked at his captain. "You're sure she's… Duke Wellesley said…"

"I'm sure, sir. Some of the men, ah, they know the type. They can tell. We ought to have a word with the airship officers, though," mused the captain. "Fallen women onboard, a long ride ahead and all of the men riding high after combat and thinking of their bonus pay. There's some opportunity, sir."

"What are you suggesting, captain?" Ostrander asked, glancing from another batch of captives rising to the airship to frown at the man.

Instead of answering, the captain stared over Commander Ostrander's shoulder, his eyes wide, his breath coming fast.

"What?" muttered the commander, spinning to see what the man was looking at. "Frozen hell. To arms! To arms!"

From the jungle, in the direction of the spice caves, several hundred spear- and knife-wielding natives were emerging from the vegetation. Behind them loomed four giant lizards.

"S-Sir, if we hurry…" stammered the captain.

"We'll hold while the women and children evacuate," declared the commander.

"Sir, they're fallen—"

"We are royal marines, Captain. Act like it!"

Ostrander began shouting orders, his voice calm and steady, his heart racing like a thoroughbred at the tracks. Around him, his men picked up their weapons, checked their harnesses and kit, and formed into three lines. His captains flanked him, and when the men were assembled, they began a slow march forward.

Above, he could hear shouts of alarm from the airships. He knew they would turn and open fire on the lizards. If the creatures got close enough, they could drop bombs on them. They knew the monsters, whatever their nature, could be killed by such means. But, if the airships were dropping bombs, that meant Ostrander and his men couldn't stand below. Behind them were the captives and the docks. The only way to go was forward.

Hundreds of natives poured from the jungle like water from a burst dam. Hundreds then thousands. He swallowed uncomfortably. Two thousand of them, he guessed. If he was right or wrong, it didn't much matter. There were a lot. There were enough.

"We march one hundred yards and then hold for the attack," Commander Ostrander called to the men around him. "Just like we did on the first engagement. Our training will win the day, lads. Have no fear. These scoundrels have never met the likes of the royal marines. They've never faced a fusillade from an airship, ey?"

He gestured overhead, drawing the eyes of his men to the three vessels floating above. Men were scrambling about on the decks. He could hear them. Hells, he hoped they could turn in time. Without the big guns…

At that moment, the pack of lizards cleared the jungle. They were still half-a-league away, but their giant legs were covering ground quickly. They'd started behind the native horde but were outpacing them. Then, a quarter-league away, the largest of the lizards paused and reared on its hind legs. It opened its mouth as if to roar a challenge, but instead of a thundering bellow, a burst of bright orange fire erupted from the thing's maw, billowing a hundred yards above it.

"Spirits forsake it," whispered the captain on his flank.

"Hold the line, men!" Ostrander cried. "Hold the line!"

The lizards, moving faster than he would have thought possible for creatures that size, lurched forward, each step covering a dozen yards. The four of them shook the earth as their clawed feet raced over the turf. He thought he saw dark shapes atop their backs — riders? He didn't have time to ponder it, no time to do anything but hold steady.

"Hold the line!" screamed Ostrander.

Shouting a victorious roar, the natives ran after the four monsters. Thick black smoke trailed from the jaw of the one in the lead, an awful reminder of what it was capable of.

Around him, Commander Ostrander could feel his men panicking. No shots had been fired from above. Nothing was happening to slow the charge. He looked up and saw the airships drifting higher, men on deck scrambling at the guns, but no one was firing yet.

"First rank!" Ostrander shouted, hoping his voice carried above the attackers. "First rank, raise your weapons!"

There was no response, and glancing to his left and right, Commander Brendan Ostrander saw the royal marines break. Slowly, at first, they stepped back, their eyes fixed on the approaching nightmares. Then, backpedaling, they turned to run. The enlisted men, then the sergeants, and finally, his two captains. One of them offered an apologetic shake of his head. The other, terror filling his eyes, simply fled.

Ostrander drew his saber and faced the lizards. He raised the blade to his shoulder, tilting his body and clutching the wooden hilt of the sword with both hands.

A shadow fell across him, the midday sun vanishing.

"For the Crown!" Ostrander screamed then swung at the massive clawed foot that loomed over him. He felt his blade bite into the tough hide of the lizard's foot, catching on the rough skin. Then, the foot came crashing down on top of him with the weight of a palace.

THE CARTOGRAPHER VIX

"IT'S COMING FASTER, I THINK," said Mister Samuels.

"It's not coming faster," barked Ainsley. "Go get more buckets of water. Hurry!"

The captain glanced behind them, where from Imbon's peak, thick white smoke was billowing into the clear blue sky, a little faster than when they'd first arrived.

Oliver knew that in the ten years the Company had occupied Imbon, there'd never been a report of volcanic activity, but since they'd arrived, the peak was shrouded in thick smoke that rose straight into the blue sky, scattering fluffy ash on the warm tropical breeze. Could it be a coincidence, or did it have something to do with the breaching of the tomb?

He heard an ominous rumble and jumped, panicked until he realized it wasn't the mountain threatening to explode. It was cannon fire.

Leaving the rear of the airship, he scrambled ahead to the forecastle, trying to peer around the steep slope of the mountain. Somewhere on the other side, Admiral Brach and his airships were engaging in combat again. The initial barrage was what had sent Oliver and his companions racing back to the airship, but shortly after they boarded, the sounds stopped. What did it mean that it had started again?

They didn't have to wait long to find out.

As the Cloud Serpent rounded the edge of the mountain, they saw a furious battle taking place down by the spice piers. Swarms of armed natives covered the ground around the warehouses. Through the spyglass, Oliver saw sickening spots of royal blue lying on the dirt beneath them. Commander Branden Ostrander's company, he guessed, but those fallen soldiers were not what held his gaze. Instead, he looked to the airships, which were furiously firing cannon and lobbing red saltpetre bombs over the sides.

Admiral Brach's airship was in the thick of it, battling four massive lizards that rose on their hind legs, snapping jaws and thrashing with the claws of their forelegs.

One of the other airships trailed black smoke and was tilting to the side just two hundred yards above the sea. It looked to be trying to escape, but its main sail was quickly becoming engulfed in flame. The side of the airship was scored with black char, and Oliver could see water spilling from where they must have been dumping the tanks, trying to gain elevation.

"Did a bomb go off too early?" wondered Sam.

Then, one of the lizards below Brach's airship belched a torrent of roaring fire. The flames bathed the already damaged keel of Enhover's Slayer in baking heat, and from a distance, they could see men scrambling away from the edges of the airship as the fire roared over the gunwales.

"Frozen hell," hissed Sam.

Oliver was speechless.

"You didn't say the things breathed fire!" cried Sam.

"They didn't," he muttered. "Not that I saw, at least. And these are... they're bigger. Twice the size of what we faced."

Enhover's Slayer lurched upward. Half-a-dozen barrels rolled over the side, dropping down past the hull into the open air.

Two of the lizards were caught in the bombardment, and when

the barrels landed and exploded, flinging the lead payload, the creatures staggered away, gaping rents torn in their flesh.

But the other two lizards were not done, and they leapt, twisting in the air as if trying to take flight, screeching an angry retort and blowing fire after the rising airship. Oliver could have sworn he saw tiny figures clinging to the monsters, like riders on a horse, but he decided he must have been mistaken as the lizards turned and leapt again, blowing another gout of flame into the heavy salt air.

The flames licked around the ruined bottom of the airship, and a corner of the rear sail caught fire. Oliver could see sailors scrambling on deck with water-filled buckets, trying to put out the flames. With no pretense of trying to stay low and continue the fight, Enhover's Slayer climbed out of range of the lizards.

A thunderous crack resonated from behind, and Oliver turned to see a shower of rock exploding from the peak of Imbon's mountain. It appeared to move slow, like it was happening beneath water, but as he gauged the distance, he realized that hunks of rock the size of houses were flying through the air faster than his airship could fly. Smoke, lit glowing red from below, billowed into the sky, lightning flashing deep within the cloud, the rumble of thunder barely audible beneath the roar of the explosion.

"Hells," Oliver shouted, "take us higher, Ainsley, higher!"

He grabbed the gunwale as the airship jerked, and he watched in panic as the distant mountain peak vanished in a cloud of dust and debris. The volcano was erupting right before their eyes.

"Duke," said Sam, gripping his arm and pointing toward the spice piers.

The airship that they'd first seen attempting to flee was listing terribly and dropping quickly. The tanks above the levitating stones must have been breached. It was a fatal position for an airship, as the levitating rocks could be soaked on one side, and rising on the other, making the list worse, and eventually flipping the thing over. Oliver cursed. Two leagues away, out of reach and on the other side of the battle, they could do nothing. The airship crashed down into the sea, water pounding onto the deck, washing over it. It was just a matter of time before that water spilled down into the hold, through the passageways, and into the chambers that held the levitating rocks. Drenched in so much sea water, they would sink like any stone.

The Cloud Serpent sped higher, and Ainsley yelled for the men to put on sail, to take them farther from the exploding mountain behind them, and toward the battle.

Oliver looked on in shock as Brach's wounded airship rose, the lizards stalking beneath it, seeming to watch for it to come back within their range. Enhover's Slayer was making it out over water, none of the crew even bothering to fire cannon at the creatures behind them.

The lizards kept hopping into the air and crashing back down onto the ground. They screeched and breathed flame but stayed well back from the water. Scattered around the lizards, the native horde was moving frantically. It seemed they at least saw the exploding volcano and understood the threat it posed.

"Where's the third airship, Franklin's Luck?" asked Oliver suddenly, looking for evidence it had gone down, but seeing nothing. "Did it…"

Sam, at his side, could only shake her head.

"There!" cried Mister Samuels, pointing aft.

In the distance, Oliver saw the white sails and brown hull of an airship. It was already three leagues away, headed south.

"I don't understand," said Sam.

"The natives," growled Oliver. "I don't know how they did it, but they figured a way to take an airship."

ENHOVER'S SLAYER LIMPED OVER THE HORIZON, LOOKING AS IF IT WAS sailing directly into the setting sun. The orange glow from that giant orb cut through the thick smoke and choking dust that suffused the sky around Imbon. The island's top had blown, scattering the entire landmass with fire and scorching hot, liquid rock. The lizards and the natives had fled, running panicked before the deadly heat, or they were struck down by the shower of loose debris that crashed in a fatal rain.

Grim-faced, Oliver had watched them die or seen them escape where they were likely to die soon enough. Perhaps a few of them might survive. The spice caves could grant some protection, he imagined, though there was a steaming river of molten rock flowing between the pier and the caverns now. There could be some other way they avoided the inexorable flow, but Oliver wasn't going to go down there and look. If anyone survived the bubbling heat that was still pouring liberally from the peak of the mountain, they would have earned it.

Instead of pursuing those below, the Cloud Serpent sailed close beside Enhover's Slayer where Oliver could yell across the open space to Admiral Brach. The man's airship was severely damaged, both from the initial trickery in the Company's compound and then much worse by the engagement with the lizards. Brach and his crew could sail it, he claimed, but they would make straight for the Vendatts to find a friendly port for repairs. The longer they were aloft, the more they risked a breach of the hold, exposing the levitating rocks within.

Both Brach and Oliver agreed it was too dangerous for Enhover's Slayer to proceed, and with Imbon a flaming disaster behind them and the open sea all around, there was nowhere they could settle down to swap crew and supplies.

That left Oliver and the Cloud Serpent to pursue Franklin's Luck into the unknown. It had been headed directly south at the last sighting, which left little doubt where they were going. There was only one thing on Enhover's maps in that direction — the Darklands.

For some reason, the natives of Imbon had sacrificed everything, including thousands of their fellows, to abscond with an airship.

Oliver couldn't help but wonder if they were running home. He grunted, forcing the thought down and turning to duck into the captain's cabin. On Ainsley's table, they'd already spread what maps she had, though there was little he could glean from them. Rough outlines of the coastline, a depiction of a wide, slow-looking river, and a capital deep in the interior. There were a few coastal towns, though the scale made them appear to be fishing villages rather than proper ports. There were some known road-ways that led to the Southlands, but they had almost no informa-tion about what those were like.

Traders from the Darklands would venture to Durban and the Southlands' markets, but it never went the other way. Most of the bulk commerce was conducted at the border and small depots that functioned as temporary towns, growing and shrinking depending on the season. Oliver had approached Darklanders while he had been stationed in Durban, but they had refused to speak of their homeland. And if anyone from the Southlands had been past the trading depots at the border, none of them had admitted it to the young Company cartographer. None of it offered any clue as to where the refugees from Imbon could be headed.

"Captives and a hostile crew," muttered Captain Ainsley, leaning beside him to study the maps. "I can't think they'll stay far enough ahead of us that we'll need these, m'lord. Our crew is experienced hands. We'll chase them down within a day, two at the most."

"Don't be so confident, Captain," argued Oliver. "They've already gained five turns of the clock on us while we were confer-encing with Brach. I don't think they'll be the easy quarry you imagine. Don't forget they managed to steal an airship manned with a company of royal marines. That wasn't dumb luck. They know what they're doing."

"Fallen women and thieves said the admiral. They can't out sail me," assured Ainsley.

"And the captain of Franklin's Luck?" wondered Oliver. "It's quite possible they encouraged the man to join them. Offers of riches to come, threats to his life, that sort of thing. We should expect the best crew the royal marines can put on deck and plan for that."

"Those marines should have died a bloody death before surrendering their airship," complained Ainsley.

Oliver shrugged. "Maybe they did. Brach and his officers said there'd been a commotion aboard, but their attention had been elsewhere. Perhaps the natives and their captives overcame the crew and immediately learned to sail an airship, or perhaps they have help from the crew? It doesn't matter for our purposes, as they're all enemies of the empire now. Whoever it is, someone on that airship is sailing the damned thing."

Ainsley grunted.

"If it was the regular crew, would we stand a chance of catching them?" questioned Sam. "Which airship is faster?"

"We are," insisted Ainsley. "We're designed for quick trips between Enhover and the atoll. They're designed to stand and fight. They've a heavy structure with additional material to absorb cannon shot." She began marking distances on the map, rubbing her fingers on her lips as she calculated in her head. Finally, she said, "If we pile on every yard of canvass we can, we've a chance even if they're well-sailed. With an empty hold, the wind at our backs will be like a rocket's ignition. It's all an estimate, of course. I know their rated speed, but how much will they be able to get out of her? How accurate are these maps, even? I don't think anyone's actually sailed this way in the air or on the sea in the last twenty years, have they? To be honest, I'm more concerned with what happens when we do catch them. Franklin's Luck boasts twice the cannon we've got, and they've got a few twelve-inchers in that mix. Twelve-inch shot is going to smash through us like a rock through a plate of glass."

"We'll worry about that when we catch them," said Oliver.

"If it's all the same to you, m'lord, I intend to worry about it until we catch them," declared Ainsley.

"Fair enough, Captain." He turned to Sam. "We need to talk."

She crossed her arms over her chest. "Yes, we do."

"Grog's in the cabinet," offered Ainsley. "I'll be on deck doing what we can to gain a little extra speed. It's been two turns since we last spotted them, and we've only got one more before the sun sets. We're not going to have visual confirmation until morning, m'lord. If we can't see them when the sun comes up…"

"Keep due south," instructed Oliver. "They're headed to the Darklands. I'm sure of it."

THE PRIESTESS VII

"WHAT WERE THOSE THINGS?" asked Duke.

Sam grimaced, stalking to the cabinet to retrieve Captain Ainsley's grog. She opened the door and saw dozens of bottles filled with the clear liquor. Frowning at the variety of choices, she took one and turned to Duke. "I wish I could tell you, but I can't. I have no idea what those were. They weren't sorcery, I don't think."

"Druid magic?" he asked.

She shook her head, unstoppering the bottle of grog with her teeth, spitting the cork into a hand, and taking a swig. The liquor burned harsh, a bit of lime juice and sugar the only ingredients to cut the sturdy punch of the rum. Terrible, unlicensed rum, if Sam guessed correctly.

"You need to pay Ainsley more so she can afford a decent pour," complained Sam. "This stuff is awful."

"Don't let her hear you say that," muttered Duke. He held out a hand for the bottle.

"I don't know if those things were druid magic or natural creatures," Sam admitted, sitting at the table across from him. "In truth, I don't know what the difference is. I've never met a druid, you know, and the Church's records of such magic are curiously silent. I asked that priest, Adriance, about druid magic. He acted like it was a myth, like dragons, just stories told to entertain children."

"Well, someone built those keeps that dot Enhover's coast," said Duke. "Everything in the histories says it was druids, and there is something special about those old fortresses. You felt it, did you not, when we faced Ca-Mi-He? There was a... a warmth, that flowed up from the rock of the place, through me, and into you. Didn't you feel it?"

She nodded, taking back the grog bottle and gulping another slug. She wiped her lips with the back of her hand and said, "I felt it, but I don't understand it. If that was druid magic, it wasn't anything like sorcery. There were no patterns, no bindings, no bridge even. And where did it come from? The keep? From you?"

"Druid magic is different," he said. "You told me that when we first met. Sorcerers compel, right, and druids, ah, negotiate?"

She shrugged. "Sure."

He collected the grog bottle and drank.

"Duke," she said, "if what we experienced in that fortress was druid magic..."

"What?"

"Then it was something you did."

He blinked at her.

She waited.

"I'm not a druid, Sam," he assured her. "I don't even know what that means. There's something... I think there might be a spirit housed within that keep, like in the levitating stones, or the fae. Don't look at me like that. I don't even know the first thing about druids."

"Then how do you know you aren't one?" she asked quietly.

She had felt the warmth, felt it suffusing her body, filling her veins and her lungs, keeping back the cold of Ca-Mi-He. In the freezing air atop the roof, facing the bitter cold of the great spirit, something supernatural had happened. Somehow, they'd been protected. She told Duke true. She didn't understand it, but she understood enough to know it was no trick of their imaginations. It could have been some lingering effect of the magic the druids infused into the fortress... or it could have been him.

Duke drank deeply and brooded.

"Before, you said the lizards that attacked Imbon felt warm," said Sam. "We both felt the warmth atop the fortress. What about this latest battle? Did those things feel the same?"

"They were blowing fire," he mentioned. "A volcano was erupting behind us. We're in the tropics. Of course it felt warm!"

Sam laughed. "Fair enough."

"What kind of lizard belches fire?" wondered Oliver.

"The kind born in the heat of a volcano, I suppose," she replied. "What kind of people would sacrifice everything for one airship? There couldn't have been more than a handful of them that made it onboard, hidden amongst the captives or controlling them like puppets."

"Born in the heat of a volcano," mused Oliver. "Fire could hurt them, though. Remember what happened when Brach dropped his bombs? Those were natural creatures, I think, even if their origin is supernatural. How are lizards born? From eggs?"

"I'm a priestess, not a naturalist," replied Sam.

"I think they're born in eggs," continued Oliver. "The heat from the volcano could have hatched them. How does that relate to the uvaan found in the tomb, the mechanisms there that were triggered, the uprising, and the natives stealing an airship to fly south?"

"I don't know the answers, but I know where we'll find them," answered Sam.

"The Darklands," responded Duke.

She nodded.

He took another pull on the bottle of grog and passed it back to her.

She drank, and they sat.

Later, a rap on the door jolted them out of their melancholy.

Ainsley ducked her head in. "We've got full sail on, heading due south. Night's fallen, and there's nothing we can see of Franklin's Luck. Hopefully at daybreak we'll get a visual to confirm our heading. Unless you've further need tonight, I'll bed down in the officer's bunks."

Without word, Duke waved Ainsley away, and she shut the door.

"We ought to get some rest as well," remarked Sam.

She stood, looking down at him. He was an attractive man, as much as any of them were. Experienced but self-aware enough that she suspected he would take direction. Knowing him, she guessed he'd enjoy doing so. As good a lover as she could hope to find, when softer fare wasn't available.

They were sailing to the Darklands, to the root of sorcery. The dark path would not be narrow and hidden there. It would be a part of daily life. Secrets and power would be at her fingertips. The lure would be nearly irresistible. She could walk down the path and gain what she needed. The thirst for more was like the allure of poppy syrup, and it was only her grip on life that would keep her from sliding all the way into the shadowy reaches of the underworld. Swimming the current of life was all that would prevent a final descent into darkness.

With what her mentor had taught her, what she'd seen battling Isisandra, Yates, and the others, with what she'd learned from Timothy Adriance, from Kalbeth, the Book of Law, with what King Edward had shared from his wife's trove of materials, Sam had all that she needed to walk the dark path. It would be open to her, if she wanted to take the steps.

At the table, Duke tipped up the bottle of grog. He made a sour face, unaware she was studying him.

If she was to avoid the temptation to fully immerse herself in darkness, she had to maintain her grip on life. She felt the thirst for more skills, more knowledge and wondered if it was already the path taking hold of her. Should she avoid it? Could she?

Duke stood and stretched then adjusted his trousers,

muttering slurred words, "If we don't have some laundry done, I'll be out of clean clothes within days."

"You can change if you'd like," she said, pointing to a trunk of his garments in the corner of the small cabin. "I can look away."

"Like you haven't seen it all before," he guffawed then began to strip, mumbling to himself as much as to her. "I wonder how often the sailors do their laundry. Do they do their laundry? That man Samuels doesn't seem the type…" He shook his head then scowled at the nearly empty bottle of grog. "That stuff tastes a bit shit, but it's gone right to me."

Sam knew she had to swim the current of life if she was to maintain her grip on it, to prevent the slide into darkness. She knew that. She'd always known that. It was the only way to avoid walking the dark path.

Suddenly, she asked Duke, "You'll sleep on the couch again?"

Shirtless, he grinned at her. "A gentleman always considers a lady's comfort, but you know, if we make it back from this voyage, I'm having Ainsley put another bed in here."

Sam smirked and then crawled into the bed, rolling over and facing away from him. She spoke to the wall. "Darken the lights, will you?"

FOR DAYS, THEY SAILED SOUTH. THE WIND CRACKED THE SAILS AND whipped by them as they soared five hundred yards above the sea. The sky was bright blue, dotted with puffy white clouds the consistency of cotton hanging far overhead. The water was the rich cobalt of the deep ocean. There were no landmasses and no vessels on the water to break the monotony, just the one far ahead that they were ruthlessly chasing.

"No one's flown within fifty leagues of the Darklands in twenty years," remarked Captain Ainsley.

She was standing beside Sam on the forecastle of the Cloud

Serpent, one tall leather boot propped on the wooden rail, her fingers restlessly toying with the hilts of her pistols.

"Why is that?" questioned Sam.

"Because the last time someone did, they didn't come back," remarked Ainsley. "It was in the early days after the Coldlands War. The empire was looking to expand. Expeditions were heading out in all directions. They quickly found there was softer meat elsewhere."

Ainsley didn't turn to Sam when she said it, and Sam didn't look at her. Instead, both of their gazes were fixed on the vessel ahead of them. Franklin's Luck hung five hundred paces above the surface of the sea, just like they did, and for two days since they spotted it and fell into its wake, they'd only cut the lead from six leagues to four.

It was just a spec in the distance to the naked eye, but with the spyglass, they could see it clear enough. It had full sail piled on. People scrambled about the deck, and the airship showed no signs of changing course.

"They could lose us at night if they wanted," remarked Ainsley.

"Why haven't they, do you think?" wondered Sam.

"We're gaining one league a day on them at this rate," mused the captain. "Darklands are what, three days away?"

"They're not changing course because they know they can beat us to land," acknowledged Sam. "But what then?"

The captain shrugged. "I told you. The last airship to see that evil shore didn't make it back."

Sam grunted.

"We've got you now," said Ainsley with a mad grin. "Whatever spirits they throw at us, you'll take care of them. I've seen enough of your work."

Sam shifted uncomfortably.

"Any change?" asked First Mate Pettybone, joining them at the rail.

Ainsley shook her head.

"We'll need to pause for resupply, Captain," warned the first mate. "I just finished an inventory. We've got six, maybe seven days of water before we need to dip into the tanks. We've food for another two weeks. Enough to finish this chase but not enough to return to Enhover."

"Aye," said Ainsley. "The water is the problem. One way or the other, we're going to have to find shore."

"What happens if we dip into the tanks?" wondered Sam.

"We need that water to douse the stones," explained Pettybone. "If we can't wet the rocks, we can't lower the airship. No airship I've known has taken the risk, but the only way back down to earth would be to rip up the deck, expose the levitating stones, and pray to the spirits it downpours. That, or start freeing the things and letting them float off while we try to manage a soft landing. As you can imagine, neither one is something I want to try."

Sam swallowed, looking up at the distant, innocuous, puffy white clouds.

"We're better off not having to dip into the tanks," stated the captain dryly, dropping her boot to the deck and hitching her pistol belt. "At sea, if we have to, we can take her down and pump the tanks into our drinking water while resupplying those with seawater. It's not as effective with the salt, but it's safe enough. The problem is that it's incredibly difficult not to mix the two. Even a little contamination can ruin our entire store of drinking water, and then we're really in trouble. Of course, if we don't find water in the Darklands, there's no choice."

Sam grimaced.

"If it comes to that, you talk to the duke, will you?" asked Ainsley. "He trusts you for some reason."

"Three days until land," responded Sam, "and you think we can catch them in four days? Unless their destination is on the coast, we might have time. Once we've dealt with Franklin's Luck, we'll be able to find a safe place to come down, I hope."

"FROZEN HELL," MUTTERED CAPTAIN AINSLEY.

"That's not natural, is it?" wondered Duke, staring at the massive wall of boiling cloud mass in front of them.

"No, I'd say not," replied Ainsley. She glanced at Sam. "Well?"

"Well, what?"

"Can we fly through that?" asked Ainsley.

"You're the captain!" replied Sam.

"Aye, and you're the sorceress," retorted Ainsley. "I'm not sure it's my captaining that's going to get us through that cloud bank. What... what is it?"

Sam frowned. Spreading across the horizon, as far as they could see, was a roiling wall of steel gray clouds. The formation was shifting constantly, flickers of silver light bursting in erratic webs from within. It was like a bold line scrawled between the dark sky and a darker sea

"Can we fly over it?" wondered Duke. "Looks like it goes, what, a thousand yards into the air? If the stones are dry, can we clear it?"

"I'd guess that's a bit higher, m'lord. Maybe two thousand yards? That's about the peak of our range," muttered Ainsley. "Regulations are to keep to one thousand yards elevation except in case of emergency. Higher up and the air gets thin and tricky."

She left it unsaid that they weren't just talking elevation. They were talking that elevation above a sorcerous storm wall. There was nothing Ainsley could do to estimate what kind of ride they would find up there.

"Franklin's Luck is going straight in, looks like," remarked Duke. "I don't suppose we'll have much of a chance of keeping sight of them in that mess."

Ainsley shook her head.

The roar of the storm was beginning to reach them, rumbling over the sound of the sails and the blowing wind.

"We can't go around it," said Sam. "That means it's over or straight through."

"I could jettison the cannon, our water..." murmured Ainsley. "Lighten us up, maybe give us a little extra loft, but I can't make any promises. Well, I can make one. No matter what we do, if we try to fly over that, we're in for a wild ride. I pride myself and our crew, but I've got to advise against it. There are physical limitations we cannot sail around, and even if we did, what's the point of catching them if we've no cannon."

"We've got four or five leagues until we run smack into the storm front," said Sam. "It won't move from that point, I don't think. Can we catch Franklin's Luck before that?"

"It'd be close," muttered Ainsley. "I think we could, if we didn't have to drop sail and turn before running into that mess. Is it... Will it be as bad as it looks?"

"Worse," remarked Sam. "This storm is not natural. It's..." She trailed off, unsure if what she was feeling was correct, unsure she should tell them if it was. "Put your men at stations, Captain, for combat if we can catch them, for the storm if we cannot. Let's clear the forecastle. Until we get through this, no one but me should be up here."

Duke and the captain both stared at her expectantly.

She sighed and explained, "I believe that storm is a reflection of the shroud. It's a simulacrum of the barrier between our world and the underworld. There are things I might be able to do which will offer us some protection but not complete protection. Anything I try up here will be dangerous to the others."

"Hells," breathed Ainsley.

"We could turn around," suggested Sam. "We achieved our mission back on Imbon. After what we saw of that volcano's devastation, we can assume the natives are all dead. This isn't necessary. Your father, Duke, would encourage us to turn around. He tasked me with assisting you, protecting you from the supernatural. I'm not fulfilling that pledge if we proceed."

"Captain," asked Duke, staring ahead, "will the crew sail into those clouds on your word?"

"Not for their current pay, m'lord," said the captain, subdued, her white-knuckled hand gripping her pistol.

"Tell them I'm offering a bonus," suggested Duke. "Ten — no, twenty times their annual compensation on return to Enhover. When we get back, any man or woman who wants out of their contract may leave. If anyone wants to stay, they'll do so at double their current rate."

"If we're going to do this, I need time," warned Sam. "I need to get some things from the cabin. Then do your best to make sure no one interrupts me."

Duke nodded and glanced at Ainsley. Pale-faced, she nodded, turned, and began issuing orders and promises to the crew.

"We don't have to do this," said Sam once the captain was out of earshot.

"You're right," acknowledged Duke, "but we both want to, don't we?"

Despite the tension, despite the looming wall of darkness they were approaching, she laughed. "Better to be crazy together, I suppose."

He offered her a wan smile.

His mother. Sam knew he was thinking of her. They were so close, and he couldn't force himself to turn back. He didn't know what she had done, what the king had told Sam in confidence, but even so, he had guessed that Lilibet was hiding somewhere in the lands ahead of them. It was true. She was hiding — and walking the dark path. Twenty years of sorcerous knowledge obtained in the fount of the practice.

Sam couldn't turn back. She and Duke both sought the same thing, the same person, but for different reasons.

"You'd best get to it," he said. He paused then leaned close. "There's something you're not telling me."

She shrugged.

"Ca-Mi-He," he guessed.

She cringed.

"Tell me," instructed Duke.

"How did you… Ah, it doesn't matter," she muttered.

She found herself nervously touching the scar in her side where the dagger had wounded… no, killed her. She'd been bound to the spirit, not through ritual and pattern, but by something more primal. She'd died, and the spirit had used the connection to save her. It had ridden her back from the underworld.

Approaching Ca-Mi-He's sorcery, she could feel the connection was there still, still pulsing like a thin tether, holding them together. The great spirit had fashioned the wall. She could feel it. She could feel her connection to it, but she couldn't explain that to Duke. Not now.

Instead, she said, "The wall was formed with sorcery, of course, and not that of the dark trinity. There are no other spirits powerful enough to control something like this."

"What is it, Sam?" questioned Duke. "What are we sailing into?"

"It's part of the shroud, bleeding through to our world," she explained. "A reflection, but something more, I think."

"And what will that do to us when we sail in?" he asked.

"My presence will offer some protection," she said. "If the great spirit recognizes this vessel has a connection to me, to it, then we might gain a reprieve from the worst of the storm. I need to bind myself to the Cloud Serpent, to infuse a part of me into this airship, to trick Ca-Mi-He into granting us passage."

"Hunh," mumbled Duke.

She turned to him and offered him a grim smile. "I'll get my materials from the cabin, and Duke, I'm going to need some of your blood."

A HUSH HAD FALLEN OVER THE DECK BEHIND HER. THE CREW STILL worked frantically. They still adjusted the sails, still carried powder and shot to set it beside their weapons, but no one spoke. They had strapped on armaments and offered their hopes to the spirits. There was nothing else to say.

It wasn't silent, though.

Ahead of them, the constant growl of thunder filled every moment with the promise of violence. The cloud bank, dark gray, nearly black, frothed with menace. Lightning burst with each beat of her heart, casting a ghastly glow beneath the surface of the impossibly large storm clouds.

The sailors didn't need her to tell them it was unnatural. They'd spent years at sea, decades in many cases, and they'd seen their share of brutal storms. Nothing like this, though. No one had ever seen anything like this and lived to tell of it.

It hadn't deterred the Franklin's Luck, though, and it wouldn't deter her.

Their quarry sailed just five hundred yards ahead of them now, and within minutes, it would be sailing directly into the storm. Five hundred yards. Tantalizingly close. Another hour and they would have had them. But at five hundred yards, they couldn't risk veering off course for a chance to use their cannon. The speed they would lose in the maneuver could put them out of range, and it'd be impossible to regain that momentum quickly enough to keep track of the other airship in the massive storm.

They had their deck guns which could be swiveled forward, and it was possible they could fire on an arc and strike the other airship with the three-inchers, but the small shot would do nothing to stop the Franklin's Luck. Any holes they blew in the sails would be insignificant. Any damage they did to the structure of the airship would be unnoticeable. Perhaps they could kill a person or two, but even with the spyglass, no one had been able to identify who was in charge. They could be killing royal marine hostages just as easily as the enemy. From the distance, there was no discerning between captor and captive. From what they could see, the crew of the other airship never looked back. They just went about their tasks, holding the line due south.

Sam drew a deep breath and settled her feet on the deck of the airship.

Around her waist, she'd tied a line of hemp rope and secured it to the rail. She'd spent the last hour scratching chalk symbols and phrases in ancient Darklands along the top of the gunwale. At her feet, she'd laid a spiraling pattern painted in a mixture of that chalk and blood from both her and Duke.

She'd taken as little from herself as she could and got the balance from him. She had to stay awake, alert. Duke had suffered the effects stoically. Last she'd seen, he was lying in the captain's cabin recuperating from the bloodletting, drinking potions from her rucksack and, she suspected, no small amount of grog.

That was probably for the best.

The blood of kings had power. She'd taken his and hers and bound them to the airship. It wasn't a perfect binding, and she knew in time it would break down, but she hoped it lasted long enough to get them through the storm and find safe harbor. Inexorably, they were tied to the fate of the airship now until the binding was broken. If it went down, they would go down. The crew may have some chance of survival, but she and Duke did not. She'd gambled it all on her ability to protect them from the storm.

Her ability and Ca-Mi-He's reluctance to destroy her. She was tied to that spirit like she was to the airship, and she suspected if her soul departed this world and passed beyond the shroud, she would take Ca-Mi-He with her. She was pretty confident of it but not certain. And she had no idea if the great spirit itself would feel the connection and hesitate, but the pull of the Darklands, the path to Ca-Mi-He, was inescapable for her now. No matter the risk, no matter the danger to her and the others, she had to continue. She had to see where this path led.

"You're sure about this?" called Captain Ainsley from the stairs to the forecastle, her eyes wide on the towering mass of ferocious weather in front of them.

Sam glanced over her shoulder and nodded. Yelling to be

heard over the growing roar of the storm, she advised, "You'd best strap yourself down, Captain."

Captain Ainsley nodded, her tri-corner hat flapping on her head like the thing meant to take flight. Her hips were still adorned with her paired pistols, but what she meant to shoot with the things was a mystery.

"Captain…"

"You mind the sorcery. I'll mind the sailing," shouted Ainsley. Then she pointed ahead.

Sam turned to watch as the Franklin's Luck began to be buffeted by tumultuous gusts of wind. The sails whipped frantically, and the ship bounced, as if being drawn over a rocky shore. In the dark wall ahead of the airship, a spiral appeared, spinning into a vortex, and a tunnel formed, lit by crackling lightning. Sam could feel the electrical charges raising the hairs on her arm from a quarter league away.

The sails on the Franklin's Luck fell, as if becalmed, and like it was drawn forward by invisible ropes instead of wind, the airship was pulled into the churning vortex. The crew aboard the airship stood stock still, watching and waiting as they were dragged into the belly of the maelstrom. As the airship entered the conflagration, the twisting clouds closed behind it, sealing it inside, presenting an impossible wall of storm to the Cloud Serpent.

Unnecessarily, Sam yelled over her shoulder, "Hold on tight!"

Moments later, they entered the darkness.

A powerful gust of wind slapped her across the face, jolting the forward progress of the airship, stalling it in midair, but another arm of air caught them from behind and shoved them forward. Like jostling through a crowd, catching shoulders and elbows of those who did not appreciate being passed, they continued forward in staggering fits and starts, the frame of the airship creaking alarmingly beneath their feet.

The wall of clouds loomed above them, blocking out the sun, the bright blue sky behind them belying the terrible mass they were facing. Like a pit fighter taking a shot to the body, the airship was buffeted to the side, jolted and thrown on the temperamental wind. Above her, she heard a spine-tingling rip and glanced up to see a flap of sail tear loose.

"Drop the sails!" screamed Ainsley, her voice a tiny whisper above the storm. "Drop the sails, or the whole damned mast is going to crack!"

A blinding blast of ball lightning exploded around the airship, bolts of raw energy crackling two dozen paces away on both sides of them. The thunder from the lightning rattled the wood of the airship, and for a brief moment, Sam worried the deck was going to simply shake apart.

The lightning blazed around them, unceasing. Her hair stood on end, and heat bathed her skin from the unrestrained energy. She blinked, but the afterimage of the first explosion was seared into her vision, half-blinding her. She could hear nothing except the concussive rumbling of thunder. Then, bitter cold assailed her, blown away by bursts of hot lightning and returning like a wave against a shore.

She felt spirits lingering in the clouds around them. She felt the spirits drawing closer to the airship. The space between their world and the underworld was thin, frayed in this place. The spirits could seep through and exist within the storm. It was a reflection almost strong enough to serve as a bridge. The wracking wind and crackling lightning were inconveniences, dangers that they might survive, but the spirits would clutch them and, howling with rage, drag them to the other side of the shroud.

Sam felt cracks forming as more of the shades pressed against the barrier, seeking to burst through, seeking her and the crew. The wall between the worlds flexed and shuddered. She could feel it, recognize it, from when she'd met Ca-Mi-He before.

Grimacing, Sam realized that with no intervention, those spirits would scour the airship, ripping the souls from the crew. The meagre protection she'd tried to invest into the airship with Duke's blood and her designs would be fruitless against the raw presence of the underworld. If those spirits came unabated against them, there was nothing she could do.

Cursing and realizing that she had no choice but to play her last card, she drew Ca-Mi-He's tainted dagger from behind her back and slashed it across her open palm, sawing deeply through the flesh. Blood spurted from the painful wound, whipped by the wind. It sprayed across the deck of the airship in front of her, twisted and carried in droplets over her body and into the sky.

Kneeling, she slid the dagger back into the sheath behind her back and wiped three fingers across the deep laceration. On the wood of the deck, she traced Ca-Mi-He's symbol over and over again. She used her blood, tainted with the great spirit's presence, to draw its symbol on the deck.

It was sloppy and imperfect, but immediately, she could feel power fill the pattern. The great spirit, present in this world and the other, loomed over the airship. Ca-Mi-He had been nearby, she suspected. Its power was what drove the strength of the storm.

She'd drawn the great spirit to them, using the connection in the dagger and in her blood. It was a gamble. She had no idea what the great spirit would do. Would it be angry at her call? Would it bring their airship down with the same twist of the sorcery that powered the storm? Could even Ca-Mi-He do anything about the spirits that were pressing the barrier? Would it take her and shove her through the shroud to them? She didn't know if Ca-Mi-He would help them or hurt them, but she had no choice but to lay her cards down.

It was a desperate choice, but the only one she had. The protection she'd placed upon the airship was keeping the lightning and the worst of the wind from them. They might make it through the wall of clouds if it was not too broad, but she couldn't protect against the spirits. There was nothing she could do when those awful shades slipped through the cracks in the shroud and took them. She whispered a hope to Ca-Mi-He and, with her blood, kept drawing its name.

There was a swelling in her mind, cold pressure, the sense of an impossible, immense presence. The sense of the spirits clustered on the other side of the barrier fled. They simply vanished with the flexing of Ca-Mi-He. The shroud settled, unstressed by the battering pressure. It shifted and moved away, as if shoved from the proximity to their world.

The storm tossed the airship like a child's toy floating on a spring-swollen stream, but the threat of the spirits was suddenly, entirely gone. The spirits in the underworld, at least. Ca-Mi-He was tethered to the pattern she'd drawn in her blood. When she wiped it away, the spirit would be free to leave, no longer called to her, but she was afraid to release it before they passed the thin piece of the shroud. She was afraid to hold the spirit longer, as she was certain it could snuff out the candle of her life the moment it decided to.

Torn between risking the spirits on the other side of the barrier and Ca-Mi-He's presence, she clutched the rope that was tied around her waist, kneeling on the deck of the airship. She didn't know what to do.

"Sam!" cried Duke, stumbling up next to her. "It's so... so cold. What have you done?"

She could only shake her head. He was right. It was cold. She was cold. It felt like ice was creeping up her arm, freezing her physically, mentally. She turned to Duke but could not speak. The cold was engulfing her, a smothering embrace from the great spirit. She knew now Ca-Mi-He would not tamely answer the call of a mortal woman. She hadn't bound it, and she had no protection. Ca-Mi-He was going to take her to where she'd originally found it. It was going to take her to the shroud.

"What have you— Ca-Mi-He?" he gasped. He lurched toward her, falling to his knees and clasping her with his hands. "You're freezing, Sam!"

She couldn't speak, couldn't move. She felt herself drawing away, as if the spirit was tugging her soul from her body.

Then, warmth suffused her, and Duke grabbed her head and turned it so he looked into her eyes. He looked, but he was not looking for her. He was looking for Ca-Mi-He, feeling for that awful spirit that he'd felt before.

The warmth spilled from his hands into her face, into her body. She shivered, helpless, held between the grip of the spirit and Duke. He snarled, and she knew he meant it for the spirit. He was... he was pushing it away, somehow. The warmth began to grow, not a trickle coursing through her, but an enveloping sense that filled her body, that forced out the cold.

The storm raged around them, but the spirit was fleeing. At least, for now.

"I think it's—" began Duke, but his eyes widened and his cheeks bulged out. He turned away from her and coughed. Bile spewed from his throat, spilling across the bloody drawings she'd made of Ca-Mi-He's name. Duke tried to speak but couldn't, as tremors wracked his body, and he heaved again.

She stared aghast at the pool of sickness obscuring Ca-Mi-He's symbol drawn in her blood. What the frozen hell did that mean?

THE CARTOGRAPHER X

HE WIPED his mouth and staggered to his feet, the deck of the airship rocking like it was on a storm-tossed sea. All around them it was black, sporadically lit by brilliant bursts of incandescent lightning. Heat and cold lashed him in waves, and any thought he'd had that they might be able to follow Franklin's Luck through the storm had vanished the moment he'd stepped onto the deck. His stomach felt like an ale shaken in a jug, frothy and bubbling with pent-up explosive force.

Glancing down at Sam's designs and his sickness pooled on top of them, he asked, "Is that bad?"

"I-I… I don't know," she stammered. She turned, looking behind them, and shouted, "Samuels, get up here with a bucket! Wash this deck off!"

"Right now?" cried the sailor from where he was crouched down near the gunwale, not trusted to tend to the sails in such violent weather but not allowed to hide below, either.

"Now!" shouted Oliver and Sam as one.

The recalcitrant sailor stumbled up the ladder, a bucket of water in one hand. Half of it spilled by the time he made it to Sam, but he dutifully dumped it on the mess in front of her.

"More," she shrieked. "Now!"

Samuels shuffled off, one hand gripping the wooden railings, the other his bucket.

Oliver and Sam stared at each other, mouths agape. Ca-Mi-He's symbol painted in her blood. What had she done?

Samuels returned along with another sailor, and both of them splashed buckets onto the deck, washing his sickness and Sam's blood away.

Moments later, the rocking and crushing wind subsided, and rain began to fall. The world was blanketed in a steel gray sheet of water, but it felt like natural rain, coming straight down from above. The howling winds faded, though the lightning still crackled behind them.

Oliver stood, stooping to help Sam to her feet as well. The rain, increasing in tempo, doused both of them from head to toe. He swept a lock of sodden hair back from his face and asked, "Are we through?"

Shaking her head, looking around, Sam said, "I think we are."

Overhearing them from the stairs, Mister Samuels shouted to the crew, "We're through! We made it!"

Oliver did not look back to watch the men cheer with relief. Yes, they were through the curtain of storm clouds, but their journey had just begun.

"I SUPPOSE THAT'S THE LAST AIRSHIP THAT TRIED TO VISIT THE Darklands," mused Oliver, looking down at the shattered wreck on the rocks below.

"Barely made it to shore," remarked Captain Ainsley.

Broken timbers, canvass near rotted from exposure, and scattered brass cannon marked where the airship had fallen just fifty yards inland. It had hit hard and shattered on impact. Certainly no one had survived, but Oliver couldn't spot any bodies. Maybe over the years they'd been dragged away by scavengers.

Evidently guessing what he was thinking, Sam said, "They

were dead before they landed. Back in the storm... the shroud is thin. Spirits from the underworld almost broke through. They would have dragged all of us back to the other side with them. They might have taken the life spirits imbued within the stones as well, which could explain why that airship had such a violent landing."

"It's a good thing we had you," said Oliver. He frowned. "The cannon is still down there. Even after a hard fall, those barrels may be intact. Why would no one have looted the wreck? Do you think it's possible they didn't know about it?"

Sam and Ainsley had no response.

"That stuff would sell well in the Southlands markets," added Oliver. "A full complement of Enhoverian cannon would be worth more than most merchants could earn in several years."

"Aye, and if they didn't want to sell it, they could have used it," said Ainsley.

"That wreck below is not the last airship to enter the Darklands," mentioned Sam.

She pointed ahead of them. In the distance, Franklin's Luck sailed on calmly, still tacking due south.

"Doesn't look like they slowed at all coming through that storm," remarked Captain Ainsley. "I hate to say it, m'lord, but we can't catch them like this. Torn sail, light on water, the rigging is a mess. We're not catching anyone until we've had a chance to conduct repairs, and m'lord, we're not going home just yet, either."

Oliver a stole a glance behind them where the thick band of storm clouds clung a quarter league offshore. Ainsley was right. They wouldn't survive another passage through that without repairs. They were stuck in the Darklands with no way home, and their quarry was moving out of sight.

"According to the maps, there's a river west of here," he said. "Let's find it. We can restock our water tanks, try to obtain food if we can locate a village, and take time for repairs. No parties disembark without one of the three of us with them. No one but us speaks to any locals. No one shoots a firearm or swings a blade unless there's an explicit threat to their life. We're over foreign soil, and while we have no quarrel with the Darklands, I don't know how they'll react to seeing us. Let the crew know, if they decide to use violence, it could be tantamount to declaring war with a sovereign nation. If they attack when it's not absolutely necessary, they're better off running away than trying to get back on this airship."

"I'll call a meeting," said Ainsley.

"Captain," said Oliver, "no grog until we've no longer got the Darklands beneath our keel."

A SHIMMERING BAND OF SLOW-MOVING WATER SPREAD IN FRONT OF them like a tiny sea. Oliver could see it coming from the south, flowing north and piercing the far horizon. Where they were approaching the river, it spread a league wide. Farther north, toward the sea, it grew even wider, expanding into a huge delta. Small islands, sand bars, and bunches of tough grass and water plants sprouted irregularly from the temporary islands in the center of the channel.

Along the banks of the river, they spotted the only signs of life they'd so far encountered in the Darklands. The nation evidently had none of the small villages and hamlets that dotted Enhover's coast. There was nothing at all along the barren shore except scattered rock and abandoned hovels. Oliver supposed the storm wall made fishing the sea impossible. Instead, in the Darklands, life concentrated beside the river.

Verdant fields grew in the river's flood plain in an irregular patchwork where farmers had tilled and planted the land. They were linked to the river with rudimentary irrigation systems, looking to be no more than shallow canals painstakingly dug across the dry soil. In between the fields, it was the same brown expanse they'd been sailing over. The difference was that near the river, the soil was darker, fertile.

On the river, they could see the occasional boat trawling the sluggish brown waters with fishing nets trailing behind or loaded with bales of goods traveling up or down to some market. Docks jutted into the river like grasping fingers, and Oliver spotted several low-slung, dung-colored villages. Each village was dominated by a domed structure that was surrounded by a score or two of wattle and daub homes. Some of the places had open markets. Others had long, narrow buildings that he couldn't determine the purpose of. There were few distinguishing features to tell between any of them.

The construction looked easy to build and easy to maintain. The thick walls were probably also natural insulators, which would help in the brutal summers of the place. He speculated whether the people along the river were partially nomadic, moving along the river as the flood stages changed. And it did flood, he assessed. Presumably a seasonal deluge, but he could see half-a-league inland where banks had formed amidst the arid landscape. All of the agriculture was located within that flood plain. He said as much to Sam, but she'd looked back at him like he was speaking in ancient Darklands.

"You ready, m'lord?" asked Captain Ainsley.

He shrugged. "As much as I can be. Any of these villages look as promising as any other."

The airship dropped slowly.

Oliver and the crew clung to the gunwales, looking down at the village, watching the buildings, the scrub, and the fields around it, and waiting for someone to appear. Instead, it seemed as if the place was abandoned, though there were animals in pens that spoke the lie to that. The people who lived there must have gone into hiding.

"Bring us down to a dozen paces above the ground," Ainsley called to Pettybone.

Nodding, the first mate relayed instructions down the open

stairwell that led into the hold of the airship. A crank was turned, and water splashed down on the levitating stones that kept them aloft. The air spirits imbued within the stones retreated deeper into the rock, and the airship descended. Moving slowly and carefully so close to the earth, the crew expertly lowered the vessel until Oliver, Sam, Captain Ainsley, and a trio of sailors went over the side on thick ropes.

Behind them, on the other side of the vessel, another group of crewmen dropped down with a heavy canvass hose. They would stretch it to the river and use a manual pump to pull water from the river onto the airship. While the crew worked, Oliver led his party slowly toward the village.

His hand gripped his broadsword. Beside him, Sam had one hand on a kris dagger, the other tucked behind her back. Ainsley had drawn both of her pistols, though after his admonishment, she no longer pointed them toward the village. The other three members of the group were armed with blunderbusses and cutlasses.

If there was any threat, they would scatter shot at the locals, and all of them would retreat back to the airship. The Cloud Serpent was turned so the aft cannon was facing the village, and three of the deck guns were on pivots where they could be trained on anything that came after the ground party. It was far more firepower than was necessary to subdue such a small, rural village, but in the Darklands, everyone felt it was better to be safe than sorry.

As they reached the outskirts of the village, only a handful of skinny chickens offered any signs of life. The birds moved restlessly, pecking at the dry, dirty pathways between the small mud huts. From somewhere, Oliver heard a goat bleating, but no people appeared to resist their approach or to offer them welcome.

"Ho the village!" he cried.

One of the chickens squawked at them then continued pecking.

"Could they have run away or, ah, all gone out fishing?" wondered Oliver, peering around the village at the empty, wooden dock that thrust into the sediment-laden river.

Sam shrugged. "They probably don't speak the king's tongue."

"We mean no harm!" called Oliver, directing his voice into the village.

"And they've probably never seen an airship before," reminded Ainsley. "Perhaps we scared them all away."

Oliver turned to Sam. "Do you sense any sorcery?"

She shook her head.

Hesitantly, Oliver walked through an opening in the thin, wooden barricade that surrounded the village. It was head-high, formed of twisted branches as thick as his wrist and bound together by woven grass. The tops of the branches had been sharpened into spikes. He grabbed the barrier as they walked by and shook it, frowning. It would take little effort to hack through the dried grass that had been braided into cords to form the fence, and a charge by a motivated squad of marines could easily trample the flimsy wall.

"For animals?" he guessed.

No one replied. No one knew.

Inside of the village, he peered into one of the two-dozen mud huts, seeing the apparatus of a simple life. A hearth in the corner, a pile of discarded fish bones, a few tools, clothing, some pieces of rudimentary furniture, but no people.

They walked around the village, looking into open huts, seeing that some of them had been recently occupied. Outside each of the huts was a rough sack filled with barley, seeds, wheat, or small purple fruits. The crops that were grown in the area, evidently, but Oliver couldn't understand why one full bag would be carefully placed outside of each structure. Instead of the sacks, one hut had a freshly slaughtered goat on the doorstep, and two had chickens. Blood from the slaughtered animals still leaked onto the dusty entryways. When Oliver glanced back at

Sam and Ainsley, they could only shrug, evidently as confused as he was.

Finally, they circled to a lone door in the exterior of the domed structure at the center of the village. A door of woven reeds was shut, covering the entrance. Unlike the other buildings, this one was fashioned entirely from mud bricks stacked high to make it into a large dome twenty yards across. From its top, he could see a thin streamer of smoke rising before vanishing into the bright day.

Ainsley gripped her pistols and positioned herself behind his left shoulder. One of the crewmen took his right. Reaching out, Oliver shook the door then shoved it open.

Inside, two-score people were arrayed facing a thick wooden pole at the center of the room. Men, women, and a handful of children. They were all on their knees, their heads bowed.

"Hello…" said Oliver.

No one moved.

"Well, this is rather odd," remarked Ainsley, both of her pistols still held up, pointed at the people kneeling in the room.

They were alive. Oliver could see movement as they breathed, but each person's eyes were closed, and none moved at the sound of the door opening or at the strange voices.

"This is some sort of temple," said Sam, leaning past him and glancing around the room. "Look at the walls. They're covered in pictures and symbols. It's Darklands script, though these are not completed sentences or thoughts. It's just discrete words and pictures."

"Perhaps they're not literate?" wondered Oliver.

Sam nodded. Then she stepped by him and walked inside.

"Wait!" he hissed.

"If these people meant to harm us, they wouldn't be crouched like that," said Sam.

Oliver grunted. He turned to Ainsley and her men. "Step inside and watch our backs. Keep your weapons trained on them. Shout if anyone moves. Don't shoot unless you have to."

Nodding, the crew spread out by the door, the barrels of their firearms moving slowly back and forth over the kneeling villagers.

Sam, ignoring the people on the ground, walked around the edge of the room and studied the designs etched into the mud bricks that made the walls.

Nervously, Oliver followed her, his glance skipping over the words and symbols, finding the pictures and trying to make sense of them. There were hundreds, most seeming to depict the struggles of day-to-day life in a rural agricultural community. Sheafs of wheat, the sun, and the river, were all major themes. Interspaced amongst them were depictions of curious, stylized violence such as a man holding another man's decapitated head. What Oliver thought was a grimalkin was devouring an unfortunate figure that looked like a child. Perhaps that was the explanation for the wall around the village?

There was one picture that showed a lizard-like creature swimming the river behind a boat. Other lizards that were depicted as encircling the village. They would have to be... He swallowed. They would have to be the size of the ones they'd seen in Imbon to do that.

He walked on, seeing more casual violence and what he began to understand were sacrifices. Crude rituals, maybe akin to the sorcerous rites that they'd investigated in Enhover and Archtan Atoll. There were several scenes of large, dangerous-looking animals.

He nearly stumbled into Sam, finding her paused at a scene that was larger than the others. It was directly opposite the doorway and seemed to show a city, but it was floating in the air above a pit of fire. Around the city, more of the massive lizards were curled up like cats, sleeping, or maybe waiting.

"Spirits, what does any of this mean?" wondered Oliver.

Sam pointed up. "Phases of the moon, seasons."

Oliver blinked, noticing for the first time a row of symbols high above their heads.

"I believe this is a calendar of sorts," explained Sam. "I think it's showing when the river is expected to flood, when it's best to plant seed, when to harvest. Our own farmers back in Enhover follow such seasonal directives. These others, they appear to be calling for... for other activities to be conducted during certain phases. See, here, I think this might be instructions for conducting a sacrifice."

"A sacrifice, but to what?" asked Oliver.

Sam shook her head, walking the rest of the room, scrutinizing the pictures of violence.

Oliver followed her, focusing on the lizards. There was one that could have been looming outside of the village. In that picture, beside crude drawings of huts, were sacks filled with the same goods they'd seen outside.

He frowned, glancing at the silent villagers. Were the sacks an offering to the lizard? Had the villagers thought the airship was... was what, a flying lizard?

He peered closer at the kneeling people and saw on their cheeks, distinct marks. Two or three dashes the length of his fingernail. Children had one or none. He didn't know what it meant, but it was impossible to ignore the similarity to the face on the sarcophagus they'd found in Imbon. He shook his head, hurrying to walk beside Sam.

"The Cloud Serpent should be topped off on water by now," called Ainsley from the doorway. "We could use some provisions, though."

"Take the sacks that are placed outside of each hut," instructed Oliver. "Take them all, but nothing else."

"Nothing else?" asked the captain.

"It should be sufficient for a week to ten days," guessed Oliver. "We can resupply at another location if we need to add more stores. I believe these people left that food as an offering."

"Why would they do that?" wondered Sam.

"These villagers are not the ones everyone is afraid of," explained Oliver. "They're not the ones who frighten off the Southlands merchants or who called that storm wall to guard the coast. They aren't the ones who first explored the dark path. They didn't create the uvaan that were hidden away on Imbon, but someone did."

At the word uvaan, he saw several of the kneeling villagers jerk.

"These people are not walking the dark path," continued Oliver, "not in the way we're accustomed to. They're afraid of someone else, and they must think we are like those people. Perhaps they're afraid of any outsiders, I don't know, but I believe they left that food at their doors so that we can take it. It's an offering to appease us. They're giving a tithe, or a tax you could say, asking us to take that and nothing else."

"I think you're right," admitted Sam. "These walls are filled with pieces and hints, but none of this is sufficient to perform even a basic ritual. It's unorganized and illiterate. Someone in this land, though, knows more."

"Well," said Oliver, "let's go find them."

In the captain's cabin of the Cloud Serpent, Oliver leaned over the maps he'd taken from the ship's library. They were sparsely inked and had already proven to be inaccurate. He doubted anyone had updated the charts in twenty years, the last time an expedition had visited this strange land. It must have been before the storm wall had been raised, which surely even the worst of cartographers would have noted.

On a blank page in his notebook, Oliver sketched the bit of coastline and river they'd seen thus far. It looked as though the maps from the Cloud Serpent's shipboard library were drawn based on tales from traders rather than direct observations, and he'd nearly thrown the things across the room when he saw how hopeless they were. He didn't, though, and a practical urge to correct the record had overcome him. Now, while they were sailing south, two leagues east of the massive river that split the continent, he was calming himself by drafting a new map and noting on the old where they needed adjustment. All of the maps did have the river, so there was at least one thing they got right.

Two hundred leagues south along that river was the one city that each of the maps had in common. It looked to be a capital, though there was no name on the maps or in the legends. On the maps, the city was typically depicted as large, geometric structures, like cubes half-buried in the sand. He doubted that was the truth, but he couldn't begin to guess what they would find.

So far, they'd only seen small villages that clung to the banks of the river like parasites, slurping at the life that flowed by them. None of the settlements housed more than a few hundred people, and most were a fraction of that. Inland, the crew on the airship didn't spy anything except the occasional roaming herd of livestock with a few tenders following behind. Those men were carrying the only armaments they'd spotted anywhere — wide-bladed spears, slings, and crooks that could be used to snag attacking predators. The crew had seen several grimalkin, hyenas, and other creatures that no one could identify stalking behind the herds. The barren landscape of the Darklands was filled with deadly predators, but it was all the natural order that one would expect near an undeveloped community. There was nothing there that Oliver and his crew had any interest in. It wasn't what they'd come for.

Every time they passed people, in the villages, on boats, or watching the herds, the people bowed down, touching their foreheads to the ground and not looking up until the airship passed. No one tried to interfere with their passage, and no one questioned what a strange airship was doing flying beside the river. Even for a member of Enhover's royal family, the flagrant groveling was disconcerting. What sort of terror did these people's rulers inspire? What sort of trouble were they flying into?

Oliver sat back and frowned at the maps in front of him.

Half a dozen, likely all copied from the same erroneous narrative. Why was that? Why had no one from the empire of Enhover explored this land? His father and his ancestors had an abiding fear of sorcery, but the people of the Darklands weren't posing a threat to Enhover. They'd never ventured out of their own territories as far as Oliver knew. No one in the Southlands seemed to fear attack from the Darklands. That pirate nation didn't even have a proper standing army. Instead, the Southlanders simply did not venture east. They acted as if the Darklands was not there, and it was only the occasional forays by traders from the secretive land that even proved its existence.

The storm wall would have deterred many an adventurer, but prior to their sighting of it, Oliver had never heard of the thing. Had it existed the last time an Enhoverian visited these lands and returned to tell of it? He didn't know, but he didn't think so. It certainly wasn't shown anywhere on the maps he had, and something like that would have made it there if the cartographer knew of it. Hells, it would be the talk of every pub near the harbor in Southundon if a sailing crew had seen such a thing.

Aside from those traders who visited the Southlands, there was no record of anyone leaving the Darklands. Maybe no one did. Except for Imbon. He was sure of it, now, seeing the similarities in the pictures on that tropical island and in the villages along the river. The Imbonese hailed from the Darklands. Why had they left, and why were they returning? Where in the frozen hell were they going now?

Frustrated, he stood and stomped to the door, exiting onto the deck of the airship. The sky was clear, the dry wind brisk across his skin. The sails flapped above, and the deck was filled with the comfortable sounds of the crew hard at work.

He walked to the side of the airship and looked out at the shimmering band of light that was reflected off the river. It was only broken by the occasional thrust of a dock into the tranquil waters and the slender skiffs that darted across the surface. The people aboard cast nets for fish, hauled in their scaly harvest, and bowed in the center of the tiny vessels when they saw the airship passing above.

The people of the Darklands bowed at the sight of the airship, never looking up once they initially noticed it. They were used to seeing flying vessels, Oliver realized. It was why they didn't show panic. They merely bowed and let the Cloud Serpent past unmolested. Whoever ruled the strange land normally approached the villages from the air. It had to be related to why the Imbonese made such an effort to steal an airship.

He frowned. It was related, but how?

HE STALKED THE DECK, PEERING AT THE HAZE ON THE HORIZON. IN the orange and pink glow of the setting sun, it looked as though a massive cloud was rising straight up, lit from below by the light of thousands of bonfires. It wasn't unlike the plume above Imbon when the mountain erupted, he decided, but so far, the Darklands was flat, the terrain only broken by arid hills and sharp, broken ridges. They hadn't seen anything like the volcanic cone of Imbon.

Above the column of smoke, the rest of the sky was crowned in thick, gray clouds. The first clouds they'd seen since crossing the barrier at the coast. It seemed as if all of the moisture had been drawn from the air and gathered there. There was no rumble of thunder from the distant formation, though, no flicker of concealed lightning. Nothing at all to suggest an oncoming storm except for the clouds themselves.

"That smoke has to be coming from the city, no?" asked Sam beside him.

He ran his hand over his hair, touching the leather thong that held it tied back. "Yes, I suppose so. It's odd, though, isn't it? We've seen fewer and fewer signs of life along the river. If we're approaching what passes for a metropolis in this land, then shouldn't it be getting more congested, not less?"

"Down river from a large city probably isn't the best place to fish," remarked Sam. "The water could be filled with sewage."

He grunted.

"Another half turn of the clock until nightfall," said Sam, wrapping her arms around herself. "Is it my imagination, or is it getting colder each evening?"

"The dry air can't retain heat," explained Oliver. "The farther from the coast, the larger the swings in temperature once the sun goes down. It's difficult to tell, but we could be gaining in elevation as well. That would make it cooler. Also, there's some literature that predicts a center point of the world somewhere near Durban, and we're below that mark now. As the climate gets warmer going from Enhover to the tropics, it could be getting cooler going south from that line."

"A center point?" questioned Sam. "The center of the world is Durban?"

"Well, there's no proper center," said Oliver, grinning. "It's a globe, of course."

"A globe, like a circle?"

Oliver nodded, frowning. "The world is a globe, like a ball."

Sam tilted her head as if she couldn't quite believe him.

"If it was flat, how would you explain the movement of celestial bodies?" he asked. "The rise and fall of the sun, the moon? Why do you think the horizon disappears in the distance instead of extending forever? The motion of the seas, the wind…"

She shrugged.

"The… Never mind," he muttered.

"The Church always claimed our world was a circle, that all of us were constantly rotating through life and death," said Sam. "I thought it was meant to be an analogy to help the parishioners understand the cycle between our world and the underworld."

Oliver blinked. "Well, I think that bit is an analogy. I meant that… I'm not talking about an analogy. The physical world is a globe. Here." He pointed to a thick glass globe filled with swirling faes that hung behind them. He walked to it, holding up a fist. "Now, pretend my hand is the sun. You see how the light from it would shine on half of this globe?"

"Shouldn't the globe of fae light be the sun?" asked Sam,

eyeing the brightening swirl of tiny creatures inside. "Do they seem agitated to you?"

"Sure," said Oliver with a sigh. "The globe is the sun. Look at how the light is only cast on half of my fist. The backside is dark. That's how we experience night and day. The world, my fist, spins as it moves. The light rises and falls, and that's a day. A year—"

"What does that have to do with it getting colder south of some arbitrary point?" wondered Sam.

Oliver barely heard her. The fae, instead of flitting about in typical random fashion, had slowed. Their bodies glowed brighter than before, and as they stilled, he could feel them, feel their anticipation, the warmth of each individual speck of light.

"That's odd," muttered Sam, stepping beside him and peering into the glass.

The fae shied away from the priestess. Experimentally, Oliver held his hand closer to the globe. The tiny creatures drifted toward it, and as his skin touched the glass, they pressed against the interior, directly opposite of his hand.

"Oh, that is odd," whispered Sam.

Oliver moved his hand away, and the fae drifted away. He moved his hand back to the glass, and the fae pressed against it again. He gestured, and the cloud of small, glowing creatures flew to the edge of the globe in a wave. He could feel them, like tiny pinpricks of light shining through a thin curtain. He could sense their warmth and knew they could sense him. He directed his thoughts, and they responded, dancing to his silent tune. They were eager, like they'd been starved for attention, like they wanted to play.

"Spirits," gasped Sam. "How are you doing that?"

"I have no idea," he breathed.

The final rays of sunlight faded as the sun dipped below the horizon. Oliver stared at the globe of fae light, amazed.

"Shall we lower the sails, m'lord?" called Ainsley from the main deck. "We can drift here and then start again at dawn so we come across this city of yours in daylight. Probably better to see it then instead of the middle of the night."

"It's not my city," complained Oliver, "but yes, I think during—"

"Duke," said Sam, pointing ahead of them.

He looked and saw that the huge plume of smoke was still visible in the dark, lit from beneath by an angry red glow. Fire, or some other source, blazed light up to the bottom of the cloud bank, producing enough heat and light that they could see it from leagues away. Oliver gaped at the image, wondering just how much fire it would take to cast such a bright glow.

A flicker of shadow passed in front of the distant light.

"Did you see that?" queried Sam, a nervous trill in her voice.

"Captain Ainsley," Oliver called. "Have the crew prepare at stations."

"For what?" she shouted back.

"I don't know," he whispered under his breath, then louder added, "Prepare for combat!"

Around them, crew members scrambled to get in place, calling in curious voices but none of them failing to hasten to battle stations. Whether or not they knew the nature of the threat, they knew they were in the Darklands. They were prepared for anything, they thought.

Quietly, Sam whispered, "What was that? It looked far away, but... but if it was, then it must have been as big as us. Duke, no airship could have moved like that."

He didn't answer. His gaze was roving, looking out into the night sky. With the sun down, the world had faded to a dark blue. In the darkness, he couldn't see anything, but he could hear something.

"What is that?" questioned Sam, taking his side and looking futilely into the night.

Long moments passed. The airship quieted as the crew found their stations and held ready.

"Sails?" wondered Oliver, ignoring Captain Ainsley who'd come to join them. "That could be the creak of sails?"

On the deck behind them, a man screamed.

Oliver spun to see the sailor staggering back from the deck gun, a bolt of feathered and stained wood sticking from his chest.

Another man cursed, gripping his arm where a bloom of blood was staining his shirt. Across the deck, a steel-tipped wooden arrow skipped to a stop.

"We're under attack!" bellowed First Mate Pettybone.

The crew crouched beside what cover they could find, the gunners grabbing the deck guns and pivoting, but they had no targets. There was nothing they could see.

"Take cover, m'lord," insisted Ainsley, grabbing the sleeve of Oliver's jacket.

He shook her off, looking into the black, trying to locate the thumping he'd heard. The sweeps of the Franklin's Luck, maybe, clawing at the air? Why would a fully armed airship be shooting arrows at them?

Another missile struck the deck, narrowly missing a man. Then two more whistled in from the opposite side, striking a sailor in the chest and the neck. He fell with a gargled yelp, his feet kicking briefly as he died.

"The fae lights!" cried Sam. "Hide them! They can see us but we can't see them."

"No!" roared Oliver. "Don't hide them. Break the glass. Release the fae!"

"What?" asked Sam, glancing at him, confused.

Oliver darted to the globe behind them and yanked it from its hook. He smashed it on the deck of the airship.

The fae swirled up in a frenzy, and he waved them toward where he thought he heard the thumping. A dozen of the tiny creatures raced into the night, casting their glow on the sails of the airship and then onto something else.

"Frozen hell," muttered Ainsley. "What is that?"

Big, the light reflecting dully on it, something thrashed and undulated in the air. Another globe of fae light was broken, and Oliver willed the little creatures into the sky. They raced around a body. A giant body. Clawed feet on short legs, a sinuous tail, and a long, muscular torso.

"Hells," said Ainsley, peeking out from behind the gunwales. "It's a lizard, like in Imbon."

"Except this one's got wings," remarked Sam, her voice stilted and stunned, heavy with fear.

"It's not a lizard," hissed Oliver. "That is a spirit-forsaken dragon."

"What?" cried Ainsley and Sam at the same time.

"It's a dragon!" said Oliver again, his voice rising. "Hells, a—"

Another arrow came winging at them, and Oliver ducked, cursing.

"Captain," he instructed. "We need to shoot back. See if we can strike that thing before it blows— Oh hells."

"The ones in Imbon blew fire," said Captain Ainsley, echoing his realization. She blinked, confused. Then suddenly the captain was bolting to the stairwell, leaping from the forecastle to the deck below. "Evasive action. Evasive action. Fire at will. Spirits forsake it, move! That damned thing can breathe fire!"

THE CAPTAIN II

SHE REACHED the rear of the airship and yanked on the handle of the simple wooden box there. It remained stubbornly locked. There was a key to the thing somewhere in her cabin. Hells if she knew where. She yanked a pistol from her belt and stepped back, aiming the firearm at the locked box. The weapon cracked when she pulled the trigger, acrid smoke and the loud bang startling her and those around her. After opening the shattered door to the box, she grabbed one of the ropes and tugged it.

Beneath the deck of the airship, a series of gears turned, tubes opened, and water began to pour out of the keel. They lurched higher, several crewmen falling to their knees from the unexpected speed of the ascent.

She spun, looking at the men near the deck guns. "Fire on the damned thing!"

They stared at her, dumbfounded. The airship rose, and the lights of the fae passed out of sight.

Snarling, Ainsley yelled to Pettybone. "Get below. I want every cannon ready. I'll dump water on the rocks, and we'll drop back down. When we pass, those damned cannons better be firing!"

"Captain," shouted a man.

She turned and blinked. On the other side of the airship, more fae were swirling around a second giant, flying lizard. She refused to admit it was what the duke had said. It couldn't be. Dragons were a myth.

The lizard's mouth was open and it was making a strange, gargling noise.

Her eyes went wide. "Fire, you motherless sons, fire!"

A man spun a deck gun and lit the wick, splitting the night with the loud retort of the three-incher. It was an ill-aimed shot, and she didn't need to look to see it was wide. In the open maw of the lizard, heat was building in wisps of orange and red.

She pulled the other cord in the box she'd broken open, dumping a tank of water on the stones in the hold. The airship dropped, and she felt her feet lift off the deck, and then suddenly, she crashed back down, cursing.

Drawing her second pistol, she pointed it up and aimed it at the lizards. She fired, knowing the small shot from her pistol wouldn't stop a beast that large, but she had to do something. Around her, the crew had regained some, if not all, of their senses. More cracks of small arms popped off like children's fireworks at the new year.

Like a master puppeteer, she gripped the second rope and pulled again, shutting off the water tanks, readying to dump it again and send them soaring. Hopefully, Pettybone had the cannoneers whipped into order now, and they would get a clean shot.

One of the circling lizards craned its long, sinuous neck down and belched a billow of scalding flame. The main sail caught fire.

"Cut the sail," she snarled to a handful of crewmen near her.

Duke Wellesley came staggering up beside her. "I have this, Captain."

"Do you even—"

"Deal with that!" he said, pointing at the burning sail. "Then get the men to fire those damned cannons. We're not going to kill a dragon with a pistol!"

The lizards above were circling, warm glows emanating from their open jaws. Another whoosh of jetted flame came down across the sails of the airship as one of them swooped close. One of the two, three... Was that a fourth? Hells, she couldn't tell how many of the damned things there were.

Ainsley reached the mast and began slashing lines. Crewmen scrambled to help her. They had to put the fires out, or the whole ship would go up in flame.

Those who weren't dealing with the fires were aiming their blunderbusses and rifles skyward, taking shots at the creatures above. From belowdecks, she heard Pettybone yelling the cannon were primed and the duke offering a muffled response.

Suddenly, they lurched higher again, rising rapidly through the air.

The lizards, squawking startled cries, weaved out of the way as the masts of the airship suddenly rose in their midst, threatening to spear them. Their bodies undulated like snakes as they twisted out of the way, and for the first time, she saw the massive wings spread out from their backs.

The Cloud Serpent ascended through the middle of them, and the starboard bank of cannon erupted. At point-blank range, unloading the entire starboard artillery at once, they couldn't miss. A terrible, pained roar tore from the throat of one of the creatures, and it flapped weakly and then plummeted.

From the aft side of the airship, a billow of flame blasted along the gunwale. Several crewmen fell away screaming as they were roasted by the searing, orange fire.

A man crashed into her, his skin charred black on one half, bright red on the other. He was unrecognizable. A low moan escaped his lips, and she pushed him away, steeling herself to ignore his torment. She stomped across the ruined canvass of their main sail, shouting for men to bring down the rest of the sails and use them to smother the licking flames that were growing along the railing of the airship.

They jerked again, spinning unnaturally in midair like a

dancer on the stage, causing her to stumble like she'd just finished her second bottle of grog.

She made it to the rail, falling against it. Half of it was char. The other half was licking with merry flames.

A man, gripping his leg with one hand where an arrow was stuck into his thigh, was trying to lift a water bucket with his other hand. After taking the bucket from him, she splashed the contents along the rail and then lunged for another of the containers that had been placed near a deck gun.

Below her feet, the cannon roared again, and another of the lizards screeched in agony.

Two down. A quick look above showed there were two left. Maybe three? Had there been four or five of them? Was that it, or were there more? Glancing around the flame-scarred side of her airship, she didn't think they could survive more.

They twisted again, and she stumbled, cursing. The airship was moving in ways she could not explain, but the jerky rises, falls, and spins were clearly distracting and flummoxing the flying lizards. It was the only thing that had kept the beasts from training their fire on them and dealing a fatal blow.

But it took time to reload their cannon, and no matter how nimble they were, the flying lizards moved with the ease of snakes in water. They'd acted stunned when the Cloud Serpent first bit back, as if they hadn't anticipated the cannon, but already she could see their flight was coordinated. It was evident the creatures had never faced an airship before, but they were adjusting. The lizards were circling above them, out of range of the cannon, the tiny pinpoints of fae light trailing them like phosphorescence on a night sea. If the things got smart, it would be nearly impossible to defeat them. The airship couldn't take many more blasts of that furnace-like flame before the fires grew out of control.

They needed something more maneuverable than their cannon. They needed—

"Spirits bless you, Mister Samuels," she cried.

THE CARTOGRAPHER XI

CAPTAIN AINSLEY RUSHED to deal with the burning canvass sails, or at least Oliver hoped she was doing that. Flame was the worst nightmare for any sailor on an airship. With limited supplies of water, blazes quickly became incredibly difficult to battle.

Well, flame had been the worst nightmare. Based on the last few moments, Oliver amended that. Giant, flying, flame-breathing dragons were the worst nightmare.

The creatures were swirling around them, building the heat in open mouths then breathing it down on the airship. Sails caught fire easily, and the masts smoldered and sputtered.

On the backs of the lizards, Oliver could see figures somehow steering the massive reptiles and firing arrows down on the defenseless crew of the Cloud Serpent. In the swirling light of the fae and hidden by the huge bodies of the dragons, the figures were difficult to see and impossible to aim a blunderbuss or a pistol at. He wondered if it would do any good if they did manage to kill one of the riders. Would the dragon keep attacking or fly away?

Their cannon, when in position, could tear massive holes in the creatures just like it had on Imbon. The problem was that the heavy brass was impossible to aim fast enough to catch the darting monsters, but there might be another way.

He let his senses drop, tried to control his breathing, and felt for the warmth he'd sensed when he'd placed his hand on the globe of fae light earlier. He tried to feel for the spirits he knew inhabited the levitating stones deep in the hold of the airship. Instinctively, he closed his eyes and reached with his mind.

"We're ready!" called First Mate Pettybone from somewhere down below.

Oliver willed the life spirits in the stones to rise, and they did. He opened his eyes and saw they were ascending into the center of the swirling mass of dragons. He shouted, "Now!"

The airship surged upward, his stomach seeming to fall from his body. It felt like he was lifting a mechanical carriage onto his shoulders. He fell to his knees beneath the invisible weight.

Cannon roared from one side of the airship, a deafening cacophony of exploding powder and crashing brass and wood. A creature cried in pain and anger, but on the other side of the airship, flame raked across their gunwales, catching several crewmen, wreaking terrible destruction while the dragon responsible swirled away into the night.

Snarling, Oliver twisted, his hand following the flight path of the dragon.

Beneath his feet, the airship twisted as well, the levitating stones moving, pressing the wooden superstructure of the airship in ways they were not meant to. His hand trembled and a wave of dizziness washed over him. Teeth gritted, he kept them moving, kept the spirits below turning to follow the lizard.

The cannon erupted again.

The lizard jerked in mid-air, its back punctured by the flying iron shot.

Oliver's arm was shaking, and for a moment, he lost the connection with the spirts. The airship slowed its spin, and he could see above them, the lizards were circling cautiously, as if preparing to dive. Two or three of them were left. He couldn't tell. If they all struck at once...

"A taper, someone bring me a taper!" cried a muffled voice.

Oliver turned and saw Mister Samuels with an arm full of yard-long, paper-wrapped tubes. A dowel and a wick stuck out the rear of them.

Oliver's eyes widened. The rockets, of course!

"Spirits bless you, Mister Samuels!" cried Captain Ainsley from across the deck. Then, she added, "Frozen hell, you fool, don't walk into the fire."

Surprised, Mister Samuels peered around the bundle of rockets to where half-a-dozen crewmen were frantically stamping out burning canvass.

Oliver struggled to his feet. "Samuels, give me one of those rockets."

Ainsley and Sam appeared beside the startled sailor, and each collected their own munitions.

"How do these work?" asked Oliver.

"Light the wick. Wait for the kick. When it ignites, it's about three seconds until it explodes," said Ainsley, peering up at the dragons above them. "That doesn't sound like much, but they move fast. In three seconds, they'll fly well past those lizards."

Oliver winced. Each of the creatures had their mouths open, and even from below, he could see the building glow in their throats where they would capture it until they were ready to release an inferno. Three of them at once...

"Got it," said Oliver.

"We need to hold onto the rocket after ignition for about a second and a half, I think," said Ainsley. "And we've got to make the first launch count. Also, we don't have the racks set up, so we're going to have to actually hold them."

"Hold..."

A sailor appeared with sets of the thick leather gloves they used to climb down the ropes when disembarking. In his other hand, he held three of the smoldering tapers they used to light the deck guns.

The three of them quickly pulled the gloves on, and Ainsley asked, "Ready?"

"Not really," muttered Sam, staring nervously at the dragons circling above them. "But I don't think we have time to wait."

Oliver nodded to Ainsley.

The crewman with the tapers passed them out and instructed, "Light 'em all at once. Best if we don't give 'em a chance to learn to evade the rockets."

"All right," said Oliver. "We'll do it—"

"Now!" shouted Sam, wide eyes peering above where the three dragons had started to spiral down toward them.

Oliver held his taper to the wick, and a sizzling sparkle began burning up the cord. He looked up and cursed. The dragons were swooping down, their mouths trailing flickers of fire.

In his hand, the back of the rocket blasted with a screaming shower of sparks that roared over his leather gloves and the sleeve of his jacket. It jerked with the ignition, and he barely held onto it. He looked away from the blinding motes of light and glanced up where a dragon was twenty yards above their mast, flame already roaring out of its mouth.

Oliver tilted the rocket and let go. It screeched into the sky, joining two others in streaks of white-orange as they raced toward the lead dragon.

Within the space of a breath, three distinct bone-jarring thumps, and the dragon was knocked off its flight path like it'd taken a punch to the head from a giant. Flames leaked out the side of its face and its neck where the impact from the rockets had torn its flesh open.

The dragon called, loud and high-pitched, and then fell within yards of the airship, flashing out of view to where, Oliver offered a hope to the spirits, it crashed on the dry earth and died.

Above them, one of the dragons had pulled up and was circling again far above them. The other had veered away but was now banking back toward them, its maw open like the door to a forge.

"Another rocket!" yelled Ainsley, holding her hand out.

Mister Samuels ignored her and dropped all of the rockets but two. He held them wide, one in each hand.

The dragon had completed its turn and was flying straight at them.

"We don't have time!" screamed Sam. "Everyone, take cover!"

Samuels ran, his bare feet slapping against the wood of the deck.

Oliver dove onto his knees, scrambling to collect another rocket, but he knew it was too late. By the time the wick burned and the rocket ignited…

The dragon cried out, flames pouring out of its mouth. On its back, Oliver saw a hooded rider, eyes gleaming in the light of the flame, and then Samuels' silhouette covered Oliver's vision of the figure.

The sailor had run to the side of the airship, put a foot on the gunwale, and launched himself into the open air. Flames encircled him, embracing him in a scorching inferno.

Ainsley screamed, Sam gasped, and Oliver was speechless, kneeling beside the pile of rockets. Samuels, arms pointed directly ahead like spears, rockets in his fists, disappeared in a billowing cloud of flame.

The dragon swept closer, disgorging devastation toward the side of the Cloud Serpent, strafing the deck with its deadly blast.

The rockets Samuels carried exploded.

The dragon's head burst. A shower of flame and gore flew against the side of the airship and blasted the startled rider from between the dragon's shoulder blades.

Headless, the creature continued its momentum and slammed into the side of the Cloud Serpent, rocking the airship with the impact, shattering boards, and knocking Oliver onto his back. Wood creaked and nails popped from the blow as the wooden structure absorbed the jolt from the massive beast, which punched the airship a dozen yards to the side.

"Frozen hell!" yelled Captain Ainsley.

Oliver sat up, stunned. The dragon was gone. They were still floating in the air, but flames were growing all around them.

"Samuels," said First Mate Pettybone, staggering out of the stairwell from the cannon deck. "Was that Mister Samuels?"

"The fires!" roared Ainsley, stabbing her finger toward crewmen. "You, you, you, get more water. You, throw that canvass over the flames. Try to smother it."

Oliver ignored Ainsley's frantic instructions and Pettybone's charge to gather handfuls of unburned canvass. Instead, Oliver found another rocket and collected the taper he'd dropped. He looked up to where a swirling cloud of fae light illuminated the final dragon. It was moving in an irregular pattern a hundred yards above them. Oliver was estimating the range and how long he'd need to hold the rocket, when the dragon banked and soared on spread swings, heading due south.

"Mister Samuels," muttered the captain, coming to stand beside him to watch the departing dragon. "Who would have thought?"

THE PRIESTESS VIII

WHEN THE SUN ROSE, Sam was still poking around the flesh and blood that had been splattered across the deck with the explosion of the final lizard's head. Thick blood, the same crimson as any human or animal, and chunks of flesh that were covered in tough, hide-like skin. There were bits of bone amongst the gore as well, white like hers but porous, lighter. It made sense, she supposed, as the things flew.

She wondered if a naturalist would have determined the dragons were closer to birds or lizards. None of the crew had any sort of expertise in those matters, and after a brief consideration, she decided that she didn't care.

Sam stood, stretching her back and glaring at the mess in disgust. For two hours, she'd been assembling every bit and piece she could that might have belonged to the dragons, but she was no nearer to discovering any truths about the creatures. Bird or lizard, natural or sorcery, she didn't know. Most importantly, she hadn't discovered anything that may help them if they encountered another one.

She kicked a hunk of muscle and skin and cursed as the piece miraculously sailed through the gap where a post had been destroyed on the gunwale. The chunk of meat vanished over the side of the airship. Grumbling, she walked over and looked down.

Three hundred yards below were several massive stains on the dirt marking where the other dragons had fallen. The problem was, they were not there. They were gone, somehow removed in the middle of the night while the crew of the Cloud Serpent had been recovering from the battle. Who had snuck below them? Who had taken so much flesh without raising any alarm from the airship above?

Not that the crew had been paying attention to anything on the ground for the last several hours. They'd been either elbow deep in triage treatments for the wounded or posted on watch, firearms in hand, eyes hopelessly scanning the dark sky. It was only in the last hour that enough crewmen had broken free long enough to begin clearing the deck.

Sam had already arranged all of the pieces of dragon in a horrific pile and surreptitiously tossed several pieces of human over the railing. The former owners weren't going to need those bits, and she meant to spare the crew from having to decide if they needed to match severed limbs with the charred corpses in some macabre puzzle on the way to deciding proper burial wasn't an option anyway. Still, she wasn't sure the rest of the crew would appreciate her so casually disposing of their mates.

Around her now, the crew was hard at work. It wasn't just the bodies and the blood they had to clean up. There were wide swathes of the deck charred black from the dragon's flame. All of the sails had been cut down in a panic and either burned where they lay or rolled into disorganized heaps.

Blood soaked the planks of the deck, both reptile and human. Arrows were studded in random places. Heavy iron shot was scattered where piles had been kicked over, and empty buckets of water were everywhere. She hoped that in the heat of battle, they hadn't used so much of their water that they could no longer descend.

First Mate Pettybone, his eyes sunken, his knit cap pushed

back and showing half of his scraggly, gray hair, was morosely walking about, directing the crew in their efforts to straighten up the deck. There was little they could do for the charred wood and bloodstains outside of days' worth of scrubbing or replacement, but they could clear a path to walk, and they had to do something about the sails.

Sam approached him. "How are the tanks?"

He blinked at her, as if confused, then finally answered, "Full enough. Ainsley probably would have dumped the whole lot of it if your duke hadn't taken over and done... done what he done."

Sam nodded.

"Any insight into, ah, what those things were?" asked the first mate, looking out of the corner of his eyes at the grisly pile of mutilated lizard flesh she'd assembled.

"Without a chance to examine a whole one, I don't quite know what to think," admitted Sam. "One thing struck me, though. They moved like the ones in Imbon, didn't they?"

He frowned at her. "These were flying..."

"Well, obviously," she muttered. "I meant the way their bodies turned, the size of them. It's an awful coincidence if we come across two different breeds of lizard that big in the space of a week, don't you think?"

Pettybone grunted.

She shrugged. "They're of a size. The coloring seems the same, and they both breathed fire. The only difference was the wings. If I had to guess, I would say that the ones in Imbon had been recently hatched, probably when Governor Towerson opened the tomb, and last night, we faced the mature version. I think it could have something to do with why the natives were so desperate for an airship. What do you think?" The man didn't respond, so she asked, "Where are the captain and the duke?"

"Below deck in the hold," answered the first mate, his hands clasped anxiously in front of him. "With the sun up, and us still in the Darklands without a sturdy enough rig to make it back through that storm, they're thinking it's time to move forward."

"Then why are they down there?"

"If we move forward, we'll need every able hand," said Petty-bone. "If the injured can't fend for themselves… The captain and the duke are deciding who has a chance, and who don't."

"Who don't… Oh," said Sam. "They're going to… they're going to make sure everyone with us can pull their weight."

Grimly, Pettybone nodded. "A sailor's life is a hard one, at sea or in the air. The crew knows the deal, but that doesn't make it easy. About the worst day any sailor can imagine, being far from home, their mates deciding they can't carry them any longer."

"The worst day," said Sam, glancing around the ruined deck and the arid terrain of the Darklands that spread all around them. "Can't argue that. They're in the hold, you said?"

Pettybone nodded and then turned back to his work on the deck.

Sam walked to the narrow stairwell that led into the hold of the airship. It was dark, the fae light globes that normally lit it shattered by the crew the night before. She descended, inhaling the copper scent of blood and the sickeningly sweet stench of burned flesh.

Unlike the stairs and the interior corridors of the airship, the hold was well lit. The fae, somehow still living, had swarmed inside, clustered unmoving near the ceiling of the space. Their glow was subdued, but there were enough of them that it bathed the area in a bright, multi-hued aura.

Blankets had been spread on the floor, and a dozen men lay on them. Half-a-dozen others moved between the injured, dispensing care and offering what comfort they could. Not a one of those was uninjured, but they were mobile, and they were capable of contin-uing on. They were the lucky ones.

Duke and Ainsley were huddled together in one corner of the room, shooting quick glances at the injured, debating fiercely.

Sam waited, not wanting to interrupt.

After evidently coming to some agreement with the captain, Duke walked slowly to stand at the feet of the injured.

Quietly, he said, "Every man who can stand and move on their own should get up now and make your way to the deck." His voice was low, but everyone in the room heard what he said. Low sobs, moans, and muttered curses greeted his statement. "Those of you who cannot stand, I'll see to it that your families receive their bonuses. What I promised you will go to them. They'll be taken care of the best I'm able. I-I am sorry. We have to do this if any of us are to leave this place. I—"

Captain Ainsley placed a hand on his shoulder.

"Go now," rasped Duke to the injured, his voice thick.

From the blankets, men began to struggle, biting back pained cries, forcing injured limbs and bodies to work. A few of them were able to stagger to their feet. More of them could not. Half of those thrashed painfully. The other half seemed to have accepted their fate.

Duke put his hand on his broadsword, watching as those healthy enough stumbled away. Some of the walking injured were supported by their peers who had been tending to them, shooting nervous glances at Duke to see if he would object.

His jaw set, his lips quivering, he was looking purposefully away from the stairwell where the injured struggled with the help of the slightly more hale. The man had a kind heart, Sam knew, but he was a Wellesley. He wouldn't act out of malice, but he would make the hard decision to save the rest of the crew. He would give them all the best chance that they could have of survival, even if it meant deciding that some of them would not make it.

Captain Ainsley watched as the shuffling line of the wounded climbed the ladder and exited the hold. There were another five who couldn't rise, who didn't have the strength to care for themselves.

"I'm the captain," murmured Ainsley. "It's my duty."

Duke shook his head. "It's on my orders, Captain. I will do what is necessary."

Sam stepped beside them. "You're both honorable, trying to do the right thing for these men, but you have to consider the others as well."

"The others?" asked Duke.

"The rest of the crew is going to resent whoever... whoever does this work," said Sam. "As their captain and liege, neither of you should bear that burden when we're in such a dire position."

"We need their respect, and if I order something that I'm not willing to do myself..." worried Duke.

"You're willing. The other injured saw it," argued Sam. "Duke, you don't need to do this."

"I have to," he challenged.

Sam looked into his eyes. "I will do it."

"Sam—"

"Duke, First Mate Pettybone is on deck getting this airship cleared and ready to sail," claimed Sam. "Ainsley can instruct the crew, but you're the one who's got to tell us where to go. You need to be there when the city, or whatever we're going to find, comes into view. You and the captain are needed on deck. This task is mine."

Frowning, Duke shook his head.

Sam glanced at Captain Ainsley and met her eyes. "It's only going to pain you both to watch. You've made the right decision, but there's nothing to be gained from witnessing it."

Ainsley grabbed the sleeve of Duke's coat and tugged on it. "She's right. Come on, m'lord. We need your guidance above."

Duke muttered further protests, but he let himself be pulled away. Sam could see in his eyes that he felt obligated to stay, but he didn't want to. Of course he didn't want to.

Sam watched as he and Ainsley disappeared up the stairwell. Duke was a good man. He knew what had to be done and didn't shy from doing it. It was unfortunate, but they had to think of those with a chance to continue and jettison those who were still breathing but already gone.

It took a strong leader to make that decision, and it took an even stronger one to enact it. Sam thought it would have broken him, though, to kill wounded men under his command. It would be a waste to ruin such a good man on such a heinous act.

Blank-faced, Sam turned to the wounded and reached behind her back. She slid the tainted dagger from its hidden sheath.

"Ca-Mi-He," she whispered, "carry them swiftly to the other side."

After taking a deep breath and releasing it slowly, she strode forward.

The first man was charred to a crisp, an unfortunate victim of the dragon's fire. His right arm was blackened and motionless, and much of his face was singed meat. His eyes were open, though, watching her. He tried to move away, to fight back with his one good arm.

She knelt, pressing her leg down on his struggling limb. She promised, "It will be quick."

Thrusting the sharp steel beneath the man's chin and up into his skull, she watched the flicker of life fade from his eyes. The dagger was ice-cold in her hand as she moved to the next sailor, and in the space of two dozen breaths, she killed them all.

THE CARTOGRAPHER XII

THE AIRSHIP LIMPED ALONG, patched canvass and hastily nailed wood creaking alarmingly but holding in the gentle breeze.

"I don't think it's enough to get us through the storm wall, m'lord," said Ainsley, glancing back at the masts. "I could fix a little bit more canvass up there, but if we face another attack like last night…"

"Hold it," said Oliver. "One of the dragons escaped. If it and its rider had friends, let's keep something in reserve in case we need to, well, in case they burn these sails too."

He didn't comment on the corpses of the other dragons going missing. He didn't mention that they were days away from the coast. They didn't discuss that they wouldn't have the water and the food to travel all the way back to Enhover and maybe not even to the Vendatts or the Southlands where they could find a safe harbor. Hells, he was finding it hard to even say the word dragon. That's what the creatures had to be, though, even if everyone knew such a thing was a myth.

Ainsley shifted, kicking at the char on the foredeck and looking ahead. She stated the obvious. "It doesn't look like anyone lives down there, m'lord."

Oliver grunted. She wasn't wrong.

The land ahead of them was ripped apart by thermal activity. Pools of glowing, molten rock were scattered like puddles in Westundon's cobblestoned streets after a hard rain. Bubbling pots of boiling mud were mixed with swirling spots of vibrant color where minerals melted and combined. Steam rose from both small and large vents in the earth. Oliver had heard of areas like this, where the heat that was buried deep within the world rose to the surface. He'd even visited an area in northern Rhensar which was dotted with scalding hot pools. Even in winter, they could melt a block of ice in seconds. Imbon, they knew for certain now, and likely most of the Vendatts had been formed from such activity.

The difference was those places were isolated and quiet, or the thermal activity violent and rare. Here, a city-sized area appeared to be in constant upheaval, as if the world atop and the world below were in an unending battle, fire and heat consuming stone and air. It was an unpleasant reminder of the proximity between their world and the underworld that they'd all felt passing through the storm wall.

Surrounding the blackened, melted center of the place were giant pyramids. They were built of the same mud bricks that the villages were constructed of, except these bricks were far larger, and the structures rose ten stories high. The amount of effort to construct the things couldn't have been any more than one of Enhover's giant keeps, but they spied no roads, no rail, no sea access with which to transport the building materials. The small villages they'd passed didn't appear as though they had nearly enough people to supply the labor for such gargantuan projects.

Oliver frowned, his fingers drumming on the railing.

"Well, wherever she went, Franklin's Luck didn't come here," remarked Ainsley. "Or if they did, they didn't stay."

Oliver nodded.

"Maybe there's another city somewhere else in this crazed land," speculated Ainsley. "Could be people lived here once, before the place got burning hot. Maybe they moved the capital, took it somewhere more hospitable. I know I wouldn't want to live in this awful desert. I know it sounds crazy given my chosen profession, but I like the grass beneath my feet. These folks've probably never felt grass like we have in Enhover. Outside of those fields by the river, there ain't much more than scrub and twisted, stunted trees, but surely there's somewhere in this awful land people would want to live."

Not responding to the captain's musing, Oliver looked up.

High above them there was a heavy bank of clouds. They'd been hanging there since the Cloud Serpent had first come over the horizon the day before, but it didn't look like a drop of rain had fallen from the formation in weeks. Despite a steady breeze, the clouds weren't moving.

"Captain," said Oliver, "I'm beginning to think that cloud is not natural. Can you take us up into there?"

She blinked at him. "I don't know if…"

"You and the crew steer. I'll bring us up," he said, not looking toward her.

His eyes were fixed on the giant formation above. Hanging over the boiling pools and the pyramids, it could have been some residue from the steam of the earth, but what if it was something else? If the Darklanders could call upon a storm wall that encircled their entire coast, then a simple stationary cloud did not seem too much of a challenge. The Imbonese had taken an airship for a reason, hadn't they? They'd intended to fly somewhere.

Ainsley turned and began to address the crew.

Over his shoulder, Oliver called, "Captain, just in case, have the men assume battle stations."

THE AIRSHIP ROSE SMOOTHLY, DRIFTING TOWARD THE THICK CLOUDS on half-sail. The wind had quieted to nearly nothing, and Oliver thought it possible they would need to extend the sweeps once they entered the clouds, but for now, he wanted the crew on the cannons. After losing so many men the night before, they didn't have the numbers to do both.

Cool mist surrounded them, enveloping them in a blind fog. He wrapped his arms around himself and frowned. Despite the burning sun that scorched the rest of the Darklands, it was cool, almost cold.

In the hold below, he felt the life spirits that imbued the levitating stones grow sluggish from the change in temperature, and perhaps something else. Mentally, he encouraged them, and they continued to ascend, the tiny droplets of water beading on his face the only sign they were moving through the still, opaque clouds.

He felt a stir in the air and demanded, "Ready, everyone, ready!"

From his feet, he picked up a rocket and stared into the mist.

Beside him, Ainsley did as well before whispering, "What are we looking for?"

He didn't respond.

Long, quiet moments passed, and then they heard a powerful flap.

"Another of the lizards!" shouted Ainsley.

"Hold until you've got it in sight," cried First Mate Pettybone. "No one fire until you know you'll hit something."

They waited. The booming flap sounded like a full main sail being filled with wind over and over again. The sound circled them, and the men turned, trying to follow the hidden motion. A crewman cursed, and Oliver heard a thump. He guessed it was Pettybone cuffing someone before they fired a deck gun at nothing.

"Show yourself or we'll fire!" shouted Oliver, calling into the fog.

"Do they speak the king's tongue?" wondered Ainsley.

Oliver shrugged. He closed his eyes, and a moment later, from below the decks, a swarm of brightly colored fae poured out. Oliver, reaching out to the minuscule creatures, encouraged them to fly out. The twinkling lights spiraled up around the mast of the airship, and then they drifted off higher, heading into the clouds where Oliver was directing them. He could feel something. Something big.

Finally, the swirling fae began to coalesce around a position. They'd found what he felt was there. It was fifty yards above them and almost two hundred yards ahead, well positioned to avoid the field of fire from their cannon.

A sudden gust of air blew into Oliver's face, and the mist parted, revealing a massive lizard, its body twisting in the sky in front of them, its giant wings pumping steadily to keep it aloft. It was nearly twice the size of the ones they'd seen the previous night, far larger than the airship.

On its back, a hooded and masked figure rode. Unlike they ones they'd battled the night before, this one did not appear armed, but Oliver was not fooled. If they were attacked, it would not be from bows and arrows again, it would be the dragon itself, or sorcery. This was the reason the villagers bowed and trembled in fear. This was the true power in the Darklands.

Sam stepped up beside him, gripping her kris daggers, though what she intended to do with them was a complete mystery to Oliver.

He leaned forward, putting hands on the railing and peering at the figure.

A gloved hand moved up and tugged down the leather mask that guarded the flyer's face. It was a woman, but from two hundred yards away, he could see few details. She sat straight up on the back of the flying beast. Black hair whipped in front of her face, blown by the power of her mount's pumping wings. She brushed the hair aside, and it felt as if she was looking directly at him.

Without speaking, the figure tapped on the back of the lizard. The creature's neck dipped lower and it surged forward, sweeping in a smooth arc carrying it below the Cloud Serpent and then off to the side where it wheeled and disappeared back into the clouds. Behind it, a stream of twinkling fae rushed in its wake.

"Raise more sail if you need to or run out the sweeps," instructed Oliver. "Follow that… that dragon."

Sam cleared her throat.

"What?" he asked her.

"You don't think… Ah, that woman did not appear to be from the Darklands," said Sam. "She looked… familiar, did she not?"

"Oh, hells," gasped Captain Ainsley, covering her mouth with a hand.

Oliver turned to the captain and frowned. Glancing between Sam and Ainsley, he asked, "What are you talking about? You think that woman was from the Franklin's Luck?"

"No, I… Ah…" stammered Sam. She glanced at Ainsley then back at him.

"What?" demanded Oliver, glaring at Sam.

Ainsley took advantage of his focus on the priestess and slipped away, giving brisk instructions to her crew.

Oliver took a step toward Sam and lowered his voice. "What is it?"

Pale-faced, Sam swallowed. "The katars, I think you ought to get them. Get them and be ready for anything. Duke, I mean anything."

BEFORE THEM, THE FOG PARTED TO REVEAL AN EXPANSIVE CITY. IT SAT atop a giant, floating mountain. The edges were wreathed in verdant green forest, and in several places, they could see where streams poured over the sides, the water spraying in the light wind and then vanishing into the mist.

Beyond the forest, pale gray stone rose in distinct tiers forming buildings that seemed fashioned from the mountain itself. People moved about on the streets and in large open squares. They were clothed in dark robes with hoods pulled over their heads. There was little color other than the green of the forest and the black of the resident's clothing.

A light rain fell, presumably fueling the streams that ran over the edges. The entire place looked damp, as if the moisture was a constant, though surely sunlight must shine on the floating city periodically for the plants to grow. As they came closer, they saw that the structures of the city grew larger as the tiers rose. The top of the city was ringed in what looked to be palaces, but even at the edges near the forests, they saw no mean hovels. There was nothing like the poor villages that clung to the riverbanks that they'd seen on the way south.

"No sense wasting our time at the bottom," remarked Oliver. He urged the life spirits within the stones in the hold to rise.

The palaces at the top were much the same as the buildings below but far larger. They were built of the ubiquitous pale gray stone and ringed with columned porticos. A dozen of them surrounded a huge, open garden. It was carefully manicured, small trees and shrubbery ringing a large, pebble-strewn circle in the center. In the circle, sat a massive dragon. Its sides were painted in vivid purple designs, and it turned to look at them as they sailed closer.

"Same one, you think?" questioned Sam.

Oliver nodded. "I don't see any others, and it looks to be the same size."

"There was at least one smaller one we fought last night that escaped," worried Sam.

Oliver looked over the rest of the city, but he saw no signs of another dragon, just the one, sitting in the center on top of the mountain. A small figure stood beside it.

Without word, Ainsley directed the crew, and they drifted closer to the open court. Oliver smirked when he felt the vessel turn, showing their side to the huge lizard beneath them. Ainsley was making sure the heavy guns faced it, though the creature showed no inclination to attack.

"I'll go down," said Oliver.

"I'm coming with you," insisted Sam.

He nodded. He suspected she would. Sam wasn't going to miss this.

"I as well," declared Ainsley.

Used to the women's insistence on coming every time he disembarked, Oliver didn't bother to argue. He knew it would get him nowhere. Instead, he turned his thoughts to what waited below.

"Captain," called one of the crew. He was pointing up, far above them.

Oliver gasped. The Franklin's Luck was drifting there, half-hidden by the cloud. Its sails were down, and there appeared to be no one onboard. The airship looked like it had simply sailed there, battened down, and then been abandoned.

"This is weird," whispered Sam.

Oliver and Ainsley could only nod.

Half an hour later, they were in range to drop lines over the edge. The trio pulled on their gloves and climbed over the side. Oliver wished he could bring more of the crew with them — a few more blunderbusses in the party would give him some comfort — but as short-handed as they were, he wanted every able-bodied man standing ready to man the sails or the cannon, depending on how they were received.

Their boots touched on the pebbles, and he let go of the rope.

Ainsley checked her pistols, Sam her daggers, and Oliver patted his broadsword.

"You brought the katars?" asked Sam, looking at him.

"I did," he confirmed.

"Be ready with them," she warned. "Duke... be ready for a surprise."

He nodded, looking at the person standing beside the dragon. The woman who'd ridden it out to greet them in the clouds, he realized. He wondered, "What? She thinks we're going to walk into range of that thing's flame?"

"What else are you planning to do?" asked Sam. "She doesn't

look like she's in any hurry to come to us. We've already come all of this way, so we may as well go talk to her."

Muttering under his breath, Oliver glanced back at the Cloud Serpent to make sure Pettybone and the crew were prepared to unleash the cannon if necessary, and then he led the party forward. They walked two hundred yards and stopped a dozen from the woman. Close enough Ainsley would have an accurate shot with her pistols, or Sam might be able to land one of her daggers if she had to throw it, but also close enough that they wouldn't have time to flee from the dragon's fire before it torched them.

The woman appeared unarmed, but she was dressed in intricately fashioned armor. A sturdy, black-dyed leather brigandine covered her torso with thick pauldrons on her shoulders. Her legs were covered by stiff greaves and she wore articulated gauntlets that rose all the way up to her elbows. The lower half of her face was guarded by a leather mask.

"Who are you?" he asked her.

"You don't know?" she replied, sounding curious.

He frowned. The voice was familiar, but...

"What are you doing here?" asked the woman, her king's tongue confident but slow, as if she was fluent but had little chance to speak the language. "What does Enhover want with the Darklands?"

"How do you know we're from Enhover?" he demanded.

The woman stared back at him, silent.

He glanced up at the Franklin's Luck and then to the woman. "Why did the Imbonese abscond with one of our airships and sail it here?"

"How else would they get here?" she wondered.

"What's the answer?" he demanded. "What's the reason they came here?"

"Come with me," she said and then turned and began walking toward one of the palaces that ringed the field.

Oliver glanced at his companions. If they went inside, they

would be out of sight and out of range of the cannons. If they were ambushed, Pettybone and the crew wouldn't even know. They would have no chance to intervene, not even a chance to flee.

"No," said Oliver, shaking his head at the woman. "We're not going anywhere until you tell us who you are and where you're taking us. Tell us what happened to the captives from Imbon and why the natives stole our airship."

"You have a lot of demands," remarked the woman. "They stole the airship to return home. They are not natives of that trop-ical island but of here. Surely you can guess why they needed an airship to perform such a task? As to the captives... I am afraid they are no longer as you may have known them. Their souls were severed from their bodies and then retied through ritual. They are no longer truly living, though they still breathe and their hearts still beat. They are merely thralls to those who bound them. I am willing to turn them over to you, but I do not think you would appreciate it. In time, the bindings will break and their souls will pass to the underworld, or perhaps I shall break the bindings myself and grant them some mercy."

"W-What..." stammered Oliver, unsure what he should ask next, unsure of what it was she was even telling him. He shifted uneasily then demanded, "The airship those people flew here belongs to Enhover. It must be returned to us."

The woman nodded. "You may have it back."

He blinked and ran a hand over his hair, touching the knot at the back. "And, ah, the people who stole it, perhaps their ances-tors were from here, but they were living within a Company colony. They are subject to Enhover's law. They killed hundreds of people before fleeing, and we demand justice for the fallen."

"Yes," said the woman. "They spoke of what happened before they fled. There is one who still lives, the sorcerer behind the binding of your people, but the others have been dealt with."

"Dealt with?" snorted Oliver.

"They are all dead," explained the woman. "You say they are

subject to the laws of your empire, but they are also subject to the laws of ours. In the Darklands, the children are responsible for the crimes of their parents. These people, these refugees, forgot why their ancestors fled. They forgot the crimes that they had committed, what they had stolen, and the punishment that was due."

"Well, I guess it's sorted, then," muttered Ainsley, glancing nervously at the dragon sitting dozens of yards away. The huge creature eyed them passively, shifting slowly and resting its carriage-sized head on the pebbles of the courtyard.

Oliver crossed his arms over his chest, trying to suppress a shiver. He felt the hilts of his katars against his arms beneath his jacket. This woman claimed that justice had been served and that they could recover the airship. Their mission was accomplished, and they had no reason to stay longer, but he had so many questions. There was so much left unanswered. The woman was hiding something, despite her apparent openness.

"There is one more matter we should attend to," said Sam, giving Oliver an apologetic look.

"What is that?" asked the woman, pale, tattoo-rimmed eyes studying the priestess over the leather mask that covered half of her face.

"Lilibet Wellesley, we have reason to believe you were behind the sacrifice of Northundon," said Sam.

The woman stared back, blank faced.

No one spoke.

Oliver's heart raced and his stomach roiled. Lilibet Wellesley, his mother? Her voice was not the same, but it was familiar, like another spoke through her lips. Could it… He studied her face, what he could see above the hard, leather mask. Tattoos were scrawled on her pale, white skin. They swirled out from around her eyes, an ever-present mask. Those eyes were cold and flat. They were not his mother's, but the shape was the same as hers. The brows, the hair, the rise of her cheekbones, now that he was looking closely, it was just as he recalled, even if the woman's demeanor was nothing like what he remembered.

The woman turned to him and reached up to unhook the mask that covered the bottom half of her face. She pulled it down, and he saw the curve of her chin, her lips, his mother's lips...

This was his mother.

Unable to stand any longer, Oliver sank to his knees.

He wanted to feel her hug, to hear her laugh, to know what had happened. He wanted to see her eyes twinkle at his antics, see those lips curl into the smile he remembered. He wanted to smell her, to touch her smooth skin. He wanted her to whisper into his ear, to tell him all would be right. He wanted so much, but he couldn't make himself ask it. He couldn't make himself speak at all.

"Come with me," she said and turned.

He watched her walk away.

Sam and Ainsley helped him to his feet, evidently unsurprised at the revelation. They held his arms and supported him as they staggered after the woman— his mother. This time, no one voiced a complaint at following her into the palace, out of sight of their airship and their crew.

Behind them, the dragon snorted and stretched, laying its giant body down on the pebbles as if it was readying for a nap.

Like walking in a dream, they passed through giant stone columns into a wide opening and a hallway. It was an entrance fit for a palace, but there was no door, just empty, open arches. The corridor was the same stone as everything in the city. It was uncarpeted and bare. The palace was hushed, but their boots rang loudly as they hurried after his mother.

His mother...

Oliver nearly jumped when they passed an alcove with two people standing in it. The pair were wearing plain cotton robes, dyed black, with cowls pulled over their heads. Their hands were clasped on their chests, and while the party passed, they stared straight down at the floor.

The hallways and rooms that they passed were sparse, bare stone with no ornamentation, though there was elegant furniture and ample space. They saw more people who Oliver took to be staff. Uniformly, their eyes were downcast and none of them looked up at the strangers in their midst. He saw no luxury materials, no gratuitously displayed wealth, nothing that would signify this was a palace other than the scale of it.

They reached the back of the building and emerged onto a broad, covered patio. Chairs, low couches, and tables were scattered about. A cart on one side held clear decanters filled with wine and an array of silver cups, but it was the view which drew Oliver's eye.

The patio looked out over the city and the ring of forest beyond. It caused a momentary sense of vertigo, looking down at the successive tiers of buildings falling away below them then the thick band of forest and then nothing but mist. There was no horizon, no land below or in the distance, nothing to anchor the perception that they were on a sturdy floor instead of falling into bottomless ether.

"I presume you'd like a drink?" asked the woman — his mother. "I have wine from the Darklands. An unusual terroir compared to what you would drink in Enhover, but I don't think you'll find it unpleasant. I have gin as well, but it all passes through the Southlands before coming here. It is not of the first quality, and I'm afraid sometimes not of the second. Still, there are times when I have a taste for it."

Oliver worked his mouth, unable to find his words.

"Yes, a drink," croaked Sam. "For all of us."

Oliver saw Sam glance at Ainsley, and the captain scurried to the drinks cart and began pouring full cups.

"You are my mother," said Oliver.

The woman tilted her head, studying him. Finally, she acknowledged, "Yes, you are my son."

His legs trembled, and he was glad he was still half-leaning on Sam.

Ainsley arrived with a silver cup filled with gin. He drank

deeply, struggling to figure out what he wanted to say to the stranger in front of him.

"Why did you sacrifice Northundon?" questioned Sam, one hand still gripping his arm, the other on the hilt of a dagger. She hadn't yet taken the cup Ainsley offered to her.

Lilibet looked at Sam blank-faced. "Why do you suspect me of sacrificing Northundon?"

"You're the only known survivor," said Sam. "You lived. Everyone else died. Who else would we suspect?"

Lilibet pushed back her hood and shook out her long black hair. "Yes, I suppose that makes sense. I understand why you think I was involved, but I was not responsible, not in the way you think. I merely took the opportunity presented. After the event, I came here, and I have remained here for these last, ah, fifteen years?"

"Twenty," said Oliver, watching his mother's face. Aside from the mask of tattoos around her eyes and the flatness of those pools to her soul, she looked much as he remembered. Her hair, her skin, it was all the same. It was as if she'd aged months instead of decades.

"The passage of time has little meaning for me," remarked Lilibet, evidently guessing his thoughts.

He started. He hadn't seen her looking back at him. He'd been staring, but it was as if he couldn't see.

Lilibet moved to the railing and gazed down at the city below them. "When the ritual began, I felt it immediately. It was a great pull, a swirling whirlpool that drew me inexorably toward its center. Not understanding, I scrabbled and clung to what I knew. I set hooks and dug in, but I was ripped away, cast into a strange place, a strange land, but not all of me. Part of me held, and I was sundered, confused. I raged, and I fought. I knew I could not win, not as I was. I erred when I held on so tightly. I should have let go, but I took what I needed from the arrangement and fulfilled what was required. And then I fled. I've hidden the last... What did you say?

Twenty? The last twenty years, I've bided my time. My enemies had been felled as a part of our bargain, but I had gained a new one. I felt myself growing weaker day by day, the longer I remained apart and not whole. I maintained my protections. I stayed in hiding, and I waited. One way or the other, I knew I would return to my strength. It is only recently that has happened. I have you to thank for that, Samantha. You allowed me to be nearly whole again."

Oliver stepped away from Sam, struggling to understand.

"What are you talking about?" demanded the priestess.

Lilibet did not respond, her gaze still down at the city below them.

"We saw the remains of the ritual you conducted," accused Sam, speaking to the other woman's back. "The sacrifices you made in that garden. You killed people!"

"Don't we all?" remarked Lilibet casually.

"I... I..." spluttered Sam. "You admit it? You admit your culpability in Northundon?

"I did not sacrifice the city," claimed Lilibet, turning to face them, "but I have done many other unspeakable things, as have you."

Sam growled low in her throat and stepped away from Oliver.

He staggered, like he'd been punched. His mother... Her face, her voice, they were familiar but not the same. Her words swirled in his mind like leaves blowing in a windstorm. He recognized them but did not understand them. He couldn't fathom the form they should take. Her enemies, a part of herself, none of it made any sense.

Sam looked as if she was ready to pounce, to slash and cut with her knives, to do as she always did.

"You're a sorceress," accused Oliver.

Lilibet laughed.

"You think it's funny?" cried Oliver. "You... you—"

"I am not the mother you once knew, Oliver," said Lilibet. "I think it will be easier for you if you understand that. I cannot offer what you seek. I cannot answer what you ask of me. You should not have come here. You should go home. Go back to Enhover. Do… do whatever it is that you do. This is not your place. You cannot stay here."

"You cannot stay, either," snapped Sam. "You're coming with us. You must face justice or… or else."

Her lips curling into a mirthless smile, Lilibet shook her head.

"This is not your place," said Oliver quietly. "Come home with us. Whatever has happened, we can fix. We can… It can be like normal, like it was."

Lilibet walked to the drinks cart and began pouring herself a cup of wine. "You are right. This is not my place, but Enhover is not my place, either. Perhaps someday I will return there in full, but not yet. I am more than I was recently, but I am not what I was twenty years ago. I am not free. I must gather strength before I face the one who brought me here."

"Here?" wondered Oliver. "The one who brought you…"

Lilibet turned and raised her glass. "You are better off not knowing, Oliver. You should not have come."

"No," he said. "No. Tell me—"

"I will not," interrupted Lilibet. "Perhaps someday you will understand, and you will know the pain I have tried to save you from. I don't know if you will thank me, then, but it does not matter. I will not tell you anymore."

He stared at her, flummoxed.

"You should not be here, but since you are, I will offer our hospitality," continued Lilibet. "Spend the night. Rest. Provision your airship for the journey home, and I will grant you whatever supplies you need. Do you have enough crew to pilot the other airship back? It seemed many of your men died in the confrontation with our outriders."

"We have enough," mumbled Ainsley.

"Then I will grant what provision you need for that airship as well," said Lilibet. "My servant is coming, and he will show you to rooms that you may use. You can inform him of what you need for your crew."

"We are not leaving so easily," said Sam, taking a step toward Lilibet.

Oliver raised a hand to slow her then dropped it. He knew what the priestess was thinking, what she intended for his mother. He knew he should stop her, but he could not. He couldn't think straight at all. Couldn't—

"You yearn to harm me, Samantha, but you cannot," claimed Lilibet. "You are tied to a part of me, and the only thing you can offer me is completeness. When I sensed you coming through the storm wall, I thought to ask you to make me whole, but I am not sure. Not yet."

Sam reached behind her back and drew the tainted dagger from beneath her vest. The steel whispered against the leather sheath as it emerged. It gleamed in the diffuse light of the fog-bound air.

Before anyone could move, Lilibet sprang at Sam, grasping her wrists.

Sam cried in surprise, but Lilibet was too fast. She pulled Sam close, their faces a finger-width apart, and then she shoved Sam back.

The priestess stumbled away, her mouth open in surprise, her hands empty.

Sticking from Lilibet's stomach was the hilt of the dagger.

"Mother!" screamed Oliver.

He tried to rush forward, but Ainsley caught him, held him back.

"I-I didn't mean to..." stammered Sam. "Duke, I'm sorry. I didn't mean to! She grabbed my hand. She—"

Lilibet smiled at the three of them and then drew the dagger from her body. She spun it and offered it back to Sam, hilt first. In her open palm, the blade of the dagger shone bright silver. There wasn't a speck of blood on it.

"I am not your mother any longer, Oliver," she said to him. "Do yourself a favor and forget me. Move on. Your potential shines like the sun. You can provide the balance that the world needs. You can strike down the dark tree that has taken root and fulfill the prophecy. It is by your hand that it may become a true foretelling. That is a task worth your effort. I am not. Leave here. It is a waste of time to dwell on the past, on what you cannot change."

THE PRIESTESS VIX

THEY WALKED from the room in stunned silence. Sam had felt the tip of the dagger slide into the other woman. She'd felt the resistance of the armor then of the flesh. The tainted blade, touched by Ca-Mi-He, had penetrated until the cross-guard stopped it. When the weapon had been removed, she'd seen the hole in the other woman's armor. Sam knew the weapon had punctured flesh, but there had been no wound. No blood.

She shuddered. Lilibet Wellesley had told the truth. She was no longer Duke's mother, no longer what she had once been. Spirits forsake it, what did that mean? What was she?

Sam looked back through the open doorway, but Lilibet had turned and was looking down over the city. Was Lilibet a sorceress or something else? Not even Yates or William Wellesley had power to do what they'd just witnessed Lilibet do. Had the woman bound some great spirit like the cabal had attempted?

Shivering, Sam hurried after her companions, trying to ignore the absolute chill that had encased her when she had realized the blade had not marked Lilibet, that the woman had grabbed her wrists and forced the blow because she wanted them to stop wasting time thinking of harming her. The utter disdain for their abilities to do anything in the situation was breathtaking.

Sam caught up to Captain Ainsley and saw the woman looked as if she was ready to start directly back to the airship.

Sam touched her shoulder. "We need supplies, don't we?"

"I hate the idea of taking anything from this spirits-forsaken place, but… yes," admitted the captain. "Do you think… do you think he's all right?"

Sam could only shake her head. She walked beside Duke, but she didn't know if he heard them. She didn't know if he was aware of anything going on around them. He simply strode forward, blank-faced, following their direction. It was like he was sleep walking, moving through a dream.

She didn't blame him. She'd never known her mother or her father, but at the moment, she was glad of it. Lilibet Wellesley was no mother, not anymore. She was… Sam didn't know. She couldn't fathom what had become of the woman.

A cowled man was waiting halfway down the long, stone corridor. Silently, he gestured for them to follow and took them to a room that had wide windows barred with wooden shutters. There were couches, chairs, and a table. There was nothing on the walls and nothing on the floors.

"Who should we see about supplies?" asked Captain Ainsley.

Their guide ignored her and left.

Ainsley stood in the center of the room, hands on the butts of her pistols, frowning. "Do you think they mean to capture us in here?"

"If so, then we're already captured," remarked Sam, "but I haven't seen any doors in this place. If they mean to hold us here, how would they?"

Duke slumped into one of the chairs, staring at the wooden shades on the windows.

Sam moved across the room and found them closed by only a simple catch. They were not locked. They were not prisoners. "Shall I open the window?"

Duke didn't respond, and behind him, Ainsley shrugged. It

was obvious the captain was waiting on Sam to bring it up, to get him to talk.

"So, ah, that was your mother," said Sam, sitting down across from Duke.

"Was she?" he asked.

"No, I suppose she was not anymore," replied Sam quietly. She glanced at Ainsley, but the captain offered no help.

Duke stared morosely at his hands.

"The woman you knew, the one you thought we would find here, is gone," said Sam, leaning forward with her elbows on the table. "That woman in the other room, she is something different, something I do not understand, but I know she is not your mother."

"What do you mean?" questioned Duke. "She's... she's controlled by a spirit or something?"

"I don't know," admitted Sam. She stood and opened the shutters, looking out at the mist beyond, more to give herself something to do than to see the featureless sky. "She's a sorceress, Duke, but not like any we've encountered before. Isisandra, your uncle, they were trying to achieve power. Your mother is striving for something else, I think, perhaps power in a way that we do not understand. She's cold. Not her demeanor, but her aura. It's like how the shades from the other side of the shroud felt. Could you not sense it?"

He grunted. He had felt it, she decided, but he did not want to admit it.

"This city, this entire land, is not concerned with power as we know it," continued Sam. "Maybe they're chasing a higher form of sorcery. Maybe there's some religious dogma that we do not know, but they're seeking something beyond our world."

"Seeking what?" questioned Ainsley.

"I don't know," admitted Sam.

"Truth," said a man from the doorway.

The three of them turned and saw a gaunt figure garbed like the rest of the residents of the floating city. He wore plain, black robes, bound at his waist with a simple rope. His hood was thrown back, and his bald head was decorated with a web of intricate tattoos. From a distance, it gave him a skull-like appearance. The sides, top, and back of his head were black. Around his eyes, nose, and mouth were the only unmarked skin, though Sam saw a network of pale scarring there. As he walked into the room, Sam could see the details of the tightly drawn scrawl. It must have taken ages to make all of those tiny, intricate lines.

He smiled at her, showing white, even teeth.

"Who are you?" asked Duke.

"I apologize. My name is Absenus," he said. "Few of the others understand your king's tongue. I've come to assist you in gathering the supplies you will need for your journey home. I am told your airships require water? And of course your crew will require food. Do you have enough men to crew the other airship, the one the outcasts arrived upon?"

"We'll make do," said Ainsley. "I don't suppose there is anything you can do about that storm wall?"

The man nodded. "It is meant to keep people from coming here. It is not there to impede your departure. There is a totem I can provide which will ensure safe passage through the storm. I would appreciate after you are clear, you throw the totem overboard into the sea. We have little need or desire for more visitors."

"Why?" asked Duke. "Why do you want no one here? What are you hiding?"

"We are not hiding," claimed the man. He stuck his hands into the opposite sleeves of his robes. "Let me see if I can explain. I was taught that your nation follows the teachings of the Church. They believe in the circle, correct, an ever-spinning cycle between life and death, this world and the underworld? We have an understanding of the wheel as well, but we do not worship it. It is a natural force, like the wind or the tide. No amount of worship, begging favors of the circle, will garner a result. The circle, the cycle as we refer to it, is unthinking. Our work, our religion you could say, is not to worship the circle but to manipulate it. It is a difficult undertaking, and we've found that your world only offers distractions. To complete our work, we need isolation. Hence, the storm wall, our floating capital... We do not hide. We merely seek to study and work with no distractions."

"You said religion. If not the circle, what do you worship, then?" questioned Sam.

"Why, the spirits, of course," said the man. "Where students of your land try to bind the spirits, to control them, we seek a different relationship. We seek their blessing freely given. We seek a communion."

"Like the druids," hissed Oliver. "Are... are you druids?"

The man smiled wanly and shook his head. "Quite the opposite. Druids strive to commune with life and help it to flourish. We strive for death."

THE CARTOGRAPHER XIII

HIS QUILL SCRATCHED across the fine parchment, inking confident lines as he outlined the great, floating city of the Darklands. Tier after tier of plain stone buildings, vast open courtyards that he now realized were for the sole purpose of providing room for the nation's dragons to land. The marketplaces in the city were small, the buildings of government non-existent, those of religion profligate but unassuming. There was nothing he'd observed that afternoon, walking around the top of the mountain and looking down, that resembled anything set aside for entertainment.

His quill swept dark outlines defining the creamy pale texture of the parchment. The colorless contrast may as well have been the city itself. There was the verdant green of the forest around the island, the pale stone of the city, and nothing else. The people moved about the place like shades, mere shadows neither effecting nor effected by their surroundings.

He understood now why the people they'd first encountered had simply bowed at their presence. Those people thought the airship was akin to the dragons and their terrible riders. They offered tribute to the floating city and whispered hopes that the lords of the place would leave them alone. The dragon riders collected tithes from the farmers along the river to support the city and its unceasing pursuit of sorcery. There was no agriculture in the city. There was only consumption. This place was about death, while the people along the river struggled for life.

The city itself was designed in all ways to support study of the dark path. The forms of behavior, the activities of the citizens, were all part of a pattern to assist the masters — the sorcerers. One was either of an esteemed rank and strode the corridors like a self-appointed king, or one was a menial servant, so cowed that they refused to raise their eyes from the floor. There was nothing in between.

Oliver and his companions traveled freely through the palaces. None of the servants had the courage to challenge them, and they carefully avoided the masters of the place, warned by the sound of their confident strides.

He and Sam had walked the ring at the top of the city after they'd deposited Captain Ainsley back at the Cloud Serpent with his mother's tattooed seneschal. Ainsley could handle resupplying well enough on her own, and they needed her to calm the crew. Oliver could not leave, not yet. He hungered to understand this place, to understand who his mother had been, and how she'd become what she was now.

What he did understand gave him no comfort, though. His mother was as cold and uncaring as the pale stone of the city. Everyone in the place was. She was a master, an iron-fisted ruler, who commanded the servants with little regard for anything other than her own needs. The hushed reverence the bald seneschal used when he spoke of her hinted that perhaps she was something even more. What that was, the man would not say.

Quiet like a graveyard when night fell, the city made Oliver's skin crawl. He and Sam had been given rooms. They'd been provided a feast for the two of them, and wordless servants poured wines that had traveled all of the way from Ivalla. All just for the two of them, apparently at the instruction of his mother. He hadn't seen her since they'd left her rooms, and he wasn't sure they would see her again before they left the Darklands.

It felt hollow, knowing that, but the meeting with Lilibet Wellesley had awoken a horror inside of him. He'd started second-guessing all that he knew. He couldn't reconcile his memories of a smiling mother in the palace at Northundon with the blank-faced woman they'd met. The woman he'd known never would have left her family. Not for the dark path, not for anything.

He set down his quill and picked up his wine.

The soft sound of the feathers on paper and the scrape as he lifted his glass, along with Sam's gentle snoring from where she'd dozed off on a comfortable couch, were the only noises in the dead city. The staff walked through stone corridors on wool-wrapped feet, terrified of interrupting a master. There was no music, no sounds of revelry that rose from the buildings below. Just silence. Like the underworld itself.

Oliver was caught by surprise when the strange bald man who'd spoken to them earlier cleared his throat in the doorway. Cursing and jumping to his feet, Oliver's hand went to his hip, but his broadsword was not hanging there.

"You do not need that for me," assured Absenus, the seneschal, "though if you'd like to bring it, I understand."

"Bring it?"

"Something is happening that you should see," explained the man. "There are sometimes disagreements within our people about how to best pursue our journey. We have no king as you do. No elected council as the Southlands did prior to your occupation. In the Darklands, we follow the mantra that strength decides. In recent weeks, Lilibet has grown stronger and has begun asserting that power over other factions in ways that have not been done in hundreds of years. Those who have been independent no longer are. Strength decides. There has been quiet resistance, but everyone was afraid to challenge her in case what they sense is true. Your arrival, and the confrontation between your airship and our dragon riders, has torn open a barely hidden rift. A challenge has been issued."

"A... a challenge?"

"Do not fear. Lilibet has answered."

"I don't understand," muttered Oliver, casting about for where he'd laid his broadsword earlier.

Sam, rubbing sleep from her eyes, was arming herself as well.

"Rijohn, the dragon rider who survived the fight with your airship, has challenged you to individual combat," said the seneschal. "Lilibet stepped in, as is her right as your mother. If she wins, he will be dead. If he wins, you will have to face him."

"But we were promised—"

The man held up a hand. "You were promised by Lilibet, and she is upholding that promise. If she had not spoken of your protection, then she would not be standing for you. As it is, she will defend you as necessary. I suspect Rijohn heard of her promise and believed it meant she could not be what she is. He thinks she is still your mother."

"I can fight my own battles," growled Oliver.

"Not this one," said the tattooed man, shaking his head. "I'm afraid one against one, without the benefit of your technologies, you would not last long. Rijohn and his fellows are young and arrogant. They were not prepared for you because they did not understand the nature of your airship or the weapons inside. He understands now, and it is not some mundane bow and arrow he'd bring against you. But have no fear. It will be a short fight. Rijohn and the others do not believe Lilibet is what she is, either. She has not declared it, and she has not demanded the respect she is due, but some of us have determined her nature. Because she is a foreigner, a woman, they think we must lie. It is not a lie, and she has the strength to lead us all. Tonight, Rijohn's death will show us what she is capable of. I believe you should witness this as well. Maybe then, you will understand."

"Hold on," said Sam, taking Oliver's side.

"No, we have little time if you want to witness the challenge," said the man. "Come with me."

Oliver and Sam fell in behind the seneschal, walking through the darkened, silent hallways of the floating city's palaces. They moved from the building that Lilibet seemed to inhabit and then through several others, seeing no one except quiet servants shuffling through the corridors with their heads ducked. The little lighting was provided by sparsely spaced oil lamps. There were no fae lights, which struck Oliver as odd since the fae were sold in the markets of the Southlands, adjacent to the Darklands. The stench of the underworld, he decided. The small life spirits could not survive the exposure to the shroud.

After a quarter hour of walking, they heard the murmur of quiet conversation and entered a room better lit and more populated than any they'd seen so far. There were tiers of benches rising around a circular, marble floor. The floor was inset with intricate patterns in gold, and a short wall around the open space was covered in similar designs.

Oliver had seen enough to know that the designs were sorcerous in nature. He glanced at Sam and saw her lips were pressed tightly together and her nostrils were flaring with excited breaths. He raised an eyebrow at her in question, but she shook her head, glancing at the robed figures in the room.

There were dozens of them, dressed much like the servants except around their necks they wore silver pendants. Where their flesh was visible, Oliver saw the dark ink of tattoos. The bald man led them to a bench, and they sat. They drew several curious glances from the crowd, but no one spoke to them.

Oliver studied the group as they waited, suppressing a wave of panic as he considered that each person in the room was likely a powerful sorcerer.

In front of them, a woman turned to glare at Sam. "I sense the spirit on you."

Sam blinked back at the woman.

The woman growled, "Do not interfere with the challenge."

"She will not need to," said their guide.

The woman snorted. "We shall see. Rijohn is impetuous, but he has reason to be. He is strong and he has the blessings of many spirits. Lilibet claims none. She glides through our halls propelled by nothing more than rumor. Rumors started by you, Absenus, if I had to guess. She is hesitant, afraid to show her power, which is all I need to determine she does not possess what you think." The woman glanced back at Sam. "I can sense the spirit's presence on you but not its blessing. You are weak. Do not seek to thwart the contest, or I will slay you."

Oliver swallowed, and Sam shifted uncomfortably on the marble bench.

The woman turned back to observe the open space in front of them.

Absenus seemed unconcerned.

In time, the room hushed, and from one side, a man emerged. He was shirtless, displaying bands of tattoos like lines of script on a page encircling his torso and his arms in distinct lines. It evoked the markings of one of Archtan Atoll's tigers, and the man moved with the same lethal grace. Oliver didn't need Absenus' explanation to guess this was Rijohn, the dragon rider who had faced them.

The man walked confidently onto the circular floor of the room, and the air grew noticeably colder. In that room, with no distractions, even Oliver could feel the underworld clinging to the dragon rider. Rijohn wore the taint like a cloak.

As if he was a prize-fighter at the pits, Rijohn began to circle, nodding greetings to those who must have been supporters, glaring at those who Oliver guessed were not. When the preening man reached the side of the room where Oliver and Sam sat, he stopped. He smiled, and Oliver grimaced. The man's teeth had been filed into sharp points.

"Imagine accidentally biting your tongue with one of those," Sam whispered under her breath.

Despite the ominous scene, Oliver found himself grinning at her jest.

In a loud voice that echoed off the marble in the room, Rijohn declared, "Foreigner, after I have slain your mother, I will challenge you. And then you," he said, looking at Sam. "You and Lilibet have been foolish in your selection of a patron. What was once the great spirit no longer is. For decades, it has been diminished, pathetic, and weak. Tonight, I will slay the last of its adherents, and then I will bind it. Tonight will mark the ascendency of a new order, the casting down of the great spirit Ca-Mi-He, like the dark trinity twenty years ago."

Rijohn held up a fist as if he would grab the great spirit and throttle it before them.

Oliver glanced at Sam and saw her sitting tight-lipped and silent. The taint of Ca-Mi-He on her, on his mother? The dragon rider Rijohn clearly sensed something, something that Sam had been reluctant to tell. Lilibet had claimed she and Sam were connected, but what did that mean? She kept staring straight ahead at Rijohn, ignoring Oliver's look. Soon he would ask her, but not now. Not there.

"You as well, Absenus," crowed Rijohn, taunting the bald man. "After these two, I will challenge you. The mother, the son, the priestess, the acolyte. The blood of the four will stain this floor. I will draw a pattern in it tonight, call upon the—"

"If you wanted to fight," snapped Oliver, a sudden rage coming over him, "why did you run away the first time I saw you? You could have saved us all the time and stayed so I could kill you then like we killed the others. Please, spare us the babbling exhortations of a proven craven."

Rijohn staggered back as if he'd been slapped.

Sam, rubbing her lips with her hand, whispered, "I'm not sure that was wise."

The sorcerer Rijohn, shaking his head like he was physically brushing off the shock of Oliver's comments, let his hands curl into claws. The room watched quietly, evidently everyone having comprehended enough of what Oliver said to understand the sorcerer's reaction.

Beside them, Absenus tensed, but he did not move to intervene. In the center of the floor, white mist began to curl around

Rijohn's fingers. They elongated, darkening, into jagged claws. The man's gaze locked onto Oliver, staring murder.

"This isn't good," hissed Sam, a hand dropping to grip the hilt of a kris dagger. "You shouldn't have said that, Duke. You shouldn't have said it."

"Are you retiring from our contest?" asked a sharp voice, drawing everyone's attention to the opposite side of the room. "Do you already concede and are prepared to grovel for my mercy?"

"No," growled Rijohn. "Your son chirps like a beetle. He is just as loud, just as easy to crush."

"You need not worry about that for much longer," declared Lilibet coldly. "Take your position and let us finish this, unless you are too frightened."

The dragon rider, bristling at Lilibet's imperious tone, stalked to a distinct point in the pattern on the floor. Oliver could tell the man was searching for a pithy quip to throw back in Lilibet's face, but he couldn't come up with one. He'd issued the challenge, and anything he said may appear an attempt to delay it. It did not take much exposure to Rijohn to see he was a man who could not stand appearing weak.

Lilibet took a position on a similar point to the one Rijohn occupied and waited.

Enhover's pit fights involved a great deal of posturing, and Oliver suspected any organized fight did, but once the bell rang, it was time to begin. Lilibet, evidently, had already rung the bell. Dressed as she'd been when he first saw her, she held no weapon and waited calmly.

Rijohn stretched, corded, ink-covered muscles taut in the lamp-light. He collected a black spear from an ally in the crowd and twirled it, displaying a time-earned confidence with the weapon, and then he crouched into a fighting stance, the point of the spear aimed menacingly at Lilibet. With no referee and no indication something should begin, Oliver was shocked when Rijohn sprang into motion.

He raced across the circular floor, the spear leading the way. Around him, a wave of spectral shadows flowed into view. Like a quickly moving wave, they spread and grew then shot in front of Rijohn, streaking toward Lilibet. The lights in the room darkened. The temperature dropped, and in the space of a heartbeat, the shades manifested physically.

They formed into a pair of creatures that ran like dogs but looked like no natural beast Oliver had ever seen. Powerful fore and rear legs propelled slender bodies. As they ran, in the blink of an eye, they seemed to thicken, to grow. The heads, thin and beaked like a bird, extended forward, the mouths opening, revealing rows of small teeth that gleamed. Black fur, maybe feathers, reflected the light, and that was all Oliver could see in the seconds before Lilibet calmly stepped forward.

The creatures flashed by her, muscular legs churning, clawed paws clutching, jaws snapping where she'd been the moment before. Teeth and claw both missed, and the pair of creatures skidded by, struggling to arrest their momentum on the marble floor.

Rijohn came behind them, stabbing with his spear directly at Lilibet's body. Oliver stood, crying out, but Lilibet looked as impassive as she always did.

With one gauntleted hand, she brushed the tip of the spear aside. Her other hand slapped against Rijohn's chest, stopping him as if he'd run straight into a stone wall. Faster than Oliver could follow, Lilibet drew back and punched the man in the face. A single blow, delivered with aplomb, and Rijohn fell back, his shirtless body crumpling onto the stone floor.

His head lolled to the side, and Oliver gasped. The man's face was now a mess of bloody meat, shattered bone, and leaking fluids. His skull had been crushed by a single blow. Rijohn was dead.

"Hells." Sam gasped. "Did you see that?"

Lilibet Wellesley, shaking blood from her gauntlet, glanced at

Oliver and Sam. Without word, she turned and walked out of the room.

"I'm told your captain has made good progress but needs a few more turns to finish provisioning the two airships," said Absenus. "You are welcome to leave as soon as she is ready, but your rooms are still available should you care to spend the night here."

THE PRIESTESS X

DUKE WAS SLUMPED on one of the comfortable couches that apparently served as the only beds in the floating city. He was still dressed, his broadsword lying across his lap. He'd been asleep for half an hour, long enough that his breathing was deep and even. Sam had seen the man sleep enough by now that she knew his habits, and she thought there was little chance he would awaken soon.

Walking on bare feet, she moved to the open hallway that led from their room. There were no doors in the floating city, and as quiet as the place was, they seemed unnecessary. She hesitated then set her boots down on the floor and continued barefoot, the stone cold under her feet.

It wasn't lost on her that it was the second time she'd set out while Duke was sleeping. The first time, she'd meant to kill the old man they'd met in the wilds of the Coldlands. This time, it was to kill Duke's mother.

Lilibet Wellesley, once the Queen of Enhover, was something entirely different now. She was both more and less. She wasn't the woman who had raised the young peer. She wasn't the woman King Edward had known, though Sam wondered how much the old man suspected. Had he understood that if Lilibet survived

Northundon, it was because she was far along the dark path? Had he known even twenty years ago what she'd done, where she'd gone?

Sam pondered the question as she skulked through the halls of the palace atop the floating city. Hours after the sun fell, there was no one about, but flickering flames in the lamps hanging in the corridor lit her way. There were no guards that she'd spotted during the day and evidently none at night. She was hoping that Lilibet's bedchamber would be near the room the woman had received them in earlier that day. If it was, gaining entry and finding her should pose little difficulty. There were no doors to lock, after all.

King Edward had charged Sam with protecting his son. Would killing Lilibet fall under that command? Sam didn't think the king would shed a tear at news of his wife's death. Lilibet had been gone for twenty years, pursing her own interests and turning her back on the Crown. No, King Edward would not forgive that. The only mourning he would do at her loss had finished two decades prior.

Approaching the halls outside of Lilibet's rooms, Sam checked her daggers. The sinuous blades of her krises had been sharpened and polished before they'd disembarked the airship. The two katars she'd pressed into Duke's hands before they'd left for Imbon were hanging from her shoulders. Ca-Mi-He's dagger was hidden in the small of her back. Lilibet had already proven that weapon could not harm her, but King Edward's words were like a spirit lurking in the depths of Sam's mind. He'd insisted the katars might be needed on the journey to Imbon, that Sam's own weapons were insufficient. What had the infuriating man known?

Sam's fingers touched the handles of the katars, and quietly, she drew them. She had no idea if King Edward had been referring to this moment when he'd given her the blades, but it never hurt to be cautious, and they couldn't do any worse than Ca-Mi-He's tainted blade.

Lilibet Wellesley was blessed directly by the great spirit. Not a binding, not a taint, but a touch. A true blessing. Sam had suddenly understood it during the challenge. The words the woman said in front of them, the connection she implied between Sam and Lilibet, it was Ca-Mi-He. In Northundon, Lilibet must have gained the favor of the great spirit, and that was why the dagger had not wounded her.

At least, that's what Sam hoped. If it turned out the katars could also not injure the woman, then Sam was about to be in a great deal of trouble. It was a risk, but she had to take it. The awful power, a direct connection to Ca-Mi-He, it could not be allowed to exist. Sam's mission, everything she claimed to stand for, was empty words if she left the Darklands while Lilibet still breathed.

Ducking quietly into the room, she saw the shutters were thrown wide, and the lights of the floating city reflected on the unceasing mist that encompassed it with a ghastly glow. The room itself was dark. No lamps were lit inside.

Breathing a slow sigh of relief, Sam stalked across the naked stone floor on bare feet. She was counting on Lilibet being asleep. If the woman had been awake, Sam would have returned to her room. She'd seen what Lilibet was capable of, and regardless of the weapons Sam had available, attacking the woman straight on would be futile. Even with the designs Kalbeth had restored on her skin, Sam was self-aware enough to realize that she could not face Lilibet. The reason it was necessary for the woman to die was the same reason it would be impossible to confront her directly. No, slaying her in her sleep was the only option.

Not that killing the sleeping woman would be easy. They would have to flee immediately, and Sam thought it possible they'd have dragons in their wake when they did. She had to do it, though. She had to kill this woman who commanded power that Sam struggled to understand, at the end of a path that Sam shuddered to think maybe she did understand.

The sorcery of the Darklands was not the simple grasping for more power as they'd seen in Enhover. The Darklands sorcerers enjoyed power, to be sure, but their power was merely a means to an end. They had something grander in mind.

Silent as a breeze over stone, Sam crept through the halls and rooms of Lilibet's private quarters. There was sitting room, a room for ablutions, a dining room, and a bedchamber. All were dark. All were quiet. She found the woman's armor, hung on a dressing rack. A neat hole from where Ca-Mi-He's dagger had punched through it was still there, but there wasn't a scratch on it from the woman's battle with Rijohn.

Sam found texts and artifacts, which at any other time, she would have stolen, but she did not find the Lilibet. She returned to the sitting room, adjacent to the patio Lilibet had received them on, and looked around. Lilibet wasn't there.

Sam moved back toward the open doorway, intending to slip away, but she heard voices approaching. She crouched behind a couch and shifted her grip on the two katars, holding the punch daggers up near her chest. There was only one hallway out, and she was stuck.

As the voices neared the room, Sam identified Lilibet and the seneschal, Absenus. They were at the doorway, blocking the only way in and out of the suite of rooms. If Sam sprang from hiding now, there would be no chance of attacking unseen. If she attacked the two of them, after what she'd seen Lilibet do to Rijohn, Sam knew she'd be throwing her life away. She prided herself on her skills, but she wasn't blinded by that pride. Lilibet, with whatever sorcerous enhancements she had, was a far superior fighter than Sam.

She would wait in hiding, hoping the other woman would retire to bed, and then she'd have an opportunity. And if not, perhaps there would be a better chance to get away unnoticed. Either way, attacking now was certain death.

"Leave me," said Lilibet, her voice crisp in the quiet room.

Sam listened and thought she heard the man retreat into the hall, but he moved as silently as a shade. She waited, sweat on her palms against the handles of the katars. She heard rustling, liquid pouring, and then the creak of furniture as she imagined Lilibet sitting down.

"Few in the Darklands drink alcohol," said Lilibet suddenly. "Syrup of the poppy or the smoke of more esoteric herbs are the vices of choice in this region. I find those make this body lethargic, so I keep to wine and the occasional gin. Unfortunately, I find myself drinking alone more often than not. Do you care to join me?"

Sam cursed and stood.

"The presence of Ca-Mi-He clings to you like a banner," remarked Lilibet. She sipped a glass of wine. She nodded toward a cart in the corner where another one sat, already poured. "You should know there are few sorcerers in the Darklands who would not immediately sense you lurking inside of a room. I could feel you the moment you entered the boundary of the storm wall, and I could name every room and every path that you've walked while in our city. If you mean to sneak about this place, you should take pains to hide the connection."

Sam shifted nervously.

"Go on. Take the drink," instructed Lilibet, "and then, tell me of Oliver."

Sheathing the katars, Sam walked hesitantly toward the wine glass.

"You meant to catch me sleeping," said Lilibet, her gaze following Sam's hesitant movements. "Is your plan now to move so slowly that I doze off? Come on, girl. There are only so many turns of the clock before dawn. By then, I suspect Oliver and his captain will be eager to return home."

"He came here to find you," said Sam, picking up the glass of wine.

"Not to chase the rebels and the stolen airship?" questioned Lilibet.

"He wanted to come here before that happened, as soon as we guessed that you'd survived Northundon," replied Sam. "We suspected you might have come here. He had to know. He was desperate to search for you."

"He is from a family of seekers," acknowledged Lilibet.

"King Edward was not so eager for us to come," said Sam.

"No, I imagine the king would not want to deal with your discovery," remarked Lilibet. "Do you believe the king will be forced to act when Oliver reports back what he found? For two decades, I have existed here unmolested, but as a shadow of myself. It is only recently, with our connection, that I've begun to feel whole. If the king understands what has happened… Well, I don't think he would have allowed you to come here."

"He didn't allow us," admitted Sam. "He directed me to keep Oliver from the Darklands. He doesn't know what happened in Imbon. He doesn't know we came."

"Ah," said Lilibet.

Sam, unsure if she should offer bluster or honesty, claimed, "He knew you were in the Darklands, but he was content as long as you stayed away from Enhover. Another airship that was in Imbon is already returning to Southundon. They'll report that we came here, and he will guess what happened if we do not return. You cannot fight the king and the entire might of Enhover. You… you must flee."

"I will not flee," replied Lilibet, her cold eyes fixed on Sam. "I have gained strength in recent months, and I do not believe the king has the power to defeat me. I thought about confronting him, but it is a risk. I assume the king feels the same. Perhaps once the king believed he could end me, but now, he is not sure. It does not matter. I am patient. Eventually, the king shall pay the price. They always do."

Sam swallowed. "The price?"

"Ascending to great heights requires great sacrifice," said Lilibet. "Those who attempt to bargain never truly understand that, how great the sacrifice is. They forget how long others can wait."

Sam, gripping her wine glass in her hand, said, "I don't understand. What are you saying?"

"I got what I wanted," said Lilibet, gesturing at a shelf behind Sam, "and I did my part. Our bargain was completed. I've been trapped here, a part of myself, because he thought to keep me close and use me again, but now, I could break the chains that bind me. I wonder if I should take the opportunity your presence provides instead. Perhaps I should return home."

"Home?" questioned Sam, shaking her head, confused. Then, she paused, looking at the three small figurines Lilibet had pointed to. They were roughly carved of black obsidian and shaped like three hunched old men. They looked familiar. "Are those…"

"Uvaan," confirmed Lilibet. "My rivals. That was our bargain. Eventually, the people of this land will entomb them in pyramids like those that litter the ground below us, but it is not necessary. These are not the crude devices the Imbonese stole, those shoddy prisons they were so afraid would be breached."

"W-Who…" stammered Sam, her gaze fixed on the uvaan. "Those are the same as what was discovered in Imbon?"

Lilibet nodded. "Much the same. Long ago, there was a disagreement between factions here. One group cast down their foes and bound them into the uvaan. They trapped them there, outside of the cycle that passes through this world and the under-world. There is no greater crime in the Darklands. The rest of the sorcerers in this land combined forces and the winners were forced to flee. They took the prisons of their enemies and they established a settlement on Imbon. They lived there in exile until your people uncovered their secret. They came here hoping we would save them."

"Save them?"

"Yes," confirmed Lilibet. "They thought we would help recover the uvaan and prevent them being opened. The Imbonese were terrified about what would emerge, as they should be. Unfortunately for them, we will not save them. They will pay for their crimes."

"One escaped in Southundon," admitted Sam. "A reaver, we called it."

"As good a name as any," said Lilibet. "Was it recaptured?"

"It was stopped," said Sam. She described facing the reaver, and the golden circlet that stopped it. "Tell me what you know of them."

"Impressive," said Lilibet, pursing her lips. "Reavers, as you call them, are exceptionally dangerous. When you return to Enhover, you should seal the remaining uvaan away somewhere secret, somewhere safe. Once a spirit is removed from the cycle, it will never return. In this world and the underworld, those spirits are unbound by the natural forces that command the rest of us. They cannot be destroyed because they are no longer part of the cycle. They can only be recaptured and imprisoned. The reaver you stopped in this world merely passed to the underworld. There, it will continue to torment its enemies. The Imbonese and their ancestors will feel incredible agony, forever. Alive, dead, and around and around the circle, the reaver will pursue them. They will always be its prey."

Sam looked at the three dark statues behind Lilibet. "If creating uvaan is so dangerous, then…"

"Great rewards require great sacrifices," responded Lilibet. "My enemies are removed from the cycle, and if they were to escape, they would do great damage to me. I allowed myself to be torn apart to seal their prison, and now, only I can open it. These uvaan serve the same purpose as the ones you found, but they are not entirely the same. These are secure. When you return to Enhover, bury the ones you have found."

"Tell me—" began Sam.

"I've said enough," interjected Lilibet. "Bury the uvaan and forget them. That is all that you need to know. Now, tell me of Oliver."

Sam, not sure what other choice she had, did just that.

Lilibet listened quietly as Sam gave what details she knew of Duke's life. The other woman studied her intently as Sam described their recent pursuit and battles with the sorcerers. Lilibet nodded knowingly as the priestess revealed that William Wellesley was upon the dark path and laughed when Sam said he nearly bound the dark trinity. When Sam brought up Lilibet's other sons, the sorceress waved her hand, insisting Sam remain focused on Duke.

Perplexed, Sam asked, "You do not want news of your other children?"

"They are no longer my children," stated the sorceress. "I care nothing for them."

"Why Duke, then?"

"Duke?"

"Oliver," explained Sam.

"You were with him on the roof of the druid keep outside of Southundon," said Lilibet. "You could feel what he did, the power that he drew from those old stones. That magic has been untapped in Enhover for over two hundred years. How did he do it? How does he keep doing it? He communed with the fae, scattered them after the dragons. He is the one who maneuvered your airship, calling to the spirits living within the stones. Who taught him these things? How did he learn?"

Sam gaped at the other woman, astonished. "How... how do you know all of this?"

Lilibet stared at her impassively.

"How could you know that?" whispered Sam.

Lilibet stood, looming over Sam.

"What does the king know of Oliver's power, girl?" Lilibet demanded. "Is the king aware of the strength he commands, the control he exhibits? Does the king know that Oliver is a druid?"

Sam's mouth flapped like the jaw of a fish thrown from the river. She was powerless, suffocating.

"Answer me, girl!" snapped Lilibet.

Sam could not.

Hissing in frustration, Lilibet set down her wine glass and leaned forward to grasp Sam's head. "We are connected, girl. It is easier for us both if you simply tell me, but if you will not, I have other ways."

The woman's fingers were like spears of ice, making Sam shiver, but she could not move away. Lilibet's grip was iron, and as her power poured through Sam, the priestess found she was frozen. Her body did not respond to her mind's frantic commands. She sat, rigid, unable to move. She was unable to do anything other than look into Lilibet Wellesley's face.

The sorceress, jaw set, stared back into Sam's eyes.

Memories welled unbidden, images flashing by, scenes replaying themselves, the mumbled droning of half-forgotten conversation. Interactions with the sorcerers that they'd faced, battles they'd won, times they almost hadn't. It rose to the surface like the corpse of a fish floating atop the water, and then the memories were flicked away. Sam, powerless to stop it, sat frozen in Lilibet's grasp. The woman was sorting through her mind like a clerk through a file cabinet, surfacing memories and discarding them when she realized they did not contain what she was looking for.

Lilibet's lips twisted in amusement as she pawed through, from Harwick, to Yates, to William. Each flashback burst into Sam's mind for seconds then was flung back into the depths of her memory. Lilibet took her time sorting through interactions with the king, the things he had told Sam. Other memories were sorted through quickly. Sam's mind was an open book, the pages perused and flipped. Finally, after long moments, Lilibet returned to certain memories and lingered.

The old man in the Coldlands, the furcula, the message Sam had seen hidden inside of the reliquary. The chamber deep within Southundon's palace where Lilibet's effects were stored. The king showing Sam around the room, pointing out books and artifacts to her.

Lilibet chuckled at the conversation. She told Sam, "You would make a great sorceress. With resources, you could have walked far down the path. Farther than anyone could have imagined, I think. Farther than one should walk."

Sam sat helpless. Her body would not respond. She couldn't even squirm in the other woman's grip. She could only sit as her mind was looted, as her entire life spooled out, was pored over, and then was shoved away.

Time passed, but Sam did not know how quickly. Minutes, easily. Hours, she thought. Nothing changed except the steady deluge of her memories, and Lilibet's sharp expressions as she sorted through.

Sam, seated on a pew in Westundon's Church, the massive arched ceiling rising far above her head. Her mentor, Thotham, telling her that the time of his prophecy was nigh, that balance would return between maat and duat, and that the seed of the tree of darkness would bring salvation.

Lilibet murmured, "Interesting. The line has been laid. The possibility is open, but is it enough?" She looked at Sam, a question in her eyes. "The old man died, didn't he?"

Sam couldn't answer, but unbidden by her, Thotham's death flashed through her mind.

Lilibet nodded thoughtfully at the shadow of the memory. Sam wanted to fight, to struggle, but she was stuck as thoroughly as if she'd been sealed in cement. She couldn't move, couldn't protest.

Eventually, Lilibet returned to the memories where Sam had seen Duke exploring his power. His experiments with the fae on the airship, when he'd known to set them free. The confrontation with William. Slowly, piece by piece, Lilibet pulled Sam's memory of that night apart. She examined each moment, watched as Sam watched Duke. Sam didn't know what the other woman was looking for, but over and over, Sam saw Duke as she burst onto the rooftop of the fortress. She felt Ca-Mi-He, and she threw herself between them.

Over and over, she remembered falling to her knees, remembered Duke kneeling beside her, putting his hands on her, and the warmth. She felt the warmth. Sam felt Lilibet grasping at it in the present, trying to understand it. Slow, agonizingly, Lilibet replayed the memory, searching Sam's mind for every detail, every second, every stimulus that Sam had remembered or had forgotten. Like cold honey poured from a pot, the memories oozed out, and Lilibet savored them.

Sam felt the warmth suffusing through her from Duke's hands and pushing back the bitter, deathly chill of Ca-Mi-He. It coursed through her, growing in waves and filling her with life. She felt it. She blinked, the memory cycling over and over. Lilibet examined it for more and tried to see what Sam could not recall, had not noticed.

The warmth bled through Sam's veins and filled her in the memory… and now.

Lilibet was lost in the flow of Sam's recollection, her entire being focused on how the warmth felt, what Duke had said, and how Sam had responded to the power that coursed through them.

The warmth grew. A finger twitched. Lilibet's eyes were scrunched tight and she leaned closer, replaying the memory again. Warmth filled Sam like the rising tide of the sea, bathing her. The current of life rose around her, and she rose with it.

Slowly, Sam's hand shifted.

Relentless, Lilibet scoured her memory and forced her back through the moment over and over again. She replayed the moment when they'd faced down Ca-Mi-He.

Sam smiled.

Lilibet's face was blank.

Sam's hand ripped up from her waist where it'd sat immobile, trapped in Lilibet's cold prison. The warmth infused her entire body, drawn from her memory. She jerked one of the katars from its sheath beneath her arm and she plunged it into Lilibet's chest, sliding between ribs and punching the dagger into the woman's heart.

The memory of the moment when Oliver poured his warmth

into her flashed through her mind again then skipped and then faded.

Lilibet staggered back, clutching the bloody wound. She gasped, "The seed from the dark tree, the balance. Let us hope it is enough, girl."

Sam surged off of the couch, shoving the other woman back to where she'd been sitting, kicking her wine glass over, and holding her down against the cushions. Sam plunged the katar into Lilibet's chest, making damned sure that it was enough. Like the woman had replayed Sam's memory over and over, Sam stabbed.

Finally, breathless, she stood. Her hand dripped blood from where Lilibet's life had spurted over her, soaked her. The sorceress, eyes still open, blood leaking from her still lips, lay dead.

"Frozen hell," muttered Sam, scrubbing a bloodstained hand across her face.

THE CARTOGRAPHER XIV

"DUKE," hissed a voice in his ear.

Oliver blinked, his eyes thick with exhaustion, unable to make out the shapes in the room. The room in the floating city. His mother. They were in the Darklands, in the floating city, and his mother was there.

"Duke," continued the voice.

It was Sam, he realized slowly.

She told him, "We have to go."

"What?" he muttered, brushing her hand away and sitting up on the thin couch that he'd fallen asleep on. "What are you talking about?"

"We have to go right now," said Sam. "Put your... leave your boots off. Get your sword."

"What's happening?" he asked, struggling to his feet and glancing around the room they'd been staying in. It felt like a dream, like he was waking into a dream.

She tugged at his sleeve. "Put your jacket on. Come on. I've got your sword."

Shaking her off, he found his jacket where he'd tossed it over a chair earlier in the evening and tugged it on. "What's happened, Sam?"

"I'll tell you when we're on the Cloud Serpent," she said.

"I don't understand. Is something—"

Shoving his boots into one hand and his sword into the other, she spun and walked out the door.

Cursing, he scurried after her. He called to her, and she hissed for him to be quiet. Walking quickly ahead of him, she didn't slow at his urging, barely acknowledging him hurrying behind her in the bare stone corridors. Then she stopped.

He caught up to her and saw his mother's seneschal standing in front of them, blocking the hallway. Sam's hands dropped to her daggers.

"Death is but a transition," said the man, eyeing the priestess. "A breaking of the bindings that life has tied to us. She returned home."

Sam waited, as if she expected him to say more, but he didn't. She reached back, grabbed Oliver's hand, and dragged him along, skirting around the strange man.

Oliver looked into the seneschal's eyes and saw a grave sorrow there, but the man did not speak again.

Following Sam into the cold, misty air of the open courtyard that capped the city, Oliver insisted, "What is it, Sam? Why are we rushing out of here?"

"Your mother is dead, Duke," claimed Sam as they approached the airships. "I-I don't know how it happened. I know she's dead, though, and we could be too if we stay here. We found Lilibet, but we can't do anything for her. She can't answer any of your questions. We have to go. This place is far more dangerous than I anticipated. It's— We have to go."

"You're sure she's dead?" he asked, grabbing Sam and dragging her to a stop. "How do you know?"

"I was speaking to her," said Sam, her eyes falling to stare at his boots. "I was in the room, and she just… she just died." She looked up at him. "It was sorcery, I think. Maybe some friend of that man Rijohn sought vengeance. She looked at peace, though, as if she anticipated it. I am sorry, Duke. I am sorry, but there's nothing we can do here."

"Someone... Did someone assassinate her?" he demanded. "What did you see?"

"I didn't see anything," said Sam, tugging at him and forcing him to move again toward the airship. "She's dead. There's nothing here for us except death. We have to go."

Grunting, he followed her, glancing over his shoulder at the quiet palace behind them. His mother dead, killed by her fellow sorcerers? The victim of some Darklands plot? Had his arrival in the floating city led to her demise?

He didn't know. He felt sad and angry. Sad, he realized, not because he lost her tonight, but because he'd lost her twenty years earlier. The time they could have had was gone, and there was no chance of bringing it back. Not because she was dead, but because she'd left. She'd turned her back on Enhover, the Crown, her husband, and her sons. She'd left them, and that was what he was angry about. He was furious.

The woman that they had met was not the same woman his mother had been. His mother would never leave her family. Never. That... That wasn't her. He told himself it over and over, but he wasn't sure he believed it. He wasn't sure what to believe at all.

The dark path was seductive. It was so seductive that it'd lured his mother away from her home and her kingdom, lured her from her husband and her sons. The woman they'd met the day before, she was no longer his mother. She'd been right. She was something else, something sorcery had turned her into. Whatever had happened tonight, who she was had been killed long before. Sorcery had killed his mother. Sorcery had caused her to turn her back on everything she loved, everyone who loved her. Sorcery was responsible for her betrayal of her family.

"Ho the Cloud Serpent," yelled Sam. "Duke Wellesley is coming aboard. Prepare to sail. It's time to go!"

"You did well, Oliver," assured the king.

Oliver shook his head as he stalked back and forth in his father's study.

"We lost the colony of Imbon but due to natural circumstances," his father continued. "There is nothing Crown, Company, or Church can do about that. We lost... we lost Lilibet through internal machinations in the Darklands. Whatever she was involved in, it seems it had nothing to do with Enhover, yes? She abandoned us, her family! She was already gone, Oliver. There was nothing you could have done about that, either. She made her decision twenty years ago. We survived that, and we'll survive this. Given those awful outcomes — which you could do nothing about — you still managed to salvage a stolen airship. You handled the loss of Imbon as adroitly as could be expected, and we know more of the Darklands than we ever have before. We'll leave that possibility for another day, but gaining knowledge of our enemies is never an empty pursuit."

"A failure, whether or not I could have prevented it, is still a failure," declared Oliver.

"What happened, happened long ago," replied the king. "Your care for your mother is touching, a noble sentiment, but it is time to move on."

Oliver reached a hand toward his hair then stopped himself and forced his hand back by his side.

"The Crown needs you," continued the king. "Your brothers are solid, dependable men. They've a talent for what they do, but they never would have discovered the hidden trove in Imbon. They never would have chased the Franklin's Luck all the way to the Darklands, through the storm wall even, and then located the capital of that lost nation. Your brothers never would have done as you, and we need that! Enhover needs that! Your brothers and I need that in our family, Oliver. Twenty years ago, your mother made her choice. Now, it's your time to choose."

"You want me to be prime minister," stated Oliver.

"I do," confirmed the king.

"Running the ministry, the bureaucrats," retorted Oliver. "The way you talk, that seems the province of my brothers. The ministry is made of solid, dependable men, is it not?"

The king laughed. "It is, which is why they need a dynamic leader to stir them to action. We suffered a great loss with William, even though it's not publicly known just how far and dark his fall was. His sudden death, the recent calamities with sorcery returning to our nation... we need a strong hand guiding the functions of our government. We need you."

"I'm no leader, Father," claimed Oliver. "I'm as like to be caught in an ale sink or crawling out of a young woman's window as I am behind a desk."

"You led an airship crew into the Darklands and back," remarked the king. "No one has done that for a generation. Your crew followed you there, Oliver. You are their leader, a good one, from what I understand."

"I offered them a rich bribe," argued Oliver. "Twenty years pay. For sailors, that sum will change their lives. Men would do much for an opportunity like that."

"Changing their lives is only valuable to them if they live long enough to enjoy it," said his father. "I'm told you also offered them a chance to leave their contracts early. Given their newfound wealth, how many of your sailors took the offer of an early retirement?"

Oliver crossed his arms over his chest and looked away.

"Those men and women are loyal to you," said the king. "They sailed with you to Northundon, the Coldlands, and Imbon. They chased the Franklin's Luck across unknown waters. They trusted you to guide them through that storm, and they were behind you in a battle with dragons of all things! You earned their loyalty, son, and they showed it by accompanying you to the most dangerous places in this world. And they're still with you! That is the sort of inspiration Enhover needs to get us through this troubled time. That is why we need you!"

"Father..."

"Lilibet abandoned the Crown and her family," barked the king. "Will you follow her path or mine?"

"That is unfair, Father," complained Oliver.

King Edward leaned back in his seat. "It's a dirty trick to get you to accept, but it's not unfair. You're a Wellesley, and we have a weight we must carry."

"And what of sorcery, Father?" challenged Oliver. "Shall we abandon the investigation into the dark practice?"

"As prime minister, the inspectors are your purview," reminded the king. "You may do with them as you see fit. I hope you'll see fit to keep our shores clear of this darkness. You, more than anyone, has seen what terrible harvest such activities will reap. Who better than you to lead the inspectorate?"

Oliver grunted. It wasn't the first time the old man had strong-armed an unwilling individual into serving the Crown. King Edward had prepared for this, and he'd pinned his son exactly where he wanted him. Aside from outright flight, Oliver wasn't sure there was a way out.

Trying to think and buy himself time, he looked around his father's study, at the piles of parchments, books, and scribblings, the mess of a man who spent his days reviewing proposals and complaints, studying history, and drafting solutions. His father had once been a sportsman, Oliver knew, but it'd been decades since the old man had been riding, much less participated in a hunt.

Edward had been a respectable fencer as well, and he and William were said to have spent a week each summer on slender ketches exploring the quiet areas of Enhover's coast when they were young. His father had a taste for adventure once, but now, he cared only for the management of the empire. The loss of Northundon and the campaign in the Coldlands had changed the old man. Now, his sole concern was the empire and his family.

One and the same. The Crown. Being a Wellesley came with great privilege and great cost.

His mother had ignored that. Could Oliver fault her if he did the same?

He turned to his father. "I'll accept."

"YOU MADE THE RIGHT CHOICE," SAID PRINCE PHILIP. HE RAISED HIS glass. "To our little brother becoming a man."

Oliver snorted but raised his glass as well.

"Better you than I," said John, clinking his goblet against Oliver's. "I wouldn't last a month listening to the droll reports from those dreadful under-ministers."

"Thanks," muttered Oliver.

"You'll do well, little brother," said Franklin, his face gaunt, his frame smaller than Oliver recalled. "It is good to see the position pass to someone we can trust. After William's unfortunate demise, I wasn't sure who Father would select. You, well, we had our worries about you in the past, did we not? But today, we are proud of you, Oliver."

Franklin seemed to have aged five years over the last one, bowed under the demands of the eastern province and his penitent wife. They'd all changed, Oliver supposed. Perhaps him more than anyone, though he didn't feel different. He was the same man he had been racing carriages through Finavia's midnight streets, the same man who'd had a regular drink order and girl to accompany it in several of the Southlands' finest gambling halls and brothels. He was the same man who'd boarded the rail to Harwick for an investigation. The same man who'd flown an airship south to face his treacherous uncle and then his mother. He was the same man, just in a different suit.

He tugged at the garment. A royal blue dinner jacket that was embellished with gold buttons and trim. Underneath it, he wore black trousers and a crisp, starched white shirt that felt more brittle than his wine glass. There'd been a gold neckerchief laid out for him as well, but he'd quickly tossed it into the fireplace. Winchester, his valet, had merely shaken his head when he'd spied the gleaming threads at the edge of the embers on the hearth. The two of them were going to have to get used to the formality of the palace's tailors or train the uptight wretches to take a breath from time to time.

The tailors, the servants who tended to his room, the sycophants clustered around his father's throne, and every man and woman who worked in the halls of the ministry. Not a one of them had let down their guard for a moment. They had not even dared to crack a smile since he'd been announced as the next prime minister. Men and women he once could have trusted to share a jest and a laugh had the mien of weather-worn stone now.

"Why so glum?" asked John, putting a hand on Oliver's shoulder. "I was jesting about how long I could last in the ministry. I'd make it two months, at least."

Shaking his head at John, Phillip assured Oliver, "You'll be fine, little brother. There's very little to it, really. The King and the Congress of Lords establish the laws, and your only task is to uphold them. The Company and the military handle international affairs, of course, so I imagine tending to domestic matters will be quite simple."

Attempting a weak smile, Oliver could only nod. Very little to it, simply following the rules, running an empire. Perfect.

"Are you four done in here?" asked their father from the doorway to the room they'd hidden away in.

"Just fortifying Oliver for his first official duties, Father," said John, raising a glass.

"Ah," said the king. He made as to step into the room, but his chief of staff, Edgar Shackles, caught his sleeve.

"The royal family is to be seen," chided Shackles. "Isn't that what you always tell me, m'lord?"

"I tell you that to push my sons out the door," retorted the king. Sighing, he turned to them and waved them out. "Come on, then. If I must go, then you must as well. Our kingdom awaits."

Like scolded children, the four brothers quaffed their drinks, sat down the glasses, and shuffled dutifully out the door into the hallway.

At the end of it, the sounds of music and gaiety bounced merrily down the corridor. The Spring Ball, the first public event since Oliver had been appointed prime minister. It had turned into a celebration for his promotion as well as the change in weather.

He was dreading the smiling faces, the eager hands outstretched to take his, the whispers in his ear hoping for favors, for special treatment, for attention. He was part of the ministry now, the engine of Enhover's government. As a royal, he had been above the fray of conniving and rung climbing, but as a minister, he was fair game. He was the one they were all going to swarm around.

Edward Shackles fell in beside him as they marched toward the party. Leaning toward Oliver, he said quietly, "Baron Josiah Child left me the kindest letter today on his personal stationary, an invitation to join him for dinner. A baron inviting me to dinner? Such an honor."

Oliver rubbed his bare chin. "Yes?"

"If Baron Child wants something, he asks your father," said Shackles, "unless, of course, he thinks your father will say no. Then a man like him might befriend me and hope I could use my influence to get him what he wants."

"And what does Josiah Child want?" asked Oliver, wincing as he anticipated the answer.

"Both of the twins are here in Southundon," said Shackles. "You know why."

"He wants me to court one of the girls, then?"

Shackles smiled. "You're a settled man now, no longer an adventurer sailing over the far horizon. You've still got a treasure trove of Company stock, and as prime minister, you're in position to grow that into a legendary fortune. Every man in the room with an eligible daughter would be happy for you to court her."

"To be here this evening, the baron must have bought tickets for the rail the moment the announcement was made," complained Oliver. "Bringing them here on such short notice, he's treating his daughters like courses at a feast! Do you care for the pork or the fowl, m'lord?"

"You've sampled both, have you not?" questioned Shackles. "Apologies for my direct question, but are they not both tasty dishes?"

Oliver grunted.

"Before you become outraged at the way the man positions his daughters, you might think of how you've positioned them," remarked Shackles dryly. He placed a hand on Oliver's arm. "Not all of the tasks of the prime minister are unpleasant ones. This is a choice with no wrong answer. If you make such a fuss about spending time with those women, I cannot wait to see you meet with Salke in the sewage administration or Davidson in accountancy."

Sighing, Oliver looked at the entrance to the ballroom ahead of them.

"Your father trusts my advice, and I hope you do as well," continued Shackles. "A son of the king — the prime minister — is a man who ought to choose what he wants and lets the others fight over his leavings. It gets you what you want, for one, but also sets a precedent. The lords in the congress, the ministers, the merchants, they should expect you to take what you desire, and only then can they come scuttling out to pick over the rest. Do not allow some bold young man with a title and promise in the Company choose for you, m'lord. Pick one of the girls yourself. Either one will have you."

They walked on, and just before the doorway to the grand ballroom, Oliver admitted, "You make a clearer point than my family has done."

"Baron Josiah Child is no innocent lamb amongst the wolves," said Shackles. "He'll make a good grandfather to your children, but as his son-in-law, never turn your back on him."

With that, Shackles stepped away.

Oliver drew a deep breath and followed his father and his older brothers into the ballroom.

"I SAW A LIVELY LOOKING PUB ACROSS THE STREET," ISABELLA SAID before her full lips closed around the heavy, silver spoon. When she brought it back out, it gleamed in the candlelight, each drop of soup sucked away. "My sister said you took her to a place like that once."

Oliver shifted on the padded chair and coughed uncomfortably.

"It sounded fun," Isabella purred, leaning close across the cloth-covered tabletop. "Surely just because you've been named prime minister you don't intend to stop having fun."

He sat down his spoon and picked up his wine. "A different kind of fun, perhaps."

"Already prepared to settle down into your role, are you?" she asked with a laugh. "Oliver Wellesley, tamed by the ministry."

"Tamed... I suppose that's as good a term as any," he muttered, glancing around the room.

It was filled with suited and wigged patrons, all speaking quietly over sumptuously prepared dishes, cradling wines that cost several months of a laborer's wage. The staff was immaculately coifed, the place settings gleamed, and the tablecloths were spotless. It was a place to be seen. Dining with Isabella at such a place was as good as a formal announcement of their courtship. Tamed. Indeed.

"My father long lost hope I'd ever be tamed," remarked the baroness, taking another spoonful of soup.

"I cannot imagine a man who could tame you, Isabella," replied Oliver.

"And no woman could tame you," claimed Isabella. "No amount of ministers, either. I'm sure it feels like an endless wave of stuffed jackets and feckless demands, but in time, you'll mold the organization to you. They'll figure out you're a different man than your uncle, the Shackles, or anyone else they've served under. I daresay, the functionaries will appreciate the fresh air once they realize they're allowed to breath it."

Oliver smiled. "No need to flatter me, baroness."

"I mean it honestly," she said. "You've an adventurous side, which is why I've enjoyed our time together. You've a serious side as well, which is why I'd like to keep enjoying time together long into the future, if I had my choice."

Oliver remained silent. He didn't quite know what to say.

"You should know my intentions," continued Isabella. "You are an honorable man and would not take advantage of a young woman like me, would you? I'll stand beside you as long as you allow me, but I'm no longer the girl who is free to frolic as she pleases. I'm a woman now, and I must think of my future."

He forced a smile onto his lips and glanced at the near empty carafe of wine at the side of the table. "Shall we have another bottle, then, and talk of the future?"

"Yes," she replied, her smile growing. "Perhaps the pub is more appropriate for a younger, wilder pair than us. We can still have fun, though, can we not? I know you were not vying for the position, but prime minister, Southundon... it does not have to be all bad, does it?"

Grinning, he nodded. "You are right, it does not have to be all bad. Baroness, I thank you for reminding me of that."

"Please, call me Isabella," she said. "I no longer want to be a baroness."

"Of course," he replied. "Let's have that bottle of wine, shall we? Then perhaps I can give you a tour of my new rooms in the palace? No one will miss you, will they? Your father, Aria?"

"They know where I planned to be."

THE PRIESTESS XI

HER FINGERS PRESSED against her eyes and she tried to rub away the fatigue. Hours, days? She didn't know how long she'd been sequestered in the cramped, dark room at the bottom of the king's tower. She'd been poring over Lilibet's effects, trying to determine the reason for the woman's flight, what goal the queen had been trying to achieve. Standing and stretching, wincing at the crack of her joints and the protest of her muscles, Sam looked around the room.

The bed was rumpled and unmade. She slept there in fits and starts, never more than an hour or two and only when her eyelids had grown so heavy she could no longer continue. There were dirty plates left on several surfaces where she'd brought food from the kitchens and never returned with the cutlery. Empty bottles of wine and pitchers flecked with dry ale foam were scattered like bodies fallen upon the battlefield. Half her candles had burned down, which wasn't helping the strain on her eyes.

Muttering to herself, she moved to a cupboard in the corner of the room and began digging for more candles. She pulled two out, the last ones in the drawer, and scowled. She would have to get more, which meant a visit to the palace staff and an explanation that she was, in fact, in the employ of the Crown.

Days before, she'd tried fae light, but the fickle creatures only stayed lit for an hour before blinking out. They did so as a group and with little warning. After several attempts that left her stumbling in the pitch-black room trying to find more light, she gave up and began doing it the old-fashioned way. She purposefully did not consider why the timid life spirits were so reluctant to show themselves in Lilibet's old rooms.

Holding the two waxy sticks, she lit the wicks from the other candles and arranged them as close as she felt was safe near the open books she was struggling to read.

A man cleared his throat at the doorway to the stairwell that led out of the hidden room.

She jumped. She hadn't heard him coming down.

"M'lord," she murmured, bowing to the king.

"I should send my maid down again, I suppose," he said, eyeing the mess she'd made of the room.

"Yes, m'lord, that would be welcomed."

"You could clean up after yourself, as well," mentioned King Edward.

She shrugged.

Sighing, the king stepped into the room, glancing at the materials on the desk. "Have you learned anything?"

"Some," replied Sam. "Lilibet kept copious notes on her studies and her speculations. It's unclear how much of it is truth and how much theory, but I did find one thing. The source of her knowledge came from a forgotten vault in the Church's library of all places. She was made aware of the trove and removed all of the items to here. That is good news. She was not part of a larger cabal that shares her knowledge. What she knew died with her."

"And any word on how that occurred?" questioned the king, clasping his hands behind his back and pacing on the other side of the table.

"I have not learned anything new, m'lord," she said.

"She is dead, though? You are certain of that?" asked the king. "Oliver said that he never saw the body."

Sam swallowed and nodded. "She is dead, m'lord. There is no doubt."

"How did it happen?" questioned the king. "You've been avoiding me after sending that terse note to hide the uvaan. Oliver told me of the tainted dagger thrusting into her stomach. He said there was no blood."

"The katars you gave me, m'lord," said Sam, "they proved effective."

"I'm glad. I thought they might be, but there's never been a chance to test their efficacy," said the king. "Why are you so reluctant to share the details?"

"I-I killed your wife," stammered Sam, her eyes fixed on the table in front of her.

Her heart hammered in her chest, and she found it difficult to breathe. King Edward knew that, of course, but so far, she'd avoided saying it so explicitly. She wasn't sure how he would react to the knowledge being dragged into the open.

He stopped walking but wasn't speaking.

Tentatively, she peeked at him and saw him using a finger to push through the papers she had scattered on the desk. He must have sensed her gaze because he looked up and met her eyes.

"Our marriage ended twenty years ago," he said. "I am not mad, and long ago, I stopped being sad. What happened, happened. As in all things, the only way forward is ahead. All but history has already forgotten Lilibet Wellesley, and it is time we do as well. Do you understand?"

"I understand," acknowledged Sam.

She meant it. It was best if Lilibet was forgotten, though she knew it'd take more than a single comment to convince Duke. Plus, there was another matter.

She told the king, "I have a problem."

He raised an eyebrow.

"Lilibet and several of the other sorcerers in the Darklands spoke of being able to sense the presence of, ah, a spirit that clings to me, tainting me. If I am to continue in this role, I need to sever the connection."

"What spirit?" asked the king.

"Ca-Mi-He," croaked Sam. "I need guidance on how to perform the ritual, and I think I know of someone who can assist."

"Ca-Mi-He," muttered the king. "Yes, that makes sense. Of course it clung to you after the battle with William. That explains how you were able to… You are right. The connection must be severed. After the Darklands, it is imperative. We must not allow the great spirit any further hold upon this world. Who do you seek? Bishop Constance, the Whitemask? I caution you, girl. If she believes you've bound Ca-Mi-He to yourself, she will not help you. She's going to kill you."

"No, not Constance. No one from the Church," said Sam hurriedly. "I need to go to Westundon."

"Who is in Westundon?" questioned Edward.

"A friend."

"A friend who knows more than you of sorcery?" pressed the king. "You've only been in my service a short time, but already I feel it is important to warn you that you're here to eradicate sorcery, not encourage it."

"I aim to do that, m'lord," assured Sam. "That's all I aim to do, but sometimes, that requires compromises. It requires dipping one's toes into the muck. I beg you to trust me. The people I will consult with represent no threat to the Crown. They are no more than tricksters and hustlers, but they know a little bit of truth."

King Edward frowned.

"If they ever become a threat, if they ever seek to learn more than they do, what better way to monitor them than as a friend?"

"And as a friend," questioned the king, "will you be prepared to do what is necessary, should it become so?"

"I will," said Sam. "I-I've done it before."

Looking skeptical, the king nodded. "Very well, then. Go to Westundon. Inform me when you return."

He turned on his heel and walked to the doorway.

"M'lord," she said, "there is one other mystery. I cannot find why Lilibet pursued sorcery so arduously. There is nothing here that explains why she fled to the Darklands. There is no hint at what she considered so important she left behind everything and everyone. The only clue, she had three uvaan with her in the Darklands. She told me of their properties, which is why I gave you the warning when I first returned. Her enemies, she claimed. I don't know who they were, what they were, but perhaps they are why she agreed to whatever dark bargain was completed in Northundon."

"Sometimes," said the king, looking over his shoulder, "the allure of the dark path is its own reason. When one walks too far, the only way is to keep moving forward. Remember that when you're in Westundon."

"SHE WON'T SEE ME?" ASKED SAM. "I DON'T BELIEVE IT."

Mistress Goldthwaite snorted.

"What?"

"You use her, girl," explained the mistress, leaning forward on her bar. "Perhaps once, when you were girls, you had a real relationship. You don't any longer. Sex, trading favors, it is not what Kalbeth wants. It's not what will keep her here."

"Keep her here?" questioned Sam.

"In the current of life," explained Goldthwaite. "You know what Kalbeth risks every time she dips her fingers into the shroud. That darkness clings to her, and she must cling to life just as hard, or she'll slip to the other side. A roll between the sheets, an occasional visit when you need something, it's not enough."

"I'm not responsible for... I'm not trying to use her," muttered Sam.

"You're not?" Goldthwaite laughed, her braids bouncing merrily around her round face. "You came to tell her you mean to court her, then, or that perhaps you're looking to move with her away from the city? A nice cottage by the sea, is it? You think that you two will settle down and grow old and gray together? Please, girl, don't take me for a fool."

"Kalbeth voiced no complaints the last time I was here," snapped Sam, glaring at the mistress, and knowing as she said it, it wasn't entirely true.

"She was clear with you, girl, had you been listening," declared the mistress. "When you first came back, she would have done anything for you. She gave up a part of herself for that tattoo, in fact, but you didn't take the hand she was offering. You turned your back on her, and she declined to follow. When you first arrived, she would have gone into that old keep without thinking twice about it. It takes two to form a relationship, though. I don't know how many times I told her, but you were the one who finally showed her the truth. That's why she doesn't want anything to do with you."

"I need her!" cried Sam.

"And she needed you, but you didn't give her what she needed," replied Goldthwaite. "She's moved on. You should as well."

"The spirit of Ca-Mi-He is loose in this world," growled Sam, lowering her voice and leaning close to the mistress. "I need her help to banish it once and for all."

"Is it loose?" replied Goldthwaite, a disbelieving smirk on her lips.

"Kalbeth can look into the shadows that cluster around me," said Sam. "She'll see the truth. The taint of Ca-Mi-He is on me. The spirit is tied to me, bound by ropes I cannot break. I wouldn't even know where to start… Kalbeth may be able to sever those ties, Goldthwaite. She can send the great spirit back to where it belongs. For me, for everyone. You know the power of that spirit as well as I. If it is able to use me as a bridge to come fully into this world…"

Frowning, Goldthwaite squinted her eyes, peering at Sam. Sam picked up the mug of ale the mistress had reluctantly poured for her earlier and drank deeply, letting the older woman study her.

"How?" whispered the mistress.

"You can see it?" questioned Sam.

"Who do you think taught Kalbeth?" grouched Goldthwaite. She reached below the bar and retrieved a clear glass bottle. "Come with me."

"What is that?" wondered Sam.

"Gin," remarked the woman, pausing and then selecting a second bottle. "We're going to need it."

"You'll take me to Kalbeth?"

"Spirits, girl," snapped the mistress. "I wasn't going to take you to her before I knew what shadows trailed in your wake. You think I'll let you go anywhere near her now?"

"Don't make me force you," warned Sam.

"She wasn't born from my loins, but Kalbeth is my daughter," said Goldthwaite over her shoulder, leading Sam through a curtained doorway behind the bar of the Lusty Barnacle. "Some-day, I will die for her. I will not take you to her no matter what you threaten, but I may be able to help."

Sam grunted.

ACROSS THE TINY TABLE, A BALD-HEADED, TOOTHLESS OLD MAN licked his lips, staring lasciviously at Mistress Goldthwaite. He was naked in the warm room, giving Sam ample view of the curling black tattoos that scrunched together on his dry, crinkled flesh. His skin sagged across his frame like a sheet, no meat between it and the bones. Now that he was seated across from her, Sam couldn't see below his ribcage, but he had strutted about earlier like a peacock in mating season, except instead of colorful plumage, he sported a small, flaccid penis. Unlike the rest of his body, she couldn't see even a hint of bone beneath that floppy skin. She'd wondered how many years it had been since the old man had gotten the thing erect.

The decrepit condition of his equipment seemed to do little to dampen his ardor for Mistress Goldthwaite, though. He eyed her like a pauper stepping off the streets into the Church for the New Year feast.

"What do you aim to do with her?" Sam asked the old man.

He winked at her. "A better question, girl, is what will I not do?"

"I'm trying to concentrate," muttered Goldthwaite, not looking up at either of them.

The old man laughed, displaying his toothless gums.

Sam rolled her eyes.

"Maybe after I'm done with the mistress, you'd care to give it a ride?" questioned the old man, looking lecherously toward Sam. "I've quite a bit of experience, girl. I've traveled far, and I know the fervor of a Southlands lover, the wanton exuberance of those of Finavia, the forbidden techniques of the Darklands. In my day, women flocked from all over—"

"I'll give you ten sterling if you can get that thing erect right now," challenged Sam.

The old man frowned at her.

"That's what I thought," said Sam, sitting back and glancing at Goldthwaite to see how much more time she needed.

The mistress, still clothed despite the old man's cajoling, was arranging a neat array of consecrated objects. A silver bowl etched inside with intricate geometric patterns traced in copper, a flagon of water blessed by life spirits in the Southlands and transported all of the way to Enhover, a thin vial of gleaming mercury, a decanter of yellowed oil that Sam hoped was from olives but suspected was actually something rather foul, three wax candles infused with the ashes of Goldthwaite's own ancestors, a stick of chalk, a leather strap to bite down on, the long steel dagger that had been tainted by Ca-Mi-He and used to send Sam to the edge of the shroud, and several worn towels from upstairs in the brothel that would be used to mop up the blood.

"You understand I do not have the skill or the strength to banish a spirit such as this?" asked the mistress, glancing at Sam. "All I can hope to do is sever its tie to your soul. I do not know what such a powerful shade may be capable of, so I cannot promise that this ritual will go well even if I execute it flawlessly. If Ca-Mi-He comes here, it may take you, and there is nothing I can do to stop it. And if it attempts to invest in you, I'll send you to the underworld myself. Ca-Mi-He is too strong for us to play around with. You understand I will act quickly if it looks like it might become necessary?"

"Could Kalbeth—"

"No," said Goldthwaite.

Sam nodded.

"You may not survive this," said Goldthwaite, evidently wanting to make absolutely sure her point was understood.

"What are the odds, do you think?" asked Sam.

Goldthwaite shrugged unhelpfully.

In truth, Sam was glad the woman hadn't answered. There wasn't a number Goldthwaite could say which would soothe Sam's nerves.

"Before we begin—" started the old man.

Both Goldthwaite and Sam interrupted him with a firm, "No."

"We shall start soon," said the mistress.

From a chest behind her, she collected a small censer of incense and a long, dark stick of it. She lit both. The censer smelled of jasmine, cardamom, and musk. The stick smelled of burning pitch.

She scrunched her nose and said, "Sorry."

With the foul-smelling stick, she lit the three candles, which smelled no better.

The old man shifted, his eyes glistening brightly in the candlelight.

"What is your name?" Sam asked him, suddenly realizing Goldthwaite had not introduced him.

He winked at her then nodded to the mistress.

Her eyes were closed, and she was whispering quietly beneath her breath. She seemed to have entered a meditative trance. Without looking, she picked up the flagon of water, pouring the silver bowl half full. She stopped right at the midpoint where the extensive copper inlay began on the inside of the container.

Still with her eyes closed, Goldthwaite unstoppered the mercury and put three distinct drops into the bowl. She did the same with the decanter of oil, though it was more like three splashes.

The liquids swirled in the bowl, maintaining distinct globs of three, moving though there should be nothing propelling them in the still water.

Goldthwaite, whispering below an audible volume, picked up the chalk and began to draw. Eyes closed, she operated from some other sight, and Sam realized she recognized none of the symbols or patterns the seer was producing. They were distinct, though, and as the woman continued, a clear design emerged, swirling, beautiful, and then severed in sharp streaks.

Rising onto her knees, the seer continued the pattern, circling the bowl in several concentric loops, drawing closer and closer to the container, and then she made one last dramatic slash toward Sam. Goldthwaite sat back, pinching her pointer finger and thumb together, the chalk perfectly expended by her art.

The old man, a sorrowful smile on his face, nodded to the leather strap.

Wincing, Sam collected it and stood. She opened her mouth and bit down on the leather.

Silent, so as to not interrupt Goldthwaite's incantation, the old man mimed removing a shirt and raised an eyebrow at Sam.

She shook her head no. Instead, she simply pulled up the tail of her shirt, exposing the puckered scar on her ribs that Ca-Mi-He's dagger had left when William Wellesley had stabbed her. She put a finger on the scar and glanced at the old man to make sure he understood.

He picked up the tainted dagger, hefting it, trembling as he held it in his fist. He faced her, no longer full of the confidence he'd displayed earlier.

She could see him sweating, little beads of liquid rolling down his brow. He shifted on his bare feet, flexing his arms, his fingers barely gripping the dagger.

Sam suddenly wasn't sure the old man was going to be able to do it. She met his eyes and then glanced down at the man's limp phallus. When she looked back to his face, she raised an eyebrow questioningly.

He laughed, and then he stabbed her.

SAM WOKE TO EXCRUCIATING PAIN. SHE GASPED AND TRIED TO SIT UP, but firm hands held her down. She didn't have the strength to fight them. She was in a dark room, lit by a pair of fae light globes that had been covered in thin sheets to further dim the illumination. The sheets were stitched with some sort of creature, a bird maybe, and it cast odd shadows around the room. From those shadows, a shape leaned forward. Sam thrashed weakly, unable to free her arms from the constricting blankets that were tucked tightly around her.

"Calm down, girl," whispered a comforting voice. "The stitches are still fresh, and if you go on like that, you'll rip them open again."

Sam stilled, eyeing the dark shape. Goldthwaite? It didn't sound like her.

"Mistress will have me flayed if you end up bleeding out," complained the voice, which definitely did not belong to Goldthwaite. "Told me to keep you company. Told me 'cause she trusts me to care for you. All of my customers leave happy after all."

"Every customer leaves every flophouse happy," cried a

woman from the other side of the bed. "You ain't doing anything that everyone else in this building doesn't do every night."

Sam turned, seeing another dark shape looming closer out of the shadows. Two of Goldthwaite's girls, she realized. Fallen women.

"Everything I do?" snarled the first woman. "If you did everything I do, why they lined up outside of my door every night and you're always down on the floor trolling for drunks?"

"Half the time, the drunks can't get it up, but they pay just the same," guffawed the second woman. "I get paid the same for half the work. Besides, they ain't lined up outside your door 'cause you got some special talent. They lined up 'cause they'll give you a few copper shillings, and you'll let 'em do anything. If the mistress knew you was offerin' the full menu without making the customers pay the full bill, she'd toss you out on the streets!"

"You tell her that, and I'll strangle you with your own hair!" snarled the first woman.

Sam, slowly recovering her senses, realized she was lying directly in the middle of an impending whore fight.

"Go ahead and try it, you two copper—"

"Can someone fetch me some water," rasped Sam. "I'd really appreciate it, and I'd like to talk to the mistress when I can."

Snorting, the second woman removed her hands from Sam's shoulders and stomped to the side of the room where she splashed water into a filthy-looking earthenware cup.

The first woman said, "The mistress isn't on her feet yet, girl. Took a lot out of her, doing what she did."

Sam blinked. "Out of her? I'm the one who... What do you know of what she did?"

"We know Goldthwaite's secret, girl," said the second woman, returning with the cup. "She's a seer. She, well, I don't know all of the details, but I know she musta communed with the spirits on your behalf. It pains her to do so, you know? Takes a lot of strength from her. She'll get right, though. She always does."

"Aye. The beggar took the brunt of it," agreed the first woman.

"The beggar?" asked Sam.

Both women stared down at her.

"The old man," realized Sam.

"Cost him his life," said the first fallen woman, "if you can call what he was living a life. Hope it was worth it, girl, whatever it was the mistress did."

The women moved away, and Sam laid back, the cup of water untouched. The beggar, the old man, he was dead?

TWO DAYS LATER, AS BEST SAM COULD JUDGE IN THE DIMLY LIT ROOM, Goldthwaite finally came shuffling in. The mistress — the seer, Sam supposed she should think of her — looked like she hadn't eaten in a week. Her eyes had the haunted look of one who has seen too much and knows she will do so again.

"Well, you lived," offered Goldthwaite.

"The old man did not?" Sam questioned.

Goldthwaite shook her head. "I was worried he wouldn't. He was old, and the feedback from what the blade did when it pierced your flesh would have been extraordinary. The heart of a man that age isn't as strong as ours."

Sam raised an eyebrow.

"Don't get sassy with me, girl," growled the mistress. "I'll show you the back of my hand just as quickly as I would one of my girls. You'll find I'm young enough for that."

Nobly, Sam remained quiet.

"We severed the connection," continued Goldthwaite. "The taint of the great spirit may waft around you for a bit, detectable by anyone attuned, but it has no hold upon your soul any longer. Shortly, even the aura will fade to nothing. I would avoid any encounter with Ca-Mi-He, of course. Even though you are no longer bound together, it's possible the great spirit could remember you."

Sam nodded. She hadn't planned on contacting Ca-Mi-He, regardless of a previous affiliation. "Who was he?"

"The beggar?" asked Mistress Goldthwaite. "He was someone I once knew, but now, he is no one."

"Everyone is someone," retorted Sam.

"He is no one." Goldthwaite gestured to the blankets near Sam's waist. "You ought to be able to travel within a few days. The girls did their best to patch you up, but I recommend you stop by the royal physician to be certain there is no infection or missed stitches."

"I owe you," said Sam.

"You do," agreed Goldthwaite, her braids bouncing around her face as she nodded.

Frowning, Sam asked her, "What do you want?"

"I want you to stay away from Kalbeth," replied the seer. "The great spirit wasn't the only shadow trailing in your wake. Your soul is steeped in darkness, Samantha. It runs through you like a river. I can see it growing, and you're drawing it to you, filling your soul with the cold of the underworld. I'd tell you to shed the darkness, to embrace the light and the current of life, but your mentor has told you that before. I won't waste my breath. Instead, all I ask is that you stay away from my daughter."

"Who are you to judge?" cracked Sam. "You and Kalbeth both dabble in the underworld."

"I am a mother," responded Goldthwaite. "I am a mother looking out for her daughter. If you have any care for her, Samantha, stay away. Do not take her down this dark path that you walk."

"I'm not walking the dark path," insisted Samantha.

Goldthwaite clutched her hands together in front of her and said, "Two days, and you should be able to travel. I've a business to run, and I expect you to be out of this room at that time, unless you've a mind to take on customers."

"Don't ask me to—"

"Swim the current of life?" interjected Goldthwaite.

Sam gaped at the mistress.

"It's no different than what you do for free, is it?" continued Goldthwaite. "I chose to get something out of it for myself, to make something and leave a legacy for my daughter. You should think about that, what legacy you'll leave behind."

"I—"

Goldthwaite shook her head. "You and your mentor, always chasing shadows. You might as well be chasing your tails. Years ago, I thought that you might be the one for Kalbeth, her anchor in life, her way of staying free of the pull of the shroud. You could have been, as your mentor and I were for each other, but you would rather be chasing those shadows, never slowing long enough to understand what it is you seek. At the cost of a man's life, we peeled the one shadow from your wake, but there are others. It's best if you leave, girl, and forget about Kalbeth. If you need me, you know where to find me, but send a messenger. I want nothing to do with the Church or the Crown."

Sam, speechless, watched as the mistress turned and exited the room.

THE CARTOGRAPHER XV

"THE MEN?" he asked Captain Ainsley, who stood on the other side of his desk looking around his new offices curiously.

"They're content," she replied. "Word got out about your generous bonus, so the pleasure houses laid out the carpets for them. Women, drink, smoke, everything a black-hearted sailor could desire."

Oliver grunted.

"Don't worry, m'lord," she said. "I'll let them have their fun for a day or two and then dry them out. I was thinking about doing some training expeditions to break in the new hires next week. A little fresh air on their faces will sort them."

"And no one has left my service?" he asked.

"You're paying them twice the going rate for crew, now," she reminded. "They've been lined up the airship bridge trying to hire on."

Oliver smirked. "I thought it was adventure that drew the lads and lasses to the open skies."

"Aye, it is," agreed Ainsley, stooping to pull a small statue from a box on the floor. "Is this solid gold?"

"Probably," said Oliver. "This was William's office. I haven't had time to toss out his effects yet."

"A bit morbid, isn't it, taking over the place?" questioned the captain, weighing the statue in her hands.

"It was easier than explaining to every man and woman in the ministry why I would want new offices," responded Oliver. "If it's adventure that calls our crew to the skies, why are they staying? They know we aren't making for the Westlands now, right? Domestic flights, perhaps a few excursions to the United Territories, but nothing farther. My scope has no room for international diplomacy, and I'm afraid there's going to be very little in the way of excitement."

"With you, m'lord, I doubt that," remarked Ainsley, looking at him like she was scolding a naughty cat. "But, as it turns out, while a thirst for adventure may drive a man to raise a sail and seek the horizon, sterling silver is all that it takes to keep him on our crew."

Oliver snorted.

"You mind if I take this?" asked Ainsley, holding up the golden statue.

"Take it?" barked Oliver.

"You're just going to throw it out, aren't you?" challenged the captain. "I'll get it out of your way. One less thing to look at from your uncle."

"It's solid gold, Captain," he said. "That statue is worth a year of your pay."

"Rather ugly at that price," she complained.

"Put the statue down, Captain Ainsley," said Oliver. "It will go into the king's treasury along with the rest of William's valuables, but if you want a chance to earn some sterling, I'll fund an expedition and give you, ah, a quarter share. Crew's bonuses to come from your bit. Make your training exercise a trip to Ivalla. It's offseason for the vineyards there. This time of year, the undercapitalized vintners start having financial troubles. Spend a little time in the wine sinks, find out who's struggling, who's offering barrels on the cheap, and then offer to buy up a portion of that estate's stores. Rent a warehouse and fill it up. We wait a year and then sell the stock for three to four times what you paid. If you can be patient, that will earn yourself and I both a tidy profit. It's a good chance to let the men show what they're capable of before it matters."

"Aye, that's what I thought," said Ainsley. "When it matters. What are you thinking, m'lord? Another foray down to the Darklands? There have been rumors the king…"

He frowned. "It's just a saying, Captain. I'm the prime minister now, a proper, settled gentleman. Isn't that what they're saying in the city?"

Ainsley winked. "If you say so, m'lord. Let me know if anything comes up the next few days. Otherwise, I'll take your advice, sail the Cloud Serpent over to Ivalla, and buy us some wine. Good practice, ey?"

He rolled his eyes and waved for his captain to be dismissed.

The moment she left, a thin-faced man poked his head in. "The baroness inquired about supper this evening, m'lord, and perhaps a night at the theatre?"

"Supper, yes," he said, looking grim-faced at the stack of parchment on his desk. "Bah, we need to be seen in public. The theatre as well. Arrange a mechanical carriage for us this evening, will you, Herb— Shackles?"

"It's Herman, m'lord," said his assistant with a grin. "I know you're used to speaking to my brother, Herbert. A curse on my father for naming us near the same."

"You look just like your brother," remarked Oliver.

"Only a year apart, m'lord," said the man. He winked. "Must have been a quiet year in the empire for my father to be spending so much time with my mother."

Oliver smiled at his new chief of staff. "Indeed."

"I'll send a response to the baroness, m'lord," said the man. "I'll arrange the carriage and tickets as well. Best seats available, of course?"

"Yes, something in one of the better boxes. Thank you," agreed Oliver.

Herman Shackles glanced over his shoulder and said, "President Goldwater has just arrived, m'lord. Shall I send him in?"

"Please," said Oliver, rubbing his face with both hands.

The white-haired President of the Company strolled into the room, an amused grin on his lips. "Duke Wellesley, I don't think I've ever seen you looking so glum. Is service in the ministry that bad already?"

Oliver snorted. "What can I do for you, Goldwater?"

Alvin Goldwater shook his head and took a seat across from Oliver's desk. "Nothing at the moment. The Company incurs favor whenever we can, and we hold our chips until we need to use them. I came to give you an update on some of our affairs and offer a bit of friendly advice."

"An update on Company affairs?" asked Oliver.

"While you're no longer a managing partner, you do have a substantial ownership in several of our expeditions. Imbon, as you know better than I, is a total loss. The Southlands are productive still, and we've never had better luck in the atoll than we did this last year. Recently, we have the other chartered companies to contend with in the Vendatts and the United Territories. They've grown rather aggressive, so we're opening inquiries into, ah, lesser markets. We want to force these upstarts out of business. The directors have found that with Imbon gone, we have more ships than we do profitable trade routes."

"Hams. Salted ones," said Oliver with a wave of his hand. "There was a man importing hams from Finavia to Enhover. I'm told he'd nearly cornered the market and was making a rather tidy profit. Janson Cabineau. He's dead now. It won't replace Imbon, but it will keep a few of our freighters busy."

"I thank you, m'lord," murmured Goldwater. "I wouldn't have thought the President of the Company and the Prime Minister of the Empire would ever have need to discuss importing hams, but it's where we are. The Company is on firm footing, but we took a grave loss in Imbon. Ah, on that subject, have you heard anything about your father requesting compensation for the damage the royal marines suffered? Several hundred men and, worse, an airship… Thank the spirits you recovered the other. Admiral Brach evidently brought up fair consideration to a Company man at a social engagement. No formal request, you understand, but I've no doubt he'll be bringing it to the king."

"You don't need anything, ey?" Oliver laughed. "Don't worry, Goldwater. If it comes up, I'll knock it down. The Crown took the risk sending our marines, and we'll bear the cost of that decision. Coming back to partners and demanding payment is not the way the Crown will conduct her business. We'll stick with the terms as they were initially agreed."

President Goldwater smiled. "Already filling William's shoes. I don't doubt you'll do a far better job than he. He had a firm hand, and he represented the Crown's interests loyally, but he was not bold. Not like you. It was always your father who pushed Enhover ahead. When Philip sits the throne, it will be you who keeps us growing. Your father startles me sometimes. He seems such a bookish sort, but he is wise, and his strategy of expansion has paid incredible dividends. Perhaps there's something to all of that study he does."

"No need for the flattery," remarked Oliver.

Goldwater winked. "I wanted to soften you up for the next discussion, the Westlands."

"You want to lower my share?" queried Oliver.

"Not yet," replied Goldwater, shifting in his chair. "We raised it, you recall, in consideration of your leadership, your airship, and your work with the Crown. If, ah, if you mean to continue service as prime minister…"

"I'll take a five percent share," said Oliver. "I'm no longer in position to serve as the cartographer and leader on the expedition, but I can still manage the political side of things. I believe the Company ought to handle the financing and the material needs as I'm no longer directly involved, but if additional financial backing is required, we can discuss along the usual terms."

The Company president nodded, pinching his chin, appearing to do a quick calculation. "That is fair."

"Do you have another selected to lead the voyage?" wondered Oliver.

"Not yet," admitted Goldwater. "I wanted to establish a gentleman's agreement with you, m'lord, before we began organizing the logistics, and to be honest, that might take some time. We may be speaking further about resources. At the moment, our sights are on the tropics and re-establishing our presence in those seas. Only then will we gaze westward again. When we do, you'll be amongst the first to know. Thank you for agreeing to the change, m'lord. With more shares available, we can attract the right sort when it's time to launch."

"Understood," said Oliver.

"One other thing," said Goldwater. "What I hope is a happy piece of advice. William and his predecessor were both members of the Hunt Club. A comfortable place to get a drink, yes, but even better, it is a place you can find Enhover's dignitaries but not its functionaries." Goldwater leaned forward and tapped his finger on the sheaf of papers sitting on Oliver's desk. "When you need a break from this, or you need to conduct some business outside the watching eyes of the denizens of the ministry, come by the club. As prime minster and a duke, I'm certain the membership will vote your way in a heartbeat, and if they don't, I'll make sure that they do."

"I appreciate that, President Goldwater," acknowledged Oliver.

"Alvin," replied the Company's president. Then he stood, nodded, and left.

Oliver was standing to pour himself a drink when Herman Shackles poked his head back into the room. "Bishop Constance, m'lord. She's here from Ivalla. She's—"

"I know who she is," he muttered, sitting back down. "Send her in."

THE PRIESTESS XII

SHE PUT a hand on the banister that ran along the wall beside the stairwell and climbed up from the rail tunnels beneath the ground. Steadying herself with the banister so she didn't slip on the fog-slick stairs, she felt like she was crawling out of a grave. Her hand felt slimy, and when she looked at it, she saw it was black with wet soot. Cursing, she glanced at the railing and saw a gleaming trail of brass her hand had polished clean.

During the day, countless hands brushed over the banister, constantly brushing away the soot that belched from the chimneys sticking up from the tunnels. During the day, thousands of feet would stomp a clear track through the piles of ash on the ground. Now, an hour after midnight, she kicked up jet black clouds of powder with every step. The soot was like black snow clinging to her damp boots and covering the city with a constant layer of grime.

Not for the first time since arriving in Southundon, she wondered if she could return to Westundon. There was no one to stop her, but she would have to leave the archives that King Edward had opened for her. She'd have to leave the knowledge Lilibet had spent years collecting. She'd have to leave the easy comfort of life in the royal palace. She'd have to leave Duke.

Though, if the infuriating man kept scheduling middle of the night meetings at far-off taverns, she might. She just might do it.

She trudged down the street, counting intersections. Three streets, take a left, walk two blocks, right, find the tavern. Evidently, Duke had something to discuss he wanted no witnesses to. Of course, in the middle of the night, nine out of ten rooms in the palace were empty. When she'd taken the message and hurried to the rail station, she hadn't given it much thought, but not for the first time since she'd boarded the rail car, she wondered why would Duke want to meet her in such a wretched place at such an odd hour.

Isabella Child wasn't the jealous type, was she? She didn't seem like one to worry about his female companions, but maybe things had changed now that they were courting and the woman's reputation was at stake. Or...

Sam paused, looking down the silent street she was supposed to turn on. If there was a tavern that way, they were doing an admirable job of hiding it. She counted again from the stairwell and muttered a curse beneath her breath. She kicked at a clump of soot fouling the avenue then started down the dark street. Someone had requested a meeting. Duke, or someone pretending to be him. There was only one way to find out for sure.

Two more turns, and she stopped.

Find the tavern, the message had said. It was a dead-end street, only one set of lights on at the end of it, a brace of lanterns hanging around a tightly shut door. The glow of more lights on the inside of the building traced the closed shutters over the windows but not a sound escaped. It was no tavern, she was sure of that.

Steeling herself, she walked into the dead-end alley, figuring that since she was there, she might as well get it over with.

She wasn't surprised to hear the scuff of feet behind her. Turning, she saw a dark shape with a heavy cloak. A masked, white face looked at her from beneath the cowl. Two figures stepped out from around the first.

Sam drew her daggers. An ambush, obviously. But who? Why? Couldn't a sorcerer have sent spirits to take her quietly? If they'd—

Cursing, she tucked into a roll, throwing herself in a mad scramble across the cobbles.

There was no sound, but a brush of cold behind her told her that her guess had been correct. They had sent spirits. Jumping to her feet, she spun the daggers in her hands, looking futilely into the darkness, trying to see the shades that had come from behind.

Then, they came from above.

Not shades, but creatures, slender and dark. She saw them only by the gleam of the faint light on their glossy skin.

She dodged away as one thumped down where she'd been standing. It hopped, batting thin wings to lift it higher. Swinging one of her daggers at it, Sam almost dropped the blade when her wrist smacked against a bone-hard leg.

Retreating, she was confused for a moment, but as the creature pursued her, she saw it scrambled on six legs, the clacking against the stone giving her a discomfiting warning that each of those six legs ended in a hard point. A second of the monsters came behind the first, hopping and flapping its wings, trying to work itself around its partner.

Sam couldn't see the figures who'd originally pinned in her the street, but she doubted they would wait long to become involved.

The first of the strange, six-legged monsters hopped and feinted a sharp-tipped leg at her, and the second darted to the side, trying to circle her.

Sam lunged forward, clacking a dagger against the bone of one of the legs and then whipping her second blade against the body of the thing. The tip of the dagger bounced against hard skin, scrapping a shallow laceration, not slowing the creature.

She ducked underneath it and bumped against a leg trying to escape, the bony protrusion bruising her arm when she smacked it. Crouching, she tried to dart the other way, but another leg

AC COBBLE

barred her path, and then the hard body forced her to her knees. She heard a chittering over her shoulder.

Squatting and trying to move quickly, she saw from the dim light of the two lanterns that the thing's head was braced by two mandibles the size of her arm. They clicked as its head tried to curve underneath its body where she crouched.

It couldn't twist to scissor her with those jaws, but she couldn't escape out from under it, either. She was trapped by the solid legs splayed all around her like bars of a gaol.

She stabbed upward, and her dagger bounced away again.

"Hells," she muttered and then offered a silent apology to Kalbeth.

Duck-walking beneath the chitinous skin of the creature, she sheathed her daggers and pinched her wrists. Fingers pressed against the endpoints of her tattoos, she felt a surge of burning heat and strength.

The mandibles clacked a breath from her ear.

She reached out and gripped them with both hands, twisted, and yanked the thing down. It collapsed on her, and she shoved up with her shoulder, still pulling on the mandibles. The creature flew into the air and flipped over, its six legs scrambling help-lessly as she flopped it onto its back. She launched herself, sensing the second monster was coming, and spun over the head of the one she still gripped, yanking on its jaws, twisting its head around as she cartwheeled across its flailing body.

The thing's neck turned and then snapped, brittle bone and skin shearing in half from the force of the pressure she put on it.

She landed lightly and turned to face the second of the monsters. Swinging the first creature's decapitated head like a club, she beat away a sweeping leg from the second. Then, she dropped the head and grabbed another leg that stabbed toward her.

She ripped it from the creature's body, her veins burning like fire was blowing through them, the spirit-bound strength coursing in her blood and muscles. Another leg came within her grasp, and she tore it away as well, the sound of it separating from the creature's body like splintering wood.

Falling, scrambling, the monster tried to flee, but she came after, grabbing limbs and ripping them off, removing the creature's defenses until she was close enough to punch down on its head, crushing the hard skin like it was a metal helmet, pounding the material into the thing's brain. She let loose several more blows until the creature stilled and slumped to the wet cobblestones.

The bone of her hand, fortified by the strength of the spirits, still cracked from the force of the blows. Stifling a cry, she turned, holding her fractured hand close to her body, drawing a kris dagger with the other.

In the faint light from the lanterns, she saw the white-masked figure approaching slowly, flanked by two indistinct shapes.

"Well done," said a woman's voice from behind the mask. Gloved hands clapped together as the cloaked figure approached.

"Bishop Constance," said Sam, suddenly recognizing the voice and realizing the title of Whitemask was evidently quite literal.

Constance stopped within a dozen paces of Sam. Three paces behind her, two taller men wearing black masks stopped. They looked like they could have walked straight out of a meeting of one of Enhover's secret societies, which, Sam wondered, perhaps was the point.

"What do you want?" demanded Sam, shifting nervously, staring at her three opponents, trying to ignore the sharp ache of her broken hand. The scalding heat of the spirits still coursed through her, but already, the supernatural strength was fading. If she was to act against the three of them, she would have to do it quickly.

"What you did was sorcery according to Church law," accused the Whitemask.

Sam shifted her stance, preparing to charge. "Aye, and what were those creatures?"

The two cloaked figures moved around Bishop Constance,

taking places in front of her, their robes trailing along the cobbles, their feet dead silent. They did not raise arms or pose an overt threat, but their intention was clear.

Sam sprang forward, jabbing at the leg of the one on the left with her kris dagger and then reversing it in her hand and stabbing the blade into the abdomen of the one on the right. Her blade met nothing but cloth, and the two figures collapsed into a pile of lifeless fabric.

She gaped at the limp robes and then looked to Constance, who stood still, her white mask reflecting like the moon, the rest of her near invisible.

"Shades," said the bishop. "Minor summonings used to intimidate more than anything. Had they attacked you, I've no doubt you would have prevailed. Did you break your hand on the head of the last formicidae? Their hides are quite tough."

Sam stared at the bishop, confused. She did not reply, afraid of what would leak out of her throat.

"This was a test, girl, and I am pleased that you passed it."

"A test?" snapped Sam, rising to her feet, nervous eyes shifting, looking for more attackers. "What game is it you play, woman?"

"The Council of Seven has gotten old," replied Constance. "Old, and we are no longer seven. But our role is still vital. The threat of sorcery is as great today as it was one hundred years ago. We need fresh blood to sustain us, someone with the strength to do what is necessary. I flatter myself that I am the youngest amongst our leadership, but I am not young. I was grooming Raymond and Bridget to take seats at the table beside me and, in time, my own. They are both dead now. I offered a seat to Thotham, your mentor, but he is dead as well. Everyone I have tapped on the shoulder to succeed me is dead."

Sam frowned.

"You do not have the experience we expect for a council member, but tonight, you've proven you have the skill. The others will object, but I know we need you. Samantha, will you join me on the Council of Seven?"

"What?" asked Sam, stunned. "Since I last saw you, I defied a direct order of yours. I-I fled the responsibilities you'd assigned me, and now you want me to sit at the council table?"

"You were not my first choice," admitted Constance, "but there is no one else."

"Right, you mentioned that," said Sam sardonically. "They're all dead."

The Whitemask nodded but did not reply.

"Well, unfortunately, you're too late," said Sam. "I already have a job."

"The duke," guessed Constance. "He pays you well?"

Sam didn't answer.

"Are you lovers?"

"We are not," said Sam. She hadn't meant Duke, but she figured there was no harm in letting the woman believe that. Sam didn't know if King Edward meant for their arrangement to remain secret or not. When in doubt, best not to tell.

"Leave Duke Wellesley. Come take your rightful role in Romalla," instructed Constance. "If you mean to do more with your life than collect silver, sit on the council with me, and make your mentor proud."

"I believe you've misunderstood our relationship," said Sam. "I don't do what you say, and if you want to throw names in my face, you can forget Thotham's. He declined your offer to join the Council, and I see no reason I should do different."

"We do important work," said Constance. "You can do important work, answering only to me."

"I answer to no one," growled Sam.

"We are all children of the Church."

"The answer is no," declared Sam.

She started to walk around the woman, heading out of the alley, her ears perked for any sign that Bishop Constance would try something. The woman had claimed it was a test. Failing would have meant death. Constance had put Sam's life in grave danger while she still wanted Sam on the council. Now that Sam declined...

"The two creatures you killed are called formicidae," said Constance, speaking to Sam's back. "Forming them and binding them is similar to the way a sorcerer creates and controls wolfmalkin."

Sam slowed but did not turn.

"It is more challenging than calling simple shades, but with enough preparation, it is not difficult. There are advantages to controlling creatures that have physical forms but are not direct manifestations from the underworld," continued Constance. "Utilizing the tattoos as you do is more dangerous than tools such as the formicidae. Your flesh, your soul, is at risk when you activate those patterns. I can teach you to gather strength safely. I can teach you how creatures such as formicidae and wolfmalkin are summoned so that you may defeat them easily or utilize them when you have a need. There is so much you do not know, girl. Do not turn your back on this opportunity."

Glancing over her shoulder, Sam stated, "You're a sorceress."

"I am farther down the path than you, girl, but make no mistake, we are both on it," replied the bishop. "Would you like to see what is ahead, to have a mentor guide you down this dangerous road? All is possible within the circle of the Church."

"I need time to think about it," muttered Sam.

She could hear Constance shaking her head, the silk whispering at her movement, the only sound on the silent street. "A day, a week, if I give you a deadline you will say no. If I force you to decide tonight, you will say no. I see that now. It irritates me, but not enough that I will rescind my offer. It is a standing overture, Samantha. When you are ready to learn what is possible, to take the power necessary to truly do your job, then come find me in Romalla."

Wordlessly, Sam walked out of the alley, booted feet falling quietly on the soot-covered street. Her entire adult life, she'd been dedicated to finding and destroying those on the dark path. She'd committed herself to fighting them with every breath, every beat of her heart. Over and over, she'd been told it was a difficult path to walk and even more difficult to turn from. She'd been told it was seductive, that it would catch her and draw her along. She'd believed it. She had thought she understood, but she'd had no idea.

Shivering in the cool spring air, holding her broken hand close to her chest, she walked the dark, silent streets of Southundon.

THE CARTOGRAPHER XVI

"CARDINAL LANGDON'S interference and now Bishop Constance is in town?" muttered Oliver. "I don't like it."

"Bishop Yates was a sorcerer," remarked his brother John. "Constance is the leader of the Council of Seven, yes? Shouldn't we expect her to be here? Her role in the Church is to hunt down sorcerers, and I can't imagine a much larger failure in the organization than one of their own being a practitioner. Bishop Yates, spirits, he was on track to become cardinal! If she wasn't here, wasn't poking around trying to save face, I imagine the prelate would have her scrubbing pots in the kitchen, or whatever it is the Church does with failed priests."

Sighing, Oliver forced his hand down from his hair where he'd been absentmindedly touching the tie in the back.

"What are you so worried about Bishop Constance for, anyway?" asked John.

"I don't like the politics the Church is playing," responded Oliver.

"The Wellesleys have never been a religious family," reminded John. "We've tolerated the presence of the Church and her priests because they give the commons something to think about other than us, but tolerating is the extent of what we've done. The

Church has never defied us openly, but they've never been comfortable with our presence on Enhover's throne, either. As the empire has expanded, so has their trepidation of the Crown. It's natural. There is only so much power to go around. We'd be well-advised to keep an eye on the Church's machinations, but it's no different than any other time in our history. You'd know that, Oliver, if you had paid attention to our tutors."

Oliver shrugged. "That may be true."

"Just don't say anything in front of Franklin," warned John. "He's in their thrall, you know? Philip and I have been watching, and we could use your attention on him as well, now that you've decided to settle in and become a productive member of the family."

Oliver rolled his eyes but admitted his brother had a point. Langdon, Constance, and Franklin. The Church was reaching into Enhover, curling its fingers around anything it could grasp, but perhaps it wasn't so different from what any powerful organization would attempt to do.

"Come on, brother," said John, raising his wooden practice sword and pulling down the meshed mask that guarded his face. "You bested me the last two bouts, but I was just warming up."

Grinning, Oliver pulled on his own protective gear and launched a wild attack at John.

His brother parried then riposted, and Oliver fell into the rhythm of fencing, letting his brother push him back before he caught John's sword on the side of his own and let it slide past, leaving John open to counterattack.

Cursing, John rubbed his arm where Oliver's wooden blade had thudded into his muscle. "Hells, Oliver, you've gotten a lot better than I recall."

"There were a few tutors I paid attention to," said Oliver with a laugh. Then he raised his practice sword again. "After I'm done bruising you, I'll show you the best way to recover — a trip to the baths, a rub down from the staff there, and a cold ale. You'll be feeling spritely by dinner."

"Matilda is going to regret you staying in Southundon," remarked John. Then he charged, trying to gain by surprise what he'd failed to earn by skill.

Oliver danced out of the way, letting John's momentum pull him off balance. As his brother went stumbling by, Oliver delivered a crack with the flat of his wooden practice sword to John's bottom, cackling at the hearty slap it made.

John yelped and dropped his weapon, clutching his backside with both hands. Scowling at Oliver, he grumbled, "I think that's enough for me."

Oliver offered a mocking bow and suggested, "To the baths, then?"

John shook his head. "I've got work to do, brother. Don't you as well?"

Casually spinning the practice blade in his hands, Oliver responded, "I do, but first, I might take a walk and get a little exercise to clear my head. I've appointments with the minister of rail later this afternoon and dinner tonight with Admiral Brach."

"Better you than I," grumbled John. He frowned. "What was all of that about the baths and the ales? Were you planning to skip the meetings?"

"The rail has been running without my help since our grandfather built the network, and I suspect it will continue to do so long after I'm dead," replied Oliver. "And Brach only wants to meet so he can beg for more resources. He wants the Company to hand us more of Archtan Atoll's levitating rocks than the contract allocates. I will say no, and then we'll have to finish the dinner in awkward small talk. We can reach the same result by avoiding the conversation entirely."

John frowned at him.

"Without the entertainment of corrupting my older brother, I suppose I've no choice but to carry out my duties," said Oliver loftily.

"You do that," instructed John, "and don't think you're going to go sneaking off any time soon. Father, Philip, and I are counting on you. Even Franklin, though he doesn't know it yet. The Crown needs you, Oliver. It's men like you that will keep the empire growing."

John turned and left, and Oliver was alone in the open-air gallery near the top of Southundon's palace. He hung their practice swords on the rack and stared at a twisting bit of vine that climbed from a dirt-filled pot, curling along the balustrades and arches that opened over the rooftops of lower sections of the palace. Verdant green in the early spring, the plant was only a week from budding and providing a bright purple accent to the cold, gray stone. Soon, it would fill the tiled space with the heady scent of flowers, competing with the thick salt air that blew in from the sea.

Oliver leaned on the railing, taking care to avoid the creeping vines as he did. Slate rooftops sprawled below, marking the expanse of the palace. Down from that was a mixture of the same slate and fired-clay tiles. Near the harbor, it was wooden shingles or flat blocks of mortar. It was a jagged range of rooftops, as cold and lifeless as the scree on the north side of the Sheetsand Mountains that bounded Northundon.

Northundon was just as damp as her southern cousin, but outside of the walls, it was a sprawl of bleak terrain only broken by the occasional stand of hearty trees and heather. Outside of Southundon, it was thick forest and grassy, emerald green hills, though Oliver could see little of them from his present perch.

The gallery he was standing on was off a quiet hallway in the royal residences. He'd come there decades before as a child when he wanted to feel like he was back in the north. The descending slate roofs had the same mien as the foothills of the Sheetsands. It was the one place in Southundon he could trick himself into believing was like the north, his mother's home.

There was no warmth in the thought anymore. Southundon, whether or not it felt like it, was his home. Everything in Northundon had been dead for years, and any connection he'd felt to the place was severed the moment he'd spoken to his mother in the Darklands. She wasn't the same as his memory. Nothing would ever be the same.

Lilibet Wellesley had turned her back on her family. She'd abandoned them in a single-minded pursuit of the dark path. Northundon, the Coldlands, Imbon... all of it destroyed, all of it for a relentless commitment to sorcery. She was dead, just like her victims, and all of it had been a waste. It was always a waste. Those memories of her he used to cherish were bitter now.

He held out a finger, pushing aside a leaf on the vine beside him to see an early flower bud not yet splitting into bloom. Soon, that flower would spread wide and soak in the spring sun, the color and the fragrance a call to little insects that would come sup and help the flower spread its seed. By the middle of summer, it would wither in the heat and die. Like people on the Church's wheel, it would die to be reborn again at the next turn of the cycle.

Was Lilibet in the underworld now, grinding under the wheel, awaiting new life? Or had she delved too deeply and entangled herself with connections to spirits who would be reluctant to let her go? Ca-Mi-He, the dark trinity, they'd been on the other side for centuries if what Sam had said was true. They were immortal or, he supposed, the opposite of immortal. They may never again experience life. His mother, his uncle, they'd been trying to achieve similar. They'd meant to balance eternal life with those powerful spirits' eternal death.

Oliver didn't know if it worked that way.

Everything was about balance, true. Sam, the Church, even the sorcerers — they all said it, but what was the balance to those powerful spirits of the dead? Surely not the fragile life spirits he was familiar with. The fae, the dumb forces that were imbued in the floating islands in the atoll, they couldn't be the opposite of the eternal spirits on the other side. He'd felt the presence of Ca-Mi-He. He knew the power and intelligence the spirit commanded.

Maybe he was wrong, though. The strength of the spirits in the levitating stones was a mystery. Was that the same force the Darklands had built their capital on? Did the home of sorcery reside on a floating platform of life? Was that a balance that they had achieved?

He didn't know.

He gently caressed the tightly clenched flower bud, pondering. Maybe all life, all death, was the same. A sudden bloom, a bright presence, and then inevitable death. Natural, persistent, and dumb. They were all mindless energy, struggling to stay alive with no idea why.

Smirking and shaking his head at his own navel-gazing, he flicked the flower bud. Live vivaciously, little flower, he told it, and hells forbid you're ever inflicted with the torment of self-awareness.

He stood up and frowned.

The bud was opening, vivid purple petals creeping into view. The air was chill, but he could feel the warmth emanating from the flower, or was it going into the flower? Had the plant caused it, or had he?

He looked down at his fingers, stunned. Before his eyes, the flower bloomed bright and full. Had he done that?

Silently, he studied his hand. Then he looked up, over the gray roofs of Southundon, past the bustle of the western half of the city, across the river, and to the forest that surrounded the ancient druid keep. A fortress that had been standing for hundreds of years. A permanent fixture there, uncaring of the busy lives of men that swarmed around it. Uncaring of the Wellesleys and the empire they'd fashioned. For what purpose had those old magic users built such a structure? What possible reason could they have for such an effort?

A monument to the forces of life, anchored in the world for as long as anyone could remember. Was there a mirror to the fortress in the underworld? Was that a balance?

Turning on his heel, he decided the minster of the rail could wait. He needed to go for a walk in the forest.

THE PRIESTESS XIII

SHE SPUN AND DUCKED, leapt and twirled. Her daggers thudded against wooden targets, and then she was rolling across the stone floor, lashing out with a foot to send a stool tumbling away. She kicked a boot against a wall, propelling herself into a cartwheel, and flung her daggers at a target at the far side of the room. They thunked into the wood, two yards from a red painted circle.

She cursed. A decade ago, she would have made that throw, even upside down in the middle of a spin. A decade ago, she wouldn't have been breathing so heavy, and her hands wouldn't ache from gripping the hilts of her daggers so that she didn't lose them with each impact against a target. A decade ago, none of these skills had been of much use to her.

At the time, she had been half-convinced Thotham was a crazy old man and sorcery had been driven from Enhover along with the Coldlands raiders. Now, she needed to be deadly. Assassins, summonings, sorcerers, or priests — she expected a threat around every corner and every time she closed her eyes to rest.

She paused for a break, moping sweat from her brow and untying her hair so the jet-black locks fell around her face. She drank deeply from a flagon of water, wishing it was ale. Was it too much ale slowing her down, or was it age?

Was it fear?

She slammed the flagon down. Slowing her or not, she wanted an ale. She needed an ale. She was still thinking about it when she heard quiet footsteps outside of the open door to the dilapidated warehouse. She waited, watching the doorway.

A scraggly-haired head poked around the door. The young girl asked, "Duchess Samantha?"

Sam snorted. "Goldthwaite sent you?"

The urchin shuffled into the open doorway. "She said ya'd give me three pieces sterling silver."

"Did she now?" asked Sam.

"She did," insisted the girl, putting her fists on her hips, puffing out her chest, and tilting her head so that her chin rose into the air.

Rolling her eyes, Sam fished the silver from her purse and flicked it toward the girl's feet. When the girl bent to collect the coins, Sam sprang at her and caught her arm.

Spitting and snarling, the girl tried to pull her arm away, punching at Sam with her small fist.

"Foundling or the Church's creche?" asked Sam, deflecting the young girl's blows with her other hand, keeping her grip locked around the girl's arm, though not so tight as to injure her.

"None of yar business," snapped the girl, still struggling to free herself.

"Foundling, then?" questioned Sam. "If you'd been taken from the Church, you wouldn't still be fighting."

The girl glared at her.

"Where'd Goldthwaite want me to meet her?" asked Sam.

"Befuddled Sage," snapped the girl, evidently deciding quick answers were the fastest way to free her arm.

Sam let go of her. "Never spread your legs for coin, girl. There are other ways, no matter what Goldthwaite tells you."

"Easy for a rich girl to say," retorted the child.

"It's a slippery path," said Sam. "If you've done it once, it's easier to do it again, and before long, it's all that you know. By then, it's too late. It's all anyone will want from you."

The girl eyed her up and down. "What? They don't want that from ya? Goldthwaite knows ya, so ya can't tell me ya never laid on yar back. Maybe ya turned from the path of a whore, but lookin' at those fine clothes ya wear, I'm guessin' ya just reached the end of it and got yarself a rich patron."

Sam frowned.

"So righteous," growled the little girl. "So sure yar path is the right one. I bet ya was from the Church, so ready to tell everyone else what to think, what to do. I'll do what I gotta do, lady, and yar path ain't mine."

"I—" started Sam, but the girl spun and ran away, her bare feet slapping on Westundon's cobblestone streets.

Her path. Why had the girl used that word? What had Goldthwaite told her? Had the mistress meant it as a message, or was the girl simply repeating Sam's own term back?

Grimacing, Sam collected her daggers, her pack, and looked around the empty space. A warehouse, not long abandoned. A Company property that was empty following the disaster at Imbon. She'd sent a message to Goldthwaite from there, requesting a meeting on neutral ground where no one would expect to see them together.

They king wouldn't have had Sam followed, probably. He wouldn't set his inspectors on Goldthwaite's tail and have her brought in. At least, Sam didn't think he would do it while he thought the seer could be of some use to them, but better to play it safe. The Befuddled Sage, not what she'd had in mind for a meeting place, but spirits forsake it, she could use an ale.

"Didn't think I'd see you around here any longer," said the barman, pouring her an ale without asking.

"Aye, I've moved on," replied Sam. "Westundon still feels like home, though."

Andrew nodded and let his gaze flick over her shoulder.

Sam turned and saw Goldthwaite standing in the open door of the pub. The lanterns hanging outside of it backlit her, and it was obvious to everyone in the room she was wearing little underneath of her thin dress.

"Isn't that cold?" asked Sam as the mistress crossed the room and took a seat beside her.

"Is this where you've been going all of these years after you stopped coming to the Lusty Barnacle?" wondered Goldthwaite. "There's not a single other woman in this building."

"I know," said Sam.

"You left the Lusty Barnacle for this?" asked Goldthwaite again incredulously.

"You paid men to kill me," reminded Sam.

Goldthwaite waved a hand dismissively and told Andrew, "Gin. A big mug of it. The biggest mug you got."

"I need your advice," said Sam as the barman moved off to fill Goldthwaite's order.

"That's what your message said," replied Goldthwaite. "I thought we were done with each other. I'm a bit leery of what sort of advice you'd ask of me, girl."

"I worry I've gotten in over my head," admitted Sam.

Andrew guffawed from the other end of the bar where he was eavesdropping on their conversation.

Goldthwaite rolled her eyes. "You're just now realizing that?"

Sam pursed her lips, flexing her hand, feeling the stiffness still in her bones a week after they'd fractured. "I've had it under control until… Yes, I'm realizing it now. I found employment with the king. That's why I came to you to sever the binding. Edward has tasked me with protecting his son and fighting sorcery. I couldn't do that with ties to… to that spirit."

Goldthwaite shook her head. "I suspected it was someone high up, but the king? Spirits, girl."

"When I returned to Southundon, Bishop Constance tracked me down. You've heard of the Whitemask?" asked Sam, ignoring the scowl on Goldthwaite's face. "That is her. She tested me, sending two giant ant-like creatures against me. I killed them both, and then she offered me a seat on the Church's Council of Seven."

Goldthwaite's look was shifting from disgusted to concerned. "I've heard of them. Thotham told me all about the Council as a warning. They... they want you to sit at the council table in Romalla?"

"To do as they ask will require commitment, a sacrifice," said Sam. "To fight sorcery, one must know sorcery. It's a risk, of course, as they're liable to stab anyone in the back that they can. If I join them, it's dangerous. If I don't join them... I have to learn more to protect myself whatever way I choose."

"You're wanting to walk the path in earnest," surmised Goldthwaite.

"I don't want to," said Sam, "but if I knew nothing of the dark arts, I wouldn't have survived as long as I have. If I knew nothing of sorcery, I'd be dead in Harwick, Archtan Atoll, Derbycross, here, Southundon, and without a doubt, the Darklands. I'd be foolish to ignore the simple fact that the little knowledge of sorcery I have is the only thing that has kept me alive through everything. Constance offered me a chance to learn more, thinking I cannot learn on my own, but I do not trust her. It doesn't matter. Whether I join her or if I refuse her, I've realized the only way is forward. This is not a journey I thought I'd ever make, but to continue my work, I must walk the path."

Slowly, the mistress nodded. "Yes, it is like that, sometimes. There is only one way to go. You want me to mentor you?"

"Will you?" asked Sam.

"Ignorance is dangerous," said the mistress. "I imagine you are right. Not knowing could have gotten you killed several times over by now. What Thotham taught you, what you've learned on your own, has given you strength. The dark path is no walk in the park, though, Samantha. You should know the risks. There are grave risks to you, to those you love, to your soul on the other side. Do not take it lightly. Death is only the beginning of the price you may pay."

"I do not take it lightly," said Sam, "but it is the only way."

"It is not," interjected Andrew. The barman was looming over them, his hands braced on his bar, his thick forearms bulging with tense muscle. His bearded chin quivered with barely contained anger. "You seek to hold onto life by embracing death? It is not the way."

"What do you know of it?" asked Sam.

"I know what any fool knows about balance," he growled. "Two sides trying to balance on a point need equal weight. Putting everything on one side is certain to result in a fall. This isn't the way, Sam. To triumph against darkness, you must swim the current. You must dive fully into light and life, not death."

"Trying to get into my pants?" she chided.

He cringed and shook his head. "You've never understood what Thotham taught you, about life, about living. You continue on this way, Sam, and you're going to become what you oppose. You'll gain the skills to kill sorcerers, sure, but that won't be all you use it for. The temptation is too great. The allure of the dark power is far more than you can imagine. Think of Lilibet and what she sacrificed. Is that what you want for yourself?"

"Without sorcery and the help of the spirits," hissed Sam, "Lilibet would still be alive. I couldn't have faced her without the skill I've gained."

"And?" questioned Andrew.

Sam blinked at him.

"He has a point," murmured Goldthwaite, eyeing the barman appreciatively. "I'd heard of this place. Thotham told me about it, but I wondered…"

Andrew shot the mistress a glare, and she smiled, letting her thoughts trail away unspoken.

"Lilibet was evil," declared Sam, ignoring the secret looks

between the two of them. "She had blood on her hands, more of it than I can fathom. I saw her kill a man with my own eyes! She crushed his skull as easily as I'd drink this ale. That kind of power should not exist in this world."

"Aye, she killed some men, did she?" replied Andrew, standing up and pointing a finger at Sam. "So you killed her, ey?"

Sam frowned at him, suspicious.

"There is evil in the world," said Goldthwaite, gesturing with her half-full mug of gin. "I'm not any more sure of this girl's plans than you, barman, but I do know someone's got to stand up to people like Lilibet Wellesley. Someone's got to hold the road between despair and hope."

"The dark path isn't the way," insisted Andrew. "It is too dangerous. The allure is too great."

"It can be trod safely," insisted Goldthwaite.

Andrew glowered at the mistress. "You have the knowledge, but you did not seek it. You've survived the path for so long because you don't walk it. You're standing upon the same spot your mentor left you. That's a world of difference, seer."

"Pour me another ale, will you?" asked Sam, sliding her mug toward the barman.

She'd known the Andrew for years. She trusted him and knew that he wanted the best for her. He cared for her more than just a frequent customer, and the man would feel real sorrow if she fell to sorcery, but he was just a barman. He spent his days behind his counter, pouring libations, listening to his patron's stories. He hadn't seen what she'd seen. He didn't know.

Sam turned to Goldthwaite. "I wouldn't ask if I didn't think it was necessary."

"I know that," said the mistress, shaking her head, her braids swaying with the motion.

"You'll do it, then?"

"I have one condition," replied the mistress. She drew herself up. "I will teach you what I know, everything that I know, but you must promise me that you'll never seek Kalbeth again. That is the price I ask. I will lead you as far along the path as I'm able to walk, but you must forget my daughter exists. No matter what happens to me, I ask for your word that you will not go to her."

Sam sat for a long moment, ignoring Andrew as he plonked a full ale in front of her, spilling the golden liquid on his bar.

Goldthwaite waited patiently, watching her.

Finally, Sam nodded. She reached to the floor of the bar and picked up her pack. She flipped it open and fished out the Book of Law and the sheafs of parchment where she'd taken notes, struggling to translate the obscure grimoire. Even with the resources of Timothy Adriance and Lilibet Wellesley's trove, she'd only gotten every fourth or fifth word, enough to give her tantalizing clues but not enough to conduct the rituals she sought.

"Can you translate this?" she asked Goldthwaite, flipping open the black leather cover.

Goldthwaite, her eyes scanning the yellowed pages over the rim of her cup of gin, nodded slowly. "Yes, girl, I can help with this."

Disgusted, Andrew stalked away, muttering under his breath, snatching up an empty mug and filling it for himself.

Sam tried to ignore the man as he glared at her from the other side of his bar counter. She and Goldthwaite had much to do.

THE CARTOGRAPHER XVII

"HERMAN," complained Oliver. "Is this really necessary? Surely not every piece of correspondence at the ministry needs to pass over this desk? We have thousands of people working hard on these matters, and I'd like to think a few of them can handle their responsibilities without my involvement."

"It's not ministry business," apologized his chief of staff. "This is all personal correspondence."

Oliver looked aghast at the pile of sealed envelopes on his desk. He poked a finger against the neatly stacked tower, and it collapsed, thick paper rustling as the envelopes spread across the polished wood in front of him in a slow avalanche.

"There must be... there must be fifty of these," he stammered. "I hardly know fifty people, much less that many I want to get letters from."

"Fifty letters?" queried Isabella Child. She tugged her dressing gown tight around her body and walked over to look down at his desk. "This seems a rather light post for a prime minster and a duke, if you ask me."

Oliver frowned, scooting his chair back apprehensively.

Isabella turned to Winchester. "Did the duke not receive personal letters while in Westundon?"

"He did, m'lady," replied the valet, looking up from where he was stoking the fire. "Red wine, m'lady, and a plate of cheese and breads?"

"That would suit," she responded. "Some of those dried fruits too, Winchester?"

"Of course, m'lady."

"Wait, Winchester," demanded Oliver. "I never received anything like this in Westundon. A letter or two a day, nothing more. I know I'll get more correspondence as prime minister, but this is outrageous. Surely this is not right..."

"Ah," responded the valet, "in my capacity as your trusted servant, I tossed most of the correspondence addressed to you into the fire. I penned some responses myself, when the sender was of high importance, and I laid out one or two letters a day that I thought you might be interested in. Anymore, and I assumed you would disregard them. Chief of Staff Shackles is managing your post, now."

Oliver frowned, standing up and staring at the pile of correspondence in front of him. He shook his head and repeated, "This is outrageous."

"I'll take these," offered Winchester, scooping up the stack and turning back toward the fire.

"You can't just throw those away!" barked Herman Shackles, clearly offended at the thought. He moved to take the envelopes from the valet.

Winchester handed them over with a shrug and stated, "I am certainly not going to read through that stack, and if you think the duke will, you're horribly mistaken."

"I, ah, I might," mumbled Oliver. He thought perhaps that he should. Fifty letters, though. Fifty!

Shackles deposited the stack back on the desk, and Isabella began sorting through them.

"Sycophants, beggars, and thieves," she murmured, pushing several of the envelopes to one side. She glanced at Oliver's valet. "There are a lot of letters from women, Winchester."

"Always unopened, I assure you, m'lady."

She laughed. "Come now, Winchester. I'm no blushing virgin, and everyone in the empire knows that Oliver is not. How many of those letters each day were from his conquests? How many did he reply to?"

"None of them!" protested Oliver. "I never received letters from women. Certainly none I ever responded to."

Winchester shifted, tugging at the sleeves of his livery. Under his breath, he said, "Perhaps the fire is stoked a bit too hot—"

"You wrote all of those responses?" questioned Isabella, staring at the valet and laughing. "I thought they sounded a bit... formal. Did you read what I wrote?"

"I read them," admitted the valet, pulling at his collar now.

"And what did you think?" asked Isabella.

"You're, ah, quite an evocative scribe, m'lady," said Winchester, twitching like he was being drawn on the rack.

"I'm glad you got something out of it, then," she said, shaking her head at the blushing and sweating man.

"The wine?" he gasped.

"Yes, Winchester, fetch the wine," allowed Isabella with a stern look at the valet.

"You are not angry, are you, m'lady?" asked Winchester suddenly. "I, ah, I've always strived to serve m'lord as best I'm able. With a lady in the house, I know I'll need to adjust..."

"You are right. A lady is in the house now, Winchester," responded Isabella. "I suppose I cannot complain given where our correspondence has gotten me, but from now on, any letters from aspiring paramours should be handed to me. And, Winchester? Do not read my private letters again. Understood?"

Flushing, Winchester shot Oliver a guilty look, nodded, and left.

Herman Shackles cleared his throat. "M'lord, these letters deserve some response."

"We'll figure out a system," said Isabella. Shackles made as if to comment, but she declared, "Oliver is done for the evening, Herman."

The chief of staff swallowed and then left as well.

"I think I may enjoy helping to run the household," murmured Isabella, turning back to the envelopes. "We really must find you a system, though, or perhaps a social secretary? Aria and I shared a girl in Westundon who worked wonders for us. I've never met a more organized person. Unfortunately, she was quite pretty…"

Oliver grunted, looking at the letters as if they were some ominously marked snake. The thought of responding to such a pile was quite impossible, but how was he to know if important business was ignored? Winchester, as well as being intensely loyal, was a bit lazy. It didn't surprise Oliver that the man had a habit of simply throwing things into the fire. As often as Oliver was away on expedition, a dearth of responses would be expected by the minor peers and merchants who tried to get his attention. As prime minister, he would be involved in official Crown business, and he wouldn't have the excuse of travel. He cringed. Things were going to have to change.

"The Befuddled Sage, what is that?" asked Isabella, holding up an envelope. "Is that a pub? Do you get letters from a pub? My, you have an interesting life…"

Grunting, Oliver leaned forward and snatched the envelope from her hand. He tore it open, noting it seemed to have been sealed with candle wax, which flaked away cleanly as he put a thumb underneath of it.

The Befuddled Sage. It sounded familiar. Frowning, he read the page and then tossed it back down on the desk. He rubbed his face with his hands.

Isabella picked it up. "Sam needs help?" she asked. "That is the priestess who clung to your coattails?"

Oliver nodded. "The Befuddled Sage is a pub she frequented. Andrew is the barman."

Winchester knocked on the door and then poked his head in. He had a decanter full of wine and a tray full of cheeses.

"Was one of these incinerated letters from Ainsley?" Oliver asked his valet. "Is she back from the United Territories?"

"I believe so, m'lord," replied Winchester, setting down the refreshments.

"Let her know we sail in the morning," instructed Oliver. "We're going to Westundon."

Nodding, Winchester left, perhaps still thanking the spirits he'd escaped with only a laugh from Isabella.

Oliver watched as his valet shut the door. He stood and walked across the room to pour himself a wine.

Sam in trouble. The barman hadn't written anything else, hadn't provided any details. Sam in trouble. Oliver wondered what she'd gotten herself into. He supposed it didn't matter. She was working for his father now, he suspected, chasing the same spectres she always did, both those brought into the world by sorcerers and those from her past.

Sam was no stranger to trouble or to the Befuddled Sage. If the barman thought it worth writing about, Oliver surmised it was worth going to help. She was his friend, though the oddest, grumpiest, most ungrateful one he recalled ever having. Sipping his wine, he realized he should have told Winchester to pack him a trunk as well. His trunk and his broadsword. Whatever Sam had gotten herself into, he would do what he could.

"I'm going with you," declared Isabella from where she leaned against his desk. "I want to meet this priestess of yours."

"WHERE IS SHE?" HE ASKED THE TATTOOED BEAUTY SITTING ACROSS from him in the small alcove at the back of the bar.

Kalbeth glanced away from Isabella and frowned at him. "I assume you mean Sam, but I've no idea where she is. Did she not move to Southundon, to the royal palace?"

"She did, but yesterday, I received a note from Andrew, the

barman at the Befuddled Sage," explained Oliver. "He said she needed help."

Kalbeth pursed her lips but did not comment.

"Can you really tell the future?" asked Isabella, holding out her palm. "I'd like to pay for a reading."

Kalbeth took Isabella's hand and began kneading the flesh, tracing the lines on the peer's hand with her fingers.

"Andrew said she left with an older woman," added Oliver. "He hasn't seen her since. Said the woman was, ah, perhaps a lady of the night."

Kalbeth winced.

"What?" asked Isabella, looking down at her hand in surprise.

"Not you," hissed Kalbeth. She glanced at Oliver. "My mother. Sam must have been with my mother. She's the proprietress of the Lusty Barnacle. It's, ah, a pub, where one can relax…"

Oliver nodded. "I'll go there and ask around."

Kalbeth shook her head. "Duke Wellesley, it is not a place for you to be seen. I will go there, and I'll tell you what I find. I assume the barman was of no help? Are you staying in the palace?"

Oliver nodded. "You're right. Andrew was worried but offered us no clues. He… Your mother, is she, ah… Does she—"

"Yes," said Kalbeth. "She is more than a simple mistress. She taught me what I know, and she taught Sam's mentor Thotham as well."

Oliver smacked a fist on the table in frustration.

Isabella cleared her throat, and Kalbeth glanced back down at the peer's spread hand.

"When I was a girl," lilted the baroness, "my sister and our friends would pretend we could read each other's palms. We'd make up futures for ourselves — who we'd marry, which palace we'd live in, how many children we might have, the kinds of fantasies little girls dream of, you know?"

"Not much has changed," remarked Kalbeth.

"It is no longer a dream," responded Isabella.

The palmist looked up at her and then to Oliver.

"What do you see in my future?" questioned the baroness.

"I see your dreams, the same as a girl and as a woman," said Kalbeth. "They are clear and fluttering just out of reach. What you desire is not what you need, and what you need will hurt you deeply."

"What does that mean?" asked Isabella. "Why must you seers be so obtuse? My father says it's because you are charlatans, that you see no truth. Tell me plain, what do you see?"

Kalbeth shook her head and brushed a strand of jet-black hair behind her ear. "True seers see possibility, not certainty. We see the potential outcomes of chance."

"And what of my dreams?" demanded Isabella. "What do you see of them?"

"You will live a life much different from what you imagine," said Kalbeth. "Will you become bitter and let it poison you? Will you realize the new life is better than what you dreamt? I see those possibilities, but you are the one who will choose between them."

Isabella frowned at the palmist.

"Sam's tattoos," interrupted Oliver, "they're linked to spirits, aren't they? Could you contact the spirits and find out where she is? I imagine it'd be a bit like scrying except the connection is already there. Easy, no?"

Kalbeth frowned and shook her head. "I have no way of finding those specific spirits."

"Her tattoos?" asked Isabella.

"She has them on her chest and over most of her back," said Oliver. "Kalbeth inked them and tied them to spirits of the underworld. They can grant Sam, ah, certain powers, which helps in the hunt for sorcerers."

"How do you know all of this?" wondered Isabella.

"Because he's seen Sam naked," answered Kalbeth drolly. "He's seen me naked as well. Has he told you about that?"

"Hold on!" protested Oliver.

"He has not mentioned it," said Isabella, taking her hands back slowly. She turned to Oliver. "Do we have something to talk about?"

He shook his head, glaring at the seer. "She's just trying to provoke you because she doesn't like me. There's never been anything sexual between Sam and I. Not between Kalbeth and I, either. They both prefer women. They're lovers."

Isabella looked at Kalbeth, and the seer winked back.

"Andrew told me that when Sam left with this woman, your mother, he was afraid that Sam was walking farther down the path," said Oliver, leaning forward and grabbing Kalbeth's wrist, "farther down the path than she already is. You know Sam, how impulsive she is. You know the risks she'll take, the danger she'll be in... the danger she'll put your mother in."

Kalbeth freed her wrist and tugged her shawl around her shoulders. "Come with me. I'll take you to the Lusty Barnacle. You wait outside while I speak to my mother. Where Goldthwaite is, we'll find Sam."

WHEN THEY GOT TO THE LUSTY BARNACLE, THE PLACE WAS CLOSED. The sounds of saws and hammers bled out from the open doorway. A pair of men looked to be hanging a new door, though it was rectangular, and the doorway itself was tilted far off-kilter. The men were kicking the doorframe in consternation. Oliver noticed the place had new windows, and a new name was freshly painted above the door.

A thickly muscled man wearing a vest and no shirt stood with his arms crossed in front of the building. His hard glare kept away a handful of disheveled people who looked as if they wanted to go inside. Poppy addicts, Oliver guessed. Beside him, Isabella stared, fascinated at the place and the people around it.

Kalbeth ignored it all and stomped up to the muscled man. "Where's Goldthwaite, Rance?"

He shrugged.

Kalbeth's shoulders squared, and she looked as if she was about to give the man a stern lecture.

"I don't know, girl," he said. "A couple of days ago, she sold the Barnacle. I haven't seen her since. New owners ran off most of the girls, but they kept me on. Fixing the place up, see? Aiming for higher paying clientele."

"She sold the place?" questioned Kalbeth. "A couple of days ago?"

"Aye, she didn't tell you?" he questioned. "Thought she was your mum. Guess not, ey?"

Kalbeth spit at the man's feet.

Rance peered around the angry seer, looking like he was prepared to use his giant muscles until he saw Oliver's attire.

"M'lord," he murmured, "the Lusty Barnacle is no more. This new place will be fit for a man like you. Come back next week, m'lord, and I'll see you're taken care of. Just ask for Rance at the bar, and anything you need, you'll have."

Kalbeth turned. "My mother has owned this place since I've known her. She's never been away for more than a few days."

"Where would they have gone?" asked Oliver.

Kalbeth stared back at him, uncertain, worried.

"How is the ministry?" asked Prince Philip.

Oliver grunted, pacing about the room.

"I'm told Isabella Child accompanied you north?" asked Princess Lucinda. "I suppose she is accompanying you many places, now? I have to admit I'm surprised."

"Surprised she's accompanying me or that I'm allowing it?" asked Oliver, glancing at his brother's wife.

"I'm surprised you're willing to settle down," replied Lucinda. "Those ministers tamed you quickly."

He kept pacing.

"Not that we don't appreciate the visit," said Philip, watching his younger brother stalk back and forth across the plush carpet, "but what are you doing here?"

Oliver stopped and sighed. "I was told a friend needed help, but now I cannot find her."

"Can the inspectors assist?" wondered Lucinda.

"Not with this," said Oliver.

"What? Then—" began Philip, but he was interrupted by a knock at the door. He called for it to open, and Herbert Shackles peeked in. Philip asked, "Yes?"

"There's a wire off the glae worm transmission from Glanhow, m'lord." The prince's chief of staff walked in and handed a slip of paper to Philip. He glanced at Oliver. "How is my brother doing, m'lord? He was quite pleased at the appointment on your staff. Just three years out of university, he's making our father proud."

Oliver nodded absentmindedly. "Yes, yes, Herman's doing quite well. A bit stiff, to be honest, but I'm sure he'll come around."

"Not all the Wellesleys have your, ah, casual demeanor, m'lord," said Herbert with a wink.

Princess Lucinda rolled her eyes.

Philip looked up from the wire. "I don't understand, Shackles. What is this saying? The fleet spied greenery in Northundon?"

The chief of staff shrugged. "I'm not certain, m'lord. As you know, nothing has lived in that city since the attack. The fleet claims there is vegetation sprouting near the keep. It looks to be encroaching on the walls, as well."

"I don't understand," repeated Philip.

"I do," said Oliver.

As the eyes in the room turned to him, he regretted speaking. He understood, but he would not explain it. Twenty years ago, Lilibet Wellesley had escaped. She'd lived in the Darklands since then, and the spirits had haunted Northundon, bound by her sorcery. Now that she was dead, the bindings were broken, and the spirits must have returned to the other side of the shroud. It hadn't occurred to him with everything that had happened, but the logic was sound. Northundon was freed. She must have lied about her involvement. She was the one.

"The spirits are gone," he said to his brother and the others. "I-I know it is true. We must go investigate. I will go investigate."

"No!" said Philip. "It's too dangerous, Oliver."

Oliver grinned. His brother didn't know that he'd been inside of the city while it had still been haunted. Philip didn't know Oliver had confronted their mother. Oliver couldn't tell Philip all of that, so instead, he said, "There's no longer any risk. Besides, it is my duty. I am still the Duke of Northundon."

OLIVER HAD LEFT MESSAGES EVERYWHERE HE COULD THINK OF THAT Sam might find them. He'd asked his brother to alert him if she turned up and said similar to Kalbeth and Andrew, but he couldn't wait. Northundon was freed of the presence of the underworld. He had to see it. He had to walk those streets, to breath that air.

He leaned on the gunwale of the Cloud Serpent, watching as they crested the final ridge of the Sheetsand Mountains. Down on the other side, they would find the ruins of his childhood home, his duchy, the land he was to have been responsible for.

"It feels different than the last time we were flying up here," mentioned Ainsley. She held a hand out, palm up, the bright spring sun reflecting on her pale skin.

Oliver nodded but did not reply.

No doubt sensing his mood, Ainsley left him alone, turning back to harangue her crew.

The bright sun, the specks of green strewn across the mountain slope below them, the knowledge that after twenty years, his home was no longer a haunted ruin. It should feel different. It should feel entirely different. This was an awakening, a rebirth.

But it didn't feel different at all. Yet again, he was flying north, searching for answers.

Half an hour later, they cleared the top of the range and began to sail down the other side, the shadow of the airship racing out in front of them. He filled his lungs with the salt air that blew in off the sea, rising in a column against the height of the mountain range.

To the west of them, Glanhow clung to the north coast of Enhover. After the fall of Northundon, it'd grown, serving as the primary fishing port in the province, but it'd never grown to rival Northundon's old might. It would never be near the size of the large cities in the south. There was a stigma to the north, and no one from outside had ever been convinced to move there. Much of it was like the Coldlands, abandoned and empty.

But not dead. Not anymore.

As they sailed closer, Oliver could feel the pall of sorcery had been lifted from around his old home. He couldn't explain it and wouldn't mention it in front of the sailors as they had enough superstitions, but even before Northundon emerged from the haze of the sea air, Oliver knew they would find it empty of the spirits from the underworld. It felt warm despite the chill that remained in the air on the far side of the mountains. It felt full with the tentative thrust of new life. After two decades of hibernation, Northundon was ready to bloom.

"Set us down right outside of the city," he called back to Ainsley.

She perked an eyebrow, as if to ask as if that was wise, but she held her tongue. The crew had seen enough in the Darklands that they would approach cautiously. Ainsley had seen enough that she trusted Oliver.

He smiled at the thought. After all that he'd taken her through, after all that she'd seen and overheard, she still trusted him. People were funny.

It was several hours before they came beside the tumbled walls of the city and lowered the airship to where Oliver and

Ainsley could easily slide down to the ground. During that time, it'd become obvious that the city was changed, even to the untrained eyes of the sailors. The open space around the city was covered with a field of knee-high grass. The cracks between the fallen blocks of the city's walls were filled with weeds, sprouting where they hadn't been seen in decades.

As soon as their boots touched the soil, Oliver could see that light filled the streets instead of shadow. The place was abandoned, and it hadn't felt the trod of a boot outside of his and Sam's months before, but it was alive.

Ainsley, for two city blocks, kept her hands wrapped around the butts of her pistols, but as they progressed, she relaxed and released her weapons.

Desiccated corpses still lay where they'd fallen, and doors and windows gaped like the ruined faces of retired pit fighters, but there was no threat from within the dim interiors of the buildings, just the dusty scent of undisturbed air.

Unerringly, Oliver led Ainsley to the druid fortress at the center of the city.

"This is your home, eh?" asked Ainsley. "Where you grew up?"

"Here and the palace in Southundon," he responded, looking at the dark stone that formed the structure. "Mostly Southundon, actually, but my mother was from here, and this is where she spent much of her time. I would come visit in the summers and stay for a cycle of the moon or longer. In the winters, we'd visit and quickly leave. I think my father wanted to convince me the climate in the capital was far more welcoming. Of course, he still named me Duke of Northundon, so I suppose that wasn't entirely it. Back then, I don't think he ever imagined I'd be anything but the ruler of this place."

"Hunh," said Ainsley, staring at the huge building.

"With people on the streets and life inside, it was a more welcoming place," he told her.

Walking in the open door, they stepped over the same corpses he and Sam had passed before. He followed the same steps that they'd taken, walking directly to his mother's old garden. Without knowing why, he felt compelled to go there, to see it again.

Ainsley walked silently in his wake, looking curiously at the bodies and empty hallways. She muttered, "Now this reminds me of home."

He looked back at her. She shook her head, unwilling to continue the thought. Her time before she had joined the royal marines was a mystery to him, and he allowed her that. He guessed her childhood had not been a pleasant one, and that was all he needed to know.

"Here," he said, pointing at the ruined glass and iron doors that barred the garden from the rest of the building.

They were open, the glass shattered where he'd broken it. It seemed wind and weather had continued the assault, and there was more broken glass in the barrier than there was whole. Air, driven by the wind of the sea, blew steadily into their faces as they stepped outside.

The garden had exploded into a tangled mess of vegetation. Vibrant greens, bright orange and reds, flowers and herbs sprouted from long neglected beds, filling the air with their heady aroma. It was as if after twenty years dormant, the plants could not wait for full spring to burst into life. There was little of the manicured organization that he remembered from when his mother had spent time in the garden, but the return of life filled him with… He frowned. It filled him with nothing. There was no joy at seeing the garden back alive. He'd felt relief, walking through the streets and seeing that the city was free, but the garden itself meant nothing to him now. It was his mother's place, not his, and she'd left it just like she'd left him and the rest of his family. It was alive and thriving but not because of her nurturing, but because she was dead.

He walked across broken tiles and growing weeds to the structure his mother had raised in the center of the garden. The skeletons were still there, still affixed to the pillars that they'd been chained to. The block of black stone, druid stone, was still there, with the corpse splayed across it. The obsidian lance still stuck straight up from the poor creature's ribcage.

Who was it, he wondered? Who had died so that his mother could live?

The city, the building, felt warm to him, full of vigor. The keep itself seemed to bubble around them like a kettle on the fire, life and steam whistling out of it, unable to be contained, but the circular block of stone in the center felt cold. It retained some taint from the underworld. He did not know how, but without touching it, he knew it would be cooler than the space around it. It was foreign, unwelcome.

"Well, the spirits are gone," remarked Ainsley, "though this is a rather grim scene to wake up to. You planning to move back in, to recolonize this place? First thing I'd do is take this out of here. Then, I suppose, all of those corpses we walked past."

"I agree," he said.

He knelt beside the circular block of druid stone and put his hand on it. The cold froze his palm, tried to seep up his arm, but he would not let it. He could feel it pushing, as if it was sentient. Some legacy of his mother's sorcery was trying to maintain a grip from the other side of the shroud, trying to sink its claws into him.

Scowling, he pushed it back, pushed it down and away. There was a surge of resistance, as if he was sliding on an icy lake, unable to maintain his footing. Snarling, he gritted his teeth and imagined himself shoving harder, imagined the heat of the sun, the heat of the fortress, coursing through his body, and he flung the alien chill away, flung it back from where it came.

A grating crack split the air, and he fell back on his bottom, shocked at the noise.

Ainsley, cursing behind him, had already drawn both of her pistols.

Oliver stared at the circular block of stone, now split in two. The chains that had bound the skeleton crumbled into rust, and dry bones slid off to one side, falling gently onto the weed-covered lawn. Around them, the remains of his mother's sacrifice fell to the dirt, the ties that bound the sacrifices vanishing. The obsidian lance collapsed into hundreds of tiny slivers, tinkling as they fell, forming a pile between the half-circles of the altar the lance had been stabbed into.

"Hells," breathed Ainsley. "What did you do?"

"Now the city is free," stated Oliver. "Now people can return."

THE PRIESTESS XIV

MIDDLEBURY WAS a city of industry and movement. Bright steel ribbons spun out from it like the strands of a spiderweb, connecting it to the far-flung corners of Enhover. Middlebury's factories and warehouses pumped goods into that network and supplied the nation's domestic trade. In some ways, it was the heart of the thriving empire, and it wore its purpose proudly, the rail running along the surface, the factories employing the citizens of the place and intricately weaving into all aspects of their lives. With gleaming steel and billowing smoke from manufacturing, it wasn't a place one expected to find secrets.

It was a contrast to Southundon, the capital of the nation, the place Enhover conducted its international affairs. There, the rail ran beneath cobblestoned streets and layers of soot. The merchants of the place met in the dusty halls of Company House and other restricted enclaves. They congregated in exclusive clubs that common residents of the city were barred from. Few understood how those wigged, pompous men built their wealth, how they leaned on the backs of natives in the colonies, and how they seized and exploited resources that they took through force. Secrecy, the backdoor deal and handshake arrangement, was Southundon's stock and trade.

While Southundon operated outside of the view of the common man, Middlebury invited him in and asked him to work. In some ways, that was refreshing, though the economics of knowledge were law there just as anywhere. Whatever new technologies one factory owner developed would be spread like spilled milk throughout the industrial complex. Employees flowed between the buildings, met in the pubs, and spread what they knew. Industrial concerns thrived on knowing first and longest.

Few peers bothered with the frantic pace of innovation in Middlebury. The wealth there was new and volatile. The peers waited, letting others experiment, sweat, compete, and die. Then, the peers would purchase the properties of the winners. They would purchase it in silver and an open door into high society.

The peers maintained their supremacy by carefully expanding their population with the most innovative and industrious of the commons. They would tie that person into their network by titles, social connections, marriages, and business arrangements. In two generations, that new blood would be mixed thoroughly with the old, and the pressing need to innovate would be stifled. The new families would fall into line, wait for another exciting innovation, and then bring its creator into the fold the same way they'd been bought in. Like plants in the forest, new life burst from the detritus of the old.

Sam shook her head and sat down her ale. She was becoming rather intoxicated from it and from the smoke that billowed around Goldthwaite. The combination of the intoxicants and the weeks she'd spent sequestered with the seer were making her thoughts strange. She told the other woman, "That stuff is making me fuzzy-headed."

Goldthwaite smirked. "A clear head is rarely an advantage in my line of work."

"Deciphering the future or prostitution?" questioned Sam.

Goldthwaite shrugged. "Either, I suppose."

"With your talents at sorcery and prognostication," asked Sam, "why do you bother with the other? You could make a fortune dispensing truth."

"Few people really want to know their future, girl," claimed Goldthwaite. "They want to be told a story, a happy one. You can make some coin doing that, telling people what they want to hear, and sometimes it might even come true. Eventually, though, for most of your clients, it won't. Something bad will happen, and they'll blame you for not warning them, but worse is if you do tell them the truth from the beginning. Who wants to know that they'll meet an early end? Who wants to know that their partner is cheating on them? Who wants to pay silver to hear their child is going to be a lazy degenerate, drowning themselves in ale and poppy?"

"You can see all of that from looking at someone's palm?" asked Sam skeptically.

"I can see some of it from looking at their faces when they sit down across from me," replied the seer. "When I do a reading, most often, I simply tell them what they already know. If they believe their husband has been sleeping with their sister, he probably has been. I just offer confirmation. They go on, not necessarily happier, but at least content they know what they thought they knew. It's no sorcery. It's just knowing people, and that is not so different from my other occupation."

Sam nodded. Knowing people, knowing their desires, it's what Goldthwaite did. Sam wondered, was it what the woman was doing to her as well? Was she simply telling Sam what she wanted to hear so that Sam left Kalbeth alone?

Goldthwaite, guessing or knowing what Sam was about to ask, waved the tube of her water pipe at the priestess, a streamer of thick, white smoke trailing in the air. "I can show you some truth, girl, and it won't take long for you to decide for yourself whether or not you wanted to hear it, but what I will teach you is not some far-off promise. You don't need to learn to read palms. You need to learn how to breach the shroud, how to command the spirits that lurk on the other side of it. You'll know the efficacy of what I teach right away."

Sam picked up her ale mug. "We've been here long enough and I've grown tired of watching you pore over the Book of Law. Will you teach me what you taught Kalbeth?"

"Some," confirmed Goldthwaite. "Some of that and some of what I taught your mentor as well." The mistress waved her hand around the circular chamber. "It's fitting we are here, so close to the old man's nest. He and I spent a lot of time there together, studying the dark arts, swimming the current of life. We were two opposites, then. We balanced each other."

"Are you… are you saying you slept with Thotham?" asked Sam, suddenly sitting forward.

"Girl," chided Goldthwaite, grinning at her, "I've slept with nearly everyone. For a man desperate to maintain his grip on the current of life, I was like a rope thrown over the gunwale of a ship. He clung to me like I'd save him. For a time, I like to think that I did. That was before his prophecy, before he found you and Kalbeth, of course. Things changed after that."

Sam fell back and sipped her ale, uncomfortable at the revelation.

"Don't believe me?" questioned Goldthwaite.

"No, I do," murmured Sam. "Is that why you have your own nest here, so close to where his was?"

Goldthwaite nodded. "I had little other reason to be in Middlebury. This is not my kind of place, you know. Too much noise, too little fog. With Kalbeth, it was too far from her and the Barnacle. I've maintained it so I have a place to flee if it ever becomes necessary. Sorcery is about preparation, ey? I've stayed prepared."

"Let's get on with it, then," said Sam. She raised her mug. "We're suitably fuzzy-headed now, are we not? What can you teach me?"

"Everything must balance," said Goldthwaite, pulling on the tube that led to her water pipe and then exhaling a huge cloud of smoke. "Our world, the underworld. Life, death. Man, woman. Light, dark. Cats, dogs. You get the idea. It is all in balance."

"Yes," agreed Sam. "Everyone knows that."

Ignoring her, Goldthwaite kept smoking her pipe, inhaling and exhaling the sweet poppy syrup. Finally, she continued, "The shroud, the barrier, whatever you want to call the space between our world and the other, is more than just a way of keeping separation. It's a pivot point between the two opposites. It does keep them apart, but it is also an inflection where order is restored through the natural force of balance. Sorcery is the art of breaching the barrier, cutting through the shroud to the other side. Good sorcery is done without upsetting the balance."

Sam sat, listening, her mug of ale forgotten in her hands.

"What you described Raffles, Yates, and William Wellesley doing, trying to bind the dark trinity, trying to upset the natural orders of power, that is bad sorcery," continued Goldthwaite. She frowned. "Bad... I mean that from the perspective of the craft. Sorcery, as you know, frequently involves acts which could be construed as bad in terms of what we think is evil. Sacrifices of blood, of the soul, yes? For the purpose of our discussion, I mean to be ambivalent as to the cost of sorcery."

"Ambivalent?" questioned Sam.

"Sorcery, despite its steepest costs, is neither inherently good nor evil," claimed Goldthwaite. "To be certain, it is more often used for terrible purposes, but it can be used for benign ones as well. When I say good or bad in reference to sorcery, I'm speaking solely of upsetting the balance. A skilled sorceress will not upset the relationship between the worlds, while an unskilled one may. Disrupting the balance is often a greater danger than whatever the sorcerer is trying to achieve. Spirits manifested physically in our world, a breach in the shroud left open, massive loss of life like your former foes were planning to achieve an epic end. These are what I describe as bad, and they are why the Church banned the practice."

"Not because of what people were achieving, but because of what could go wrong?" asked Sam.

"Kings and queens like Edward do not need sorcery to cause havoc in this world," pointed out Goldthwaite. "He can direct his royal marines to rain bombs upon any city within reach of an airship and obliterate it. The damage done to the natives in Imbon was not from a sorcerous attack, but a mundane one."

"Northundon was destroyed by sorcery," challenged Sam.

The mistress nodded. "Aye, and the reprisal that obliterated the Coldlands was not sorcery. You see my point, girl? People can do terrible things regardless of what we know. Ignorance of the occult has never prevented a war."

Sam nodded slowly. "That makes some sense. Sorcery is a loaded blunderbuss, a tool. How it is used is up to the one aiming the weapon, but like a blunderbuss, it has the chance of a misfire."

"Sure, I suppose that's as good an analogy as any," said Goldthwaite. "In its eyes-clenched-shut wisdom, the Church banned all sorcery. Like any scared, helpless beast, it overreacted. And like any beast that overreacts, it faced unintended consequences. Sorcerers were killed. They were scattered like leaves on the wind, and they went into hiding. And in hiding, they were free to pursue their art with no constraints, no review by their peers, no one to tell them to stop. Power, unrestrained and hidden, is an awful thing, Samantha. That is how something like Northundon occurs."

Sam stood and stretched.

"Bored already?" asked Goldthwaite.

"No, but I need another ale," replied the priestess. She crossed the room and poured from a pitcher there. "If good sorcery is about balance, and catastrophes like Northundon are bad sorcery, then what was the consequence of that event? Rogue sorcerers caused death and mayhem. What brought the world back into balance? Or is it even in balance?"

"That is a good question," said Goldthwaite, "and I don't know the answer. These things may take time, yes, and the changes that happen can be difficult to discern even for experienced practitioners. We are small sparks on the grand stage of the world. Sometimes, balance may be restored quickly and violently. Sometimes, it could take years or even decades."

Sam slowly walked around the edge of Goldthwaite's nest, noting the thick layer of dust on most of the items stored there and the differences between what the seer kept and the brik-a-brak that others accumulated. There were no blood-flecked daggers, no suspicious-looking bowls that could have only one purpose, no casually stored bones or dried pieces of skin, none of the items which she associated with sorcery, except the symbols and the books.

The seer, like all who practiced the dark art, had symbols and designs scrawled about her nest. Protection, Sam guessed, or merely practice for drawing the real thing. Also like others, Goldthwaite had accumulated small mountains of ancient-looking texts. Knowledge written down and then hidden.

"Why do sorcerers feel compelled to write down what they know?" Sam asked. "I've never done it, but it must take an entire season to write a book. For a group of people so bent on gaining power, they're awfully generous with their time. Of course, they never show anyone their writing, do they? Is it so they can recall the details? If so, why organize it into consumable fashion? Lilibet Wellesley's notes were a sprawling, unintelligible disaster, but I've no doubt she knew what she'd written. She had the reminders she needed. She had an audience of one, but others spend ages on books that no one else will ever read."

"That's a curious question," admitted Goldthwaite. "Not one I've considered before."

"Do you write anything down?" asked Sam.

"Not for others to read," responded Goldthwaite.

"Neither does Kalbeth, from what I saw," said Sam, still walking the perimeter of the room. "Isisandra Dalyrimple, Marquess Colston, Raffles, Yates, William Wellesley... none of them had anything other than personal notes."

"Perhaps there is something different about the authors of those books, then," said the mistress, following Sam's steps as she perused the small library in the room. "They might be seekers of knowledge looking to understand and to classify what they learn. Or perhaps, once they understand what they've found, they are too affrighted to actually do it. The pull of the dark path is irresistible, but it does not pull us all the same way."

"What of the sorcerer who sacrificed Northundon?" asked Sam. "What happened to them, do you think? Were they killed during their ritual and that is why we've never heard from them again? Surely, someone capable of such a feat would not vanish into obscurity after. They must have had some purpose for the bargain they made."

Goldthwaite set down her smoking tube, frowning. "Lilibet Wellesley was the one who conducted the sacrifice, no?"

Sam shrugged. "She said she was not, but who else? She was there, and she survived."

"But what did she gain?" questioned Goldthwaite, guessing Sam's thought. "For such an act, the world must have shuddered violently to return to balance, but how? If she successfully completed the sacrifice, what was her reward? Perhaps she told the truth, and she was not the one. Perhaps the bargain had not yet been completed."

Sam stopped walking.

Goldthwaite stared at her.

"If whatever the sorcerer was attempting had not yet happened," said Sam, "then it may be happening now. And if it was Lilibet, then— Hells. If it was her, then her bindings are broken."

The seer stood. "Northundon. We should go to Northundon."

THE CARTOGRAPHER XVIII

OLIVER and his father stood in the garden looking down at the work happening below. Swarms of men in their shirtsleeves were trundling huge wagons filled with rubble down to the harbor. There, other men took over and rolled the heavy blocks into the sea, building new wharfs and raising the seawall that protected the harbor.

"It would have taken us years to haul that material out of a quarry," observed King Edward.

Oliver grunted. "You could make the argument that it did."

"This port will be the best protected one on the continent when they're done," continued the king, ignoring his son's jibe, "the best protected anywhere in the world, I suppose. Those walls will keep out the worst of the winter storms, and you'll be able to fit four of the Company's largest freighters on the docks. I'd guess a couple of dozen large ships could shelter at anchor behind the wall if it was needed."

"Aye, but why do we need the capacity?" questioned Oliver. "It gives us something to do with the material, but the room in the harbor will be far more than Northundon can use. There's no longer any industry in the north, no reason for the Company to come here. After the work camps break, we'll only have a few hundred hearty souls in residence. We may as well use the rubble, but—"

He frowned at his father's small grin. Oliver glanced back down at the work below, the expanding harbor, the slowly clearing streets, and the sea beyond. What was the old man planning?

"The Coldlands," said Oliver suddenly. "You mean to begin logging the Coldlands and sail the timber here. You'll expand the rail as well?"

"The budget for the rail ministry is due a review, is it not? I'm sure they'd appreciate a chance to build out," replied the king, sounding pleased at Oliver's realization. "We haven't extended the footprint of those tracks since my father's time. The Coldlands is nearly endless forest, son. Untouched and unclaimed. The people are gone. You said that yourself, did you not? There's no one to challenge the Crown's claim of owner-ship. It's an abundant resource, Oliver, and I mean to tap it. With a safe port and rail leading direct to Middlebury, Northundon is going to be bustling. The way to rebuild is through commerce, and we're not going to get there with cod oil."

"But what would we do with all of that timber?"

"What indeed?" replied the king.

Oliver waited, but his father did not answer. "I'm your prime minister, Father. Tell me what you have in mind."

"The Company has a toehold in the Southlands and little more," said the king. "That place has more pirates in residence than it does citizens loyal to the empire. We could expand our presence there, make it safe, and then push down into the steppes and the lands south of Durban. You are the prime minister. Is that what you'd advise? Or perhaps we'll need these resources when the Company finally makes a serious expedition to the Westlands."

Oliver watched his father. The old man had his goatee pinched between his fingers and he was studying the work below.

"Hells," gasped Oliver. "The Darklands. You mean to colonize the Darklands?"

The king turned and winked at his youngest son.

"Are you testing me, Father?" complained Oliver. "Why are you hiding your plans?"

The king shrugged. "I haven't spoken to anyone in detail. Your brother Philip hasn't even sussed out my intentions. You've got a lot of me in you, Oliver. When I return to Southundon, I will call Philip and Admiral Brach in for a meeting, and I'll float the idea to them. Brach will be foaming at the mouth to oversee a new conquest, and Philip will follow along with whatever position I take, as he always does."

"The Darklands," muttered Oliver. "You're doing this because of what I told you?"

His father nodded. "It's not about your mother. It's about everything else you said. A primitive people living seasonally along the river. No major settlements outside of this floating city. They have no cannons, no standing army even."

"They have dragons," remarked Oliver dryly.

"And you killed four of them with one airship," reminded the king. "With a full complement, two-dozen airships captained by the best our fleet has to offer, manned with royal marines trained for air-to-air combat? Think of it! If there were a dozen rocket banks on the deck of each airship, if the decks were treated with fire retardant, if the men knew what to expect…"

"It still leaves the storm wall and the sorcerers who called it," mentioned Oliver.

The king waved a hand dismissively. "If the storm wall can be breached once, it can be done again. Remember, we faced sorcery in the Coldlands, and it gave us little trouble. The denizens of the underworld don't fly. All we need to do is take the capital, and the rest of the nation will crumble. Not just a tribute, not a small island where the Company maintains a colony, but an entire nation. One decisive battle, and we'll build a new phase of this empire. Do you see it, son?"

"You're right," admitted Oliver, looking back down to where the men worked on expanding Northundon's harbor. He took a deep breath and released it. "One decisive battle, and we'll expand the empire."

"You're telling me some sorcerer is about to achieve incredible power?" asked Oliver, glancing between Sam and Goldthwaite and frowning.

"We're saying it's a possibility," responded Sam. "In your vision, the shades claimed Lilibet was part of the bargain, right? If she was the final piece, then the bargain is now complete, and whatever end the sorcerer was trying to achieve can come to fruition. The city is freed, which I think means—"

"The city is freed," interjected Oliver. "Surely that cannot have been the goal of the sorcerer?"

"Agreed," said Sam.

Oliver waved around them, encompassing the sunlit streets, the sprouting greenery. "While you've been in hiding, Northundon has been blooming. It certainly doesn't look like the underworld has invested in this place."

"If Lilibet was part of the sacrifice…"

"Maybe we misunderstood," said Oliver. "I don't know. You are certain she is dead? Could she have been wounded or… or something else?"

Sam shook her head. "That woman we met in the Darklands is dead, Duke. There is no doubt."

"It's been over a moon cycle since we left the Darklands," he responded. "Northundon has returned to life, but nothing awful has happened. If some sorcerer gained incredible power, why aren't they using it? How come nothing has changed except for the good? Maybe Lilibet bound these souls to Northundon as part of her escape from whoever did conduct the sacrifice!"

"Just because we have not noticed it, does not mean nothing is happening," retorted Sam. "Just because it hasn't happened yet, doesn't mean it never will. Maybe I'm wrong, but we'd be foolish not to prepare."

Oliver clenched his fist by his side and began to pace. The women let him stew, but he could feel their eyes on him.

Finally, he stopped and asked, "What do you suggest we do?"

Sam and Goldthwaite looked at each other.

Sam said, "There's one way we can be certain whether the bargain was completed or not, and what is at stake."

"And…" murmured Oliver, getting a nervous tingle.

"We contact Ca-Mi-He," said Sam calmly. "We won't attempt to bind the spirit. We won't attempt to force it to do anything, or even open the shroud enough for it to pour through, but we can communicate with it. I-I have some knowledge of the great spirit, and I think this can work. With Goldthwaite's help, we can find the answers we need."

Oliver blinked at her and shook his head.

"It's the only way, Duke."

"No," he retorted. "No. It cannot be the only way." He glanced at Goldthwaite. "You agree with this?"

The mistress shook her head. "I do not. The connection Samantha has to the spirit will facilitate contact, but it also increases the risk of something going terribly wrong. We should not underestimate the danger—"

"Tens of thousands of souls were sacrificed here!" interrupted Sam. "Think what may happen if someone used that sacrifice to bind the greatest spirit of the underworld. Duke, the trinity promised to drown Enhover in blood. Everything is at risk! Will communication with Ca-Mi-He be easy? Will it be safe? Of course not. Of course it entails danger, but we do not have a choice."

"No!" cried Oliver. "What you suggest is not some fringe sorcery, Sam. It's not some gray area. It's not toeing the line. It's illegal in both Crown and Church law. Hells, Sam, it should be! If some sorcerer attempted to bind Ca-Mi-He twenty years ago, they may not even be alive now. There haven't been any reports that hint at some new, awful power loose in the empire. If something happens, we'll deal with it, but we're not going to go about creating our own sorcerous calamities."

"It's the only way," declared Sam.

"No," he replied. "I forbid it."

"You forbid?" she said, venom in her voice, anger in her eyes.

"I'm the Duke of Northundon, the Prime Minister of Enhover," he said, lowering his voice and taking a step closer toward her. "By the authority granted to me by the Crown, I forbid it. I am serious, Sam. This is too far. You've always said the dark path is difficult to turn from. That is what is happening now. Don't you see? You're being drawn into it, convinced it's the right thing, but it is not. This is not the way."

Sam folded her arms and stared at him, her lips pressed tightly together.

"Sam," said Oliver quietly. "This is an order, and if you disobey, I'll be forced to act." He turned to Goldthwaite. "You too."

The mistress held up her hands and backed away, clearly uninterested in both defying the prime minster and risking the attention of Ca-Mi-He.

"It was all a show, then?" asked Sam bitterly. "I'll admit you had me fooled."

"A show?" he said. "No, there is no show. What do you even mean? Sam, surely you can see this is not right. Whatever evil was attempted in this city must be stopped, but not by doing more of the same. Not by following the same path that my uncle and mother trod down. Look at what happened to them. Look at what sorcery turned them into! That is not the way."

"You cannot fight what you do not know," insisted Sam. "If it wasn't for me, if it wasn't for Thotham and the Council of Seven, sorcerers would be ruling this empire, not your family. The knowledge we have is what has kept this nation free of darkness.

You need me, and you need what I can do. We have to find out if the bargain was completed. We have to know what's coming. It's the only way."

"I won't have it, Sam," declared Oliver. "I'm not going to discuss it. You're commanded to forget this. Do not attempt to contact Ca-Mi-He. I'm ordering you to drop your pursuit of dark knowledge, to stop practicing anything that might be considered sorcery. No more walking the line, Sam. It's done."

"Power is a strange thing, Duke Wellesley," she hissed. "Whether it's from the dark path or a family's iron rule over a nation, it's a strange thing. I've used my power to fight evil. Can you say the same? Would the people of Imbon agree that your way is a better way?"

He stared at her, enraged. He opened his mouth to shout, but instead, he clamped his jaw shut.

She glared at him, waiting for his response, waiting for him to explode.

"Can't you see?" he asked after a long, terrible pause. "Can't you see you're pushing me away, forcing those who care about you from your life? Me, Kalbeth, who else? You're losing your way in the current, Sam, and the dark path is what lays beyond. Do not do this."

Her lips quivering, her arms still wrapped around her, she glanced over her shoulder at Goldthwaite. "Coming?"

The mistress glanced uneasily between the two of them then nodded.

Sam turned to Oliver. "I'll be in Southundon when you change your mind. Your father knows where to find me."

She and the seer left, and Oliver stood alone in his mother's old palace.

He walked to the fireplace burning at the end of the reception hall. It was a huge, empty space meant to warm a room the size of an airship. There was just a small fire in it now, built from ruined furniture scavenged in the keep. He looked into those flames, thinking of the white inferno that had blazed in the underworld, fueled by the sacrifice of the city.

The spirits had told him that his mother was the final piece of the bargain. Sam had insisted that Lilibet was dead. If she was, did that mean the bargain was complete? Had those shades he'd seen in his vision found peace? If Lilibet had been the perpetrator of the sacrifice of Northundon and gained untold power from it, why had she fled? If she was a victim, then someone else must have been involved, but who?

HE SAT, IDLY SKETCHING LINES ON HIS NOTEBOOK, THE SCRATCH OF his quill barely audible over the distant rush of the sea and the whistle of the wind. The city, without the hustle and bustle of man, felt somehow more alive than ever. It was filled with sound, with motion, but not the clatter of mechanical carriage wheels over cobbles, not the vendors hawking their wares in the market squares, or the rumble of steel on steel of the rail. This life felt real, grounded, the way it should be.

His feet dangled down over the battlement of Northundon's keep, his mother's garden behind him, the slate and shingle roofs spreading below. The stone was warm against his trousers and skin when he brushed against it despite the chill in the northern air. He could feel the warmth stirring in response to his presence, a spirit of life welcoming him.

In his notebook, he marked the streets that led from the palace down to the harbor, streets, twisting like veins, curling back and forth as they spilled down the slope.

In Southundon, the avenues were wide and laid out in rigid grids. From the deck of an airship, it looked as if one was looking down on a piece of carefully woven cloth or a game board. Northundon followed the flow of the land. The streets would have been too steep had they been formed in a grid, he supposed, but it looked as if there was more to it than that. They were not switch-backs designed to give maximum rise in minimum space. Instead, they spread through the city like they'd grown that way, branching out like roots of a tree.

He frowned, brushing his lips with the feather of his quill. He held up his notepad, seeing the main avenue that curved around the keep and then split into branches below. A trunk and its roots.

Scrambling down from the battlement, he hurried back inside and up the abandoned stairwell that led to the rooftop of the fortress. He stepped across bare stone and rotten carpet where the workers had not yet cleared it out. He got to the roof and, with his shoulder, shoved open a wooden door that hadn't been used in decades.

Looking south, opposite of the harbor, he began to sketch again, not bothering with the details, just trying to capture the shape of the passages and byways that cut through the city of Northundon.

The main boulevard, linking the city gates and the keep, was the only piece of straight road. The rest of the paths branched off, wiggling sinuously through the stone buildings as if they were merely filling space the structures did not occupy. It was a jarring moment, looking down on it, suddenly wondering whether the roads or the buildings had come first. Were the stones stacked to form buildings beside the streets, or had someone cobbled the streets in between existing buildings?

He knew little of city planning, but he'd spent years mapping various cities throughout the world. He had some sense of how the planning was done. The lines the planners drew defined streets and the neighborhoods that would come, while his lines detailed what already existed. As he looked at Northundon, he realized no master city planner had laid out these streets. No one had designed this place. It had grown.

Below the keep, sealed behind steel gates and barred passages, were tunnels, like the druid keep outside Southundon, but these extended beneath the city of Northundon. Roots pressing into the land.

Standing atop the keep, looking at the streets below where the handful of workers were still picking up and tossing rubble into mechanical wagons, he felt the eager thrum of life pulsing within the city. He could feel the push of vegetation, the ache in the men's backs, and the warmth of the sun chasing away the shadows that had clung to Northundon for far too long. The keep was warm, living stone and from it flowed the breath of life, filling the city with possibility.

In the quiet, he could sense it. Druid magic, he realized. He was feeling druid magic. It wasn't the grand spectacle that was sorcery. It wasn't raw power harnessed to a purpose. It was subtle, and it was always there, pouring possibility into the world.

He put his hands on the stone of the keep, the druid stone grown from the very earth as a whole. It was anchored in the world, its roots snaking deep, connecting it to the land, to the buildings men had carved from it, to the quays around the harbor that men had dumped into the sea, to the water crashing and spilling around those rocks, to the wind gusting above the waves, stirring the newly sprouted leaves in the city, taking the scent of fresh growth to the men working below. It was all connected.

That was the current of life.

The cycle of living and being. The ebb and the flow as man, plant, spirit, and the forces of nature danced together. The current of life was about connection.

He felt that connection deep within the fortress, linking it to the outside. That, he realized, was the strength that had kept the druid structures standing for a thousand years. That welling of life would sustain the keep indefinitely, he guessed. It was anchored there, tied to the structure. As long as that force of life was there, the fortress would stand. It was dynamic, though, living. Like the spirits within the levitating stones, like the fae, the wind and the sea, it sought motion. He wondered if he could release it and free the spirit to roam, but then, would the fortress collapse?

He shook his head, feeling like he'd had too much to drink

and thinking that perhaps being home, seeing it awaken around him, was too much to bear. The idea of returning to Southundon, to its soot-covered streets and screeching metallic clangs, curdled his stomach, but that was where his responsibility was, his family, his home, even if it did not feel like it.

THE PRIESTESS XV

"I'm glad you came to me with these concerns," murmured King Edward, tugging on his goatee as he paced the room. "I confess I know little of how this works. If some occult bargain was completed, then what do you think the sorcerer gained from the arrangement?"

Sam shrugged. "That I do not know."

The king frowned at her. "It was my understanding that it was Lilibet who conducted the sacrifice of Northundon. She was there, and she survived, didn't she? When you and Oliver first returned, I believed this was over. Surely, if some sorcerer gained incredible power recently, we would see the results of it? Otherwise, why go to the trouble?"

Sam had nothing to say. He was right. Now that the bargain was completed, they should be seeing the effects of the ritual, either in the world where it was intended to have an impact or from a person who benefited from the connection to the great spirit.

"Do you plan to contact Ca-Mi-He?" asked the king.

"Your son demanded that I do not," she said.

King Edward nodded, his eyes hard.

"You think I should?" she asked.

"No, I agree with Oliver. You should not," he replied. "It is an incredible risk. Too much of a risk."

"The seer, Goldthwaite, believes we can do it safely," replied Sam. "We will not attempt to bind the great spirit, merely communicate with it. We won't allow it on this side of the shroud. We won't give it a finger-hold on our souls."

"It does not already have one on you?"

Sam grimaced. "We were successful breaking that connection."

The king grunted, clearly doubting her statement.

"If you command it, I will not proceed," she said, "but if I am right, there will be a tide of incredible sorcery that washes over this empire."

"That is dramatic," noted the king.

"Such are the times," replied Sam.

"Goldthwaite, you said the seer's name was? She is the one who assisted you breaking the connection with the great spirit?" asked King Edward. "And you believe she has the knowledge to contact the spirit again?"

"She is, and I do," agreed Sam.

"You are her only apprentice? She has not shared her knowledge with others?"

Sam nodded.

"We're trying to rid this land of sorcerers, not encourage them," remarked the king.

"I agree, m'lord," Sam replied.

She was willing to work with the king and Duke as long as she could, but she was seeing now there was a limit to how far they'd go. There was a point they would stop, and she would have to continue. In Northundon, it was terribly obvious the devastation that sorcery could bring. Tens of thousands had died twenty years earlier. She had to stop that from happening again, whatever it took.

THE CARTOGRAPHER XIX

"You support him on this?" questioned Oliver, lifting his reins and spurring his horse to catch up to his brother.

Philip glanced over his shoulder and shrugged. "I will if he asks me."

"He will," said Oliver, coming alongside his brother on the wide, dirt trail.

The mist that frequently blanketed the city was thick in the forest, curling around the base of the tree trunks and obscuring their vision of anything more than fifty yards in front of them. Somewhere out there, a pack of hunting dogs was coursing through the woods, yipping and barking, trying to catch the scent of a silver fox on the damp air.

Without the hounds, hunting silver foxes was an entirely futile exercise. Their coats blended into the natural mists that clung to Enhover's west coast, and moving quickly near the ground, they were impossible to spot and follow. But once the dogs were on their trail, they could be tracked by scent, and the hunters would spur their mounts into a frantic run through the wet trees, aiming blunderbusses and blasting shot through the leaves and branches, trying to fell one of the svelte animals.

In years past, common and peer alike would be thick in the

forest in the spring, searching for the silver foxes, and they'd been hunted near to extinction. Now, it was illegal to hunt the creatures by anyone without a permit from the Duke of Westundon. The scarcity made their butter-soft pelts worth a veritable fortune.

Poachers had been known to lurk in the Crown's woods, hoping to earn several months' wage by offering a pelt on the underground markets, but the Wellesleys and those peers close to them occasionally made sport of the human prey when the opportunity arose. Poaching was a crime punishable by death, after all, and the previous dukes in the Wellesley line saw little need to sit and judge a trial when they could handle matters in a more efficient manner.

Philip would not do such a thing, of course. He was the consummate rule follower, but every season, there was a rumor or two of some permit-holder granting rough justice. After decades of such behavior, it made the Crown's forest outside of Westundon a rather quiet place. A perfect place for the discussions that Oliver wanted to have with his older brother.

Adjusting his seat so the butt of his blunderbuss no longer dug into his side, Oliver tried another tact. "It'd be outright war, you know, an invasion of a sovereign nation which has given us no cause to attack. There are no resources there that I saw besides a wide river filled with fish. We've little need of fish, brother, with abundant shoals off our own shores. There was some primitive farming Enhover's dirt tillers would sicken at the thought of. It's hardly worth it."

"Aye, and what of the floating city?" asked Philip. "If it's made of the same material we mine in Archtan Atoll, but one hundred times the size of those islands, it's a bounty unlike any other. On a per cubic yard basis, there's no material more valuable in the known world, not even gold. You know that, Oliver. What you describe is several times larger than the sum of the floating islands in the atoll, not to mention a good deal easier to mine. And what if, after seeing your airship, these Darklanders begin building their own? Whether they use them or sell them, Enhover's dominance in the skies will be over the moment we no longer have a monopoly on the levitating stones. Without that advantage, the empire will be challenged from every direction."

"They don't need airships," complained Oliver. "They have dragons."

Philip snorted. "Another reason we should eliminate the threat before it becomes one."

"You sound like father," accused Oliver.

"I am his son and successor," remarked Philip. "Should I not sound like him?"

"Good governance means good balance," challenged Oliver. "You should be the foil to his impulses, keeping him in check and convincing him to steer a middle path. In this case, a path away from outright conquest and war."

"I believe that's the role of the prime minister," suggested Philip.

Oliver winced.

"Father and I both respect your opinion, Oliver," continued the prince. "We've always listened to you, but to convince either of us that we should not proceed, you have to give a reason. Why should we not campaign against the Darklands? They've always given Enhover the cold shoulder. They are a fount of sorcery, as you yourself told me. They have incredible resources that anyone could exploit, and the only thing preventing us from solving all of these problems is a little rough business. It's how our ancestors built the empire, Oliver. It's how we make progress. Tell me plain why we should not do this?"

"People will die," answered Oliver. "Countless people will die."

"Everyone dies," retorted Philip. "I won't say I like the thought, but it's the world we live in. Everyone dies, so shouldn't their death serve some purpose?"

"Some purpose?" cried Oliver.

Philip turned in his saddle and met his brother's angry look. "Enhover has brought peace and prosperity everywhere we have gone. We've settled the wild places, Oliver, made them into proper nations with laws and commerce. It's true that blood has been spilled along the way. It's true that more often than not, given the choice, no one would have asked for our rule, but they've got it. They've got it, and they're better off for it."

"I'm not sure they'd agree," challenged Oliver.

"I haven't seen as much of the world as you, brother, but I've been to the United Territories," said Philip. "I've seen the people there, and they live good lives. I've spoken to their leaders, and not a one of them has protested our rule. There are no rebels in those nations, no one seeking to overthrow us. We treat them fairly, we spare them war, and we give their children a chance at a better, more comfortable life."

"Of course they don't protest to you, Philip," said Oliver. "If they did, it'd be treason, and you'd have their heads cut off. You're correct. Some in the United Territories have become quite comfortable, but it doesn't make it right. How many were killed twenty years ago when we campaigned against them? How are those lives going?"

Philip was saved from a response by the baying of the hounds.

"Here we go!" he called and kicked his mount into a run.

Oliver followed behind him, racing down the dirt track, craning his neck, and listening for the bark of the dogs.

Philip cut across an open field, the grass beneath his horse's hooves still thick with mist, and then he plunged back into the forest, lying low on his horse while branches whipped over his head.

Oliver, more used to the deck of an airship than the back of an animal, held on tight, gritting his teeth and letting his horse follow his brother. The beast, an expensive breed raised for the hunt, knew what it was about and needed little guidance from its rider.

For a quarter hour, they tore through the forest, tracking the braying hounds, and then the barking rose, and Oliver knew the dogs had pinned the fox.

He and Philip burst into a clearing and found the hounds surrounding a young fox, its fur gleaming in the low light. The creature was barring its small, sharp teeth, yipping ferociously and a little bit comically at the larger animals surrounding it.

The dogs kept their distance, some instinct telling them those sharp teeth and little jaws could saw through flesh as easily as a blade.

Beside him, Philip slowed his horse and raised his blunderbuss. He jerked the trigger, a spark striking from the flint of the matchlock, but it did not ignite. "Hells! My powder must have gotten wet in the mist. Take it, Oliver."

Oliver drew his blunderbuss from beside his leg and stared down the cold, brass barrel.

The fox looked at him, seeming to meet his gaze with its small black eyes. They were set in its silver-furred face like deep pools. The creature was warm and free. No domesticated beast like the dogs or the horses. Oliver could feel its warmth, its fear, and its hope upon seeing him. Life welled through the tiny creature, bursting out and spreading through the mist of the forest. An animal, a spirit?

He shifted the barrel of his blunderbuss to the left and pulled the trigger, blasting a scattering of shot to the side of the fox. The dogs, stunned at the eruption of powder, stood stock still as the fox darted around them and vanished into the heavy fog.

"Spirits, Oliver," complained Philip, "that was a terrible shot."

"I'm better with my broadsword," claimed Oliver, blowing the curling wisp of smoke from his barrel. "To be honest, brother, it's been years since I've done much practice with a firearm."

"Doesn't take that much," chided Philip, shaking his own weapon and scowling at the firing mechanism. "These things will spread shot two or three yards across from his range. If you can get them to fire, that is. Hells, it's a wonder you didn't put a single pellet into it. It's been ages since I've seen someone miss so poorly. Have you already been into the ale this morning?"

"It's a cold day, brother. There's no shame in fortifying oneself a little before sport," replied Oliver. "No fox fur gloves for Lucinda after this hunt, I suppose."

"The hounds can catch the scent again," said Philip. "We just need to run them out of this clearing and let them get the smell of the powder out of their nostrils. There's still light in the day to run the fox down."

Oliver shook his head. "It won't stop running for hours after that. Let's go on back, get a glass of wine, and put our feet up in front of the fire."

Philip stared into the fog and shook out the dead powder from his blunderbuss.

"Isabella is here," said Oliver. "Perhaps she'll bring her sister along. Since I've begun formally courting Isabella, Aria has grown jealous, and her attire has gotten downright scandalous. You ought to see it, Philip. I'm shocked her father lets her out of sight with so much flesh on display."

Philip rolled his shoulders, smirking. "Fine. Let's head back to the palace and see if we can arrange a drink with your ladies before Lucinda finds out I'm back. As you say, it's wretched weather this morning. Those twins… You're a lucky man, brother."

Oliver nodded, wondering if it was true.

THE PRIESTESS XVI

SHE SLAMMED the sheaf of paper down on the table in frustration. Goldthwaite's translation of the Book of Law, the accumulated wisdom of the Feet of Sehet, was a bunch of mad scribbling for the most part. When it was coherent, an incredible number of the rituals and diagrams related to membership in the order. Glamours for an aspirant to stay interested in the order, bindings to keep initiates from speaking of what they learned, rituals that were purposefully illegal to give members another incentive to keep quiet and never let the authorities know what happened within the chapter house. It was all a self-aggrandizing circle. Tricks for those in power to use sorcery to stay in power so they could continue using sorcery — but to very little purpose.

There were some summonings that could have use, scrying, for example, with a cleaner, easier to perform sequence than what she knew. There were ways to bind minor spirits to perform simple tasks such as spying or carrying a message, parlour tricks for the most part. There was no insight on how Marquess Colston had transformed himself into a giant, flying monstrosity. There was no recipe for building a wolfmalkin and certainly nothing that pertained to contacting and safely communicating with the most powerful spirits of the underworld.

Sighing, she stood and stretched, her lithe body bending to her will, though not as easily as it once had. She needed to practice, to swing her daggers, to move. Instead, she'd spent days buried under books and papers written years before she was born. It was archaic and from a time that was no longer relevant. Who needed a spirit to transfer messages when a glae worm transmission could do it just as easily and without the mess of a blood sacrifice? Who would speed their footsteps when they could simply board the rail or, better yet, an airship? Why bother spending days fashioning a glamour when a little silver across a man's palm was just as effective?

The world had moved on from the painstakingly archived knowledge in the Book of Law. Spirits forsake it, she wondered if more than a dozen people in Enhover could even read the language. Technology ruled now, technology and a higher form of sorcery that was beyond the ancient scholars.

Northundon, what she'd seen beneath Derbycross, what Yates had summoned in his home, it was a different caliber of strength. The dark trinity, Ca-Mi-He, that was where the real power lay. Lilibet had not written down whatever it was that allowed her to transform into what Sam had witnessed in the Darklands. That knowledge wasn't to be found in her hidden, windowless lair.

Sam grabbed her daggers and belted them around her waist. She shrugged into her vest and pulled on her boots. Why bother learning lesser summonings when a spirit such as Ca-Mi-He could be contacted? She was wasting her time in study. She'd always acted on instinct. That was what she must do now. She must act. The time for thinking was done.

She walked out of the room and locked it behind her, leaving the chamber in the palace and heading into the city to find Goldthwaite. It was time they summoned the great spirit, regardless of what the Wellesleys had demanded. It was time they got to the bottom of how Lilibet obtained her power, to the bottom of the bargain which had sealed the fate of Northundon.

Sᴀᴍ ᴄᴀᴜᴛɪᴏᴜsʟʏ ᴄʟɪᴍʙᴇᴅ ᴛʜᴇ ᴄʀᴇᴀᴋɪɴɢ ᴡᴏᴏᴅ-ᴘʟᴀɴᴋ sᴛᴀɪʀs ᴛᴏ ᴛʜᴇ fourth floor of the tenement. Goldthwaite had rented a flat there, eschewing more comfortable accommodations closer to the palace. The mistress said it was the type of place she felt comfortable in, though it made Sam cringe just touching the door to walk inside. She didn't put her hand anywhere near the splintery, suspiciously stained railing that led up the stairs.

Behind loose doors, bound shut with ragged twine, she heard coughs, arguments, the clatter of crockery, and sex. Smells, mostly bad, pervaded the narrow stairwell. It was the type of place no one was like to ask many questions, and that was what Goldthwaite had been looking for. Sam didn't think the mistress would be in danger from Oliver, but someone had gained from the sacrifice of Northundon. Someone would be prepared to eliminate potential threats. Without the seer, Sam had no hope of contacting Ca-Mi-He and finding out who was behind it all. As was always the case with sorcery, secrecy was their only option.

She reached the top floor of the building and looked down the dark hall. On this floor, the flats were weekly rentals and were largely vacant. Renters would be prostitutes, poppy addicts who'd come into a little bit of silver, and those types. Goldthwaite's types.

Sam walked down the hall, watching the half-open doorways leading to empty rooms. She paused a dozen paces from the seer's. It was ajar. Cursing, Sam drew her two kris daggers and listened. She heard nothing except for the sounds of life below.

Moving slowly, rolling her heel to her toe with each step to minimize the sound of her feet on the decrepit floorboards, she stalked to the door. Drawing a deep breath, she reared back and kicked. The door flew open, crashing against the inside wall, sliding wetly across the uneven boards of the floor. She was almost sick.

The scent of blood and offal assailed her. Even in the dim light of a single, curtain-covered window, she could see the floor was slick with blood, dotted with clumps of gristle and flesh. Splatter was strewn like it'd been flung from a paintbrush. A tuft of braided hair was wedged under the doorway where it'd been opened.

There was a mark across the bloody floor where the door had swung and no other marks that Sam saw. No footsteps, nothing to show a person leaving. Clearly, the door hadn't been opened since whatever had happened. Frowning, Sam came to the discomfiting realization that there was no skin amongst the tattered remains of Goldthwaite. There were twisted, shattered bits of bone, clumps of muscle, organs, and hair, but nothing that resembled an exterior layer of skin.

Uncomfortably, she compared the scene to what she recalled of Lannia's death. The missing material seemed more akin to the carnage caused by the reaver, she thought, and there was no other body that could have been spirit possessed. Was it an intentional echo of Lannia's murder, a message? Whatever had happened, Goldthwaite certainly hadn't done it to herself.

Sam stood there for several minutes, looking into the room and letting her eyes rove over what was left of the seer. Sam's mind bounced between thoughts of leaving so that she wasn't caught standing outside the doorway and wondering what the inspectors would think when they came across the scene.

Moncrief and his men would see instantly what she had. There was no doubt it was sorcery.

Sam shook her head, thinking she needed to... do what? The woman was dead, and nothing Sam was going to do would change that. Sam paused, frowning. She supposed she ought to tell Kalbeth that her mother was dead. It would be better for the woman to hear it from a friend instead of stumbling across Goldthwaite's presence on the other side. That would be an unpleasant discovery, to be sure.

Kalbeth wanted nothing to do with Sam but perhaps a letter. She could do that, she supposed.

She shuddered, wanting to turn away and leave, but sitting in the midst of the floor, in a place clear of the worst of the gore, was a paper envelope. Cream, flecked with red specks, but not covered like the rest of the open surfaces. It must have been left there after the attacker finished.

Grimacing, Sam moved into the room quickly, trying to ignore the sticky sound of her feet walking across the tacky blood. She picked up the envelope and went back into the hallway before opening it. Thick paper, a red wax seal. Fine script in an elegant hand covered a small slip of parchment.

You have made your choice, and you follow a path that few have dared to tread. Incredible wisdom, incredible power, lay at the end of your journey, but there is a cost to those rewards. When you've decided you are prepared to pay the cost, when you are willing to commit, come find me.

The envelope, the handwriting, it was the same as she'd found beneath the dead old man in the Coldlands, hidden inside of his reliquary. The same person had left her a message there and here, the same person who thought she was upon the dark path, who evidently thought she would join them.

No longer bothering to hide her footsteps, Sam walked down the hallway. "Come find me," said the note. They expected she would know who they were, know where to go. Who—

She stopped, halfway down the stairs.

Who knew she was working with Goldthwaite? Who could have raced ahead of them to the Coldlands? The resources, the knowledge, there wasn't anyone who—

She began walking again, her stomach roiling, her head swirling. Duke wouldn't believe it. She didn't want to believe it, but the pieces slid together like a puzzle she did not know she was working. She knew who it was.

THE CARTOGRAPHER XX

HE PACED along the side of the airship, looking down at the activity three hundred yards below them. Two huge freighters were tied to the wharf, depositing their cargo of rough timber shipped from the Coldlands. It would be milled on site in Northundon, most of it used to rebuild where war and time had damaged the city. The next batch would be dedicated to a massive new warehouse complex and railyard next to the harbor. Eventually, those raw trunks would supply the material for a giant new ship works. The clamor of progress rose from the harbor, audible even from his perch on the airship.

Progress.

He snorted, shaking his head.

Northundon had been a quiet province with a quiet capital to suite it. The commerce in the region rose and fell with the shoals of fish off the shore. It had none of the heavy industry and rapidly changing technology that Southundon or Middlebury relied upon. For the most part, its people had been content with that.

Oliver had spent enough time in the southern cities to understand why. Coming north after time in Southundon used to be like dipping into a cool bath on a hot summer day. Down south, one could not escape the constant chatter of wheels on rail or the rumble as it passed beneath the streets. Soot floated above the city like spring clouds, drifting down and settling on the rooftops, the streets, and the people. The harbor was full of strange and wonderful goods, the markets packed full of shouting vendors, selling items much too expensive for the common folk. The food, brought in from the middle of the country, wasn't as fresh as elsewhere, but it was plentiful, at least for one of his means.

The entertainment in Southundon had the same frantic, demanding pace as the rest of the city. Each season, the theatre had new shows, the old ones forgotten by the time the curtains rose again. The performances were brash, unpolished, like they might have been had the show had time to mature. The racetrack was surrounded by the ebullient cries of the winners and the wails of the losers. The horse owners and jockeys were constantly pushing for speed no matter the risks. They had to keep the people coming and betting. A quarter league away, the glue factories had little need to search for supply. The sand in the fighting pits was stained red, left there for a week to build the fervor of the drunks who came to watch. The pugilists danced and weaved to the cheers and jeers of those who'd paid to see them bleed. It was a city that knew no pause, that never stopped to assess whether it was on the right path. It was busy, hectic, and loud.

Northundon had been a place where time moved with the natural rhythms of nature, unhurried, patient. The fish would come when they did. The weather would change as it wont. Northundon was no longer the same, though. As it had hibernated beneath the haunted shadow of the spectres, Enhover had changed around it. The nation was no longer a budding empire spreading from the mercantile houses and palaces out into the world. It had become a vast, hungry beast. It had sunk claws into most of the known world, and it was viciously pulling what it found there into the gaping, hungry maw of its people. They'd conquered, and now, they wanted to enjoy the spoils of that effort.

Northundon would be part of that now, a gnashing tooth, taking in the felled trees of the Coldlands and turning them into goods to feed the empire and expand it. Northundon's newly erected mills and ship works would build war ships that the empire may spread its arms wider and haul in more wealth. More wealth, more power, more.

Oliver shuddered, looking down at the work taking place below. Wealth spent so that they could earn more. Everyone struggled, climbing the mountain higher, climbing it to nowhere.

His father's and Admiral Brach's plan for the Darklands was reliant on airships. They were necessary to attack the floating capital and deal with the dragons. While Enhover's airships were engaged in a far-off land, it was necessary to maintain the empire's presence elsewhere. Their flag must be seen in the Vendatts and at the major cities in the United Territories. Enhover's flags should flutter above the world's harbors like mosquitos in the summer.

That was what they'd planned for Northundon. The northern city would become the world's largest ship works. Fed from the vast stretches of untouched timber in the Coldlands, Northundon would build a fleet with which Enhover could cover the world.

In time, those sea-going vessels would be replaced by airships, if what they believed about the Darklands' capital was true. From there, they could mine enough levitating stones to float hundreds of airships. They just had to get rid of the people first.

But that was years away. Even after a successful campaign, building airships was a complicated process, and it took time. The ships Northundon created were needed now, but they would be useful for decades. As the airships expanded the empire's reach, the sea-going freighters would hold it together.

It was his father's new model for expanding the empire, and it made Oliver sick, knowing that it was going to work. It made him sick, but he would do his part, for his family, for the Crown.

He turned to find Captain Ainsley watching him.

"Seen enough, m'lord?" she asked.

"More than enough," he responded. "Take us back down the

coast. We'll observe the progress on the new rail line, and then we'll head for home."

Ainsley nodded, and the men began adjusting the sails.

"Everything worth having comes at a cost," claimed the king.

"But for what purpose?" questioned Oliver. "A larger empire, more territory to rule?"

Edward laughed. "Yes, more territory to rule. For the Crown, for you and your brothers, for their children and yours should you get around to having them. That is why our ancestors did it, Oliver. They consolidated Enhover not for themselves, but for future generations. I've expanded our empire not for myself, but for you, and those who come after."

"And if we don't want it?" asked Oliver. "Franklin is content underneath the luminous glow of the Church's circle. Philip marches only where you tell him, and John doesn't even want to be in Southundon! He maneuvered himself out of power's path, or else he would be serving as prime minister instead of me."

A twinkle in his eye, his father said, "There was a time when I did not want power, either. A time when I thought of tending to my family and watching them grow. We knew little of the colonies when I was just a few years younger than you. We knew little of the heights that were possible. I pursued simple goals, as you do now. I wanted to marry, and I did. I wanted to excel at my studies, and I did. I wanted to prepare myself to take over the throne, and I did. They were simple things, mostly things that had been done before by many people. There came a time, though, when I realized there was more that I could achieve. Through Northundon, the Coldlands, and the United Territories, I saw the opportunity was far larger than I ever imagined. I could not turn away from it. It could be done, so I felt it must be."

Oliver stalked back and forth, uncomfortable with the idea of this new conquest, this war born of greed and lust. He was honest enough, though, to see that his father was right. It was the way it had always been. Enhover expanded, the Crown's grip upon the world grew, and it was paid for in blood. Even before their family's rule, in other empires, it had always been that way.

His father, evidently guessing at his thoughts, asked, "Oliver, if the Wellesleys disappeared from the world's politics, what do you think would happen?"

He frowned at his father.

"You do not like what we do," said the king, "What do you propose instead? You think me an awful person, carving pieces of this world out for you and your brothers. You think it selfish that we live in this palace and decide the fates of all."

"All is a bit of a stretch," muttered Oliver.

"In time, maybe it won't be," remarked the king.

Oliver grunted.

"With power, you can steer humanity the way you want them to go," continued the king. "You can decide right and wrong, the waft and the weave of how men and women live their lives. Who better than you, Oliver? Who better than our family, the Crown? That is why I do what I do. I cannot think of anyone better than I — better than us — to lead. Can you?"

"I don't think all of the people we rule would agree," said Oliver.

The king waved his hand dismissively. "I'm not asking them. I'm asking you. Who better than the Crown to lead this world? Tell me a name, Oliver."

Oliver raised his hand to his head then quickly forced it down.

"You cannot tell me a name because there is no name," declared the king. "The Church, the Congress of Lords, the Company, you know as well as I that they only think of themselves. The governments of Finavia, the Southlands? One has their nose so high in the air that they're probably not even aware there are common people fouling their landscapes. The other is worse than the pirates that they allow to flock in their harbors. It is us, the Wellesleys, who brought modern technology, law, and commerce to many of these places. It is us who have secured peaceful futures for the children. Do you know how many have died in the United Territories due to war this last decade, Oliver?"

He winced. He knew the number his father was looking for but had trouble saying it.

"None, my boy, none," crowed King Edward. "You were never a student of history, but surely you recall the bloody past of that continent. A decade without war may very well be unique. Since someone figured out how to sharpen a stick, Rhensar, Finavia, and Ivalla have been stabbing each other with them. We have eliminated war for millions of people! Yes, the cost was high. People died to make it so, but what they purchased with their lives was a better future for others."

"Death for less death," muttered Oliver, shaking his head.

"We've made those places better," argued the king. "Choose any measure you like and tell me the world is not better off due to our rule. We will bring the same order to the Darklands. Conquest is for us, yes, but also for them. Everything I do, I do for the Crown and the empire. I've done so much… You will never know how far I've gone so that you and your brothers can have this, so that everyone can have this."

Oliver glanced at his father. The old man was staring down at his hands.

"Father, you do not have to do this," said Oliver. "Everything that has been set in motion can be stopped or even redirected to another purpose. We can find use for the Coldlands' timber outside of ships of war. If we encourage the Company to further explore the Westlands, we may need every piece of wood we can get our hands on. We can still expand the footprint of Enhover without undue bloodshed."

The king shook his head. "No, my boy, it is too late for that. This empire is like one of those giant freighters the Company employs at sea. We are capable of much but slow to turn. We've set a course for the Darklands, and that is where we shall sail."

"You keep saying we, but you are the king!" barked Oliver.

Smirking, his father looked up at him. "Yes, I am."

"Then it's not too late to change your mind."

King Edward stood, stretching. "It is. We've walked too far to turn around now, my boy. Go on, then. I've said my piece, and you've said yours. I have much to do this evening, and I am sure you do as well."

Oliver turned to leave.

"Oliver," said the king, stopping him before the door. "If you think of someone who'd rule better than you or your brothers, let me know, will you? Someone you'd trust more than yourself, ey? Do you think there is anyone like that? Because if there is not, then you've a burden, Oliver. You've a burden to the Crown, to Enhover, and to all of the lands that fall beneath the keel of our airships. You're responsible for those people, just as I am. If you cannot think of another who can bring them a better life, then do not lecture me about the course I've chosen. You've a burden, Oliver. You owe them your leadership."

Oliver left.

THE PRIESTESS XVII

"WHY?" she asked.

King Edward stepped from around the screen where he'd been bathing. He wore baggy, silk trousers, and his chest was bare. His skin was dusted with a scattering of silver hairs and stretched taut over a muscled but thin frame. He looked to be in good shape, even if he'd been a fraction of his age.

He tugged on a silk dressing shirt and told her, "I find I sleep better in silk. It's smooth against the skin, soothing. You should try it."

She replied. "I've been told that before."

"No tattoos," he said, opening his shirt again as if to show her his chest and then closing it and wrapping a tie around his waist. "Is that why you pushed past my servants to intrude on my bath, you expected to see some?"

"What did you buy with such a sacrifice?" asked Sam. "Enhover was a powerful nation, and you were on the cusp of becoming its king. You had a wife, a family, and an empire. What was it you sought?"

"Wine?" asked the king, moving to a table at the side of the room. His silk trousers whispered, the only sound in the room other than the crackling fire. His bare feet padded noiselessly across the carpeted floor.

He moved confidently, gracefully. He was lean muscle and bone. It was as if his body spent no energy maintaining strength it did not need or putting on fat that it did not want. He looked incredibly healthy for his age, remarkably spry. How had she not noticed that before? How had no one noticed it?

He poured her a glass and left it on the table then turned to face her. "Perhaps you'll want it later."

"Why did you do it?"

"Everything comes at a cost," he answered, raising his wine to his lips before continuing, "Enhover was a powerful nation, I suppose, but not so powerful as you may think. We were locked into maritime skirmishes with Finavia, and they were slowly and certainly taking over the Vendatt Islands. We had the nascent airships, but they'd yet to be tested in battle. At the time, they were no deterrent, just a curiosity. The Church's grubby hands had been pushed into half the peer's pockets and their whispers into the hearts of the commons. The cardinal and the bishops commanded a respect that the Crown had not enjoyed for a generation. And there was the Company. The Company had revenues that challenged our own with none of the Crown's responsibilities. Those merchant princes, kings in their own mind, they would have ruled us, both my family and the empire. They would have ruled us and would have sold us the moment it suited them. They care for nothing but lining their own coffers with sparkling silver."

The king began to pace, agitated, but not angry.

"We were rotting from within, and it was just a matter of time until Enhover crumbled. Would the Church undermine the authority of the government? Would Finavia defeat us on the field of battle? Or my greatest worry, would the Company undermine Crown authority to the point we were nothing but empty puppets? We needed strength, Samantha. The kings of our empire are the rock that the Crown sits upon. If we are not strong, if I am not strong, then all will fall."

Sam shifted, her hands gripping her kris daggers, but the king made no move to lunge for a weapon, no move to call for his guards, no move to perform some ritual. No, it seemed he wanted to speak to her, to tell her why.

She had to know. It was burning inside of her, the desire to find the bottom of the mystery, to find out why this had all begun. It had driven her to take the foolish risk of speaking to the man before she pounced, allowing him that moment of time to prepare a defense. But he wasn't. He was talking. It made her palms sweat as she wondered if he was telling the truth, afraid that he was.

"If I'd done nothing, if I'd continued the path of our predecessors, Enhover would be a failing state," claimed the king. "In my lifetime, in that of my children, we could have fallen. All empires fall, eventually, but that does not mean I want it during my time upon the throne or during that of my children. When an empire falls, there is suffering, girl, like our people have not experienced for hundreds of years. Everything the Crown has achieved would be gone."

Sam stepped closer, trying to get within range to strike when the time came.

"You've heard that, yes, all empires fall?" he asked her.

She nodded.

"It is true," he said. "Every empire that has straddled the lines of nations has fallen. Every one but one. Enhover. It alone has not fallen. We are the latest, one could argue, but I aim for us to be the greatest. I aim to hold this nation together for centuries, millennia."

She shifted forward again, pretending she was walking toward the wine, trying to get close enough to the king she could pounce.

He laughed, watching her slink closer. "Do you think I'm a good king? Are the people of Enhover well cared for?"

She paused, frowning.

"I had a similar discussion with my son, Oliver, earlier today," remarked King Edward. "He's unhappy with my plans for the Darklands. He does not yet understand. I asked him, and I will ask you as well, who better than I to rule Enhover? Who better than I to rule everywhere? It is a serious question."

"I—" she began then snapped her mouth shut. What was the man playing at?

"There's no nation more prosperous than ours," continued the king. "There is none more peaceful. I've stopped the ceaseless border wars in the United Territories. We've halved the incidences of piracy in the waters off the Southlands. In the tropics, people have access to medicines and opportunities they never knew existed. Technology is flourishing. The world is effectively shrinking. My finance minister tells me that under my reign, it's quite possible that economic activity across the globe may double. Double! Fewer people die as children than before I sat upon the throne, did you know that? It is true."

She blinked.

"More prosperity for the empire means less need to work," he said, raising a finger. "Less work for the youngest of our citizens means more time in the schools, less time in the fields. Along with improved nutrition, access to medicines, it's led to longer, safer lives. With the technologies I am sponsoring, that will continue. Thanks to the might of my military, we're ending the small, bitter conflicts that kill so many and serve so little purpose."

Sam shifted uncomfortably.

"That is why I did it, my girl," said King Edward. "I did it so I could save our empire, so I could save the world. A terrible cost of lives, yes, but wasn't it worth it? You wondered what terrible things a sorcerer would do with the power gained from Northundon, but look. The fruits of that sacrifice are all around us."

She didn't answer. She couldn't answer. She could only listen.

"Oliver said exactly the same thing," mentioned the king, a wry smirk on his lips. "If you think my son Philip will serve the empire more aptly than I, then strike your blow. If you think Oliver would be best seated upon the throne, then you have much work to do. He has three older brothers and a number of nieces and nephews." The king took a step forward. "And if you fancy someone other than a Wellesley should wear the crown or that this empire be shattered upon the blade of your dagger, first do everyone the courtesy of thinking hard about what that future may look like. If my line dies, there will be no peaceful transfer of power. There will be war. There will be blood. What happened in Northundon twenty years ago will look like nothing compared to the carnage the fall of the Wellesleys will bring. Every two-shilling peer in the Congress of Lords will be mustering men, marching to battle. Pierre de Bussy will raise his banner in Finavia, but Rhensar and Ivalla will die before they bend a knee to that man. The Church, the Company, they'll let the others bleed then put their boots upon the throats of the survivors. Is that the future you want to see?"

The king strode across the room, turning his back to her, and looked into his fire.

Sam was speechless, unable to comprehend what the man was telling her. He showed no fear, which would worry her except he clearly wanted her to believe him. He wanted to explain himself because he wanted to recruit her to his cause. Since she'd known him, since they'd first met, he'd been trying to recruit her. The assignments with Oliver, the leeway they'd been granted to pursue sorcerers, the subtle pushes and hints, the help, the access to Lilibet's trove, it had all been an effort to draw her down, for her to follow the dark path behind him. The king wanted her as his apprentice.

Was that such a bad thing?

"Have some wine, girl," advised King Edward.

"The notes in the Coldlands and… and in Goldthwaite's room," stammered Sam. "It was you!"

King Edward turned to her, the fireplace casting his shape in a dark silhouette. "Yes, it was."

"Why?"

She had to hear it from his lips. She had to hear it before she could believe it.

"Amongst my sons, Philip and John have no aptitude for sorcery," explained King Edward. "They don't have the drive, the passion to walk the dark path. Franklin, perhaps he could, but he's consumed by the Church, unable to see past his ecumenical fervor. They may be capable rulers one day, but my sons cannot bear the true weight of my mantle."

"And Oliver?" asked Sam.

"He is the balance," said the king.

She frowned at him.

"He's a druid," continued Edward. "His affinity is with life, with the spirits of this world, not of the other. His power is the answer to my own strength, the world swinging back to the middle. He has potential to be a great man but not a great sorcerer. I thought once... but no. His path is clear, and it is not mine."

"You will kill him?"

"Of course not!" exclaimed the king. "I could have killed him a thousand times if that was my desire. No, I want Oliver to live, to support the Crown and our empire. He is like me and the opposite of me. He is the one who will expand our boundaries, draw new lines upon our maps. He is the one who will grow our empire, because when it stops growing, when we no longer find new territories to consume, we will consume ourselves. That is the day the empire will crumble, no matter what I do."

"But—"

"Oliver is a druid," interjected the king. "He expands and he grows. It is his nature. If he, and you and I, serve the Crown as I envision, our collapse is far off. Hundreds, thousands of years from now, if we manage it correctly. If you, I, and Oliver manage it correctly."

"Me?" exclaimed Sam, staggering back from the king.

"Do you want to know what is at the end of the dark path?" asked the king. "I can show you."

"I don't understand," she mumbled.

"You're worried I am going to ask you to kill Oliver," said the king. "I told you, I want him to live, to share in the burden of supporting the Crown. The price I ask is not for you to kill him, but for you to convince him."

"Convince him…" she babbled.

"Convince him that working with us is for the good of the people," explained King Edward. "By joining us, he can bring balance. He can help our people thrive. That is what I want you to convince him of. He is my child, but he does not listen to me."

"And if I cannot convince him?" asked Sam.

"Preventing rot in the empire, removing the dead wood, that will always be an important task," replied the king. "It is what you were born to do, what your mentor trained you for your entire life. I can help you fulfill your destiny. You can still play the role that Thotham's prophecy foretold."

"Oliver will not follow you onto the dark path," said Sam. "When he finds out who — what — you are…"

The king laughed. "You have no idea who or what I am, girl. From the beginning, you have been wrong, and you still are, but that can change. You can learn. You can know. All I ask is that you convince Oliver to join us first."

Sam frowned.

"And if he cannot be convinced," continued the king, "then he is an obstacle to Enhover's future, and like any obstacle, he'll need to be removed."

"You'd kill your own son?" gasped Sam.

"I told you if that was what I wanted, then I could have done it nearly any day since his birth," said the king. "It is not what I want, but if he leaves me no choice…"

Sam released her daggers, her hands still curled into claws. She stalked over to the table where he'd sat her wine glass, and she picked it up. She finished half of the glass in one gulp.

"Walking the dark path is a difficult journey, fraught with danger, and costly in ways that most women cannot imagine," said King Edward. "Oliver, the son of a king, the son of a sorcerer and a sorceress, a man who has trod the underworld in his dreams, a druid… His life and his death hold immense potential. His seed, or his blood, would be of great value to one upon the path who knows what to do with it."

"You… I don't…"

"Oliver will help us or hinder us, depending on what you can achieve," declared King Edward. "His seed or his blood, that is the price I ask from you."

"You're making the assumption I will join you," growled Sam.

King Edward shook his head. "You are on the dark path, girl. It is a walk that I know well. It's too late for you to turn. You've made your choice, and now, Oliver must make his. Go to him. Let him choose."

"And if I do not?" challenged Sam, setting the wine glass down.

"I released the rest of the reavers," said the king calmly, toying with his own glass. "Those creatures are hungry, mindless, and they will not stop. You recall the emblem you embedded in the druid keep across the river, the one calling to them? I infused a bit of my son's spit into the creation, and you assisted me with your own. The reavers will be called to the emblem, and from it, they will know you. They'll track you like a hound chases a fox. I would guess that by a turn of the clock after midnight, they'll be in the city. You cannot face them as you are. Only with the power you can gather from my son may you survive the night. He's down in the baths. I made sure he'd be alone there. His blood or his seed, girl. Let him choose. Then you do as you must to save yourself. I will be waiting."

THE CARTOGRAPHER XXI

OLIVER SHOOK HIMSELF LIKE A DOG, droplets of water flicking off into the thick clouds of mist that hung over the thermally warmed waters. His body was finally relaxed, muscles nearly limp.

Following the meeting with his father, he'd been tense, like a spring pressed too tight. He'd taken that energy to the practice yards, thrashing several marines with a wooden blade before their stifled curses and sullen looks had driven him away. Reluctant to strike at a member of the royal family or surprised by his vigor, he wasn't sure. It didn't matter. They weren't the outlet he was seeking. He'd needed release, some way to vent the boiling froth of... of what?

Confusion, he supposed. His father had twisted him like the lines of a river across a plain, forcing him down turns, coming back on himself, and losing sight of where he'd been, where he was going.

The old man had a point, though, didn't he? The awful might of Enhover was paid for in blood, but was the value the empire brought worth that terrible cost? There was no more bickering between the United Territories. Children in Archtan Atoll were given schooling, something that hadn't existed prior to the Company's occupation. Even the Southlands, with its deeply imbedded culture of privateering, was a safer place than it used to be. The world, arguably, was better off because of what King Edward Wellesley and their ancestors had wrought.

Oliver poured himself an ale from a cooled pitcher and walked through the silent caverns of the baths. It was strangely empty, at that hour, but there was only one entry and one exit. He'd spoken to the guards just a quarter hour before to order more ale, and there had been no threat, no concern. Perhaps everyone was at the new show which was getting such rave reviews down at the theatre. John had asked if he'd attend, but Oliver couldn't. Not tonight.

"Fancy sharing that ale?" asked a voice.

He nearly spilled the mug, jumping and almost slipping on the damp tiles of the steam room floor. "Sam?"

She emerged from the fog, naked.

"Ah..."

She took the ale from his hand, her wrist lingering a moment against his. She sipped deeply then handed it back, licking her lips. "That's quite good."

He nodded.

"This is my first time in the palace baths," she said. "They're... expansive. Care to show me around?"

Nodding again, he took her to where the pools were. The baths had several of them with varying levels of warmth. He showed her different rooms where attendants could give rub downs, where a barber would be stationed during the day, where one could rinse with chilled pitchers to wash away the steam sweat. Sam walked beside him, close, and he felt a bit of apprehension. What was she doing there? Trying to make up with him after the argument about sorcery? Was she up to something else?

Sam was as strong-willed as they came, and he had no doubt she would push the limits of his command, but from what he'd heard, she hadn't practiced the dark art against his wishes. She'd kept quiet, meeting with the king, training with her blades, and avoiding the seer.

She'd avoided Oliver as well, which had stung, but he understood. He had been harsh with her when they'd argued in Northundon. He'd used his authority as a royal for the first time with her. It wasn't the first time he'd done that with a friend, though, and it always destroyed the relationship. Unfortunately, there'd been no choice. If he'd said nothing, she would have ventured too far. Without his intervention, she would walk the dark path and be no better than those she sought to stop.

Why was she there? Had she come up with a new angle, a new way to talk him into relenting?

As they walked back into the steam chamber, he asked her, "Come to convince me to change my mind?"

"Convince you?" she asked, stumbling.

He caught her. Her naked body was slick from the steam that billowed all around them, and she slid against his own bare skin.

She righted herself, half a hand away from him, and shivered. "That's not what you meant, was it?"

"What I..." he mumbled. "About pursuing the dark path, trying to contact Ca-Mi-He, I won't change my mind, Sam. It's too dangerous."

"Ah, of course," she said, taking his ale from him again.

"There's more in the steam room," he said and led her there, where the mist hung thick, obscuring anything more than ten yards away.

The room was set with benches scattered around the floor where one could rest while sweat poured out, leeching away the toxins. The chamber was normally filled with sweating men and women, but tonight, it was quiet. Oliver refilled the ale and turned to find Sam standing behind him, close again.

"Ah, here you go." He handed her the ale.

He walked around her, conscious of his nudity. In the steam room, both men and women walked around with nothing more than a towel to wrap around their waists, if they were so inclined. Tonight, with the room empty except for the two of them, it felt uncomfortably intimate. He sat on a bench and stretched his arms in front of him, moving his legs awkwardly, unable to find a comfortable way of hiding his middle bits from her.

She walked around the room, drinking the ale.

"I met with your father," she said, her voice muffled by the heavy moisture in the air.

He grunted.

"The old man's quite sharp, isn't he?" she asked. "He said some things I hadn't considered. Some things that made me, well, change my mind a little, I think."

"He said some things to me today as well," admitted Oliver. "I've been wrestling with it ever since, but I've decided that he's wrong. He says because we've given medicine and technology to the Vendatts, we've improved their lives. But did we? We brought new cures as well as new diseases. We have technology that changed their industry and destroyed the old. We've opened doors that perhaps they'd already elected to keep shut. Despite what he said, he isn't considering a campaign into the Darklands to help those people along the river. He wants the levitating stone, and that is it. He'll kill everyone, tear down that city, to get what he wants. My father is a wordsmith, a silk-tongued debater, but I see through him."

"You're thinking of Imbon," responded Sam. "You're letting it sway you. What happened there was not our fault."

Oliver shook his head. "But it was. If it wasn't for us, thousands of people would have lived. It was my discovery of the pool, Towerson's breaching of that tomb, which set in motion the catastrophe that killed every man, woman, and child on that island. Without our involvement, they'd still be alive."

She kept circling the room, sipping her ale and peering into the quiet steam hanging around them. Finally, she said, "You seem tense."

She walked behind him and sat her ale on the bench he was seated upon. She began rubbing his shoulders.

He shifted. "Ah, you don't need to—"

"It's no bother," she said. "You can do the same for me, after."

Her fingers, strong from constant practice with her daggers, dug into his flesh, kneading and stroking his neck and his shoulders. He had to admit it felt rather good.

"It was our fault in Imbon, Sam. My fault," he said, trying to think of anything other than her standing so close behind him. "Before the rebellion, we brought as much sorrow as we did improvement. The fact that they were willing to sacrifice it all is proof enough what they thought of our presence." He snorted. "They're all dead now. All of them. How can we argue we improved anything?"

"They sacrificed for sorcery, Duke," she responded. "Their rebellion was over the horrific choices they'd made with the uvaan, not Enhover's rule. They had the option to live within your empire, to lead better lives, but they chose the dark path."

He grunted and picked up the ale mug. After another moment of her massaging, he shook his head and stood. "That's enough. It, ah, it felt wonderful. Let me return the favor."

Smiling at him, she turned and sat on the bench, pulling her jet-black hair over her shoulder to expose the smooth skin of her neck and back.

Putting his hands on her shoulders, feeling the warmth of her damp skin, he began to massage her, watching his fingers and hands move over her pale skin, over the black lines of her tattoos. "I've never given anyone a massage before," he admitted. "I've had plenty from the servants, but, ah, I never thought of how they did it. Is this right?"

"It is," she said. "A little more pressure?"

He stepped closer, working his hands from her neck, down her shoulders, trying to mimic the techniques she'd used on him.

"That feels good, Duke," she murmured. "You know, with a little time, I can show you how to make a woman feel really good."

He coughed on the thick mist in the air and tried to pull away from her.

She reached up and gently grasped his wrists, pulling him against her and his hands down to her breasts.

Jerking his hands away like he'd touched a hot kettle, he barked, "What are you doing?"

His wrists still in her grip, she turned and planted her lips on his hip, kissing his bare skin.

Pulling his hands free and stumbling back, Oliver touched his side where she'd kissed him. "What— what was that for?"

She stood slowly. "You know what that was for. We know each other well enough by now, Duke. That's not the first time you've been kissed. Come on. We're both here, and no one else is. Let me show you some things. I promise you'll enjoy it."

He frowned at her, his head swirling, and not from the heat in the room or the ale he'd drank. "You, ah... Do you not prefer women?"

"I do," she acknowledged. She looked him up and down. "I prefer chicken to steak, ale to wine, bread to salad, but if it's on my plate and seasoned right, I'll take any of them in a pinch."

"This isn't... Something isn't right here," he worried. "This is not like you."

Half a year ago when they'd first met on that rail car, he wouldn't have hesitated even for a breath. She was beautiful, and standing there amidst the steam, the clouds of vapor rolling around her glistening, naked body, he felt himself responding. She was willing. She was there, but... but something wasn't right. It felt wrong. Terribly wrong.

"What aren't you telling me?" he asked.

She walked around the bench, coming toward him, mist swirling around her like she was wading through a dream. He stood his ground as she approached, and she put a hand upon his chest.

"I'm ready," she whispered. "That's all you need to know."

"This isn't right," he repeated.

"Is it Isabella?" questioned Sam, smiling coyly at him. He fought to keep his eyes on her face. "Do you think she would be jealous? Maybe, but she doesn't seem the type. What if we sent the guards to go fetch her? We can get started, and she could join us. I bet you'd like that, the two of us, slick with sweat—"

He put his hand over her mouth, silencing her.

She opened her lips, pressing her soft skin against his, and then her tongue traced the lines on his palm.

"Sam!" he cried, stepping back, bumping against the brick wall at the side of the room. "What's gotten into you?"

She reached for his groin, but he blocked her.

Pouting, she said, "That should be what's getting into me."

"I'm not going to do it," he said. "This isn't… this isn't you. Tell me what's going on."

She crossed her arms underneath her breasts, pushing them higher.

He squirmed against the wall, unable to keep his eyes entirely on her face.

"You won't do it, will you?" she asked. "I'm surprised and disappointed."

"Tell me what's going on," he whispered.

"Your father released the reavers at the druid keep," she said flatly. "They'll find our scent there, and they'll come right for us. We have a few turns of the clock. With your seed, or your blood, there are rituals I can perform that will help. I can consecrate our weapons to be effective against the creatures, like that crown your brother used against the first one. It won't destroy them, but it will send them to the underworld. With the power I can get from you, we have a chance."

"The reavers!" gasped Oliver. "Wait, my blood or my seed— You said my father?"

"King Edward," she agreed. "He's the one behind this. He sacrificed Northundon; he sent us to Harwick; he was the one in the Coldlands; he led us to Raffles, Yates, and his brother; he killed Goldthwaite; he's known it all this entire time. Duke, he's been playing us since the day we left for Harwick. The curtain is pulled back, though, and his secret is revealed. We've one more test, and then we can join him."

"Join…" stammered Oliver. "My father, you're saying my father is a sorcerer?"

"Keep up, Duke," she chided. "We don't have much time."

He stared at her, finally able to ignore her naked body, but he couldn't comprehend what she'd said. The words jostled inside of his head, bumping against each other, not making sense.

"My father," he muttered. He frowned at her. "Why are you saying this? What happened?"

"He told me," she said earnestly.

"I'm going to talk to him," he said, shifting along the wall, trying to edge around her.

"That's a bad idea, Duke," she claimed.

"Why?" he demanded. "You don't think he'll back up what you're saying?"

"No," she replied. "I think if you go looking for the man, we'll lose our opportunity to get in front of the reavers. We'll lose the little time we have. He told me they are coming for us, and I believe him. Duke, without the strength I can gain from you, I don't think we'll survive tonight."

He shook his head, refusing to believe.

"Duke, think about it," said Sam. "He's the one who had the uvaan. He's the one who wouldn't let anyone else see the tablets that were found with them. Your father gave the lock and key to me, knowing that fool Adriance would stumble into releasing the creature. Or maybe he killed Adriance and did it himself, I don't know, but who else could have possibly been able to fashion the circlet to stop it? Who would have given it specifically to John? Who danced your brother Philip like a puppet to get us into this in the first place? Every time we've acted, your father has been guiding us from the shadows. You know it's true. It's been true this entire time. He's the other your uncle warned us about. We just couldn't see it."

The reavers released by his father, a sorcerer? There was no reason… no reason why.

Except his father would do anything for the empire. Except his father thought he was the best man to rule Enhover and the world. He'd said as much, that he'd do anything for the Crown.

"Duke, I am being serious when I say we do not have much time," insisted Sam, stepping toward him again. "Even with consecrated weapons, even with your help, there were two dozen of those uvaan. That means two dozen reavers, and just one of them nearly killed us in the Church's library. If you and I are to survive tonight, we have to get started now."

"Why would my father do this?" he asked softly, his voice barely audible above the drip of moisture from the ceiling, the bubble of water in the heated pools.

"He's forcing us to choose, join him or die," she said. "It's an easy decision for me. I'd rather be alive than dead, fighting for a cause rather than taking space in some grave. What is your decision, Duke? Join your father or die?"

"I have to talk to him," he hissed.

"We don't have time," she snapped. "Duke, I need your blood or your seed. You've got to decide now. Do you want to fight me or fuck me?"

"This isn't right," he said, his vision swimming.

Then, Sam's fist lashed through the vapor, and he jerked to the side, only his instinctual reaction saving his nose from shattering beneath her knuckles. Instead, she caught his cheek, snapping his head back where it bounced painfully off the brick wall behind him.

"Hells, Sam!" he shouted.

Her left fist swung at him in a vicious hook.

He ducked, taking the blow on the side of his skull, rocking him but not injuring him. He staggered to the side.

She surged against him, grabbing his shoulders and pounding her knee into his ribcage. Breath exploded from his lungs, whooshing between his lips. She kneed him again and again.

He pushed his hand down, trying to deflect the blows, fouling her strikes, but still his ribs threatened to crack beneath the onslaught. He got an arm into position and took the next shot on the point of his elbow, the bone slamming into the muscle of her thigh.

Cursing, she grabbed a fistful of his hair and yanked his head back, swinging her own elbow at his face. He twisted, and she landed a glancing blow to his cheek. The skin split, and blood trickled down his face.

"Spirits forsake it, Sam!" he bellowed. He wrapped his arms around her, clutching her tight where she couldn't throw any more elbows and knees at him. He felt her wet, naked body pressing against his.

She let him hold her tight and snarled into his chest, "You've a choice, Duke, two options, and you'll enjoy one of them."

He shoved her back, and she stumbled, landing on her bottom on the tile floor.

"This isn't right, Sam!" he yelled at her. "Stop. Let's talk about this."

She held out a hand.

He moved to grab it, to help her up.

She spun, her hand locked around his wrist, her leg lashing a back kick that caught him in the gut.

He staggered away, falling against the wall, a surge of anger burning through his veins.

She was on her feet, charging.

He met her attack, letting her slam a shoulder into his midsection, then he wrapped an arm around her neck and held her there, squeezing tight around her throat.

"Stop this!" he growled, squeezing her neck, cutting off her airflow.

She grabbed his manhood and yanked.

Squealing, he flung her away from him, tossing her like a heavy sack of wheat across the room.

Slipping on the wet floor, she crashed into a bench and flipped over it.

Chasing after her, he vaulted the bench, nearly landing on her. He lost his footing as she spun and kicked his feet out from under him. A pained grunt burst from his lips as he landed hard on the floor.

In a blink, she rolled on top of him, straddling his waist, swinging her fists down at his face.

Holding up his forearms, he took the blows, but he knew it was only a temporary reprieve. She was small, but she was strong, and in heartbeats, she would find a way past his guard. With one hand trying to protect himself from her fists, he reached up with the other, grasping for her hair.

She tried to brush his arm aside, but their sweat slick bodies slid across each other frictionlessly. Twisting on his waist, she tried to move back, but he caught her, wrapping his fist in her jet-black locks and tugging. He yanked her head down and flung his up.

She turned in his grip, shifting her face away so that the crown of his skull caught her lips instead of her nose. Screeching in pain, she was momentarily stunned.

He kept ahold of her and pulled, throwing her down by her hair, rolling on top of her, and putting his weight on her, trying to trap her against the floor.

She wrapped her legs around him, chopping at his face with flat hands.

"Spirits, Sam!" he snarled, letting go of her hair to swat her hands away and then catch her wrists.

She tilted her head to the side and spit out a mouthful of blood before turning back to meet his gaze.

Keeping his weight on top of her, he pushed her arms down over her head.

She kept her legs locked in an iron-grip around him, but without her hands and on her back, half his size, she had no leverage to throw him off.

As long as he maintained the position, his size could trump her skill. He watched her mouth, worried she would try to bite him, but so far, she hadn't.

She rolled her hips, rubbing against him, and he looked down where their waists met, naked skin against naked skin.

"There's another way, Duke," she said. "A more pleasant way, I think, for us both."

"You're crazy!" he shouted.

"Maybe," she replied.

She didn't stop grinding against him, and he couldn't stop himself from responding. Blood leaking from her mouth, she was still beautiful. Beneath him, willing, she was trying to show she knew how to use her body in ways other than fighting.

"It would have been more fun before we fought, unless you're into this," she said.

"Sam, this is not right," he growled.

"Do it, Duke. I want you to."

He held himself above her, breathing heavily, watching her face as she stared back at him. Her chest rose and fell, no doubt from the exertion of their fight, but his mind swirled, thinking of what she was asking him to do, thinking that if they did, she would be breathing just the same way.

She raised her hips off the floor, rotating them against him while keeping her legs locked behind his back. He couldn't free his waist without letting go of her wrists and risking her attacks. She was inviting him, begging him. She didn't speak anymore, but she didn't need to. His blood was rushing, and in her eyes, he could see she felt his growing excitement.

He shifted, trying to move away, but they were locked together, her legs around him, him holding down her arms. He couldn't get away without letting go of her.

Smiling, she asked, "Are you into this, Duke? I wouldn't have thought."

"I'm not," he growled, pressing down as she attempted to snake an arm free.

Still working her hips, she said, "An act of bringing death or an act of bringing life, which do you choose? I won't stop, Duke, one way or the other. I won't stop. You know that about me, and I know you can't kill me. Take the easy way, the better way for us both. I know the way you look at me. I feel you now. I know you want to. Just do it."

With a wordless shout, he let go of her and forced her legs apart. He stood, scrambling back away from her.

From her back, she wiped blood from her lips, frowning at the red smear on the back of her hand. She looked at him, first at his eyes then lower. "What's the problem? I can see that you want to. Do it quick. We can have another round and take our time later, if you like. First, though, we've got to get into that forest. We've got to meet the reavers before they enter the city. You remember the last time? It fed on the skin of people. It grew stronger that way. We can't fight these things if they're getting more powerful as they go. We've got to get out there, Duke. If we don't, we're going to die."

"My father arranged for John to have that circlet, the artifact that killed the first one," whispered Oliver, knowing he was right. "He… He's been behind it this entire time. He's the one who gave us the furcula that led to William and the others. He's the one they were worried about, the other. Even the tainted dagger, the one Hathia Dalyrimple brought to Enhover, it was from him. He set us on this mission to destroy his opponents. He's kept sorcery out of Enhover because he didn't want the competition. He's the only one who truly benefitted from Northundon. It was his ticket to true empire. He's the one who… Spirits, he's the one."

"That's what I've been saying," mentioned Sam.

"He's the one," hissed Oliver.

Sam, lying on her back, legs spread, stared at him incredulously. "We've been over that. Look, Duke, I need your blood or your seed. You've been wanting to give one of those to me ever since we first met on that rail car. Get down here and do it!"

He rubbed two fingers across his cheek and held it up to show her. "My blood."

"That's not enough," she growled.

"Get up. Let's get dressed," he told her. "You're right. We won't stand a chance if the reavers gain the outskirts of the city and start to feed. They'll follow us, right? I've got an idea, but we'll have to hurry. Bring your daggers."

Turning his back on her, he strode through the vapor and headed to the lockers where his clothes were stored. If there really were reavers out in the forest, they had to act fast. Then he could decide what to do about his father.

THE PRIESTESS XVIII

SHE STARED AT HIS BACK, her fingers unconsciously tapping on the hilt of her sinuous dagger. His blood or his seed. Incredulously, she'd failed to collect the second, but she could gather the first by drawing her blade and sticking it into him now.

A quick thrust, and his blood would pour over her dagger, over her hand. She could capture the liquid, use it in ritual. Her blades, consecrated by the blood of kings, would be enough to stop the reavers. All it would take was one quick thrust, and she would have the strength she needed.

With such power, once she'd defeated the reavers, she could turn on King Edward, if necessary. She could face anyone she needed to, alone. Her path would be one strewn with the bodies of her enemies.

She glared at Duke's back. He was practically inviting her attack.

He glanced back at her, still striding down the palace hallway. "We'll take one of the carriages from the courtyard. If he's expecting us to confront these monsters, I doubt my father left instructions to keep us here. As far as he knows, his plan is working."

She didn't respond, but she kept following after him.

"What of your friend? Do you think she'd help us?"

"Who?" she asked.

"The mistress, Goldthwaite, your friend," he said, frowning. "Do you think she'd help us? We could go by whatever hole she's burrowed into and pick her up. I've got a plan, but I won't refuse assistance if we can trust them. Unfortunately, I don't know anyone else with experience in these matters."

"Goldthwaite is dead," Sam replied calmly. She ignored Duke's surprised look. "Watch where you're going or you'll run into a wall."

Shaking his head, he turned from her and picked up his pace, almost jogging down the corridor.

She forced her hand away from her dagger. "Why wouldn't you do it? I've seen the way you look at me, and I couldn't miss that you were excited. This can't be the first time you've thought about it. Hells, I've thought about it, Duke. A quick dip in the current of life, the power we need to survive this... The grip we'd need on life, on each other, to shed the darkness that's about to wash over us. It's the easiest way."

He kept walking. Over his shoulder, he replied, "I don't think this current of life works the way you keep saying. It's about connection, isn't it, not about simply rutting? If it worked the way you think it does, then how come you've got no sorrow at the death of Goldthwaite? How'd you so easily turn your back on Kalbeth and however many others you've shared a bed with? There's no connection there, Sam, and the current of life is the way all is connected."

"Now you're an expert?" she scoffed. "I've stayed alive, haven't I?"

"Alive, but you told me that by swimming the current of life, you'd remain free of the pull of the dark path," he responded. "You were willing to kill me tonight, Sam. You can't get much darker than that. If you're so centered in the current of life, how come you keep reaching toward the underworld?"

She frowned at his back.

He led her down empty corridors, back stairwells, and eventually to a little used doorway that led to the carriage court. "I've realized it is best if we don't see my father or his minions," he said. "I have to see him but not until I'm ready. Right now, I'm too… emotional."

"We could release some of that tension," she offered again.

"Still on that?" he asked, peeking into the courtyard and then scurrying to the side of a mechanical carriage. It was puttering softly, the brakes on and the gears in neutral, waiting for a passenger from the palace. "Sam, we don't need to have sex to gain a connection. We've already got one. We're friends. That's the bond you need to work on, that's the grip you need to maintain. I felt it in Northundon, how everything is connected, how everything flows from one to the other. I felt the current of life, Sam. Your friends are what will keep you free of the darkness. Me, Kalbeth, and… I guess that's it. That's all the friends you've got."

"Thanks," she muttered, suddenly thinking of stabbing him again.

He clambered onto the driver's bench of the carriage and then reached down to help her up.

She settled beside him, deciding that if it came to it, she would need little time to enact the ritual that King Edward had described. She could spill Duke's blood on the way to the forest or maybe after they got to the outskirts. Besides, she didn't know how to drive the mechanical carriage, and he did. She could still use him alive. He could get them to the forest much quicker than she could running. There was no reason to rush, no reason to play her cards before it was time.

"What is this plan of yours, then?" she asked.

He kicked off the brakes on the carriage and engaged the gears, and the puttering contraption lurched into motion. Ignoring the startled calls from the handful of footmen and servants in the courtyard, Oliver leaned close to her and said, "We use the reavers' hunger against them."

SHE CROUCHED ATOP THE MECHANICAL CARRIAGE, LOOKING BEHIND them in the near-black of the forest. Underneath her, she could feel the steady thump of the thing's combustion engine. The pops and wheezes of the engine were the only sounds that broke the still of the night. She steadied herself against the rooftop of the carriage with one hand, the other hand gripped a dagger at her waist. She could still use it against Duke, but she wouldn't.

In the steam room, she'd been prepared to do anything. She'd gladly spread her legs for him, begged for his seed. When that had failed, she'd swung her fists at him with intent. She'd meant to strike him, to hurt him, to make him bleed. Part of her refused to admit that she would have killed him. She would have convinced him, pushed him hard enough to see that the other path was the way, but another part of her distrusted that narrative. She hadn't been thinking at the time, just acting. Lust and violence had consumed her. She would have preferred the first, but she had been ready for the second.

He, though, had overcome it. He'd not buried himself in her despite her pleading. He hadn't battered her flesh, even when he'd gained the advantage. He'd taken another way, one she hadn't seen, one she was still unsure of.

Squatting on the roof of the carriage, she looked to where he sat on the driver's bench, listening. She could be on top of him with her blade at his neck in seconds. She wouldn't do it, though. Not anymore.

What had come over her?

If his plan worked, there was another way. He'd found a choice that neither his father nor her had considered. Had the temptation of the dark path overwhelmed her, driven ideas from her mind? Had her hunger to learn more, to grow more powerful, displaced logic?

A snap drew her attention, and she strained to see into the dark around them. She heard a shuffle of slow feet on the forest floor. Branches slid around something and then sprung back, rustling their leaves.

"Wait," whispered Sam. Duke didn't respond, but she could sense he was ready. She heard the sounds growing closer. Quietly, she instructed, "Let them loose."

From behind her, a multi-hued glow burst into light. Shades of red, orange, and green fell on the trees and foliage around them, revealing the nighttime forest in a cacophony of color. The nighttime forest and half a dozen reavers coming several yards behind them.

"Hells!" she screeched. "Now, Duke, now! They're right behind us."

Cursing, he scrambled to react, and she nearly lost her grip as he threw the carriage into gear and it jolted into motion.

Behind them, the reavers leapt to the chase, shuffling dead feet faster than she'd expected they could move, their mouths open wide at the sight of her, low moans escaping where they'd once had lips and tongues.

The carriage bumped. Behind them she saw the broken body of a reaver come into view. Duke had run the spirit-forsaken thing over.

"Don't crush them!" she warned. "They have to stay mobile if this is to work."

"I'm trying," he snarled.

Several more figures flashed by, and she realized the creatures had surrounded them, forcing Duke to steer the carriage through the pack, not hitting them and not letting them catch ahold of the carriage either. The reavers were working together, it seemed. That wasn't a good sign.

She looked around and cried out. One hand gripping the brass bar atop the roof of the carriage, the other swinging a kris dagger, she took several fingers off of a reaver that was attempting to climb up.

With an outraged moan, the thing fell away, unable to maintain its hold without the fingers. It tumbled on the ground beside the carriage. Fifty yards behind them, she saw it rise again, struggling to its feet.

Over a dozen of the shroud-wrapped, walking corpses were in their wake now. She thought she could see the movement of others beneath the dark trees. Was it all of them? She didn't think so, but there was no way to know.

"Slow down if you can," she advised. "We don't want to lose them."

Duke said something rather impolite.

She turned to scold him but saw he was trying to manipulate the steering T with his hands and kicking at the face of a reaver with his boot.

"Duke," she warned, crawling across the roof and reversing the grip on her dagger, "don't put your leg near its mouth."

She raised her arm up and brought the dagger down on top of the reaver's skull, not killing it, because the things couldn't be killed, but distracting it so a better aimed kick from Duke knocked it off of the carriage, her dagger sliding free of its brittle skull as the reaver fell away.

"Duck," he called.

She threw herself flat on the carriage roof, the thick limb of an oak tree whipping a hand's-space overhead. There was a satisfying crunch as a reaver climbing up the back of the carriage caught it full in the chest, and when Sam rose, she saw Duke was finally steering them back onto the recent road that had been cut through the forest. For the moment, they'd escaped the swarm of reavers.

Tracks, worn by the workman hired to clean out the fortress from William's occupation, were burrowed through the thick-trunked trees of the small wilderness. Behind them, reavers poured out of the woods, running in their odd, disjointed gaits, following the carriage.

"They're coming three hundred yards back," she said.

They slowed a little as Duke adjusted the throttle.

"That's good," she advised. "Keep it right there. As long as this damned thing doesn't break down, we should reach the fortress just a few hundred yards ahead of them."

"I hope that's enough," he worried.

She shrugged. It would have to be. Too far ahead and they might lose some of the creatures. Too close and the awful things might catch them.

Fae swirled about, zipping behind them, illuminating the chasing reavers then whizzing around to shed light on the way ahead. The tiny life spirits should be dead. They couldn't survive in Enhover's air. Seeing the little creatures buzz about was the one thing that gave her hope Duke's crazed plan might work. It was one reason she didn't turn and ram her blade into his neck. If he could sustain the fae with whatever strange magic he possessed, then perhaps he could do the rest of it.

Hells. She hoped he knew what he was talking about.

THE CARTOGRAPHER XXII

THE REAVERS WERE CLOSING BEHIND them. The carriage was jostling painfully as it bounced over roots, ruts, and bumps in the forest track. Moments before, there'd been a disconcerting crack somewhere beneath the carriage. He didn't know enough about the vehicles to guess what had broken, but it kept running, and he kept pushing it. Sam, perched on the rooftop behind him, gave terse updates as they raced through the trees.

"One hundred and fifty yards," she called. "If we have to go much farther, I recommend you put on a little more speed. Assuming you can, that is, without this thing breaking apart underneath us."

He reached for the throttle, but it swung loosely in his hand, no longer connected beneath the floorboards.

"Spirits forsake it," he cursed.

"What?" asked Sam, turning to look at him. "Are you going to... Oh."

"There's the keep ahead of us," he said. "We just need a little more time to get there."

"They're closing on us," warned Sam. "We might have time. We might not. When we get to the entrance, Duke, we're going to have to move fast."

"If we get there," he grumbled under his breath, the carriage bouncing wildly as the iron-bound wheels thudded off a tree stump, sending them careening across the track. Louder, he said, "One more minute."

Sam slid down onto the driver's seat beside him. "Not much I can do back there if they catch us. The full two dozen of them are chasing us. We can't fight that many."

"Still thinking about stabbing me?" he asked.

"Do you think one minute is enough time for you to finish if we do it the other way?" she snapped. Shaking her head and standing up from the bench to glance behind them, she said, "We should have done it the other way."

"Let's just hope a minute is enough time to reach the keep," he replied.

The carriage jerked again, and he heard the screech of twisting metal.

"Wheel binding fell off," advised Sam, glancing over the edge of the carriage. "They're fifty yards behind us, now."

"Five hundred yards to the entrance to the keep," he reported.

She nodded curtly, crouching on the driver bench, eyes fixed behind them. "Stop outside and we run?"

"I don't think we have time for that," he replied.

"What are you— You're going right in?"

Grinning maniacally, fighting to hold the steering T steady as their carriage skipped and jostled, he aimed them directly at the wide, circular entrance to the ancient druid keep. Fae, scattering before them, lit the opening with a bright glow. He aimed for it like an arrow at a target.

Sam gripped his arm, her fingers digging painfully into his bicep, and then they hammered into the stone floor of the keep at full speed.

The carriage was knocked into the air and crashed down half-a-dozen paces farther, stabbing into the interior of the fortress and rolling up the smooth, stone tunnel.

Madly, Oliver clung to the steering T, wrestling it like it was an angry badger. He could feel it wobbling where one of the wheels must have been jarred out of alignment, but the mechanical carriage kept going, wheezing and groaning, until with a final shudder, its engine stopped.

The wheels kept rolling, heading up the incline, but Oliver knew they had little time left before the contraption slowed to a crawl and the reavers caught up from behind.

"I'm going to try to block the route," he called. "Be ready to jump clear!"

"You're what?" shrieked Sam.

He twisted the steering T hard, yanking it to the left, where the carriage promptly smashed into the side of the tunnel, the wheel running up the wall, the corner of the vehicle shattering in a cloud of splintered wood and twisted iron. Then, it tipped over.

Oliver flung himself from the seat, flying through the air with the momentum of the ride and the force of his jump. Behind him, the carriage wrecked, crashing to its side, skidding across the floor and wedging against the opposite wall in a screaming howl as metal dragged across the stone floor and wood snapped from the impact. Oliver slammed down against the stone, the breath blasting from his body, his vision momentarily flickering black. He groaned and felt Sam's hands on his arms, dragging him up.

"No time for laying about," she muttered. "Those things will be over the carriage in seconds."

Letting her pull him up, he staggered to his feet and began a limping run up the tunnel. By his side, Sam ran as well, the twinkling lights of the fae swarming ahead of them in a cloud. Turn after turn, yard after yard, they ran up the gradual incline of the tunnel, the sounds of pounding feet and low moans echoing off the stone behind them.

Occasionally, Oliver would spare a glance over his shoulder and would wish he had not. The reavers, their dead mouths open in hunger, the purple glow filling their eye sockets, chased after them just thirty yards behind.

The reavers couldn't run faster than he and Sam, but they were relentless, untiring. Oliver had no doubt the creatures could keep running for hours, maybe days. They didn't feel pain, weren't affected by wounds that would kill a man, and didn't need to breathe. They only hungered for flesh, but if his plan worked, they wouldn't get his. Gasping great lungfuls of air, he offered a hope to the spirits that it would work.

"How much farther?" gasped Sam. "I don't know how much longer we can keep ahead of them."

"You've been getting lazy," he chided, ignoring the burn in his legs, the desperate rise and fall of his chest.

Stumbling, struggling, they kept running, passing through rooms, and soon, they made it a third of the way up the keep. Behind them, the reavers were catching up, dashing across the open spaces, their awkward strides unimpeded.

"Those gates that we saw, think we can find and shut one?" wheezed Sam.

"The workmen took them out," said Oliver. "Here." He darted to the left into a narrow passage, pulling Sam behind him. "They can only come one or two abreast."

"Are you sure this is the right way?" asked Sam, staggering against the wall, shoving off and pushing herself forward with her hands. "The plan was to take the main avenue."

"I'm sure," he said, and he was.

Whether through some knowledge dredged from his distant memory of mapping the keep or some recent connection to the spirit of the place, he knew it was the right way. Just as he knew when they reached the top, he could do what was necessary. He felt the spirit around them, felt its bubbling insistence, felt its desire to be free.

Next to him, Sam pulled one of her daggers.

He winced, hoping she didn't mean it for him, but evidently, she just wanted to be prepared. Ten yards behind them, the first reaver came relentlessly closer.

Oliver thought to the fae that swirled around them, and half the tiny creatures flew back, pelting into the face of the reaver, clustering over its eyes, causing it to howl its grating, terrible cry. The monster beat at its face, slowing its jog, and Oliver and Sam put on speed, gaining a few extra steps.

"Nice trick," rasped Sam.

"That's the only time it's going to work," he admitted. They needed the remaining fae to light the way.

They fell quiet, only their ragged breaths and the dry shuffling behind them filling the echoing stone tunnel. A little bit more, a little bit more to the throne room.

"Hells," muttered Oliver, glancing behind where one of the creatures had closed to within five yards of him.

Suddenly, they burst into an open room, and he took the opportunity to draw his broadsword on the run. He lost a step doing it, but he wanted the steel in his hand if that thing caught him.

"That won't kill it!" warned Sam.

He knew, but he could slow it. At the other end of the room, right before they ran into the next tunnel opening, he spun, swinging his sword low, catching the reaver at the knees.

The creature, mindless in its pursuit, didn't see the blow coming, and it pitched forward as he severed its left leg at the knee.

Hands grasping at him, its jaw snapping in frustration, the reaver tumbled to the floor beside him. Oliver felt its bony fingers close on his ankle.

Sam kicked the thing's hand away and hauled him after her into the tunnel.

The other creatures coming behind veered off course, swerving around their fallen companion, and he and Sam gained a few more steps ahead of the monsters.

"They can't jump," observed Oliver.

"Does that help us?" gasped Sam. "Duke, I don't know how much longer…"

"We're almost there," he assured.

One more turn, and they sprinted out of the narrow corridor

into the wide-open throne room. The stone formed a tall dome far above their heads, and the gleaming rock of the floor spread out where it wasn't covered with the carpets William had laid there. Sam's blood still fouled a few of them.

In the center of the room was a huge construct. It'd been hanging in the rooms below, before Oliver had the workmen take it down and bring it into the throne room. There was space there for him to study it, and the wall was open to the air outside, in case the construct was designed for what he thought it was. He thanked the spirits, seeing the construct was still there where he'd been toying with it.

Behind them, the tortured moans of the reavers were right at their heels.

"Go!" cried Oliver unnecessarily.

Sam showed no hesitation. She raced alongside him, and when they reached the construct, they both slammed into it, pushing. It resisted until there was a sharp crack, and its ancient wheels began to turn.

Bony feet clattered across the stone floor as reavers poured into the room.

Oliver glanced back beneath his arm and shuddered. A dozen of them, purple eyes ablaze, with more coming.

He and Sam pushed the construct, its wooden wheels bouncing over the carpets, the frame seemingly less sturdy beneath his hands than when he'd last felt it. The hides stretched over it were stiff with age but not as brittle as he would have expected.

Something within the keep had sustained it, an endless fount of life welling up and around the stone and everything within. Toes digging against the floor, arms braced against the construct, Oliver felt for that fount, that bubble of life which had kept the construct from crumbling. It coursed through him, filling his veins and his lungs. It cascaded through Sam, through the stone around them, the very air, the fae swirling around them, but not the reavers. The current of life infused itself into all matter within its boundary except for them. They were no longer a part of this world or the other.

The spirit, the current he felt, was a permanent print of life upon the world, but it stayed within its boundary. It was anchored there, tied to the fortress by bindings druid magicians had set a thousand years before. It was ready to be released.

As the construct picked up speed, its wheels turning faster and faster, Oliver severed those spiritual bindings that were tied to the fortress. He released the anchor. He freed the bubbling energy from the place, encouraged it to fly out into the world, away from the stones it'd held onto for so long.

Then he and Sam reached the end of the room, and they both jumped into the rolling construct. He landed on a bed of soft, stripped bark, and she landed on top of him.

Behind, he could hear the wail of the undead creatures clamoring after them, but they had a few steps on the reavers. They had enough.

The construct rolled out of the open end of the room.

Sam gasped as it dropped, and Oliver scrambled to haul on the levers in the front of the cocoon where they lay. They plummeted into the air, falling from the side of the druid keep, and then the wind caught them, snapping the frames and the hides that were spread over them.

Swooping, the construct soared above the trees, gliding like a bird.

"Frozen hell, I can't believe this is working!" cried Sam.

Oliver's heart jumped when, to his right, he heard the ancient hide tear. He'd redirected the font of life away from the keep, and the construct was no longer maintained by the bubbling well of energy. The construct was reverting to what it should be — dust.

Oliver looked back at the keep behind them.

"Watch where you're going!" screamed Sam.

She was stuffed beside him in the compartment of the contraption, wedged between him and the thin wall of the thing where he'd pushed past her reaching for the controls. What he hoped were controls, at least. She tried to sit up, but the construct leaned as she did, and they veered to the right, following her shift in weight.

"Get back down!" he growled, pulling again on the levers, not knowing what to do with them.

He didn't have long to worry about it. The construct was sinking, the initial gust of air that supported them dying as they neared the river. Oliver was still wondering if he should try to reach the river, to land on it, when the first branch whipped against the bottom of their compartment, jolting them and causing a horrible scraping sound.

Without any options, Oliver yanked on one of the control levers, and the nose of the contraption dipped. Cursing, he braced himself as they impacted the top of another tree. The right wing of the construct was torn free, slowing their forward progress, increasing their downward momentum, and tilting them alarmingly.

"Hold on!" Oliver shouted as they fell into the trees, smashing into branches, splintering the wood around them, leaves rustling in his ears and thin sticks slapping his face.

The construct fell, bouncing off the thick canopy and descending through it in fits and jerky drops. Finally, fifteen yards above the forest floor, they cleared the last of the tree limbs and dropped straight down.

The construct shattered around them.

Oliver bounced off the bed of bark shavings and tufts of string that lined the compartment of the device. He rolled out the broken side and flopped onto the dirt of the forest floor. He lay there on his back, blinking at the ceiling of branches and leaves above him. Bits of hide and sticks of the frame were scattered through the tree limbs, torn away as they'd fallen through.

"I can't believe that worked," muttered Sam, shoving bits of wood and hide off of her.

"The escape worked," he said, climbing to his feet and looking back toward the keep.

He didn't see it. All he could see was a giant plume of rock dust.

"If a single one of the reavers escaped that place..." worried Sam.

"We'll go look," said Oliver. "I know we can't kill the things, but maybe... I don't know. We have to find out. We have to be sure each and every one of those reavers was buried under that mountain of rock. We have to be sure they're still trapped there. Trapped there forever." He patted himself, found his broadsword amongst the wreckage of their construct, and turned to Sam. "Are you all right?"

"Unbelievably, yes," she admitted. "Duke, I didn't think—"

"We'll talk later," he said.

"I'm sorry," she said. "I shouldn't have... I should have trusted you."

He waved her after him, and they began walking toward the collapsed druid fortress.

"Philip," hissed Oliver.

His brother slowed his walk and turned. By his side, his wife Lucinda looked back as well, peering curiously into the dark night.

"Is that you, Oliver?" asked his older brother.

"I need to talk to you alone," whispered Oliver.

"What's going on?" asked Philip.

He made no move to join Oliver in the bushes, and Lucinda made no move to continue walking the pebbled path back to her rooms in the palace.

"We don't have much time. I need to talk to you now," insisted Oliver, trying to force urgency into his low tone.

"What are you doing hiding in my garden, little brother?" questioned Philip. "You're lucky the guards didn't see you and shoot you, mistaking you for an intruder. Come up to my study.

We'll get a drink and settle whatever is on your mind." He turned to his wife. "You don't mind, darling, do you?"

She adjusted her dress and gave the man a frank look. "I didn't sit through the theatre, darling, to go to bed alone. Hurry along, will you?" She turned to look into the shadows beside the garden path. "It's good to, ah, see you again, Oliver. I do hope you don't get caught in Southundon and never find time to visit us. I have to admit, the city is a less exciting place without you doing, well, what you do."

She turned and seemed to float down the manicured trail, the sound of the wind whistling through the spring growth and the scent of fresh blooms accompanying her back into the palace.

"Spirits forsake it, Oliver," cursed Philip when his wife passed from earshot. "What sort of trouble have you gotten yourself into now?"

"Come here," encouraged Oliver.

Philip put his fists on his hips. "I'd rather have this conversation in my study with a glass of wine in hand, but if you won't do that, then let's do it here on the path. I'm not going to go skulking through the bushes of my own garden, no matter who you've angered."

Sam nudged him in the ribs and nodded for Oliver to step out next to Philip.

Sighing, Oliver walked to the edge of the path where he knew his brother would be able to tell it was him. With luck, any passing sentries would only see a dark figure.

"Is this about Father?" guessed Philip.

"It is," confirmed Oliver.

"Still worried about the expansion of the empire?" chided Philip. "He's the king, the ultimate representative of the Crown. He's given us great leeway, Oliver, you in particular. We may question him in private, but he is the king. I don't like the way you're approaching me. This is the type of thing men do when engaged in a conspiracy…"

Philip let the comment hang there, a half-formed question, as if he was nervous about getting the answer.

"He's a sorcerer," said Oliver. "Father is the one responsible for Northundon."

"What?" Philip asked with a laugh. He paused, waiting for Oliver to reveal the jest. When he didn't, Philip asked again, "What?"

"Philip, Father is a sorcerer," stated Oliver. "He's behind it all. Everything. He's been playing us like marionettes, dancing us to his dark plan."

The prince crossed his arms over his chest, shaking his head and frowning.

"We have to work together and—" began Oliver.

"What are you saying, Oliver?" interrupted Philip, dropping his hands to his side and taking a menacing step forward. "I'll tell you right now I don't like this."

"He's a sorcerer, Philip."

"He's the king, Oliver."

"How can you call him your king when he's... he's evil, Philip!" exclaimed Oliver. "He killed tens of thousands of people in Northundon, all for some silly notion of empire! All so we can draw new lines on our maps!"

"So you can draw new lines," barked Philip, scowling at his younger brother. "You draw the lines."

"I didn't mean literally—"

"Imbon, the Darklands, the Westlands," growled Philip. "You led the expeditions. You identified the resources, and more often than not, you were involved in claiming the territory for the Crown. I am not sure if I believe what you are saying or not, but I know Father does what he thinks is best for the Crown. As do you. As do I. Have faith that Father is doing what he thinks best, Oliver."

"It's not the same," muttered Oliver. "Those were our people in Northundon."

Philip snorted. "People are people, brother. Whether they were born in Enhover or the tropics, the Darklands or Ivalla. People are people. You've said that yourself!"

Oliver blinked at his older brother, only able to see the silhouette of the man in the darkness. He shook his head and laughed mirthlessly. His brother was right. People were people. How could Philip not understand?

"What?" asked Philip.

"People are people, brother," said Oliver quietly. "You're right. That's the way the Crown sees them. That's the way the Crown has always seen them. Natives in the islands, sheep herders outside of Middlebury, the peers in the Congress of Lords. They're all the same, aren't they?"

Philip clenched his fists but didn't comment, evidently sensing Oliver was making a different point than the one he was insisting on.

"Father cares nothing of the people — ours or others," continued Oliver. "He cares only for the Crown."

"For the family," said Philip. "Oliver, he cares about us. He's doing this for us."

Oliver shook his head.

"He is," insisted Philip.

"I know," replied Oliver. "That, Philip, is why we have the responsibility to stop him. I came here to ask your help, but I see now—"

"Stop him?" interjected Philip. "What are you planning, Oliver? Do not be stupid. Come inside with me, and we'll talk about this."

But Oliver did not. He could not. He realized now his brother would not understand, would not approve even if he did. Their father did it for the family, for the Crown, to grow the empire. Edward Wellesley was raising the empire, but he expected his sons to carry it. A mantle paid for in blood and darkness. If they accepted the charge, they'd be just as guilty as their father.

Philip, earnest and docile, believed that Enhover's rule made the world a better place, but he'd never been there, never been out to the wild places before the imperial boot fell upon the soil. Philip had never seen what Oliver had. The peace Enhover brought was not worth the blood spilled to earn it. The commerce the merchants opened wasn't worth the control they exerted. The tithes the Church claimed were too high for the glory she provided. The empire brought change by conquest, and nothing was worth that price. Oliver knew because he'd seen. His brother had not.

Their father, the king, was the embodiment of the bargain the empire made, the sacrifice it required. Edward sought to expand the empire and no doubt thought it would be a great gift to all men, but the blood that fueled his terrible sorcery, the darkness he would steep the world in, could not be tolerated. King Edward had to be stopped.

Oliver backed into the bushes and slipped behind a hedge, ducking low and scurrying through the growth. Behind him, Sam followed quietly.

He could hear Philip fumbling after them, getting caught up on unseen branches, cursing and calling for Oliver to wait, but he did not. Philip would never understand.

HE RUBBED HIS CHEEK UNCONSCIOUSLY, WINCING AT WHERE HIS SKIN still stung from the full-armed slap Isabella had delivered. The blow had reopened the cut Sam had given him in the steam room, and it was spirits-forsaken irritating.

Isabella had been in Westundon visiting her sister and father. She had literally stumbled into him as he was fleeing his brother's palace. She'd been surprised to see him and reacted to the uncertain circumstances the way she always did. She'd wrapped herself around him and tried to drag him into an empty room, whispering entreaties and questions in his ear as he struggled to extract himself from her grip.

In the midst of it, he'd realized the life she was planning was never going to be. He could not tell her what he was about to embark on, but success or failure, his life would never be the same. His life would never again be one that Baroness Isabella Child would want to be associated with. He'd tried to explain that to her, that he was giving up everything, but he couldn't give her the details. He'd tried to assure her that he cared for her and that he'd make sure she was taken care of. He tried to… He'd accidentally mentioned Sam.

That was when the slap had occurred, followed by several more frenzied strikes that he managed to get his hands up and defend himself against.

Isabella thought he was leaving her for Sam, to pursue some illicit relationship that his family would not approve of. She thought he was giving up everything for another woman. He'd decided maybe that was for the best. It was an easier explanation than what he was really doing.

Sam, standing beside him, had burst out laughing at Isabella's attack, which had not helped the situation. Oliver and Sam had scrambled away, chased by Isabella's shrill admonitions and then by Philip's guards as they were drawn to the commotion. There would be no hiding that he'd visited Westundon and spoke to his brother.

Philip would tell Edward.

Isabella might tell everyone.

His father would understand that Sam and Oliver had decided not to join him. He would figure out that, given the timing, they were moving on the Cloud Serpent. He would know enough about his youngest son to guess that they would not be fleeing to some overseas hideaway. They wouldn't gather the available sterling and live a life of comfortable exile. No, Edward would know that unlike Philip, who was content to passively follow instruction, unlike Lilibet who'd retreated to pursue her own interests abroad, unlike Franklin and John who led where their wives took them, Oliver would stand up for what he believed. Oliver would defy the king, the Crown, and the empire.

The airship banked, and Oliver lowered his hand to brace it against the table.

"We ought to be heading out over the sea now," remarked Sam.

He nodded, his eyes fixed on the maps spread out on the captain's table of the Cloud Serpent. Ainsley was out on the deck, exhorting the crew and plotting a course into the night that would take them far from Enhover's prying eyes. She would buy them time to come up with a plan.

Though, as the hours passed, Oliver was becoming more and more convinced that planning was a fruitless adventure. His father had all of the resources of the Crown. He had the royal marines and dozens of airships. He was the most powerful sorcerer the world had seen. When Oliver asked Sam what kind of strength Edward could have gained from the sacrifice of Northundon, she could only shake her head. Her look told Oliver everything he needed to know. They couldn't stand against that strength, but they had to try.

THE PRIESTESS XIX

SHE WATCHED HIM, poring over his maps, making notes, scratching them out, and then making them again. His cheek glowed where Isabella Child had struck him, which Sam felt he thoroughly deserved. Tentatively, her tongue darted out and touched the split where he'd opened her lip in their tussle the day before. It still stung something fierce. He definitely deserved what he'd gotten from the baroness.

Her heart began beating faster, thinking of their fight. Brutal and quick, though at the time it seemed to have stretched for an hour. He'd hesitated, and so had she. Neither one of them had committed to the fight, and she didn't know which way it would have gone if they had.

Had some part of her known, suspected at least, that there was another way? Had some part of her resisted the allure of the dark path, or had she merely preferred a more pleasant way of tapping the power of a king?

It was as if she was looking back at the day, the weeks before, through a clouded window. She saw herself, recalled clearly what she'd done, but only vaguely remembered why. Ever since the Darklands, her thoughts were frantic, confused. She wondered if there was some influence of the great spirit still upon her, still twisting her toward its own desires, twisting her toward the dark path.

Not easy to walk upon, even more difficult to turn from. Everyone described the dark path that way, and she finally understood how true that was, how subtle the tug had been, how desperate her actions had become. She'd come close to a point of no return, where it would have been impossible to swim up from those dark depths. Or maybe she'd already crossed it. It made her cringe, not being able to trust her own thoughts, her own feelings. She shook her head, forcing herself into the moment, fighting back the cloud of unease that clung to her.

"Any ideas?" she asked Duke.

"Plenty of ideas," he said. "I just don't know if any of them are good ones."

"Walk me through them," she suggested. "Maybe that will clarify things."

He grunted but stood, leaning over his maps.

"The new ship works isn't operational in Northundon yet, so the Southundon yard will have been busy building Admiral Brach's sea-going fleet," he said.

"But they're of no concern to us, are they?" she asked. "We'll sail hundreds of yards above them."

"They're outfitting each royal marine vessel with banks of rockets to face the dragons of the Darklands," said Duke. "We'll be hundreds of yards above them, the edge of the range for those munitions. They won't be able to make an accurate shot, but if dozens of vessels are launching at once, there could be hundreds of the explosives going off around us. We can bet that at least one of them hits us."

"Can we sail above their range?" wondered Sam, peering at where Duke was stabbing the map with his fingers.

"We can," he said, "but for us to reach my father, we have to get to the palace, and we have to come in low. The palace is just a quarter league from the waterfront, and it's possible those rockets could reach us from there. While we might be able to draw away the airships, the sea-going vessels aren't maneuverable enough to follow. They'll still be on dock. I don't think there's any way we can bring the Cloud Serpent close enough to disembark at the palace."

"We could come in high and drop bombs on it," suggested Sam. "We could get off a barrage before the other airships spot us at night. We can target the royal quarters, reduce it to a smoking pile of rubble with little risk to our own skins."

Duke frowned at her.

"If we attack your father in his nest, innocent lives are going to be lost," warned Sam. "Whether it be exploding bombs or spirits called from the underworld, there will be casualties. Remember, this is the man who sacrificed Northundon. He released two dozen reavers and set them on our scent while we were in the midst of his city. If he's capable of doing those things, I shudder to think of what else he would do. King Edward cares nothing for the lives of these people. Duke, if we give him the chance, he'll use that against us."

Duke smacked a fist on the table but didn't respond. There was nothing he could say.

"We need more than a pair of daggers and a broadsword to face him," said Sam.

He clenched his eyes shut in frustration. "Who can we ask to defy the king? Who would do it? Who has the skill to help?"

Sam fell silent. Kalbeth, her only friend outside of Duke, would be in no mood to help once she found her mother had been killed. Duke knew hundreds of people, but Edward was a popular king ruling the most prosperous nation in history. Many of those people performed functions in Edward's government. None of them would be eager to join an uprising. Edward's rule had bene-fitted nearly everyone in Duke's circle. And if they couldn't convince Prince Philip, who actually stood to gain from the removal of Edward, then they couldn't convince anyone.

They had Captain Ainsley and her crew, but asking them to serve as anything other than transportation would almost certainly result in their deaths. They would be outnumbered twenty to one against the king's airships and a thousand to one against his marines. Direct confrontation, open battle, wasn't the way. Even Sam had to admit that. Stealth, trickery, or supernatural favor were the only ways to win the day, but the king must suspect they were coming. He would be ready.

"What of your druid magic?" she asked him. "What you did to the keep, making it collapse, could you do something similar? If we bring the palace down around his head, it doesn't much matter what sorcery he's capable of."

"The druid keep was imbued with spirits of old," said Duke. "I was able to commune with them, and simply releasing them is what caused the keep to fall. It was their strength alone holding the fortress together. My father's palace is built on mortar and dead stone. Even if we weren't worried about the other people inside, there are no living spirits to contact. I can't perform the same trick."

"Could we gather those spirits back and enlist their help?" she asked.

"Maybe," he responded with a shrug. "What I do is instinctual, the opposite of sorcery. That's an art of preparation, right? The fae, the spirits in the stone, I don't think about it when I connect with them. It just happens, and I encourage them to do what they naturally want to do. I don't think I could convince them to come destroy a palace, even if that was possible."

"The spirits in the stone," murmured Sam.

He looked at her.

"We may not need to worry about the other airships," she remarked. "Could you bring them down?"

He nodded, pinching his chin. "Maybe. It'd be risky, though, so many of them. We'd have to be close, at least to where I could see them. I'm certain a few hundred yards would be close enough, but I couldn't reach out across leagues. With so many... I'm not sure how many of the spirits I could commune with at once, and my range may be no longer than that of a rocket."

"It's something to consider," she said.

"It is," he agreed, leaning back over his maps with renewed interest. "Anyone onboard of those airships wouldn't survive the crash, though. I'm not sure if I could stomach that."

"Duke, there's another advantage we have if we want it," she mentioned.

He looked up.

"Your blood or your seed," she said.

"No," he declared, standing up and raising a finger to her. "The dark path is not the way to defeat my father. Surely, Sam, you can see that now. My father thinks what he is doing is right, that there is no evil act which is not justified. We will not fall into the same trap."

"It is a trap," she said, nodding slowly. "I realize that, now. The temptation… I can feel it, Duke. It's like a call to me, like a honeyed voice begging me to step farther into the underworld, but what if I am not the one who chooses? Maybe that is the balance. I can make use of the power, but I will not make the choice to do so."

"You want… you want me to…" he stammered.

She met his gaze. "What do you want? I am merely offering a possibility, not even a suggestion. With the right materials, I can be formidable. On this mission, I will serve as a tool, a blade in your hand. Use it or not, it is up to you. It is a way around descending to the depths of the underworld, Duke. If it is not my choice, I can maintain my grip on life. I will not be walking the dark path."

"That is just words," he said. "You're just twisting the words, trying to make—"

"It is your choice," she insisted.

He was silent, looking at the map, but she doubted he was seeing it. He was thinking. Thinking about her proposal. Thinking about what other options they had. Surprise, trickery, the supernatural. It was all that there was, the only cards they had to play. They couldn't afford to ignore any one of them. She was certain of it, but she was also certain that she could not trust her instincts. She'd meant what she'd said. She would let him choose, and she wouldn't argue with his decision.

Finally, after she'd given up on him taking her offer, he looked at her and asked, "How would it work?"

She smirked. "If you need to ask me that, then I'm beginning to understand why Isabella slapped you so hard."

He frowned. "I'm being serious."

"I know," she admitted with a grin. "There's never been a more serious occasion, but you can't leave an opening like that and not expect me to take it."

"I think you are the one leaving the opening," he said, grinning back at her.

She rolled her eyes.

Sheepishly, he asked, "Do you need a drink?"

"No, Duke, I don't," she replied.

He hesitated and then slowly took a step around the corner of the table. Then quicker, he moved around the next corner, and then he was beside her.

She tilted her head, looking at him.

"Are you sure?" he asked.

Her lips curling, she said, "It is your decision, Duke, but sorcery or not, your father or not, I am sure."

He bent to kiss her, a hand sliding up her arm, her neck, to the side of her face.

She opened her lips, let his tongue twist across hers, felt his firm lips, the scratchy stubble on his chin against her smooth skin. His fingers curled into her hair, and she pressed herself against him. She moved her hands over his back, his sides, his hips. She let him kiss her, hold her head, and then she took his wrist and turned, putting her back against him.

His breath was fast in her ear, and at her direction, he let his hands trail from her shoulders to her breasts. Slowly at first then eagerly, he touched her, reaching down and unbuttoning her vest, yanking it off, and pulling her shirt free of her trousers and over her head. He was confident and assured, but she felt the tremble of anticipation in his hands. She felt its mirror in her chest.

Her skin pebbled in the cool air of the cabin, his warm hands covering her breasts, pinching her nipples. She reached behind and felt him. He moaned in her ear as she gripped him, and he squirmed with anxiousness as she moved her other hand back and unbuckled his belt. She shoved his trousers down, and he sprang free, bouncing against her back, stiff like a board.

One of his hands slid down her stomach, and he pulled her trousers down. He pushed her forward against the table in the center of the room, and she could feel his need. She turned, reaching down to grip him, and looked up to meet his gaze.

"Duke, there are a few things I've been meaning to teach you."

"What?" he asked, bending to kiss her.

She let him, growing eager as well, feeling him in her hand, his shaking hands pulling her tight. She broke from the kiss and shoved him back to the bed, forcing him down and then climbing on top of him. She swiveled, crawling over him, opposite of the direction he lay.

"Use your lips and tongue," she said. "Slow and gentle at first, and then use your fingers, and then not as slow. You'll know when it's time to stop being gentle." She looked back at him, at his face peering at her between her thighs. "I'm no lady, Duke. You don't have to pretend to look in my eyes while we're doing this."

She wiggled above him and then sat down on him.

Uncertain at first, he quickly figured out what to do. A little shiver went through her body, emanating from her core, and a soft gasp escaped her lips. She let her body react, guiding him to what she liked. She was glad to find the man was a quick study.

His hips twisted and thrust in front of her and he strained in her hand. She smiled. She leaned forward, blowing a stream of air over him, watching as he squirmed, gasping as his hands closed on her bottom. Dark path or no, King Edward or no, this was what she wanted. This was her connection, her grip on life.

She bent down, returning his attentions. She teased him, going slow, making him wait, drawing it out.

He writhed beneath her, thrusting up with his hips, and she wriggled atop him, offering suggestions, groaning with delight as he took them.

Then, he rolled her over, and crawled up beside her, whispering into her ear, "Now it's time for me to show you a few things."

THE CARTOGRAPHER XXIII

HE GLANCED up at the tin sign swaying in the steady sea breeze. Stenciled on it was the name of the establishment, the Drunken Ass, and from the sloppy way the thing had been fashioned and hung, it was difficult to tell if it was meant to refer to the pub inside or the man who'd put up the sign.

It didn't matter much either way as the Drunken Ass was the only public house in Fearndale, a tiny settlement clinging to the eastern shore of an island fifty leagues south of Southundon. The village shared the island with Southwatch, which wasn't much bigger, but that town was sheltered by a low spine of rock that ran down the center of the landmass. Southwatch was at least slightly habitable.

Oliver ducked inside of the pub, shaking water from his jacket and nearly choking on the heavy cloud of smoke that filled the place.

Fearndale survived off harvesting thick sheets of moss that grew in abundance in the constantly damp climate. The stuff was used fresh in poultices and dried in fish stews. Kissed by the sea, it sold well to people who cared about such things, but there were only so many of those people. In Fearndale, the moss was dried and then burned to heat pubs, evidently.

He let the canvass sheet that served as the door fall down behind him, sealing him inside with the heat and the smoke. He grimaced at the moisture and slime that clung to his hand from touching the damp exterior of the canvass door. Wiping his fingers on his jacket, he looked around for First Mate Pettybone. It was hard to see in the haze, but finally, he saw the man's knit cap hunched over in the corner of the pub. The first mate had two pitchers of ale and four cups arranged in front of him.

Oliver made his way through the room, the cold and tired patrons making no effort to look up at the stranger in their midst. Sam and Ainsley followed Oliver, and they drew a few interested glances. Even bundled and disguised, it must have been obvious to the moss farmers that there were actual women amongst them. After walking through the dismal place, Oliver suspected that was a rarity. Taking a seat next to Pettybone so that his back was to the wall, Oliver waited until the priestess and the captain sat.

The first mate began pouring ales.

When everyone was settled, Oliver asked, "Well?"

Pettybone scrunched his lips tight and shook his head. "He's preparing, it seems."

"For us or something else?" questioned Oliver.

"Does it matter?" asked the first mate. "Word around the city is that Admiral Brach is assembling forces to move against the Darklands. Could be some truth to that, ey? But could be they're preparing for you, too. Got at least a dozen fully armed airships floating around the city, and another two or three tied to the bridge at any moment. There are a score of man-o-wars in the harbor. Companies of royal marines are drilling in the barracks and bedding in a temporary tent city east of town. The marines are crawling all over the palace, and I didn't bother to try and count 'em. Thousands, at least."

Oliver drummed his fingers on the table, thinking.

"By now, Prince Philip will have reported to the king that you're coming for him," mentioned Ainsley.

"And he knows what we did to his reavers," added Sam.

Oliver quaffed his ale, enjoying the brew, finding the sour taste fitting.

"He's arrayed against us, m'lord," said Ainsley. "Everything the royal marines have is layered around the palace. Mayhaps if we wait for Brach to sail to the Darklands, we'll get an opportunity, but…"

"But he won't do that," said Oliver. "Not while we're still out here."

"You could always flee, m'lord," suggested Pettybone. "The captain and I would be happy to drop you anywhere you'd like to go. Without the Cloud Serpent floating overhead, you could disappear in the Southlands, Rhensar, anywhere, m'lord. No one would think to look for you in those places."

"Aye, and you'd sail off with the airship?" questioned Oliver with a bitter grin.

"Only as long as you don't want it anymore," chirped Ainsley.

"It's your airship," said Pettybone. "None of us is going to argue that, but where the Cloud Serpent goes, the king will assume you've gone. You want to hide? You shouldn't do it on that deck."

Oliver sighed, rubbing a hand over his hair and fingering the knotted leather thong that kept it tied back.

"M'lord, before I hired on with the Company, I ah, I had some experience with conducting raids," said Pettybone, scratching beneath his knit cap. "The defenders always have an advantage. They've got walls, they've got cannon, and they've got watchers. To win, all they gotta do is hold out until help comes along, and that's assuming you're even bringing enough force to threaten them. The smart raiders, the ones who'll survive for a bit, they don't attack the strength. They snatch what they can outside of the walls and then they're off. They avoid direct confrontation and live to enjoy the spoils. We can't win a battle against the royal marines. It's not possible."

"He's right," agreed Ainsley. "I'd stake our crew against any in the empire but not the entire empire. We can't be of much help to you, m'lord."

"And that's not to mention the next layer of defense," warned Sam. "Your father is a sorcerer, Duke, and not some mean conjurer like we've faced before. He's completed a bargain with Ca-Mi-He. He's aligned himself successfully with the most powerful spirit of the underworld. We won't be dodging wolfmalkin or swinging obsidian blades to banish shades. We'll be facing... well, I don't even know. No one knows what he's capable of because no one has achieved what he has. He's hunched down in a fortress, protected by stone, cannon, and spirit."

"The druid keep across the river from Southundon stood for a thousand years until it crumbled with a thought," said Oliver. "A thought, Sam, is all that it took."

"It's not just a fortress. The man has an empire!" cried Sam before quickly quieting and looking around the room to see if anyone heard her.

Oliver nodded slowly, ideas unfurling in his mind like leaves of the first green shoots breaking above winter ground. He sipped his ale, and then he smiled. A plan, unformed and raw, was beginning to grow.

"What?" asked Sam, looking at him nervously.

"All empires fall," said Oliver. "All empires crumble from within."

Sam shook her head. "A nice platitude until you're the one trying to bring the empire down."

Oliver turned to Ainsley. "You said you'd stake the Cloud Serpent and her crew against any airship in the empire. Is that true? Is it really faster than the royal marine airships?"

The captain glanced at Pettybone and then back to Oliver. "It is."

"Good," said Oliver. "I think I have a plan, but we're going to have to get close."

Without word, the other three at the table reached for the ale pitchers.

THE CAPTAIN III

"I'VE GOT to hand it to you, Captain," muttered the first mate, speaking quietly so his voice wouldn't be heard by the rest of the crew.

"Why's that?" she asked, peering into the dense fog ahead of them.

"You reached your goal," he said, "and now you're going to die a wealthy woman."

"We might not die," she responded.

The first mate snorted.

"If you're so sure we're going to die, why are you here?" she asked, turning to look at him.

"Because it's the right thing to do," he claimed. "The death I've seen, the blood that's been shed for this empire, it's not right. It's not right, and it's never going to end unless someone stops it. King Edward, that man is evil, Captain. He don't care about anyone — his subjects or his enemies. He only cares about expanding the breadth of his power. All that talk of it being for the good, that's the sweet seduction of dark power whispering in his ear. We might die tonight. In fact, I think we probably will, but if our sacrifice buys the duke a chance, it will be a small price to pay."

She grunted and turned back to studying the fog.

"You don't agree?" whispered Pettybone.

She didn't answer for a long moment, and when she did, she said, "I haven't given it much thought. Good, evil, I'm not the right person to judge. Is the king evil and his son noble? Aye, that's probably the score of things, but I'm not the Church or a magistrate. I'm not doing this because I want to settle some grand battle for the fate of the world. I'm just doing it to get rich."

Pettybone, choking on a response, shook his head.

Captain Ainsley put a hand on the gunwale of the Cloud Serpent. "This is my airship, First Mate. Mine, yours, and all the way down to the deck swab. Each of us has a share in this hunk of wood, iron, and stone. Each one of us has got a future that we never could'a dreamed a year ago. Each of us has an opportunity, First Mate. You want to do some good with your share and make a difference in the world? Have at it. If we weren't doing what we are doing, we wouldn't have to worry about making a difference, you know what I mean? We wouldn't have the resources to choose."

"And maybe that's the point, ey?" replied Pettybone. "We get to choose."

She shrugged. "I'm not a philosopher."

"But you're still doing the right thing when you don't have to," he said.

She felt his eyes on her and she shifted uncomfortably, wishing the man would go attend to his duties and leave her alone.

"You could order us to raise sail and turn this airship around," said Pettybone. "Wouldn't take much to convince the crew. Whether we help the duke or not, we'll be outlaws after this. Our fortunes won't change whether or not we accomplish our mission. What's stopping you, Captain? If it's only about getting rich, why aren't we sailing off over the horizon?"

Ainsley gripped the butt of one of her pistols and kept staring ahead into the mist. "Get to work, First Mate. We've much to do tonight."

"You're a good woman, Captain," he said, his voice fading as he left her side and walked away. "Even if you don't want to be."

SHE LOOKED AROUND THE DIMLY LIT DECK OF THE CLOUD SERPENT. The entire crew was on hand and prepared to begin.

"As soon as I light this, it's too late to back out," she said, pitching her voice to be heard by the crew but not so loud the sound reached past the proximity of their airship.

No one replied.

She imagined they thought it was already too late to back out. They weren't entirely wrong. It was well known that the duke had fled on the airship. It was well known they were working with him. She figured there was no way an inspector could prove they were aware the duke was preparing to assassinate his father, but whether the king and his marines would take that into consideration if the crew turned themselves in was anyone's guess. A gamble, and they'd all placed their chips on the big payout. They wouldn't turn back now.

She had to admit her first mate was right. The crew thought the duke was doing the right thing, and that'd earned their loyalty, even when it wasn't the wisest course they'd charted. They were loyal to her as well, she supposed, and not a voice had risen in dissent when she'd shared the plan.

"Very well, then," she said. Then she touched the taper to the fuse and gave the barrel a shove.

It rocked in its cradle but didn't roll. The lit wick sparked and hissed.

"Hells," she muttered and shoved again, barely shifting the heavy munition.

"We usually roll it as a team. Let me help," offered Pettybone.

Sparks flying from the sizzling wick, they both put shoulders against the fully loaded barrel and shoved. With the creak of wood on wood, the cylinder bounced out of its cradle, rolled down a short ramp, and then whistled into the air below them. They listened, breaths held for a half-a-dozen heartbeats, and then the thing exploded with a violent thump.

Along the edges of the airship, crewmen shouldered more munitions over the edge. Wicks crackling, the barrels whizzed through the sky and burst with deep, concussive thumps. In between the blasts, shouts of panic rose from far below. Lights flared or were extinguished as a dozen airships were kicked into motion and responded in a panic.

The Cloud Serpent hung a thousand yards above the surface of the harbor, twice the height of the royal marine airships. Those that had air spirits strong enough to float so high would keep their stones wet. Regulations stated a specific height in harbor, after all.

"We got their attention," remarked Pettybone, peering over the edge at the activity below them.

Moments later, a rocket came screaming up from one of the royal marine airships. It burst four hundred yards aft, a hundred yards below them. The billow of flame might have been enough to reflect on the bottom of their hull, though.

"Time to go!" shouted Captain Ainsley. "Look sharp, boys. We've got about half a league, and then we'll lose the extra push the duke is giving us. That's half a league to build a lead on these fellows, or we'll sorely regret not having it."

Pettybone began calling instructions, driving the men to hoist the sails, to catch the stronger breeze at elevation before they dropped, before the chase began in earnest. They would need every advantage they could muster before they sank down to the height of the other airships.

Below, they heard the high-pitched shriek of another rocket flying up from the decks of the royal fleet. It thumped three hundred yards off the starboard side.

Air filled their sails, and they began to move.

With their bombardment stopped, the shouts below them grew

focused, and the pursuit was started. Rockets still flew at them, but only one exploded near enough to rock the airship. At night, with five hundred yards of extra elevation, it was more luck than skill which guided the attacks from below.

As they moved, imperceptible at first, but then quickly, they began to drop as they exceeded the duke's range to communicate with the spirits that lifted them. He was giving them all that he could, Ainsley could tell, but it wouldn't last forever. It was time for some old-fashioned sailing.

"Come on, you air dogs!" screamed Ainsley to her crew. "You want to survive a life of privateering in the tropics? Then you'd best learn to evade the royal marines. Get the rest of the canvass aloft, and down below, bend your spirit-forsaken backs on those sweeps. They're coming after us, boys. If they catch us, we die, but if we escape, we'll be the richest damn aircrew in the history of the empire!"

She moved back to the rear of the airship and looked below where a dozen royal marine vessels were scrambling to fall into their wake. Unused to attacks from above, or any attacks at all for that matter, they were disorganized. Their confusion was buying the Cloud Serpent extra seconds as the fleet struggled to untangle themselves and find open air.

She'd claimed her aircrew could out sail anyone. She was about to find out.

"Would have been easier if we'd let some of those bombs land on their decks," advised Pettybone. "We could have knocked three or four of them out of the chase before it started, and it would have given the others something to think about before they got too close to us."

"Aye, but we're still working for the duke," said Ainsley. "The loyalty we show him will be repaid when the crew shows it to us. Soon, First Mate, soon we'll sail this thing however and wherever we please, but until then, we work for the man, and he asked us not to kill anyone, unless we have to, of course."

First Mate Pettybone grunted. His eyes were fixed on the airships that were finally getting their acts together and starting after them. "Whether or not we pull this off, I've been proud to serve under you, Captain Ainsley."

"Get to work, First Mate," she growled.

THE CARTOGRAPHER XXIV

ABOVE THEM, the clouds flashed, reflecting the red and orange blasts of bombs and rockets. Even from below, on the waters outside the harbor, the confusion amongst the royal marine airships was evident. They'd never faced an attack, never battled air to air. They had never imagined an opponent who could sail above them.

Oliver thought that the slow reaction to the Cloud Serpent's bombardment did not bode well for the planned foray into the Darklands, but if all went well, perhaps the marines wouldn't be making that journey.

He and Sam waited quietly while he cast his mind above, encouraging the spirits living within the Cloud Serpent's stones, hurrying them on their journey. He strained, reaching as far as he could, watching as the rockets chased Ainsley into the distance. Finally, his connection began to slip, and they could follow the arc of the rockets as the Cloud Serpent descended.

"I hope that's enough of a lead," he muttered.

Beside him, Sam nodded. "Ainsley is a good captain. They'll be all right. Time to row?"

"Time to row," he agreed, and as one, they bent forward, dug their oars into the choppy waters, and leaned back, propelling their tiny boat forward.

Like a leaf on the surface of a stream, they floated across heavy swells, darting silently through the harbor break, past the guards there. From two hundred yards away, Oliver could see that the men stationed on those remote posts were uniformly staring up at the sky where the airships were launching rockets and scrambling after the Cloud Serpent. All two dozen of the vessels, uncoordinated, were attempting the pursuit.

Grinning, Oliver felt a bit reassured that at least the first part of his plan was working. He'd known that Admiral Brach's marines had no contingency for an attack from above, particularly in the safe confines of Southundon's skies. Who would be mad enough to attack an airship above the capital?

It meant that each captain was on their own on how to respond, and if there was one thing about Enhover's royal marines everyone knew, it was that they feared no one. They thought themselves the most potent force on the planet and could not conceive of a threat they couldn't meet.

They hadn't seen what Oliver had, and it made them overconfident. It made them blind to the idea that the Cloud Serpent was merely a ruse, a way to draw the eyes from the water where he and Sam were slipping in silently upon a rowboat.

The Cloud Serpent would circle the city of Southundon to the west, launching half a dozen rockets toward the palace to truly garner everyone's attention, and then it would race north, charting a course over central Enhover, hopefully out sailing the pursuit.

Over the river that disgorged beside Southundon, Ainsley would drop two bundles from the sides of the airship. Two bundles wrapped tightly around simulacra made to represent he and Sam. The bundles had been invested with traces of their hair, their blood, and other fluids that had been a bit more pleasant to collect. They'd been bound to the simulacra with designs that Sam had spent hours fashioning.

With any luck, King Edward would be drawn to the dummies, and he and his shades would be watching as the decoys floated harmlessly down the sluggish river.

Oliver and Sam would approach, partially hidden by the tattoos Kalbeth had inked on the priestess and that Sam had extended through ritual. It had worked before. The plan had gotten them into the ancient druid keep and past William's watchers. Of course, his uncle had been waiting when Sam had leapt out of hiding.

Oliver kept pulling on the oars, trying not to poke holes in their plan while they were in the throes of executing it. Whether or worked or not, they were committed. It was time to bring down the empire.

"You're sure this will be unguarded?" asked Sam.

Oliver shook his head. "It will be guarded but not by my father. Years ago, I constantly snuck in and out of the palace. If they couldn't figure it out then, I doubt my father has found my secret ways since."

Sam grunted and fingered the hilts of her sinuous kris daggers.

Leading the way, Oliver climbed out of their rowboat onto the narrow fishing pier. It was open to the public, but the slender fish that populated Southundon's harbor were bottom feeders, only rising toward the surface during bright daylight. At night, the pier was deserted. In a crouch, Oliver scampered down the pier, passing its open gate and scurrying into the city.

At his side, he clutched the hilt of his broadsword, and under his arms, he felt the hard steel of the two katars Sam had given him. The punch daggers would be effective against shades, imbued with the power to banish them back to the underworld, but the longer steel of his broadsword felt comfortable. The katars were close weapons, intimate. Tonight, he hoped he wouldn't need them.

Several hundred yards away, the commercial wharfs were busy, ships loading or unloading, their masters hoping to finish the task in time for the turn of the tide. The shouts of the workmen were loud enough that they covered the sound of Oliver and Sam's footsteps as they entered the city. Off the harbor, the buildings were warehouses, some lit to receive or discharge their goods, most dark and silent.

None of the workmen paid them any mind as they scuttled by, sticking to the shadows. The goods that moved on the sea-going vessels were bulk commodities, and two individuals couldn't steal enough of it to make it worth bothering to closely guard. There were a handful of watchmen walking in pairs on patrol in the district, but when they saw them, he and Sam strode by like they belonged there. The sentries let them pass unmolested, either unable to see their faces in the darkness, or maybe they hadn't been given their descriptions.

Southundon was a relatively safe city, and as long as they didn't appear to be up to something nefarious, the night patrols would pay them little mind. Oliver suspected it would be that way until they reached the inner walls, where his father could have alerted the guards to watch for them. If not guards, the old man would have his shades clustered thickly.

Still, it gave Oliver a sense of relief to step off the cobble-stoned streets into a narrow, dirt alleyway, out of view of any prying eyes. They'd made assumptions that parts of their plan would work, but there was no certainty. If the wrong person saw and recognized them, then his planning would be for naught.

"You snuck through here as a boy?" asked Sam, her lips twisted in distaste.

He winked at her. "A young man, I would say."

"Doesn't seem a place the king would appreciate finding his son," remarked Sam.

"Didn't you tell me you were sent to Glanhow's gaol as a young girl?" he asked her.

She shrugged. "A young woman, and I don't recall telling you that."

"You did tell me," he insisted. He paused. "What did you do at such a tender age to be locked up in a gaol?"

"Probably a bit of what they're doing in there," she said, gesturing to the narrow house that blocked the end of the alley.

A roar of cheers poured out of the doorway.

Oliver started ahead. "Best if we can slip inside while everyone is distracted."

At the door, a man waited, taking up half the width of the alley. He stood beneath the solitary lantern that illuminated the entry, the mist curling about him in the early summer air. His head was bald, crisscrossed with a network of impressive scars, and beaded with moisture from the fog coming off of the sea. He wore a padded leather vest, loose trousers, and heavy leather bracers studded with steel spikes. His fingers were covered in brass knuckle-guards.

A former fighter from the pits inside, guessed Oliver. Skilled enough to have caught the interest of the masters of the place and strong enough he'd survived the bouts it took to earn such a set of scars.

With the brass guards on his knuckles and the steel spikes on his bracers, Oliver had little doubt the man could handily beat him to death in a matter of moments. The guard had probably done it before, when hapless drunks tried to force their way inside. The watchmen, their purses lined with silver, knew to avoid the narrow little house. The families of those who went missing inside never asked questions, or if they did, they didn't ask for long until someone paid them a visit.

"Password?" asked the hulking guard, his voice surprisingly high-pitched.

"Pickles," replied Oliver confidently.

The guard frowned at him.

"Pickles," repeated Oliver.

"That's not the password," said the guard. He shifted, clearly positioning himself to block the doorway.

"Silver, then?" asked Oliver, and he pulled a small pouch from within his jacket and shook it. A fistful of coins clinked at the motion.

"Silver doesn't do me a lot of good if I let a watchman inside of here," responded the guard.

"I've got a tip on a fight coming up tonight," said Oliver. "I'll have this much again on the way out."

The guard snorted. "How many times you think I've heard that, chap? If you don't know the password, do yourself a favor and turn around. You don't have enough silver for me to risk my neck. Word of advice, chap? If you don't belong here, then it's best you never get in."

Another wave of noise crashed out the door from behind the guard, but the man ignored it. He was used to the boisterous yelling, and he kept his eyes fixed on Oliver and Sam.

"Let's go," said Sam, looking behind them nervously. "We can find another way."

Oliver shook his head. The Filthy Beggar was one of the city's oldest illegal establishments. It had an entrance near the harbor, where they were trying to gain admission, but it sprawled in a network of underground rooms and passageways, twisting around the tunnels that had been bored for the rail lines, snaking beneath the inner walls of Southundon.

Avoiding the portals that led through the gates on the surface was how he'd first discovered the illicit fighting parlour, and it was the only way he knew to slip through undetected now.

Southundon's inner walls were manned constantly with guards, and now that Admiral Brach was raising additional militias, they would be thick with new men who would be eager to prove themselves and gain a position in a forward unit where the plunder would be richest. Those men would have their eyes open, not yet bored to slumber by tedious guard duty. Not to mention the fireworks show Ainsley had put on above the city. His father would have alerted spies at the inner wall and possibly set sorcerous snares as well. There would be no way they could pass through undetected. The Filthy Beggar, though, would take them underneath all of that.

"You know a retired fighter named Jack?" asked Oliver.

The guard frowned at him.

"He would have been fighting about the same time as you. He had a good record," continued Oliver. "One of the legends in this place, I was told. You don't know him?"

"Chap, the only thing people do more often than try to bribe me is to bring up some old fighter and pretend they know 'em," rumbled the guard. "Aye, I know a Jack. I know a few men named Jack. But that don't mean we know the same Jack, and even if we did, I still ain't letting you in."

Oliver shook his head. "I've only met the man once. That sure thing I told you about? They whipped him in the space of a dozen heartbeats. Someone who could do that, you think they'd be a good bet?"

The guard laughed. "I doubt that's true, but if it is, the Jack I know ain't fought for years. He's bound to be rusty. It's a fool's bet you're talking about, and there's no shortage of those."

Grinning, Oliver shook his head. "The fighter that beat Jack isn't inside. She's right here." He hooked a thumb at Sam.

The guard laughed, looking her up and down then tilting his head forward and licking his lips. "Well, if I was Jack, I'd let you beat me too, girl. What say we meet up after my shift and give it a go?"

Sam looked at the man and then back to Oliver. "You want me to knock this lug out? I suspect I'd have to kill him, and I don't know where we'd hide a body that big."

The guard grunted and raised a fist. "You've got a pretty mouth, girl. Best not let any more stupid words come out of it. Boss'll have my hide if I let you in, but he won't blink if I bloody you some."

"I don't want anyone to fight," assured Oliver. "Not out here. Not when there's no coin to be made from it."

"What you gettin' at, chap?" asked the guard.

"This girl beat your friend Jack fair and square," said Oliver. "Maybe you heard about that? He took a pounding while in Baron Child's service up in Westundon. It was her. I aim to put her in some bouts tonight."

"No one is going to fight her," growled the guard. "Ain't no fights between women."

"She'll fight the men," insisted Oliver.

"They won't—"

Oliver shook his bag of silver. "I got twenty times this in a credit note. They'll fight her for that. And when they do, there's not a man in the house that'll bet on her 'cept for me. What kind of odds you think they'll put against her? Twenty to one? Hundred to one?" He shook the purse of silver again.

The guard looked suspicious.

"Look, mate," said Oliver. "I'm not asking for your silver. I'm just asking for you to let us in. I'll give you a cut if we win, and if we lose, it's no loss to you."

"How much a cut you offering?" questioned the guard.

"Five percent," said Oliver.

"Ten," said the guard.

"Seven," countered Oliver.

The guard frowned, shaking his head slowly.

"Ten, then," agreed Oliver, "but in an hour when your shift is over, you come in and play the other side. Help talk to management and get her into the pits against someone formidable. Place some bets to get the silver flowing. Talk it up around the pit. Get people interested. Do that, and you've earned your ten."

"How do I know she'll win?" asked the guard.

Sam attacked in a flash, grabbing the collar of the man's leather vest and jerking him forward onto her knee. The big man coughed as a blast of air was knocked from his lungs. Sam put fingers under his chin and raised it so that he was looking into her eyes. She wiggled her fingers. "This could be my fist in your neck."

The guard stepped back, drawing a deep breath and raising his hands in front of himself. "Inside, they'll be ready for you. Dirty tricks won't work, girl."

"The only trick is that they'll see me and think just as you did," said Sam with a smile.

"Ten percent, and I'll see you in an hour," said the guard. He looked around cautiously and warned, "And I'd best see you. Otherwise, I'm going to come find you."

"You and plenty of others," said Oliver with a grin.

He grabbed Sam's arm and led her past the looming guard. Before he entered the house, Oliver turned and asked the giant man, "Last I was here, pickles was the password. What is it now?"

The guard eyed him. "It's still pickles. Didn't like the looks of you, though, so I thought I'd see what you said when I wouldn't let you in."

Oliver grunted, shook his head, and walked into the Filthy Beggar.

Low, smoky ceilings cut the light from the burning torches and scattered lamps to a dim, ominous glow. Patrons, mostly men, walked around bouncing on the balls of their feet, drinks in hand, pouches jingling with coin. Their faces were flushed, their eyes quick. Watching the fights excited them, got their blood pumping. It wasn't uncommon for the battles to spill out of the pits into the room. The thrill of pugilism, the emotions of winning or losing significant coin, the effects of too much ale... it was a dangerous cocktail.

The Filthy Beggar employed the biggest, nastiest bouncers in the city, though, and they had little regard for their patrons when it came time to kick someone out. A knock to the head, a missing purse, and that was it if the offender was lucky. Losing fighters weren't the only ones to occasionally leave sewn into a long, dirty canvass sack.

A roar went up, and the men near the doorway all turned to see a new fight begin.

Oliver, holding Sam's hand, guided her around the first of the open pits.

Covered in a mixture of dirt, sand, sawdust, and blood, the pits were dug into the ground so that the fighters were a yard below the floor. The patrons clustered around wooden railings and looked down, shouting encouragement at their fighters.

Oliver glanced between the legs of the throng and saw two shirtless men close on each other. Hands wrapped in cloth, nervous sweat slicking their chests and brows, they swung tentative jabs, trying to feel each other out.

Farm boys or common laborers. They'd probably been in more than their share of barroom brawls, but these men were not professionals. They were amateurs given a handful of silver and brought in to appease the commoners who simply wanted to see blood spilled. There would be no skill in the bout, just flung fists until one combatant fell and was unable to continue.

The patrons didn't care. They were there to drink, gamble, and watch two men batter each other unconscious. The crowd roared as the two amateurs fell onto each other, the sounds of fists striking flesh drowned out by the thirsty chants for blood.

Oliver and Sam moved quickly, weaving between the dozen sunken pits that kept the sailors and harbor workers entertained.

Bars lined the walls, interspaced with money changers, sellers of illicit potions and drugs, scantily clad women eager to accompany big winners back to the hidden rooms that honeycombed beneath the city, and vendors of dubious-looking paper-wrapped meat skewers and pies. There was little Oliver would rather do less than eat meat cooked in such a place.

A girl passed them carrying a huge earthenware pitcher. For a couple of copper shillings, she would refill a patron's drink without them having to make it all the way to the bar. It kept them drunk and gambling. At each one of the fighting pits, there was a representative of the house to hold the coins, settle up the wagers, and take the Filthy Beggar's share.

More bouts of fisticuffs began in the pits, and by the time they'd crossed to the opposite end of the huge room, two had begun outside of them. The combatants were quickly dragged apart in one case, and in the other, they were shoved into a pit to settle their dispute upon the sawdust. It was a strange place, far from the king's laws, but it had its own, and no one objected when the rule breakers had to face their fates.

Sam grabbed Oliver's sleeve and nodded toward two men wearing royal marine blue.

Oliver shook his head and circled around a far fighting pit to stay away from the men. A marine was more likely than anyone else to know Oliver's description, and even if they hadn't been tasked with looking for him, he was the prime minister, and despite his attempts at a disguise, anyone from the palace might recognize him.

Across the heads of two brawling men, he saw the marines were drinking and laughing. They were off duty, but it was still best to avoid them.

The crowd burst into a mixture of cheers and curses, and one of the fighters staggered around the pit, blood smeared on his face, his arms raised in celebration.

"There," said Oliver, nodding at a nondescript door hidden in the shadows.

They opened it and proceeded down a brick tunnel, lit sporadically by lanterns hung on the wall. The sounds of fighting and revelry faded behind them until they were heard again in front.

"The men back there are brawlers and thugs," said Oliver. "Ahead, we'll find entertainment for the peers and the merchants. Everyone fighting in the next room will have won several bouts and showed some measure of skill. They may have gained a patron, or the house will sponsor them. This is where the real wealth changes hands and the reason the watchmen never raid the place. No one wants to accidentally arrest a peer."

Sam grunted. "They'd have no problem tossing one of those commons in the gaol, though, would they? They certainly kept me locked up for less than many in here are guilty of."

"Aye, but many in here can pay their way out," said Oliver. He looked over his shoulder at her. "What was it you did?"

She ignored him, and around a bend in the brick-lined hallway, they found themselves facing two bouncers, each as large as the original man who had guarded the first entryway.

Sam whispered, "How will we talk our way around these two? I'm guessing they're less likely to be fooled."

Oliver nodded. He strode up to the two men and looked them right in the eye.

One of the guards nodded and turned to open the door.

Oliver walked through, Sam on his heels.

"Frozen hell, do they know you?" she asked.

"Seems so," he replied with a grin. "That first man is trained to let no one in. These two are trained to let the right sort in. I can't imagine they'll be running to tell on us to my father, though."

She spluttered, shaking her head in consternation.

The room they'd entered wasn't so different from the first fighting chamber. The vices of the commons and the peers were much the same, but the peers had better seating. Tiers of benches set with padded cushions rose around the pits. Girls, dressed in tight, revealing dresses, walked amongst them offering drinks or other intoxicants. Liveried men shuttled between their masters and the wager makers.

The pit itself had the same sawdust floor and the same shirtless men prowling within it, but these men were skilled and lethal. They followed the same rules — fight until one man could no longer continue, but broken noses, split lips, and swollen eyes were the smallest of the scars they'd carry. These were the type of men who could seriously wound or kill another with only their fists. It was their job, and they did it for a great deal of silver. In this room, a few successful prize bouts could set up a man to retire for life or, just as easily, end it all too soon.

One such loser was being dragged out near them. Two attendants held his arms and pulled him across the rough floor, his feet trailing listlessly behind. Oliver could see his jaw was swollen, likely broken, from what must have been an epic blow. As a younger man, Oliver would have been eager to see the confrontation that led to such carnage, but now, it just made him sick. He shook his head, seeing the man's eyes squeezed tightly shut, hearing his low moans.

Then, the man blinked, and Oliver gasped.

Twin, glowing purple eyes turned slowly to stare at them. The man seemed to gather his strength and pulled himself upright. The two attendants backed away, confused, but the man, or what had once been one, had no concern for the attendants. He took a shuffling, awkward step toward Oliver and Sam.

"Duke," hissed Sam, "your plan of sneaking in doesn't seem to be working very well."

He nodded and drew the two katars from beneath his jacket. "I can see that. I think it's time for the backup plan."

"The backup plan?" questioned Sam. "What's the backup plan?"

"We fight."

THE PRIESTESS XX

"WHAT'S THE BACKUP PLAN?" questioned Sam, unable to look away from the glowing, spectral eyes of the injured pit fighter.

"We fight," claimed Duke.

She shrugged and then lunged forward, drawing one of her kris daggers and slashing it at the fighter in the same motion. The sharp edge of the blade split the man's face, and in an instant, the purple glow faded from his eyes. He collapsed limply. The two men who had been carrying him stared at her, mouths agape.

"Invested with a shade, not a reaver, for what that's worth," she advised.

"There are more of them," warned Duke.

A dozen men, shirtless, most of them sporting fresh wounds from bouts of fisticuffs, shuffled toward them. Screams rose from the benches and around the room as peers and merchants realized something was terribly wrong.

A woman, dressed in a billowing silk dress more appropriate for a debutante ball than a pit fight, stumbled in front of the approaching pack of men. One reached out and gripped her head, twisting it sharply until the woman's spine cracked. The creature shoved the dead woman away, but she pivoted back, her head hanging loosely from her neck, her eyes glowing purple.

Beside Sam, Duke shifted his grip on his katars and nodded to her. The two of them advanced.

She kept her eye on the guards and attendants scattered throughout the room. If they misunderstood what was happening and became involved, she and Duke would have no way of facing them all, but against a dozen men, moving awkwardly as if they were suspended on strings, the two of them had a chance.

One of the fighters, a big, burly man with an impressive red mustache and a disturbing amount of hair on his chest, charged her.

She let him come then dodged to the side, sliding her blade along the back of his leg to cripple him. He fell, but instead of crying in pain or rising to his knees, he flopped forward and lay still.

"All we have to do his injure them!" called Sam. "They'll fall like lesser shades."

Duke ran to the side, circling the pack of possessed pit fighters, darting at them and lashing out with his katars. The inscribed blades nicked the creatures, felling them one by one, drawing their attention to the peer.

Sam plunged into the pack. Windmilling her arms, she cut through the center of the group, slashing five of them in the space of a few heartbeats. Duke cleaned up the rest, and soon, there was just one man left. Unlike the others, this one did not attack. Instead, it stood, watching them.

She shifted her grip on her kris daggers, worried.

The creature opened its mouth and with a wretched, tortured voice, uttered, "You've chosen poorly. You should have joined me or fled."

Sam lunged forward and stabbed her dagger into its side.

The fighter collapsed like the others.

Duke looked at her and shrugged. "That wasn't so bad."

"No, it—" she began. She bit off her words and cursed.

Duke, frowning, turned.

"Frozen hell," he said. "There's a door on the other side of the room. Maybe it can be barred, if we can get there."

Between them and the other side of the room, two hundred men and women were shuffling toward them, taking the slow, painful steps of the spirit-infested. It seemed every man and woman in the place had fallen under the thrall of King Edward.

"He's possessing people with a thought," hissed Sam. "This is the power of the great spirit."

"Why not us?" asked Oliver, shifting his grip on his katars.

"My tattoos might be granting enough protection, or your blood is strong enough to oppose him," said Sam. "Hells, I don't know. Maybe he's giving us a chance to fight our way through."

"He's toying with us," growled Duke.

She shrugged uncomfortably. King Edward had been toying with them for months, dancing them on his strings as easily as he did the possessed.

"What do we do?" asked Duke, edging nervously closer to the throng of slow-moving puppets. "Any ideas?"

"Run," she suggested.

Moving quickly, cutting down the stray possessed man or woman who stumbled into their way, they circled the room and the largest pack of the creatures, the huge benches around the fighting pit serving as a natural barrier to slow their attackers.

Outside the door to the next hall, she slashed the face of one former guard, banishing the spirit that infested it, then raised her forearm to block a swing from a second. Duke thrust a katar into the creature's gut, and they moved into the tunnel.

There was a heavy, steel door, which together they were able to muscle shut. They locked it with a bolt as thick as her wrist.

She muttered, "Well, they're not getting through that."

From the other side of the door, they heard thumps as the creatures reached the barrier, but she doubted even combined they had the strength to break through. The door was designed to protect against serious raids by the royal marines and buy the patrons time to escape.

Leaning against the door, she looked down another brick-lined tunnel, just like the one they'd taken between the two fighting chambers. Lanterns hung on the walls, filling the corridor with a yellow glow. The passageway undulated and bent, following the curve of the city or perhaps snaking around the underground rail lines. She couldn't see more than twenty yards away.

"What comes next?" she asked Duke. "If we run into that many of those things in a confined area like this, it's going to get messy. They're slow, but we need space to outmaneuver them."

"No more fighting pits," he assured her. "It's, ah, it's a bit of a maze from here on out. Tunnels and rooms are sprawled haphazardly. They built them where they could find room to dig, I guess. There are some areas set aside as pleasure houses, potion dens, and the like. I'd guess there are other criminal enterprises down here, but it wasn't the kind of thing they showed a young duke during the tour."

"We've got to worry about more of the possessed," she stated. He nodded.

"We'd best get going, then," she suggested. "I don't know what else your father will have waiting for us, but I know getting pinned in this tunnel with a room full of his summonings behind isn't going to go well."

They started off, stalking the brick corridors, moving quickly when the way was clear, slowly when they approached branches in the path.

She worried they would find more shambling foes, but instead, they found dead bodies. Dozens then hundreds of dead bodies. They'd been killed messily, torn apart by what looked to be tooth and claw — attendants of the sprawling complex that was the Filthy Beggar, patrons, pit fighters, and fallen women. All died in a panic, trying to get away from something. Evidently, none of them succeeded. The stench of blood permeated the space, and Sam began to sweat in the close confines of the narrow tunnels and low-ceilinged rooms.

"I had no idea this place was down here," muttered Sam, stepping over the mutilated body of a half-naked woman.

"You haven't spent much time in Southundon," remarked Duke. "After a time, most everyone hears about it, even if they never find their way here. When they do, some flee in disgust. Others become regulars."

"You were a regular?" asked Sam.

Oliver, looking queasily at a man who appeared to have been ripped in two, replied, "No, not a regular. I just passed through on my way out of the palace. Some of my associates came here often, though. They'd wager large on the pit fights, seeking a thrill that was missing from their lives. I always preferred to have my own adventures. I'd rather experience the excitement of discovery and find a new world than pay to see two men beat each other senseless."

"Aye," agreed Sam, "if I'm going to pay two muscular men to do something, it's not fight."

Duke looked back at her, frowning. Then the wall beside him exploded in a shower of brick and dirt. He was flung away like he'd been kicked by a giant, and she screamed in astonishment as a nightmarish creature crawled from the hole. It had skin the color of dead ash, thick arms and legs, and no hair on its body. A long, curved horn protruded from its forehead, catching her gaze and then almost her throat as the monster swung toward her, trying to skewer her.

She scrambled back, and the beast came after her, brushing against the wall, crushing brick as it came, smashing against the lanterns hanging on the wall, extinguishing them. Sam retreated until she found an open room, a place she would have space to maneuver and where the beast couldn't easily knock out all of the lights. Even with the extra illumination, she could hardly see the thing, like it was cloaked in swirling shadow. She saw enough to tell it was huge, four times her size, and nearly indestructible as it crushed through a pillar of solid stone. Mortar and rock rained down, but it kept coming, as if the thick stone had been no more substantial than tall blades of grass.

She tripped, stumbling over a body and falling onto her bottom, stunned.

The creature reared above her, its horn snagging on the low ceiling. It bellowed, the sound causing a rain of dust to fall from above, echoing down the brick tunnels and back. It flexed its arms wide, and a spike of steel burst from the creature's chest, the point of Duke's broadsword emerging bloodlessly. The monster whimpered and then fell to the side.

Duke was standing behind it, half his face covered in brick dust, the other half in blood. He held up his broadsword, "I knew there was a reason to bring this."

Mutely, she nodded and struggled to her feet.

"What was that?" he asked, a finger touching his scalp gingerly where the skin had been torn open.

She could only shake her head, frightened that King Edward had called upon a creature she'd never heard of, disturbed at how quickly she'd retreated and then fallen. If Duke hadn't been there…

"Thanks for distracting it," he said earnestly, looking down at his broadsword as if he meant to wipe blood from it, but the blade was as bare as when he'd drawn it. He glanced at the fallen creature and shuddered.

"Next time, you distract it, and I'll sneak up from behind," she rasped.

They started walking again, both of them looking nervously at the crater the beast had emerged from. It was a large pocket of earth and brick. There was nothing to show how it had gotten there.

"This entire tunnel could be lined with… with things like that," she warned.

Duke nodded grimly.

"We can't survive this," she realized.

"I've got an idea," claimed Duke. "We've got to… we've got to make it a little farther."

Mindless, shambling possessed emerged from darkened corridors, raising numb fingers grasping for throats. Ephemeral shades appeared from within the shadows, clutching at limbs, trying to snare her and Duke's arms where they couldn't swing their blessed weapons. Monsters, indescribable, burst from walls, and in one terrifying case, the ceiling. Wolfmalkin and grimalkin, their senses fortunately blunted by the confusing underground passages, waited for them around half-a-dozen corners.

Oliver was limping from an injured leg, and he constantly used his off hand to wipe blood from his eyes. Claws had raked Sam's back, tearing her vest, her shirt, and her skin. She could feel the parallel lines of where three talons had parted her flesh as easily as knife would cut paper. Blood leaked down the small of her back, gluing her shirt to her body. The healing potion she'd quaffed had merely slowed the flow to a trickle and reduced a myriad of bumps and bruises to a dull ache that seemed to cover her entire body. Her throat ached with every breath where several hands had tried to close around her neck. She and Duke were battered, dragging, and she'd become certain they wouldn't make it out of the nightmare tunnels when he paused in front of her.

"What?" she croaked, rubbing at her throat.

"I don't want to say anything in case he can hear," muttered Duke, a hand against the wall, his head bobbing from exhaustion and pain.

She waited, air wheezing in and out of her open mouth.

He pointed to the wall, and when she looked closer, she could see the brick was molded around a black metal sheet that rose from floor to ceiling.

"Can you… can you use your supernatural strength?" he questioned.

She nodded, unsure what he was asking.

From his seed, she'd gained power, incredible strength and speed. She'd infused that power into her tattoos, hiding them from the spirits and extending that protection to Duke as well. The shades had difficulty detecting them, and it may have been what prevented the king from simply possessing them, but their enemies were thick in the tunnels, and there was no way around. The increased strength and speed she had was churning at a low burn, but it gave little advantage when their opponents were the size of a carriage and as dense as a block of stone.

She shuddered at the thought, recalling one slavering monster they'd given up trying to fight and had simply ran. The thing was out there, somewhere behind them.

Duke tapped the metal sheet, drawing her out of her exhausted reverie. She saw bolts in the metal, sealing it shut. He mimicked opening it, and below their feet, she felt a thrum, the rumble of the rail.

Her eyes opened in surprise, and he nodded to confirm her guess.

Hells. An exhaust tube for the rail lines. It meant the locomotives and their cars would be passing directly beneath their feet. This tube was carrying the filthy air from the mechanical engines up to the surface. If they could...

She closed her eyes, whispering utterances in a language long forgotten in Enhover. She sheathed her kris daggers and pinched her wrists at the terminal points of Kalbeth's ink. She didn't call upon the full power of the spirits, did not bring the shades through the shroud and into the patterns injected into her skin, but she borrowed some.

Putting her fingers against the metal, trying to wedge the tips of the digits beneath the sheet of steel, she felt cold power coursing through her veins. The seed of kings amplified what she was already capable of. She could do this. Grunting, she wiggled her fingers deeper, pressing into the metal, forcing it apart, and then she peeled it like the skin of a fruit.

A horrible screech echoed down the hall, but there was nothing they could do about that. Wolfmalkin and grimalkin would hear the noise but hopefully not be able to follow it to the source in the confusing maze of tunnels. The shades may not have heard it at all.

She ripped the panel the rest of the way open and found a tube roughly twice the width of her shoulders. It was entirely black and smelled foul from the noxious fumes that boiled up from below. Looking down it, she couldn't see a bottom.

"Should we go back and try to find rope... somewhere?" whispered Duke.

She shook her head then held her hands and legs wide, showing him what she intended.

Wide-eyed, he looked back at her but did not argue. Both of them knew they couldn't continue in the tunnels. They'd been lucky so far, sustaining painful but not crippling injuries. Every sweep of the claw, clutch of a shade, or spinning brick dislodged from the wall could be the last. They had to escape, and buried beneath Southundon, surrounded by denizens of the underworld, there was nowhere else to go.

Leaning into the tube, she placed her hands on opposite sides of the metal cylinder. It was unpleasantly hot but not scalding. She inhaled cautiously and found she could barely breathe the foul air. She coughed it out, withdrew her head to gasp a lungful of cleaner air, and then stepped into the tube, quickly placing her boots on opposite walls, pressing out with her hands, holding herself up with the pressure.

She slipped, unable to find good purchase on the soot-covered metal, but the pressure from her arms and legs slowed her descent, and painstakingly, she slid down, the poisonous air closing around her, the light vanishing as in fits and jerks, she dropped into the earth.

Above her, the little light was snuffed out entirely out as Duke leaned in, cursing and attempting his own descent. Larger than her, he had less room to spread his limbs to get leverage against the walls. He was also twice her weight, and she could hear him slipping and sliding above her.

"Hells," she muttered.

She released some of the tension in her arms, letting her legs control what was quickly becoming a fall. They should have let him go first, but it was too late now. She wasn't climbing back up.

Grime and filth covered her, soot billowing in clouds as her feet scraped it from the metal walls. She held her breath and closed her eyes, knowing that stuff could kill her as easily as a blade, and she tried to move faster without dropping into a free fall.

Above her, Duke sounded like bone being dragged from a grave as his body slid down the metal tube. More soot cascaded down on top of her head from where he was knocking it loose, and her lungs began to burn from holding her breath. He snorted, but she didn't hear him take in more air. Like her, he was holding his breath. Like her, he wouldn't be able to do it much longer.

She looked down between her feet, blinking to keep her eyes from clogging with the black dust all around her. She couldn't see a damned thing.

If they were above a rail tunnel, she wasn't sure where it was. She wasn't sure in the pitch black how she would know when she reached the end of the tube. Would she simply drop down onto the tracks? Was there a platform, or... Sprits forsake it, they couldn't just drop onto the tracks. In the narrow rail tunnels, there would be nowhere to hide, nowhere to avoid the speeding mass of metal and combusted energy. She paused, unsure what to do.

Above her, Duke slipped and fell before arresting himself, one of his boots stomping painfully on the fingers of her left hand. She locked her knees with her back against the wall, reached up, and gripped his leg with her free hand. He shifted, and she moved her fingers.

He waited silently. She guessed that like her, his lungs were burning, his eyes watering or blind. He didn't move, though, didn't panic, yet.

Beneath her, she felt a tremble of motion in the tube and heard the deep rumble of an approaching locomotive.

She whispered, expending the last of her breath, "When I say go, you let go."

"To where?" he asked before falling into a terrible coughing fit and losing his grip on the sides of the tube. He slid half a yard down, his knee bumping against her head before he stopped himself again.

"We're going to land on top of a rail car, hopefully," she hissed, She hacked out her own coughs, unable to keep the fouled air from her lungs. She gasped. "It's the only way."

Still coughing, he didn't argue. She wasn't sure if it was because he couldn't get the breath to do it or because he didn't have a better idea.

The rail, moving quickly through the tunnel between stops, roared below.

"Go!" she cried, and she let go.

THE CARTOGRAPHER XXV

HE FELT her fall away below him.

He tucked his arms in and let go with his legs. His chest ached, and his heart hammered from lack of air. His stomach lurched at the sudden fall. His shoulders and knees bounced against the metal of the tube. Then suddenly, he was free of it. His booted feet smacked into something hard and moving very fast.

He was thrown from his feet and landed on his stomach. Inch by inch, his body began to slide backward along the steel roof of a railcar. There were dim lights somewhere in the tunnel, but he was too disoriented to identify the source. For a moment, he was confused about what had just happened, but he knew the slow slide down the railcar was not good. At some point, he would slide off the end of the thing.

He splayed his fingers against the metal roof, trying to find purchase on the smooth surface. Wind blew against his face. Above his head, he heard a high-pitched whistle as the top of the tunnel whizzed by.

Slowly, he began to get his bearings, to see that the light was reflected off the dark walls of the tunnel. It looked to be coming from within the car. Three or four yards above his head was the solid stone ceiling of the rail tunnel.

Periodically, they rushed beneath tighter sections. He swallowed uncomfortably as he felt the roaring air compress when they passed a low-hanging protrusion. Had the timing been different, Sam and his bodies could have crashed into the stone at speed.

Sam.

He looked around, not seeing her in front of him, and then realized she'd dropped first. She'd be back—

"Duke!"

She wasn't anywhere he could see in the dim light of the tunnel, so he began scooting backward, letting the wind shove him along the surface of the roof. He could vaguely spot the car behind them, but she was not there. He'd heard her, though, hadn't he?

"Duke, I can't hold! Hells, are you up there?"

He scurried across the roof and looked over the end of the railcar.

Sam was hanging there, between his car and the one behind, panic in her eyes, her fingers dug into the steel roof trying to hold herself up. As he watched, her hand slipped, and she began to fall.

He lunged forward and caught her wrists, his face half a yard from hers. Her mouth was open in a wordless scream, and he could see terror and relief battling in her eyes.

Over the sound of the rumbling wheels, he shouted, "I've got you."

Then, the car jolted as they took a hard turn, and he slid forward, toppling over Sam's head, both of them falling between the cars. He fell, bouncing off the front of the car behind them and then landing on a metal platform, his bones creaking at the jarring impact.

Sam crashed down on top of him, all knees and elbows.

For a moment, he expected to feel the steel wheels slice through his body, the weight of the car pressing the broad discs as effectively as a blade, but it never came. He realized they must have landed on the couplings between the cars. He shifted, trying to work his way out from under Sam, but he stopped. He was staring at the blurred steel lines of the rail just half a yard from his face. They were on the coupling, but his head was hanging off of it, dangling down between the cars.

He cursed and tried to arrange himself to a safer position, but Sam was lying on top of him. He couldn't risk throwing her off.

Fortunately, in moments, the car began to slow. He called, "We're approaching a station."

"Which one?" gasped Sam, sounding dazed.

"Does it matter?" he asked.

As the car slowed, he wiggled out from under her. He jumped down onto the side of the track, dirty rocks shifting beneath his boots as he landed.

"I suppose not," she admitted. She let him pull her down after him.

The car came to a final rocking stop, nudging him on the shoulder and nearly knocking him down. Ignoring it, he dragged Sam behind him, emerging from between the two cars and clambering onto the waist-high passenger platform. A handful of people, disembarking or boarding, stared at the two of them in shock.

"Annual inspection," he mumbled, moving quickly through the sparse crowd as they parted before him. He looked at Sam and smirked. Her face was blackened by soot, her clothes filthy and torn. For better or worse, she was completely unrecognizable. He supposed he would be as well.

They climbed the stairwell that led to the street, his legs aching from where some creature had smashed him against the wall of the tunnel and later when he landed hard onto the rail car. His face stung from half-a-dozen cuts and scrapes. His hand left a sickening trail of soot and blood on the brass railing of the stairwell. When they emerged onto the street, he breathed a deep lungful of air, glad to see the night sky above him. The sky and the burned-out hulk of the Church's library.

"Through there," he said. "It will take us right to the palace."

Nodding, fingers probing some injury on her shoulder, Sam followed him across the square. They ignored the startled looks from the few people sober enough to realize how out of place they were on the streets so late at night, and they entered the ruins of the Church.

THEY SLINKED THROUGH THE BURNT TIMBERS AND SCATTERED PILES OF ash. He hoped they'd worked their way around the rest of his father's traps, but he wasn't sure how the old man had known they would be passing through the Filthy Beggar in the first place. Had the shades been summoned there in preparation, or had they been sent there after he and Sam were detected? Would King Edward be aware they'd changed routes by going into the rail line? Could he reposition his forces?

As they worked their way through the ruined hulk of the Church's library, Oliver decided it didn't matter. It was too late to turn away. Now that his father knew they were in the city, it would be just as difficult to flee as it would be to move forward. They were committed, and the only way to finish was to keep going.

The doorway to the palace proper was unguarded but locked. Thick bands of iron bound it shut, along with a massive lock the size of Oliver's fist.

"Think you could use your super strength again to crush that lock?" Oliver asked Sam.

"Not without making a ruckus your father will hear all the way up in his tower," she whispered back.

A man cleared his throat behind them, and they spun.

Duke John Wellesley was standing in the middle of the burned down Church, barely visible in the shifting moonlight that bled between the clouds in the sky and the charred spars of the Church's buttresses.

"John," gasped Oliver.

His brother nodded, slapping his palm with a bit of metal.

A key, Oliver realized. The key to the lock behind them, he guessed.

"You are going to kill Father, aren't you?" accused his brother.

Oliver shook his head, grim-faced. "I have to. John, Northundon…"

"Philip told me everything," said John, "everything you told him, at least."

"You know, then," said Oliver. He watched his brother, but John made no move except fiddling with the key. "We cannot allow this to continue, John. Tens of thousands died in Northundon. Tonight, we saw hundreds sacrificed just to slow our approach. Hundreds of innocents, John! These are our people! He's killing them like they're no more than animals, their only purpose to support his awful power."

"You've turned your back on us then, the Crown, your family?" demanded John.

"If the Crown has no care for the people, then yes," said Oliver. "If our family has no loyalty to the nation, if we exist only to feast on the fruits of others, then yes. I cannot live that life any longer, John."

His older brother looked away.

"I've seen what terrible price our colonies pay," continued Oliver. "I've seen the blood that is shed to fuel our engines of conquest. You have, too. Here, in this building, you saw the reaver. You saw the bodies that it had stripped of flesh. Father is the one who released that thing, all to convince me to stay in Enhover! He let loose two dozen more of them, John. We trapped them inside the druid keep across the river. If we hadn't… You were here. You saw what that thing was."

John grimaced.

"Philip has only seen one side of the old man," insisted Oliver. "You've seen the other with your own eyes. You've seen the price that our people are expected to pay for our greed. Can you live with it, John?"

"I don't know any other way," admitted his older brother. John drew a deep breath and exhaled, his gaze rolling around the ruins of the library, the look on his face showing he was remembering that night, remembering the terrors he'd witnessed. He turned back to Oliver. "If you're successful, what will you do? Will you take the crown for yourself and become a different type of dictator? Will you come for us next?"

Oliver shook his head slowly. "No, brother. If I'm successful, I will leave. You'll never see me again. It's the only way."

John opened his mouth to reply.

Oliver cut him off. "Philip is a good man. He could be a good king, but he would never understand this. You and he, together, you could do well for our people, he as king, you as... however you see fit to serve. I do this for our family, John, and the empire. Not for myself."

"Where will you go?" asked John.

Oliver shrugged. "I haven't decided."

Sam shifted beside him, and Oliver knew that soon, she would do something rash. It wasn't long ago she'd been willing to kill him for her cause. Putting a dagger into John would barely make her blink. On the threshold of the palace, she would let nothing stand in her way.

"There's something else, John. Mother was alive all of this time," said Oliver. "She was in the Darklands, a sorceress. She fled Northundon and hid for the last two decades. Father knew that she was there. He knew and did nothing. He didn't tell us she was there. All of his talk of family, but he didn't tell us about Mother."

John's face twisted in confusion.

"Father lied to us. He's always lied to us," declared Oliver. "He lied to us about Northundon, about the Coldlands, about everything! The blood he's shed is not worth it. It cannot be. We have a responsibility to stop this."

"You're right," admitted John after a long pause.

"You'll give me the key, then?" asked Oliver.

John shook his head. "Father gave me this key. He told me you'd be coming this way. He's testing me, I think. If you walk through that door, you won't walk far. There's another way, a way I used to... It's another way. You know the Speckled Beetle, the pub?"

Oliver nodded.

"Ask for Rosie's room," instructed John. "It contains a passage into the bowels of the palace. You'll come into the servant's quarters, three floors below our own. You'll need to give them some coin, but they won't ask questions. You can find Father in the throne room."

Oliver nodded. "Thank you, John. Will you come with us and face him beside me?"

His brother shook his head. "No, Oliver, I cannot. If we failed, Father would know I did not give you the key. My life will be forfeit. I accept that, but I cannot sacrifice Matilda and our children as well. Family, you know... I haven't lost all of my loyalties."

"I understand," said Oliver. "I will try to keep you out of it, if we can. Good luck to you, John. One way or the other, this will be the last we see each other."

"The Speckled Beetle, Rosie's room," said John. He tossed the key onto the ash-strewn floor and left.

"No hug goodbye?" asked Sam after the duke passed from earshot. "You think he was lying? The trap could be the way he directed us."

"No, he wasn't lying," said Oliver. "He's my brother. I've known him my entire life. He was telling the truth. I saw the fear in his eyes, for Matilda and their children. He'd do anything for them, Sam, sacrifice it all."

"You've known your father your entire life, too," she reminded.

Oliver could only shake his head. She was right. "Let's go find that pub."

———————

THE TREK THROUGH THE UNDERBELLY OF THE PALACE WAS STRANGELY quiet. It felt as if the servants of the place, like animals in the forest, sensed something was amiss and had burrowed into their lairs. Perhaps they'd heard there was a commotion in the Filthy Beggar. Word of hundreds of people dying mysteriously would spread quickly, if anyone had made it out alive to begin the rumor. It was a well-trafficked venue, and even from the palace, there would be patrons of the place out late at night.

Or maybe the denizens of the palace felt something was off with their master. King Edward, normally even-keeled and calm, was overseeing more excitement in his realm than any time since the Coldlands War between the preparation for war with the Darklands, the loss of Imbon Colony, the threat of pirates in the tropics, and the hushed whispers that sorcery had returned to the empire. It was enough that experienced palace servants would know to disappear.

It worked well for Oliver and Sam, and limping along the floors of the stately, stone building, they climbed and snuck to the hallways outside of the throne room. Peering from within a shadowed alcove, they could see the throne room doors were guarded. A dozen royal marines stood outside, half of them clutching brass-barreled blunderbusses, the other half leaning tall pikes against their shoulders. They looked bored, up so late at night, but they were awake. Any marine guarding the king who fell asleep at their post would have been strapped to a post and flogged, sufficient punishment to keep their eyes open, even if they did look as if they would rather be in their beds or the pubs.

There were more guards than usual posted outside of the king's rooms, but Oliver supposed Captain Ainsley's activities above the harbor must have stirred them up. Any sensible commander would bolster the posting near the king after that.

Oliver and Sam retreated to where they wouldn't be overheard.

"Any way we can sneak around?" she asked.

He frowned and shook his head. There was no way around. There were no secret passages leading into the throne room. There was the front door and the back door, and both would be equally protected with a dozen well-armed marines and whatever supernatural defenses his father might have raised. He shivered. Those could be invisible.

For all he knew, they'd already been spotted, and his father was waiting for their arrival. If they had been seen, the king could know exactly where they were. He would be prepared. There would be no luring him out of the throne room, no ambushing him on his way to his bed or performing some other trickery. They had to face him and do it on his terms.

"There's no sense waiting," said Oliver, realizing that despite his hopes of a stealth approach, it simply wasn't going to happen, "and there's no way around the guards. Could you use some of your powers?"

She smirked. "I can be faster and stronger than normal, but I don't have the ability to magic us past a dozen men. We're going to have to fight our way through. On the plus side, your father probably already knows we're here, so whatever commotion we make won't give us away."

Oliver grunted. "I'm not sure that's an advantage."

It was Sam's turn to shrug.

Oliver opened his jacket and pulled out two vials of fae light. "Try not to kill too many of them."

She glanced around and then strode over to a tall, brass lampstand. She removed the lamp oil and the wick and was left with a yard-and-a-half-long brass club. She hefted it. "I can't make any promises, but this should be slightly less lethal than my daggers."

Drawing a deep breath, Oliver unstoppered the vials of the fae. The tiny creatures swarmed out, flying close around him.

"Ready?" he asked.

"Ready," she confirmed.

The fae darted out into the hall, keeping their lights dim, and shot toward the guards. Oliver and Sam waited several seconds then came running out after the fae. The little creatures reached the guards and burst into light, crowding around each of the men's eyes, effectively blinding them.

Mumbled curses and shouts of alarm hid the sound of Oliver's and Sam's boots on the thick rugs leading to the throne room. They were in the midst of the men before anyone knew they were there.

Sam lay about her with the brass lampstand, clubbing men in the head with ruthless efficiency.

Oliver, his hands balled into fists, began throwing haymakers, clouting men on the side of the head, and knocking them unconscious.

One man turned at the last second and caught Oliver's knuckles on the bridge of his nose. He shrieked in pain but was quickly cut off as Oliver swung a hook with his other fist and bashed the man on the temple. Oliver shook his hand and murmured a silent apology to his opponent. The guard was just doing his job, after all.

Without word, both he and Sam turned, stepping over unconscious bodies of royal marines and approaching the huge double doors of the throne room. Oliver placed a hand on each door and shoved. The heavy slabs of wood and metal shifted then stopped.

"Spirits forsake it!" cried Oliver. "He locked the door!"

A call sounded behind them. Another squad of guards who evidently heard the scuffle were coming to investigate.

"In fairness," said Sam. "We probably should have foreseen that."

Oliver kicked the unyielding door.

"Allow me," suggested Sam.

Oliver stepped away and watched nervously as Sam's eyes grew distant. A chill settled into the hallway, and he knew she was demanding the assistance of the spirits.

Running feet echoed ahead of the approaching guards.

Oliver held his breath. They didn't have much time.

Sam took two quick steps and slammed the brass lampstand against the center of the two doors. The impact was shocking, and noise of the blow boomed down the hallway with a thunderous crash. Metal twisted and squealed as the bar across the doors bent. They opened a hand-width.

Sam brushed her hair back from her face and then swung again, smashing the lampstand against the protesting iron bar that locked the door. This time, it snapped under the force of the blow, and the doors swung wide on well-oiled hinges.

Oliver and Sam rushed inside. He spun, slamming the huge doors shut. He looked to relock them but saw the bent and broken bar was useless now. When the guards arrived, there would be no keeping them out.

Sam was already approaching the throne, walking down the wide, crimson rug toward King Edward, who sat upon his throne, chuckling at them.

Oliver joined her, striding toward his father, his eyes darting about the room, looking for a trap he was certain they were about to spring.

"John is dead," remarked King Edward when they came within twenty yards of him. "He betrayed the Crown, and the punishment is death."

Oliver stopped. "You killed your own son?"

"It seems I'm just getting started in that business," replied his father with a smirk. "You could have stood beside me, you know. That's what I wanted. You could have been the balance to my own power. Not just the head of the ministry, but a true force in this world. You have the potential, but unfortunately, it has to be your choice."

Oliver grunted, and out of the corner of his eye, he saw Sam edging to the side, trying to get another angle to the throne. When it came time, perhaps his father could not stop both of them. Perhaps one of them would get through the king's defenses to strike a blow, but first, Oliver had to know.

"Why did you do it?" he asked. "You had the airships. You

had the royal marines. Enhover wasn't in immediate danger from any other nation. With the might of our technology, we could have accomplished anything. You had the means to expand the empire already. Why did you sacrifice Northundon, Father? Why?"

His father, sitting upon the throne, tugged at his goatee.

"None of this makes any sense!" cried Oliver, taking a threatening step forward. "What was it all for?"

His father stood and began pacing on the dais before the throne. "I've been sitting here for hours, waiting to see if you would make it to me, watching to see if you are worthy. If, despite everything, you could still be convinced to join me."

"Join you?" spit Oliver.

"The world needs balance," stated King Edward. "It's a necessary component of power, a way to grow without the entire thing toppling over. To grow my own might, for the stability of Enhover, there must be balance. You, Oliver, are that balance. I've known since you were a boy, since I rocked you to sleep and watched you take your first steps. I could feel it within you, the welling of life. You, unlike your brothers, had the instincts to use what flows within your blood. Life magic, druid magic, it is the balance to my own power. That you stand here before me is proof enough. I will ask one more time. Join me. Together, we can do great things."

Oliver shook his head, confused. He shouted, "I've already defied you! Crown, empire, I want none of it! It's not worth the price."

"If not for the Crown, then for me," said his father. "Without the energy you can call upon, without the balance of druid magic returning to Enhover, the empire will crumble. I will fall. Is that want you want, son? Think of what will happen to your brothers, to their children, to all of the children in the empire. They need your balance."

"There's another way," declared Oliver. He stepped forward again, his hand on his broadsword. "You say you need my magic to balance yours, that the empire will fall if I do not join you, but that's only if you remain on the throne. If I remove you, that will restore the balance. Your presence, Father, is what will bring the empire toppling down."

"Remove me?" King Edward laughed. "You do not have the strength to remove me. You don't even know what it is you face! You are ignorant children, playing at matters you cannot comprehend. Nothing is as it seems, son!"

"You conducted the ritual in Northundon," accused Sam. "Lilibet told the truth. Did she know it was you, that you bound Ca-Mi-He? Is that why she fled?"

Eyes twinkling with mirth, King Edward shook his head. "You will never understand."

"My mother was innocent." Oliver gasped.

His father tilted his head, smiling at him.

"But she was a sorceress!" exclaimed Sam. "I've seen what she studied. We saw her! She was a powerful sorceress…"

King Edward stood upon the dais, glancing between them as they were mired in confusion.

"Lilibet," gasped Sam suddenly. "You knew she was in the Darklands. You used her, somehow… She was part of the bargain."

"Yes, part of the bargain, but Lilibet was not the sacrifice," claimed King Edward, clearly enjoying toying with them.

"I don't understand," hissed Sam.

Oliver saw her looking at him, searching for an answer, but he had none. His mother was sorceress, they'd seen that much, but it made no sense. How had she escaped? How had his father known and done nothing? Lilibet had a connection to Ca-Mi-He, didn't she? If his father had bound Ca-Mi-He, then surely he'd—

"Lilibet Wellesley died in Northundon, didn't she?" Oliver asked suddenly. "It wasn't her. It was Ca-Mi-He we faced in the Darklands. That is why she was so cold, detached. That is why she didn't… why I didn't recognize her at first. She wasn't my mother any longer, was she? You knew! You knew this entire time!"

Fingers pinching his goatee, the king nodded. "What you faced in the Darklands was not your mother."

"How… how did the body…" he stammered. "We saw her. If Ca-Mi-He took her, then who conducted the ritual? Who…"

Sam's fists were clenched around the hilts of her daggers, her body tensed to spring, but like him, she must have been facing paralyzing confusion. He wanted to attack, but he had to know. His father, Ca-Mi-He, his mother. He had to know.

"So many clues, but you children still do not understand," chided King Edward, wagging a finger at them. "I will tell you all, my son, but only if you join me. Join me and become my balance."

"Tell us now," demanded Oliver.

"Knowledge is power," declared King Edward. "It is power in our world. It is power in the other. Knowledge is the only power. When you know more than your opponent, you will always defeat them. I tried to teach you, to show you and your brothers, but you never understood, never truly grasped. Airships, firearms, bombs, swords, silver, and sorcery, they are nothing more than an accounting of the score, the physical sum of what our knowledge has earned us. Those are not power. They are what power can buy. Since you were a boy, I tried, but I see you will never understand. I'm afraid I can no longer teach you. In this world and the next, knowledge is power, and if you do not join me, I will not grant you that power. I am afraid this is the end, Oliver."

"Teach me," mumbled Oliver. "You never—"

The sacrifice had been fulfilled twenty years before, the bargain completed. What had his father gained from the sacrifice of Northundon? Why had he given the great spirit possession of Lilibet's body?

Oliver snarled in frustration, inadvertently reaching up to run his hand over his hair and touching the leather thong that kept it tied back. A habit he'd had since Northundon, a comfort ever since he'd lost her. He maintained that habit even after what happened in the Darklands. He'd been doing it for twenty years, ever since…

His fingers traced the knot, the same one he tied nearly every morning since then. He'd been making the gesture ever since he'd lost his mother. His protector, his teacher.

"No…" he whispered.

"Do you understand, then?" asked King Edward. "Do you finally understand?"

"Why?" he croaked, painful knowledge crashing through him.

"What is he talking about?" asked Sam, but Oliver could not answer her.

He couldn't form the words, couldn't move. It was like a dam had burst in his mind, and the torrent of understanding was washing him away, taking him from where he was, what he'd known, taking him somewhere different.

"You do not understand this world, Oliver," said the king. "There is so much you do not know, but there is one thing I taught you and your brothers, one thing that you do know. Family. Nothing is more important than family. I knew what I must do, what price I would have to pay to achieve what was necessary, but I could not leave you. I could never leave you."

"What the frozen hell are you two talking about?" cried Sam.

The king turned toward her. "Priestess, orphan, Sam, Samantha, sorceress, assassin. We all wear masks, do we not? All of us wear many faces. None of us are who we seem."

"D-Duke…" stammered Sam. "What is he saying?"

King Edward turned and met Oliver's stare, their eyes locking. "Duke, rake, Oliver, cartographer, prime minister, son. You've been many things, but not the one you needed to be. Not what I needed you to be. The balance… The empire will crumble in time without a druid. It will crumble because of you."

"It will stand because of me!" he shouted, drawing his broadsword. "I will pull you from that throne. You've no right to it."

"Pull me from the throne, will you?" cackled the king. "Your powers are weak, undeveloped. You have no strength to challenge me, Oliver."

"Remove your mask," commanded Oliver. "Show yourself, Mother."

The king, grinning madly, curled his fingers beneath his goatee and then peeled it back, his flesh pulling away like the skin of a snake. Inch by inch, the old man's countenance was shed, and a cold-eyed beauty was left in his place. Lips curled in amusement, she looked much the same she had in the Darklands. She had not aged a day. Her features were the same as he recalled, but her eyes were black, filling the sockets like terrible pools of endless night, like the dark of the underworld.

"Spirits forsake us," muttered Sam.

"I am sorry, my son," said Lilibet Wellesley, her voice strong, powerful. "If you will not join me, it is time you join your father in the underworld."

His mother, wearing the king's ermine and red velvet cape as she stood before the throne, was the embodiment of royalty, but she did not belong. It was not her throne to sit upon. She'd murdered her husband, sacrificed him and herself, and had taken his body. She'd ruled the empire for twenty years, guiding its expansion with her bloodstained hand. She'd sat the throne, no one knowing, no one realizing the awful presence in their midst.

Oliver growled low in his throat. "You've no right to that throne."

His mother snorted. "Try and take it from me, then."

Several things happened at once.

Oliver and Sam surged forward, charging Lilibet. The doors to the throne room burst open, and a score of royal marines rushed inside. The air between Oliver, Sam, and Lilibet split, tearing four rents into space through the shroud. From those holes emerged the creatures of the underworld. Shambling monsters, twisted and deformed, roared their rage as they entered the world, physically manifest.

"Hells!" screamed Sam, evidently still unable to utter anything other than a curse.

From the corner of his eye, Oliver saw her dodge to the side, narrowly avoiding the sweeping claws of some malformed creature but then crashing into the thing's spiked tail with her legs. The monster turned and swept her feet from beneath her, and she flipped into the air.

Oliver had no time to look after Sam, though, as two of the summonings closed on him, one tall and lean with ghastly yellow skin, the other squat and a sickly shade of green. Bristling spines covered its body, black ichor oozing down its vomit-colored skin.

Without thought, Oliver hurled his broadsword at the face of the shorter, fatter one. The steel spun end over end. Miraculously, the tip thudded directly into the center of the fiend's face, punching half its length into the monster's skull. Gurgling blue blood poured from its mouth, and the creature collapsed.

Oliver stared at it in shock and then nearly lost his head as the taller of the two circled its dead companion and lurched toward him, bony arms extended, clutching fingers grasping for him. He staggered away and drew his katars from beneath his jacket.

Behind him, firearms exploded as the marines discharged their weapons. Pellets whistled by Oliver, most of them scattering harmlessly against the walls of the room, a few tearing into the howling monster in front of him. Meat, torn from bone by the force of the shot, hung bloodlessly on the monster's frame.

A royal marine, brave and foolish, charged past Oliver, a smoking blunderbuss in one hand, a short sword in the other. The lean monster caught the man before he could close with his sword. One long arm gripping his shoulder, the other his skull, the summoning tore the marine's head clean off with a sharp twist of its wrist. Blood sprayed across the room as the monster tossed the dead man's head at his companions, and then it shoved the body aside and continued to advance on Oliver.

More firearms cracked, but none of the shot struck the approaching nightmare.

Oliver risked a quick glance behind him and saw blue-coated royal marines pouring into the room and contending with another half-dozen creatures emerging from open rifts in the shroud. Blocked by those foul apparitions, they would be of no help. Not to Oliver.

"We have to kill your father— your mother, whoever that is!" screamed Sam from across the room. "Kill her, and they lose the bridge. It's the only way to close the rips in the shroud."

Oliver ducked a lashing arm and lunged forward to bury a katar in the abdomen of the creature in front of him. He tore upward with the sharp blade, eviscerating the summoning, and then he ducked, avoiding a flailing arm that swept at his head.

The creature staggered away and collapsed, twitching, clutching at the gaping hole in its stomach. Beetles spilled from the wound, small and black, and they scurried across the floor and over Oliver's boots.

Eyes wide in horror, he looked to where Sam was surrounded by three new monsters and where more emerged from the openings his mother had torn to the underworld.

THE PRIESTESS XXI

COLD POWER SURGED through her veins and scalding heat burned her flesh where her tattoos ignited with fury. Patterns, designed and inked by Kalbeth and fueled by the seed of kings that she'd used in ritual to activate them, drew power directly from the open rents Lilibet had left to the underworld. The torrent of raw energy was unlike anything Sam had ever experienced, but it paled in comparison to the strength it would have taken to rip open the shroud.

Lilibet Wellesley wasn't dead. She'd been right. They had understood nothing. She'd been playing with them the entire time. Hells.

Monstrosities, huge, misshapen, and strong, stumbled into the world, disoriented and hungry. Sam had to banish them back to the place they came from, and she had to close the openings in the shroud.

She shouted to Duke, "We have to kill your father— your mother, whoever that is! Kill her and they lose the bridge. It's the only way to close the rips in the shroud."

She tried to charge the dais, to reach Lilibet, but shuffling figures closed around her. Pale skin covered taut muscles. Open mouths slavered, displaying jagged rows of wet teeth. Claws flexed, glistening and sharp or dull and bone white.

Power surged through her, making her giddy and strong. She launched herself at the nearest creature, seeming to fly into the air, her sinuous daggers held wide, slashing like the teeth of the beasts she faced.

Carving hunks of flesh off of the monsters, she twisted and spun through the crowd. Like her training in the barn so long ago, she dodged and weaved, using her daggers where she could, her feet where she couldn't. Flesh parted from the swipe of her blades, bone shattered beneath her supernatural strength. Half-a-dozen of the monsters fell before her in seconds, and then she attacked, rushing the dais, her daggers raised to taste Lilibet's blood.

She faltered, the unnatural power draining from her like water from a broken pitcher.

In front of her, smiling, Lilibet lowered a hand that had traced a burning pattern in the air. She tore off her cloak and the formal suit of the king and stood before Sam in a bright, red leather bodysuit. It was sculpted to the woman like a second layer of living skin. Skin that Sam had seen, but it had been that of an old man dressing after his bath. The woman's face, her body, was a mask that she'd worn for twenty years. It was as changeable as the clothes she'd thrown aside.

Lilibet Wellesley could be anything she wanted. She had achieved the peak of dark power. She was the ultimate sorceress. She'd bound and controlled even the great spirit Ca-Mi-He. Lilibet had reached the end of the dark path.

Lilibet launched herself at Sam.

Ducking, the priestess tried to slide beneath the queen, but Lilibet caught her shoulder with a hand and twisted in mid-air. The sorceress flung Sam like she was a rag doll. Tucking into a roll, Sam tumbled across the carpets and tile to land in a heap.

Lilibet brushed aside her summonings, shoving them out of her way, rending their flesh if they were slow to move. A royal marine, somehow broken away from the tumult at the back of the room, charged the queen.

The sorceress held up a hand and caught the man's face. She squeezed, crushing the flesh and bone as easily as Sam would squeeze the juice from a lemon. The man's head burst in a sickening shower of gore. Lilibet tossed him away and kept advancing.

Duke appeared as if out of nowhere at her side, thrusting at his mother with a katar, but she did not even look at him. She kept advancing on Sam, and Duke was swarmed by a dozen indistinct shadows before his blade could reach the sorceress. Shades swarmed over him like ants on sugar. He thrashed impotently with his katars, each strike banishing one of the shades, but two more would pile onto him, forcing him to the floor and grasping him with their insubstantial hands.

Sam surged off her knees and attacked, whirling her daggers in front of her in a complex weave, trying to draw Lilibet's eye. Then she tried to surprise the other woman with a quick slash toward her neck.

The sorceress lifted a hand and brushed Sam's dagger from her grip with the ease Sam would disarm a child.

Sam's wrist was numb where Lilibet had knocked against it, her fingers twitching spasmodically. She stabbed with her other dagger, but Lilibet caught her hand. Brutal cold crept down her arm, and Sam couldn't move it. Her muscles were paralyzed by the strength of Lilibet's sorcery.

Sam flung her head forward, the crown of her skull catching Lilibet square in the face, ripping open the other woman's skin above her eye. A trickle of blood leaked down the side of Lilibet's face.

Lilibet shoved her back, and Sam tripped over her own feet, falling to the floor, her numb arms hanging near useless at her side. The wind burst from her chest as her back slapped against the polished stone beneath her.

"Priestess, you surprise me," admitted Lilibet. The sorceress held her hand up to her brow, and before Sam's startled eyes, Lilibet's flesh knitted back together. With a touch, Lilibet had healed herself. The sorceress frowned at Sam. "The patterns on your body are clever. They are not inked by that corpulent seer who helped break the binding to the great spirit, she did not have the talent. Tell me, who inked those tattoos?"

Sam, feeling returning slowly to her arms, did not respond. She scooted herself backward, franticly scrambling for a plan, but coming up with nothing.

"You should have joined me," declared Lilibet.

Then she strode forward and bent, grasping Sam around the neck and lifting her one-handed. Fingers, cold as ice, hard as iron, closed around Sam's throat. As the other woman lifted her, all Sam could do was kick her feet. Her boots thudded harmlessly against Lilibet's leather-clad legs.

Sam called upon her markings, trying to infuse her body with supernatural power, but every time she activated the designs and called to the spirits to fill her, her strength ebbed and then quickly waned.

Lilibet smiled at her, one arm raised, holding Sam by the neck. "True power requires true sacrifice, girl. You've clung to life when you should have embraced death. Now, you will die anyway. Pathetic. I will bind your shade in my thrall. Whoever inked those patterns, whoever gave of themselves to help you, will be mine as well. Everything you know, everyone you love, will be mine."

Sam struggled, thrashing against Lilibet's impossible strength, unable to summon her own. The woman controlled the shroud, as William Wellesley, Yates, and Raffles had merely dreamt of. The sorceress could pull strength from that barrier, and she was able to block Sam from doing the same.

Lilibet was impossibly powerful. She was invincible.

Specks swirled in Sam's vision, making the other woman look splotchy and strange. Embrace death. She wouldn't. She couldn't. She kept fighting, and she clung to life, but she knew she could not win.

THE CARTOGRAPHER XXVI

SHADES PILED upon him like a suffocating blanket, dozens of them, the ephemeral bodies smothering him, forcing him to his knees. He struggled to free his arms, and he lashed out with his katars at his invisible tormentors, but as the blades passed through the shades, banishing them, more came. They poured from the rents in the shroud. Unimpeded, they spilled into the world.

He watched as Sam attacked and was easily repelled. He watched as his mother advanced on Sam and began to choke her. He could see the panic in Sam's movements, see that there was nothing she could do. He struggled, but the weight of the shades on top of him increased, threatening to shove him down onto the floor.

Balance. Control. The blood of kings. His mother. Ca-Mi-He. Sacrifice. The bargain.

His thoughts, like cold-numb fingers, scrabbled against the words, trying to make some sense of them, but he found no purchase. None of it arranged itself into a pattern that he could comprehend. He had no ideas. Nothing he could have done would have prepared him for this moment. He and Sam were as his mother said — ignorant. Like babes, they'd stumbled into the room, thinking that they knew what they faced, but they couldn't have. No one could have.

He pushed against the floor, heaving himself a hands-breadth higher, shrugging off shades, and banishing them with his punch knives, but more came.

Dark mirth filled him. Had they known, would it have made a difference? He still would have come, whether he thought he was facing his mother or his father. Had he known, he still would have been woefully unprepared. He and Sam could not combat her strength. They could not match her power.

As he fought against the shades, he saw flashes of Sam still struggling impotently against his mother. Around them, battle raged. Royal marines from all over the palace rushed into the room and then quickly died. Creatures from the underworld appeared, crawling through the rents in the shroud and falling on the warm flesh of the marines. Blunderbusses discharged with thunderous booms, and the steel of pikes flashed, but the men were no match for the nightmares they faced. The marines could do nothing against the cold, white fire of the underworld.

Oliver suddenly freed an arm and whipped his katar around, banishing half-a-dozen shades with the strike, but another of the apparitions wrapped around his wrist. He struggled against it, cursing under his breath.

The cold white fire of the underworld.

The shades he'd seen in his vision of the underworld had told him they were waiting for Lilibet, waiting for her to complete the bargain. They were looking for her.

But she'd offered the sacrifice. Lilibet Wellesley had been the one who offered the souls of Northundon to Ca-Mi-He. She'd given up her city, her home, for unrestrained power. The souls searched for her and had asked Oliver to find her, to complete the bargain, but she'd done her part. She'd made the sacrifice. Would she have sacrificed her own soul to seal the bargain?

He realized suddenly that the bargain the marching spectres told him about was not with his mother. It was for his mother.

Oliver fell back to his knees, another surge of shades toppling and overwhelming him. He reached out with his mind. He could feel Sam, her life force fluttering and fading rapidly. Like one of the fae, she burned but not for long. He could sense it, could sense that her end was near. His mother, she was there too. He could feel her now that he was aware. He cursed himself for missing it earlier. It was her. How could he have not felt her?

She burned. Cold bled from her in waves. Terrible, sorcerous strength, like the power of the shroud itself was invested in the woman. In his mother.

Oliver fell to his face, shades piling on top of him, breath wheezing from his lungs as the apparitions clustered on his back. He felt the spark of his mother's life. It was there, deep inside. She'd hidden it from him somehow. From everyone. For twenty years, she'd been hidden. She'd hidden from him, and who else?

He could not kill her. It was not his way. Not the way to balance.

He was a druid. Druids fostered life. They grew it.

He grasped for her spark and poured life into her. He made her life burn bright, shining like a beacon from Southundon's highest tower. He made her life force cry out and demand notice. Shining like a spotlight, it blazed forth, illuminating the throne room to his supernatural senses and sparkling through the open rents to the underworld.

The creatures of the underworld looked to her, sensing the blaze of her soul, but they were in her thrall. They could do nothing to harm her. Lilibet was death. She cloaked herself in it. He was life. He ripped away her cloak and forced her to shine.

The shades were crushing the breath from him. He couldn't draw air. He knew he had only moments. With his last, fleeting heartbeats, he grasped his mother's life and amplified it. Poured energy into her, drew strength from the forest outside, the people in Southundon, the spirits in the stones of the airships. Even the tiny fae. He drew from them all and cast her presence as hard and as far as he could.

Her soul radiated like the sun.

His face was pressed against the floor, but with one eye, he could still see his mother and Sam through the murky haze of the shades. Sam's kicks were slowing, her eyes looked vacant, blinking slowly. Sam was dying.

Everything Oliver had, he pushed into his mother's spark, igniting her like the fire he'd seen on the other side, the fire that had consumed Northundon. She was that fire. She consumed the spirits of the underworld to fuel her power in the world of the living, and she would burn them until those souls were freed. The price of the bargain? Her soul for theirs.

Oliver let her blaze, let her mirror that impossible vision from the other side of the shroud. Balance. She was death. He was life. He put his life into hers, magnifying it, blasting it through the open rents to the underworld until, through the tears in the shroud, her presence was felt.

The slow trod of marching feet, tens of thousands of feet, boomed through the openings to the underworld. The sound of marching filled the room with palpable dread.

Lilibet heard it and dropped Sam. She spun, a slight frown marring her terrible visage. She looked at the holes in the shroud, peering into the underworld, and her eyes widened. She thrust up a hand, closing it into a tight fist. One by one, the holes closed, sealing themselves like a knitting wound until they vanished.

Except for one.

Taking a step toward it, Lilibet raised an arm, concentration twisting her face.

Oliver shoved himself up, heaving the shades above him higher so he could gasp a lungful of air. He shouted, "The blood of kings has great power, Mother, but that blood is not yours."

She turned to him. "What is it you are doing? You have no control of the shroud between our world and the other. You—"

"I do not," he said, struggling to his feet, the shades falling away from him, lessened as she sealed the pathways to the underworld, closing the wells they drew their strength from. Oliver snarled. "I am not death, I am the balance."

A chill wind blew over them, and in the opening of the remaining rent, Oliver saw a spectral figure, a shade, burning white, cold flame billowing from its body, leeching the warmth from the room.

Lilibet shrieked, "Edward?"

The spectre did not speak, but around it, others did.

"You found her, Oliver Wellesley," rasped the voice of a legion. Thousands as one, they spoke to him. "You found her. We shall complete the bargain."

"It is finished!" screamed Lilibet. "The bargain is finished! You got your souls. You got your price."

"That is not this bargain, Lilibet Wellesley," intoned the figures. "We are no longer the sacrifice. You are."

"Ca-Mi-He!" shouted Lilibet. "I command you. I command you to seal this rent."

In the opening to the underworld, the spectre of King Edward stared at his wife. He stood in the gap and held open the rent.

Around him, two columns of white shades, burning with searing cold, marched into the room. They spilled into the throne room, shuffling slowly toward the queen.

Her mouth opened as she shouted wordlessly. She turned and started to flee, but she stumbled, seeming to struggle, like a cold had was wrapping around her. Then, the marching columns reached her.

Brilliant white hands closed on her and the shades lifted her above their heads. The shades turned. "Oliver Wellesley, the bargain is completed. Our souls are traded for this one."

The souls began to march back into the underworld, the stone of the throne room shuddering at each of the group's steps. His mother, wailing, crying, cursing, was carried from the world of the living into the other. The shades disappeared except for one, the first one.

It turned to him, and the pressure on Oliver's back vanished.

Around the room, there was a startling series of deep thumps. The monsters, the denizens of the underworld, collapsed in on themselves, like crumpling parchments. The shades were dragged back through the shroud, streaming around the figure standing in the center of the rent like water around a rock.

Oliver felt an awful presence pressing against him, like a weighted blanket on his mind, but it did not come through the opening in the shroud. It hovered on the other side.

He recognized it. Ca-Mi-He was lurking behind his father. The rent between the worlds was open, but the great shade had what it wanted. The bargain complete. The great spirit had released the souls of Northundon in exchange for the one it sought, the one it had waited for — Lilibet. The great spirit had the prize it could not obtain on its own, the one who had bound it.

The figure in the center of the shroud stepped back, and the rent to the underworld began knitting shut. Oliver met the spectre's gaze, saw it watching him.

He heard, like the faint whisper of wind.

There is no life without death. There is no love without sacrifice. There is no freedom without responsibility. There is no balance without pressure. He was the balance to his mother. He was the seed that destroyed the dark tree, the completion of Thotham's prophecy. And now she was gone. All empires fall. All empires crumble from within. He was the balance, and he could tip the scales, or he could not.

The opening to the underworld closed, and the pressure lifted. His ears popped, and warmth returned to his body.

Oliver let out an explosive breath. He knew what must be done.

THE PRIESTESS XXII

THE WOMAN SLAPPED her hand on the table. "I call this meeting of the Council of Seven to order."

"Five," mumbled Sam.

The woman turned to her, only her eyes visible beneath the white silk of her mask.

"There are only five of us," remarked Sam, gesturing at the doddering old fools around the table.

"The Council of Five," acknowledged the Whitemask, "though I have no plans to change our charter. I assume it is only a desire to needle me which causes you to speak rather than concern our paperwork isn't in order?"

Sam gave the woman a wry smile.

"Very well then," said the Whitemask. She shuffled through a sheaf of documents in front of her, thumbing through the papers slowly. The others in the room remained silent, letting her steer their discourse. "We have new reports of a coven of hedge witches in Rhensar, and it seems they've achieved some skill. The mayor of a medium-sized hamlet claims they raised the spirit of his late wife. The shade evidently told the coven of an affair the man was having, the discovery of which resulted in the wife's death. The coven is attempting to hold this information over the mayor's head to gain political power. The governor of Rhensar isn't quite sure he can arrest the man for murder on the claims of a spirit, but he is sure he'd like the Church involved in eradicating the witches. Samantha, will you attend?"

"Send someone else," she responded with a wave of her hand.

The Whitemask stared at her, the papers shaking in her grip.

"I'm returning to Enhover for a time," said Sam.

"Looking for your duke, still?" questioned the Whitemask. "You think he stayed within the borders of the empire? Or perhaps you're concerned with his family? Sorcery is a family business, more often than not. Do you know something which should be shared with this council?"

Sam shook her head. "No. I have a personal matter I must deal with."

"What is it?" asked the Whitemask.

"When you need to know something, Bishop Constance, I will tell you," said Sam, steel in her voice. "It is of no concern to the council."

"Do you mean to make yourself a nuisance?" questioned the other woman. "It's apparent to anyone with two eyes that we need your help. We are growing old and frail. We need those like you who still have strength in their limbs, but we operate as a council, girl. Our organization sets foot on the dark path. We flirt with catastrophe to prevent worse. Our methods only work when we operate together, when we balance each other's worst instincts. It is when you choose to pursue dark matters alone that you risk walking too far down the path. Do not venture without us, girl. Do not make me regret adding you to our ranks."

Sam drew a deep breath and let it out. "You are right, Bishop Constance. I'm not used to working with others. You've convinced me we need fresh blood, and I may know of someone suitable."

"Very well," said the Whitemask, glaring at Sam, clearly thinking that what made one suitable as an ally of the council were the exact same qualities as what made one an enemy.

"While I hope this person will join us, I will deal with them if they do not," declared Sam, not meaning a word of it. "When I return, I will inform you of the outcome."

Constance grunted. "And when you've finished this errand?"

"Then I will visit the hedge witches in Rhensar," allowed Sam.

Bishop Constance, the Whitemask, cleared her throat and turned back to her papers. "Additionally, on the subject of recruiting, I've been speaking with the masters of the creche, and they've identified two more prospects — a boy and a girl. I've evaluated them, and with proper training, the potential is there. Are there any objections to us beginning indoctrination and, assuming they survive, finding suitable mentors?"

Around the table, there were murmurs of assent, which was all the vote Constance needed. She made notes on her ledger, the official record of the Council's actions, and proceeded to other business.

Sam's mind had already wandered.

The Council of Seven, the hand that gripped the Church's Knives. She was one of less than a dozen living souls to see the inner workings of the secretive group, but she found she couldn't focus on their machinations. Not yet. The Council dealt in death, but she understood now that she required balance. She required a connection to life.

"READ MY FUTURE?" SHE ASKED, DUCKING INTO THE CURTAINED alcove.

The woman inside scowled at her. "How did you find me?"

"Word of a palmist whose predictions actually occur spread quickly," said Sam, taking a seat opposite Kalbeth and placing two empty mugs and a pitcher of ale between them.

"What do you want?" asked Kalbeth. "I thought I was clear with you. I never wanted to see you again."

"You told me," agreed Sam, "but I did not believe you."

Kalbeth snorted and sat forward to pour herself an ale. She left the second mug empty, glaring at Sam. "Since I last saw you, you were responsible for my mother's death."

Sam shook her head. "Goldthwaite made her own choices. She died for a cause she believed in."

"She died for you," retorted Kalbeth.

"Helping me battle a terrible evil," said Sam.

Kalbeth drank her ale but did not respond.

"I wager that as soon as you knew she was dead, you contacted her on the other side," said Sam. "She must have told you what we hoped to accomplish. We found him— her, I mean. We found the ultimate source of the shadow that had spread across Enhover."

"We?" asked Kalbeth. "You and your duke? What of him? Where is he hiding? I suppose you've come to beg my favor, to scry for him, perhaps? Or has he found himself in some trouble you think I can help him out of?"

"No," whispered Sam. "I know what it costs you, and I could not ask for that."

"It costs a piece of my soul, Sam," snapped Kalbeth, turning her ale up and finishing it. She slammed the tankard down and leaned forward. "And you have asked for that."

"I've taken much from you," acknowledged Sam, "but I'm not here to take more. I came to offer to… to replace what I can."

Kalbeth frowned at her.

"I've been wrong about many things, but the one that hurts the most is you," said Sam. "I mistreated you, used you, and thought little of it. There was no balance in our relationship, and I'd like to fix that, if you'll let me."

"Fix our relationship?" Kalbeth laughed bitterly. "We have no relationship. Not anymore."

Sam looked back at her, waiting patiently.

"What?" demanded Kalbeth. "You mean to mope around my rooms for a few days, pamper me with your kisses, and then what?"

"Then I'll follow you wherever you go," said Sam.

"And if I go nowhere?"

"Then I will stay by your side until you ask me to leave," said Sam. "If you'll have me, it is your choice what we do. We could stay here. We could leave. That is up to you, but I want to be with you whatever you decide to do."

"For how long?" asked Kalbeth quietly.

"As long as you'll have me," responded Sam.

"You've said similar before," grumbled the other woman.

"I mean it this time," replied Sam.

The palmist's fingers drummed on the table, and her dark eyes studied Sam. Finally, she glanced down at Sam's hands. "Let me read them."

Turning her palms over, Sam felt Kalbeth's warm fingers press against her skin. She felt the woman's assured touch as she traced the lines there. Kalbeth's lips moved as she read the curve of Sam's future. She frowned and looked up.

"Rhensar?"

"I have a job there, if you'd care to go with me," admitted Sam. "I mean it, though, Kalbeth. It is your choice. We can go to Rhensar, or we can stay here. We can go to Finavia or the Southlands. We can find a cottage on the coast and take up fishing. If you'll have me, I'll be beside you wherever you are."

"I've heard they have good ale in Rhensar," said Kalbeth, still holding Sam's hand.

Sam smiled. "I've heard that as well."

"I'll need a few days to prepare," said the palmist. "There are things I need to sort here, bags to pack. I've had enough of this place. The streets, my familiar haunts, they remind me of my mother. She wouldn't want me... She'd understand, I think."

"I am sorry about what happened to her," said Sam. "I-I didn't realize what we were up against, and I was blinded by the dark path. I made a mistake, and she paid the price."

"She made a mistake as well," said Kalbeth. "She told me everything. It— You're right. No one could have suspected."

Sam turned her hand and gripped Kalbeth's.

"What of the duke?" asked Kalbeth. "Speculation is in all of the papers, but it seems that no one who knows the truth is talking. Is he really gone?"

"He is gone," said Sam, glancing around the room to confirm they were alone. "Far gone from here."

"Good," said Kalbeth. She stood. "Come upstairs with me, then. I have something I'd like you to do before I start packing my bags."

Grinning at the back of her friend — her lover — Sam gripped the other woman's hand and followed her to the rooms. Stay by the woman's side and swim the current of life. It'd be a pleasant bondage, following Kalbeth's lead. Sam had meant what she said. She'd do it as long as Kalbeth let her, she hoped.

THE CAPTAIN IV

CAPTAIN CATHERINE AINSLEY put a boot on the gunwale, leaning forward and resting one arm on her knee, the other hand on the butt of a pistol. Her hat flapped on her head, keeping the bright sun off of her. Clean air, warm so far south, blew by her face in a constant stream. As she inhaled, her lungs filled with heavy, salty sea air.

"Spyglass," she said, holding out a hand.

First Mate Pettybone handed it to her and pointed down at the azure sea where he'd been looking.

She held the leather-bound brass device to her eye, spent a few moments locating the tiny white-and-brown speck floating in the distance, and then watched it for several long moments.

"That's them," she said finally, confirming what everyone on the crew already knew. She was the captain, though, and they were waiting on her pronouncement. "Prepare at stations then chase them down."

Shouts rose behind her. Men scrambled to adjust the sails and lay out their armaments on the deck of the Cloud Serpent.

"Black Rodger," said Pettybone beside her. "He just struck a freighter off Nurzig. His hold oughta be filled with spices."

"Aye," agreed Ainsley. "We'll have to slow him and then board him. Can't risk sinking such a catch."

"Won't be easy," warned Pettybone. "Any thought of simply rolling a bomb over the edge and letting the bloody bastard sink? I know there's valuable cargo on board, but there's a healthy reward just for the kill. That's easy coin, Captain."

"Getting rich is never easy, First Mate," she replied. "We'll take him, and then we'll take our share of the spices in his hold."

Pettybone nodded.

"Not long ago, First Mate, you were convinced we'd be dead," she reminded. "Now, we're the richest damned aircrew in the empire — in the world!"

"Even after seeing the paperwork, I still don't believe you managed to wrangle a privateering charter out of the King Philip," said Pettybone, shaking his head and grinning.

"Someone's got to hunt these corsairs. Someone's got to end their scourge in the tropics," claimed Ainsley. "Why not us?"

"Because we spirited away Oliver after he killed their father," mentioned Pettybone. "He killed the spirit-forsaken king! Our involvement would be called treason by some."

"Aye, and if Philip had strung us up," retorted Ainsley, "he'd have to tell everyone why — the lords and ladies, the Church, the commons, the Company. He'd have to admit his family's secrets to them all, and if he didn't, you'd best believe I'd shout out afore they tightened that noose around my neck. Nah, we're safer for him out here, taking prizes and protecting his colonies from the corsairs. Everyone knows sailors tell tales. Out here, no one will believe ours."

"You wouldn't'tve had a chance to talk if there was no trial," mentioned Pettybone. "In my experience, kings lose little sleep over breaking their own laws. A pillow over our faces in the night, a dagger in the back, poison in the ale… If I was him, I'd rather us dead than in the tropics."

"That's true, and King Philip suspects that's the way we'll end," admitted Ainsley. "Told me so himself. Said he thought we wouldn't make it a season out here before we chased the wrong vessel and met someone bigger and meaner than us. Not to mention the storms and the sickness that does so many in these seas. He said he thought we'd die soon enough. I told him if I died, I planned to die the richest damned airship captain in history."

Beside her, Pettybone's jaw dropped.

"Besides," continued Ainsley, "Philip saw we can sail circles around his royal marines. We evaded the entire fleet outside of Southundon without even a scrape on the hull."

"You... you told him about that?" stammered Pettybone.

"Had to convince him we were capable," she claimed. "I needed that charter, First Mate, so we'd be legitimate. Otherwise, we're pirates, just like Black Rodger down there."

"Captain," declared Pettybone, "you are crazy."

"Let's go get those spices, First Mate," she said with a grin.

Crazy, aye, she admitted her first mate might be a little bit right about that, but it took a little crazy to make history. Not that she cared what they wrote down in the books. All that she cared about was that before her end, she would earn a fortune that would be legendary.

She held the spyglass back up to her eye and found their quarry again. Black Rodger would try to run, she suspected, but he couldn't out sail her, and there was nowhere to hide. Not from Catherine Ainsley, Captain of the Cloud Serpent.

THE CARTOGRAPHER XXVII

H<small>IS</small> QUILL SCRATCHED across the parchment, dark ink outlining the coast, noting the rivers, the forests, and the mountains beyond. He filled in a rough approximation of Enhover's Westlands settlement but left it rough. No one was interested in the layout of the lodging, meal halls, brothels, warehouses, or pubs of the place. Anyone perusing the map would want to know what was beyond, where the riches lay.

Oliver glanced at his notes and then back at the map he was drawing. The outlines on the blank page were slowly expanding the boundary between knowledge and fantasy. There were still seas of empty space, where only the wild stories of explorers gave any hint of what lay beyond, but week by week, he was filling in the gaps. He was defining this new land.

He grinned at a second map that sat on the corner of the desk, allegedly completed. It was copied from one of the Company's. A partner of his had procured it from a Company man too far gone in his cups and passed it to Oliver so he could make a rough replica, and then they'd slipped it back into the Company man's satchel before he recovered the next morning.

Oliver had quickly seen the Company's map was hopelessly inaccurate, and using it would lead an expedition astray, if not into complete disaster. His hands had twitched, yearning to correct it, but he'd left the map as it was. He had no ill will toward the Company or the men who worked on her behalf, but he wasn't going to give them any advantages that they hadn't earned.

A knock sounded at the door, and Oliver granted permission to enter.

A man poked his head in. "Ey, Cartographer, you coming down to the pub?"

"I've got work to do and ale here, Robinson," he replied.

"A ship from Enhover berthed two turns of the clock past," said Robinson. "It had our man on it. He got the official charter, Cartographer. The Allied Westlands Company has been granted leave to begin exploration and commerce in the Westlands territory! The king himself signed the document. Anything we find out there is ours to claim. We're going to be rich men, Cartographer, rich men!"

Smirking, Oliver laid down his quill. "Being a rich man isn't what you think it is, Robinson."

Robinson rolled his eyes. "Ey, you'll be giving me your shares then, Cartographer?"

Oliver stood and stretched, cracking his back, realizing he had been sitting for too long. "I'm not doing this for the silver, but I'm not going to give it away, either. Not to you, at least."

The other man laughed and leaned against the side of the doorway. "Come on then, mate. Let's hoist an ale and toast the Allied Westlands Company. Second to the continent after the Company, but we'll be the first over the Ridge, ey? We'll be the first to see what this land truly has to offer."

Oliver followed the buoyant Robinson out the door and down to the pub, weaving through the dirt streets of Enhover's Westlands colony. He stepped carefully to avoid the large piles of waste left by the odd, flightless birds that people in the place rode instead of horses. He ignored the calls from the women hanging out the windows of the brothels. He looked up the muddy street, past the two-story buildings that lined it, over the wooden palisade that protected it. He looked at the expansive, virgin forest that stretched beyond, nearly as far as he could see, where it rose to the foothills of a sharp line of mountains. He looked at a world untamed by the hand of man.

The Ridge, as the Westlands colonists called the mountain range, rose like a wall between the known world and the unknown. The colonists believed it was raw wilderness beyond, but no one had been there, no one had mapped it.

Oliver had already been out in the forest, nearly to the foothills of that range. He'd strolled around the huge trunks of the trees, beneath a canopy that rose hundreds of yards into the sky. The darkness below that natural roof was filled with strange and wonderful beasts and flora not even the botanists could identify. It offered an escape from who he had been.

He could feel the bubble of life within that forest, small sparks and large ones. They burned in that dim light with an unrestrained vigor that he'd never felt in Enhover. As far as anyone knew, this land was untouched by man except for their small compound on the coast, but it wasn't uninhabited.

The Westlands was filled with virulent life like no man had ever encountered. And there were spirits out there. Oliver had sensed them the moment he'd slid over the gunwale of the Cloud Serpent and snuck several leagues south to the colony, flitting in at night so that none knew the airship's shadow had met these far shores, so that no one knew who he used to be.

He could feel the spirits, even from within the compound. He could reach out to them, commune in a sense. He'd felt beings questing, seeking an attuned mind, but he had not yet responded. He was savoring what he did not know, what he had yet to learn.

This place was a mystery to him, like his newfound abilities. He was eager to explore out there and within, but too often of late, when he gained knowledge, he wished that he had not. Living ignorant was better sometimes. It was almost time, though. Soon, he would lead a party for the Allied Westlands Company beyond the palisade, through the forest, over the ridge, and into the unknown. He would learn the wilderness and chart it. He would open himself to the wonders of this place.

He was no longer what he had been. No longer the son of the king, no longer a member of the Company, no longer the Duke of Northundon. He didn't know what he would become. A merchant? Not like he had been, he hoped. A druid? Maybe, though he was still unsure what that meant. He could feel the spirits, could encourage them, but if there was more, he left it for the future. For now, he was merely the Cartographer, and he was content with that.

Robinson burst through the door of the pub, dragging Oliver behind him. He shouted at their partners in the corner and then back to the barkeep, demanding a fresh round of ales. The group was clustered around a thick scroll spread out on their table, the ends held down by half-empty mugs. Their charter, granting the Allied Westlands Company rights to explore and trade in the vast, unknown continent of the Westlands.

Oliver picked up the scroll, rolling it tight, ignoring the signature at the bottom. He stuffed it into his satchel, beside his quill, his ink, and his notebooks. It wouldn't do for the burgeoning company's legal authority to be so quickly stained with ale.

He slung his satchel and broadsword over the back of a chair and settled at the table, the ebullient joy of his partners infecting him with their excitement. He felt his lips curling into a grin.

"A toast!" cried Robinson, slapping Oliver on the shoulder and raising his mug. "A toast to the Allied Westlands Company! A toast to this brave crew! And a toast to our leader into the unknown, the Cartographer!"

THANKS FOR READING!

THANK you so much for taking the time to read my book! If you enjoyed it, please tell a friend about it.

A few folks who helped drag this from messy draft to complete package: Shawn T King is responsible for the cover design and most of the graphics you see on my social media and website. Bob Kehl illustrated a digital painting and whipped up the line art for me. Soraya Corcoran created the maps — which was a bit crucial for this particular series. Nicole Zoltack is back yet again as my proof reader, and James Z (no relation) is my lone beta reader. Without their help, this would be a very different experience. And while I still find this hard to believe, the legendary Simon Vance is narrating the audiobooks. The moment I heard his voice, I knew he was the guy. I'm blown away he agreed to take on this project. Finally, thanks to the Terrible 10. May we always talk over cigars, scotch, and archery.

Thanks again, and hope to hear from you!

AC

Find out what's next from AC Cobble by heading to accobble.com. There's news, artwork, blogging, maps, a newsletter, and more!

GLOSSARY

MEMBERS OF THE CROWN:

Edward Wellesley - King of Enhover

Lilibet Wellesley – deceased, former wife of Edward & Queen of Enhover

Philip Wellesley – son of Edward & Lilibet, Prince of Enhover & Duke of Westundon

Lucinda Wellesley - wife of Philip, Princess of Enhover & Duchess of Westundon

Franklin Wellesley - son of Edward & Lilibet, Duke of Eastundon

John Wellesley - son of Edward & Lilibet, Duke of Southundon

Matilda Wellesley - wife of John, Duchess of Southundon

Oliver "Duke" Wellesley - son of Edward & Lilibet, Duke of Northundon

William Wellesley - brother of Edward, unlanded earl & Prime Minister of Enhover

Lannia Wellesley - daughter of William & unlanded countess

Members of the Peerage (Council of Lords):

Gerrald Holgrave - earl and chairman of the Congress of Lords

Josiah Child - widower & Baron of Eiremouth

Aria Child - daughter of Josiah, twin of Isabella

Isabella Child - daughter of Josiah, twin of Aria
Nathaniel Child - brother of Josiah & unlanded baron
Bartholomew Surrey - Marquess of Southwatch
Rafael Colston – unlanded marquees
Ethan Brighton - unlanded viscount
Adelaide Boughton - Countess of Swinpool
Vassily Resault - unlanded earl
Avery Thornbush - unlanded baron
Victoria Thornbush - unlanded baroness

Members of the Church:
Joshua Langdon - Cardinal of Enhover
Gabriel Yates - Bishop of Westundon
Thotham - priest & Knife of the Council
Samantha "Sam" - apprentice of Thotham
Constance - bishop & member of the Council of Seven
Raymond au Clair - Knife of the Council
Bridget Cancio - Knife of the Council

Members of the Ministry:
Richard Brach - Admiral of the Royal Marines
Brendan Ostrander - Commander of the Royal Marines in
Archtan Atoll Colony
Edgar Shackles - Chief of Staff for King Edward Wellesley
Herbert Shackles - Chief of Staff for Prince Philip Wellesley
Herman Shackles - Chief of Staff for Oliver Wellesley
Joff Gallen - Senior Inspector in Harwick
Patrick "Pat" McCready - Inspector in Harwick
Jack - night watchman in Harwick
Walpole - minor bureaucrat in Westundon
Bryce – minor bureaucrat in Westundon
Winchester - valet to Oliver Wellesley
Simon Moncrief - senior inspector

Members of the Company:
Randolph Raffles - member of the Company's board of directors, Company representative in Westundon

Alvin Goldwater - President of the Company, Marquess of Southwatch

Alexander Pettigrew - member of the Company's board of directors, finance committee

Sebastian Dalyrimple - Earl of Derbycross & Governor of Archtan Atoll Colony

Hathia Dalyrimple - wife of Sebastian & Countess of Derbycross

Isisandra Dalyrimple - daughter of Sebastian & Hathia

Jain Towerson - Governor of Imbon Colony

Ethan Giles – senior factor (merchant) in Imbon Colony

John Haines - Captain of the airship Cloud Serpent

Charles - personal secretary for Director Randolph Raffles

Catherine Ainsley - Captain on the airship Cloud Serpent

Pettybone - First Mate on the airship Cloud Serpent

Samuels - crew on the airship Cloud Serpent

Others:

Pierre De Bussy - Governor of Finavia's colonies in the Vendatt Islands

Goldthwaite - proprietor and madam of the Lusty Barnacle

Kalbeth - daughter of Goldthwaite, tattoo artist

Rance - barman at the Lusty Barnacle

Lagarde - former barwoman at the Lusty Barnacle

Ivar val Drongko - perfume merchant

Duvante - historian & author

Edwin Holmes – deceased, former pothecary in Harwick

Fielding - apothecary in Harwick

Jack - body man to Baron Nathaniel Child

Marcus - adept in the Feet of Seheht

Andrew – barman & owner of the Befuddled Sage

Madam Winrod – medicine woman

Artemis – leader of a group of pirates

Janson Cabineau - merchant

Rijohn - sorcerer in the Darklands

Absenus - seneschal in the Darklands

Locations:

Nation of Enhover

Southundon - home to King Edward, Duke John & capital of Enhover / Southundon province

Westundon - home to Prince Philip, Duke Oliver & capital of Westundon province

Eastundon - home to Duke Franklin & capital of Eastundon province

Northundon - capital of Northundon province, destroyed in war

Middlebury - city in Eastundon province & major rail transit hub

Swinpool - city in Westundon province & cod fishing village

Harwick - city in Eastundon province & whaling village

United Territories – allied nations, tribute states to Enhover

Ivalla - home of the Church's headquarters

Romalla - capital of Ivalla, home of the Church

Valerno - port city

Finavia – wealthy merchant nation

Rhensar – forested nation known for hedge mages and wood witches

Coldlands - subjugated and largely destroyed by war

Archtan Atoll - colony of the Company & famous for levitating islands

Archtan Town - location of Company House

Eyies – island in Archtan Atoll

Farawk – island near Artchtan Atoll

Imbon - colony of the Company

Westlands - largely unexplored & location of Company outpost

Southlands - largely unexplored & location of Company outpost

Darklands - largely unexplored, religious state known for worship of the underworld

Lightning Source UK Ltd.
Milton Keynes UK
UKHW010715191222
414157UK00005B/542